SWEET REVENGE

Also by Tina Day/Tina Knight

~

The Kastle Fortunes Series
The Courtship of Princess and Pirate
A Soul Lost at Sea
A Pirate's Promise
The Heart of a Woman

The Watching Trilogy
Watching
Wanting
Willing

Other Novels
On Vacation

SWEET REVENGE

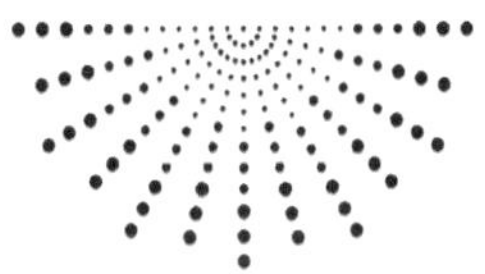

TINA KNIGHT

Day and Knight
Romance
Publications

*For Lisa, who empowered me to
send my stories out into the world.*

IT'S HARD TO SNUGGLE UP TO A MARBLE COLUMN

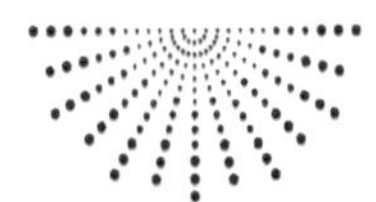

The envelope itched Tess's hand. Maybe, after so many years working in the secretarial arts, she'd finally developed an allergy to paper. Or maybe the odd reaction came from the contents, not the container. Glancing down, she read the name typed across the envelope's face: *Mason Tramont*.

Tess dragged her eyes up to the impressive building before her. With a deep breath, she began climbing the ivory stone steps as she had each weekday for the last six years, passing the all-too-familiar entry marker: *Field and Tramont, Architectural Associates*. Her heart squeezed while she continued up, still as awed by the beauty of her workplace as her wide-eyed self, fresh out of college, had been the first day she crossed the threshold.

A lot had changed since those initial moments. Back then, she'd been flustered by the captivating Mr. Tramont. Her mouth had run wild on more than one, or possibly more than a thousand, different occasions. But now, Tess prided herself on the fact that she didn't babble around Mason anymore. After six years of exposure to him, and by exposure she meant being around him day in and day out, not exposing herself to him – well, other than that one time she'd gotten the back of her skirt stuck in her underpants on the way out of the bathroom and Mason had whispered gently into her ear that she might want to return to the restroom before they walked into their client meeting together – she'd learned not to let her mouth go into overdrive just because Mr. Tramont stood near her.

Yes, she was stronger now. Strong, determined, independent. And ready to tackle everything that lay before her.

When she reached the top stair, Tess drank in the sight of the striking slate and marble building. To her, it represented the man inside: handsome, hardened, structural perfection.

But no one can snuggle up to a marble column, can they?

Tess smoothed over her blond hair, making sure it was still neatly ensconced in its high ponytail, as she reached for the towering glass front doors. She grasped the gleaming scrolled handle with determination. This was it. The first day of the rest of her life. The day she stopped being Mason Tramont's Go-To Girl, or Super Secretary, or Executive Assistant Extraordinaire, or anything else. The day she told him she would leave...for good.

MASON TRAMONT SAT at his desk, running his fingers across the deep black surface of the oversized, angular block of wood. No carvings, no ornamentation, no distraction. Nothing to detract from its simplistic beauty. It always seemed like the perfect work surface. Until today.

With unbidden curiosity, he looked out of his open door, down the elongated hallway, and into the office opposite his. David Field, his business partner and longtime friend, sat behind his desk as well. Except David's desk wasn't simply functional. It was an antique Colonial piece, covered in swirls and etchings, a conversation starter that set their female clientele atwitter. That was David's specialty: awe and beauty. Mason laid foundations, planned supports, and engineered structures. David decorated them.

Mason never envied his old college buddy before. He never wanted to be the schmoozer of their dynamic duo. He never wanted to change places. At least, not until now.

He watched David's eyes light up as Regina, David's secretary, sauntered into the distant room. Except she wasn't just his secretary anymore, since today wasn't just any Monday. Today marked their return from their honeymoon, back to the office as husband and wife.

Regina herself didn't make Mason envious. He'd never paid much attention to her, and honestly, he knew she didn't really care for him. The actual reason he envied David today was because his old friend was now a happily married man.

Mason exhaled, watching as Regina bent down and kissed David on the lips, lingering a little too long, until David pinched her skirt-clad bottom and she arched up and giggled. Mason tried to look away from the intimate scene, but David caught his eye across the distance. Mason nodded solemnly, tamping down his voyeuristic guilt, hoping that would be the end of the uncomfortable moment. But then David stood and began navigating the lengthy hall.

Mason cringed. Clasping his hands together on the desktop, he steeled himself for his friend's arrival.

"You've got your door open today," David noted as he stepped inside the stately office.

"Yes."

"Why? Usually you're holed up in here like some mad scientist."

"I prefer mad architect, thank you."

David chuckled. "Well, you're the brains of this operation, so do what you need to do. I just don't want you to worry."

"About what?"

"Me and Regina. We'll be professional; I promise. You don't have to leave your door open to keep an eye on us."

"I wasn't. I was just..." Mason wasn't sure what he'd been doing. "I was just getting some fresh air."

David folded his arms across his chest and stared him down. "What's eating you?"

"What do you mean?"

"Something's bothering you. Let me guess...Malory Catskill."

Mason turned to look out of his arched window.

"That's it, isn't it? Did you and Malory break up again?"

"A few weeks ago. Before your wedding."

"How many times is that now? Ten since college?"

"About that." He kept looking out the window to the park across the street. The urge to run out of the building and roll around in the grass nearly overtook him. "It's for good this time. She and I, we just don't..."

"Oh. I'm sorry," Tess's voice came from behind David.

Mason straightened in his oversized leather chair, pinning his eyes on his secretary. "Yes, Miss Troy?"

"I didn't expect the door to be open," she explained. "I meant to knock."

"It's no problem," Mason assured, watching Tess smile at David before turning her light blue eyes back to him.

"I, um, I just wanted to go over your appointments for the week, Mr. Tramont."

Mason heard a slight quaver in her voice. "I got your memo outlining everything on Friday. Has anything changed?"

He watched her shift the papers she held, a tiny tremble apparent in her purple painted fingertips.

"No, I guess not," she answered.

Mason focused on her bright fuchsia mouth as she nibbled her lip.

Tess cleared her throat, diverting his attention back to her eyes. "I guess I'll let you and Mr. Field get back to business, then." She nodded at David, spun on her bright red high heels, and disappeared.

Mason stared at the space she'd just occupied. "Something's wrong with her."

David's brow shot up. "Excuse me?"

"Something's wrong with Tess. She's a wreck."

"A wreck?"

"Didn't you notice?"

"Um, no. She looked as gorgeous as ever."

"Watch it, David. You're a married man now."

"Yeah, but you're not."

"What's that supposed to mean?"

"I'm just saying that dating your secretary can be quite an experience. You might want to think about it."

"Good Lord. You do realize you're talking about Tess, right?"

"Yeah. I do." With a suggestive grin, David turned and exited. The resonant sound of laughter trailed behind him all the way to his office.

Mason stared after his friend. *Why on earth would David suggest I date Tess?* Tess wasn't just a secretary; she was a professional woman. Not to say Regina wasn't, but this was different. Tess was...Tess.

Shaking his head while reaching beneath his desk, Mason pulled his laptop from its case and placed it carefully on the smooth surface. As the computer whirred to life, he put David's unsettling thought from his mind. He couldn't devote precious work time to one of his partner's random notions. He would, as always, be the sensible one. The planner, not the dreamer.

HOURS LATER, Mason caught himself staring into space for the umpteenth time. Running a hand over the tense muscles in the back of his neck, he worked to refocus. His laptop usually offered him a happy place to reside, to forget about the rest of the world and concentrate on the structures housed inside his mind. But staring at the drafts for the new hospital wing – which would normally make an eight-hour day flash by in minutes – couldn't hold his attention right now. Not after seeing the happy Field newlyweds grope each other this morning. And not after what David suggested to him. And definitely not after hearing Tess's laughter drift down the hallway.

Her lively, animated giggles stirred something inexplicable inside him. Before Mason knew exactly what he was doing, he stood and crossed his expansive floor to his doorway. He glanced at his partner, who sat in the distant office speaking enthusiastically on the phone, before stepping silently into the hall and turning left. He tried to ignore the awkward feeling that he was sneaking around in his own building.

With a few more steps, Mason arrived at the door adjacent to his. Slowly and carefully, he peered into Tess's office. He hoped to catch sight of her – her bobbing blond ponytail and her soft, kind eyes and her bright, glossed lips – but Regina stood in front of his secretary's desk, blocking his view.

"Can I tell you how awesome Cancun is for a honeymoon spot?" David's new wife spouted to Tess. "The nude beach we stumbled onto was hysterical! You know, I'd like to say I've never wanted to strip naked in public, but that would be a lie, so…"

The sound came again: Tess's laugh. Loud, boisterous, too big for her body. Mason reconsidered David's odd thought.

Could I date Tess? Could I be with a woman who laughs like that? Malory never laughed like that. Not once.

Mason wished Regina would move. He wanted to get a better look at his secretary. Which was ridiculous, since he'd seen her nearly every day for six years.

"I'm not sure about the nude beach thing," Tess replied to Regina. "All of those people staring at you, and sand up in your pieces-parts? I don't know if I could do it. Did you?"

He didn't hear Regina's response. He was too busy imagining a nude Tess covered in sand. *Damn it. That does it. Now I have to see her.*

Stepping away from the wall, he pretended to walk purposefully past her door while casting a casual glance over his shoulder. He figured she would be looking at Regina, or at her desk. She wasn't. Her eyes caught his and held them. He almost tripped on the marble floor.

Tess opened her mouth to address him but Mason kept moving, fully aware that he was inadequately prepared to respond. He continued walking to the end of the hall, finding himself in their employee lounge for the first time in years.

Chad and George from Accounting sat at a small round table, eating donuts. "Mr. Tramont," they said in unison, obviously surprised by the sight of him.

"Hello," Mason replied, watching Chad crumple his napkin.

George stiffened in his chair. "Do you need anything, Mr. Tramont?"

Apparently I need a naked, sandy secretary, he considered, but didn't think he should say it out loud. "Just, um...getting a cup of coffee."

George settled down and smiled, returning to the glazed concoction in his fingers. Mason walked to the counter by the refrigerator, opening several cabinets until he found a usable mug. He poured the hot liquid in, the deep brown color bringing to mind Malory's hair. His ex-girlfriend's dark curls were always perfectly styled. He'd learned through the years never to touch them, since Malory hated having a single hair out of place.

He continued staring into the mug as he added some fancy creamer he found sitting out on the counter. Stirring the new liquid in, he watched the color transform to a golden blond, much like Tess's hair. She wore it down on occasion, but most of the time it was like it was today, pulled up into a ponytail. He imagined how the gold waves would look against her skin if he pulled the tie out and let them fall around her shoulders. He wondered how soft that gold would feel when he ran his fingers through it, and how she would look at him while he marveled at the sensation.

With a silent curse, Mason put the coffeepot back on the burner. *Why am I comparing Tess to Malory? Or imagining touching Tess's hair? What is wrong with me? She's my secretary. That's all.*

He picked up his mug, mumbled goodbye to Accounting, and marched himself back down the hall toward his office. He kept his head stiff, eyes forward. He wouldn't look at Tess that way again.

Her inquisitive voice called to him as he passed her door. "Mr. Tramont?"

He stopped cold. *Damn it. I'm not getting away that easy.*

Retracing his steps, he glanced into her office with the most innocent expression he could muster. "Yes, Miss Troy?"

Tess peered around Regina, looking up at him from her chair. "Why are you in the hall? Do you need something?"

Mason stared at Tess's lips. The gloss she normally wore sparkled in the dull office light. He wondered how it would taste. "No," he said, speaking more to himself than to her.

"Okay. I just wondered if I could help you."

Can you help me? I have no idea. "I just got myself some coffee. Heading back to my office now."

"Well, let me know if I can do anything for you." She leaned forward in her chair and the end of her ponytail swept across her shoulder, landing dangerously close to the swell of cleavage peeking out from her dark blue blouse.

Mason cleared his throat. "Mm-hmm. Sure will." He shook his head and turned, retreating to the safety of his office.

~

Tess's eyebrows lodged into her hairline as she watched Mason walk away. She waited until she heard his office door close before looking back to her friend. "That sure was weird."

Regina's head tilted. "What was?"

"Mr. Tramont. He hasn't gotten his own coffee in six years."

"Not once?"

"Nope. Not once."

"My God, you spoil that man. Whatever you do, don't tell David. I stopped getting him coffee eons ago."

"Really?"

"You should stop, too. We've got enough to do around here; I swear it gets busier every day. Let Tramont get his own damn coffee."

Tess tried not to look guilty. Getting coffee was trite compared to everything else she did for Mason, from picking up his dry cleaning to buying gifts for his family members' birthdays. If Regina knew, her head might spin around. But Regina's judgment couldn't bother her now, not with Mason acting so strangely. Today of all days.

Tess pressed her lips together. *Could he know?* No, he couldn't know she was quitting. No one knew except her best friend, Annabelle, who'd never met Mason in her life. Although, with Tess's incessant ramblings, Belle probably felt like she'd known him forever.

"You okay?" Regina asked.

"Yeah, sure. Just a lot of work," Tess fibbed, knowing Regina would be hurt by her impending departure.

"I'll leave you to it, then. But promise me you won't work yourself to death over Mason Tramont."

Tess smiled. "Promise."

The bubbly brunette exited as frantically as she'd entered, leaving Tess alone with her thoughts. She mulled over the envelope in her desk drawer, the one she'd been working up the courage to deliver for months. Why did Mason have to pick today to act out of character?

Tess had already played out the scenario a hundred times in her head: she would walk to his closed office door, knock, be allowed entry, hand him the envelope, watch anxiously while he read her resignation, hold her head upright as he looked at her with disapproval, accept his coolly detached regards, and walk out. And get back to her desk and cry a little, probably, over how easily he dismissed her. But then remind herself that she was a professional, with her own business to run, and finish out her last weeks here with dignity and grace.

Unfortunately, her plans went belly-up the minute he'd left his door open this morning. She couldn't give him her resignation then, not with David Field standing in the same room. And now, her creature-of-habit boss was spending the morning walking the halls and getting his own coffee. Apparently, all hell was breaking loose.

The words on her computer screen blurred into hieroglyphics as she considered what to do next. Should she return to his office now? Or wait until after lunch? Or the end of the workday? It had to be today; her nerves couldn't take another night of tossing and turning.

She pulled open her desk drawer and stared at the name on the envelope. *Mason Tramont.* A man who'd spent countless nights in her bed. But only in her dreams.

Tess sighed. She'd never questioned the origins of her schoolgirl crush. It didn't take a genius to figure out why an innocent, unskilled college grad would worship a handsome, successful young architect with purpose, drive, and resplendent manners. What Tess cursed herself for now was how she'd strived, in her exuberant youth, to be more than Mason's secretary.

She'd made herself his wardrobe planner. His social calendar. His family go-between. She'd even been his chauffeur, although just once, and only because he'd sprained his ankle in a morning tennis match and needed to be at a client meeting that afternoon. And because he looked incredible in tennis shorts. Or in anything, really. The man's body was positively sinful.

Still, everything she'd done to make herself irreplaceable hadn't caused her boss to look at her as any more than an employee. No matter how short her skirts or how tight her shirts, she simply didn't tempt the ever-stoic architect. On top of that, she could no longer bear to watch him fall back into the arms of that scornful socialite, Malory Catskill, whose claws were dug permanently into his backside.

Tess had spent her first year – okay, years – at Field and Tramont mooning over Mason. Then she started to grow up and realize how futile her feelings were. Eventually, she made the decision to move on.

She dated other men; one she thought could be forever. When that didn't work out, she enrolled in night school and quietly earned her MBA. She started her own business on the weekends, small but increasingly successful, partnered with Annabelle, her best friend since college. Now, Tess was ready to be her own boss, to quit this job and not look back.

In four weeks, she would never return to this building. She would never again sit at this desk. She would never again look into Mason's gorgeous, deep brown eyes. Or watch the side of his mouth pull up during the infrequent moments when he let his sense of humor show. Or hear the deep, stirring cadence of his voice.

"Miss Troy, may I have a word?"

That voice.

Tess's breath hitched. Her eyes darted to her boss, who stood rigidly in her doorway, arms placed at his sides. Even from this distance, he watched her with an intensity that dampened her palms.

Damn, the man is magnificent. So unfair.

She slid her desk drawer closed. "Yes, Mr. Tramont. What can I do for you?"

He stepped into the room, his meticulously crafted charcoal suit highlighting broad shoulders and a carved chest she would pay good money to drool on. She studied his approach, her mind searching to uncover the drive behind this morning's unusual activity.

On the outside, nothing seemed out of place. He looked as stunning as always. She especially loved how his thick black hair pulled back from his forehead, revealing a sharp widow's peak. Tess often fantasized that the striking trait came from an ancestral vampire. She liked to imagine Mason Tramont biting her. And not just on the neck.

She coughed to suppress a laugh as her boss glanced at the artwork she'd hung on the walls. The muscle across his jaw twitched, a sure sign he was deep in thought. Tess fidgeted with the short hem of her skirt. *Why is he here?*

Normally, Mason never left his office. Not until everyone else was gone for the night. In truth, most of her coworkers were terrified of him, thinking if they saw him out in the open, they'd be fired.

Oh, crap. Is that it? Has he decided to fire me? Wouldn't it figure that the day I work up the courage to quit, he fires me first? And if so, how dare he! After all I've done for him! He's certainly going to get a piece of my mind if he...

She ceased her mental-rambling the instant Mason's dark, intent eyes refastened on her face. She swallowed hard.

He straightened to his full, exceptional height and cleared his throat. "There's something I need to ask you, Tess. Well, something I need to say."

Her breath caught at the sound of her name. He never, ever called her Tess. *What in the hell is happening right now?*

"What do you need to say, Mr. Tramont?"

"Just that I'm...I'm interested in you."

"In what about me?"

"In you. I'm interested in you."

"Interested?" she repeated, certain he didn't mean what it sounded like he meant. She'd had men tell her they were interested before, generally with bedroom eyes. But these – these were boardroom eyes.

"Quite interested," he restated, his fixed gaze as potent as ever.

She had no idea what alternate dimension she'd woken up in this morning. But after six years of working for this man, Tess knew one thing for certain. Mason Tramont was *not* interested in her.

She shook her head. "No."

"You mean no, you won't consider me?"

"I mean no, you're not interested in me."

He shrugged his imposing shoulders. "But I just said I was."

A laugh escaped her throat. "Um, no offense, but I've worked here for six years and you've never looked at me twice. Am I to understand you've developed some sort of attraction to me *today*?"

"What if I said yes?"

"Then I would say you lost your mind."

"Does that mean you won't consider dating me?"

Tess opened her mouth but nothing came out.

This isn't really happening, is it? All these years, all this time, and now *he asks me out? Today of all days?*

Part of her, a ridiculously huge part, wanted to scream, "Yes! Yes! I want all the dates! Woo-hoo!" and jump across the desk to tackle him. The more mature, slightly smaller, part of her knew she couldn't. She couldn't let him deter her.

Tess reached for the envelope in her desk. "Mr. Tramont, I actually have something to tell you..."

"Good," he interrupted. "You can tell me over lunch."

"Lunch?"

"I'll take you to that quaint little Italian place down the street. I've heard you say you love it there."

"I do love it there, but..."

"Great. Let me grab my keys and we'll head out."

"Uh..." She attempted a protest, but he simply turned and disappeared.

2

DAZED AND CONFUSED

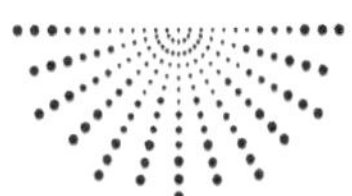

The inviting waitress who served them lunch wore a low-cut blouse, highlighting her buxom chest and multiple tattoos on her shapely arms. Yet Mason's eyes never left Tess's face. She tried not to fidget as she sat across the small table from her boss, knowing how intense he could be when he wanted something done. He'd just never tried to do *her* before.

Tess still couldn't believe this peculiar turn of events. Why on earth was this happening today? It must be some celestial event gone massively awry, or a bizarre test by the god of secretaries, or the strangest coincidence ever. Except she didn't believe in coincidence, and she really wanted to figure out the reason behind Mason's baffling behavior.

She hoped she could solve this wacky-boss mystery, but even if she couldn't, she would still fulfill her purpose during this lunch. She *would* resign. Fiddling with the envelope she'd laid inconspicuously in her lap, she watched the waitress deposit their drinks and saunter off.

Mason sipped his iced tea. "So, Tess, what do you want to talk about?"

Tess inhaled steeply. "Mr. Tramont, I need to…"

"Mason."

"What?"

"Please call me Mason."

"But I…I never call you Mason."

"Yes, I know."

"And you never call me Tess."

"Something I would like to change."

"Why?"

"Because, if we're dating, I'd like to call you by your first name."

She consciously avoided rolling her eyes. "That's not what I meant. Why do you want to change things between us? Why ask me out now? Why *today*?"

He stared at his tea, took a long drink, and set the glass precisely centered on his coaster before looking back to her. "Why not today?"

Tess had a perfectly good answer. Her pulse sputtered as she brought the envelope up and slid it across the table. "Here."

Mason glanced down at his name in writing. "What is this?"

"Just open it, please."

She held her breath as he opened, unfolded, and read her resignation. She knew the words by heart; they were professional and brief. No flowery speeches to end this relationship.

Only a few hour-long moments passed before he set the paper down. Tess watched with nerve-wracking anticipation as he refolded the sheet and slid it back into the envelope, allowing it to fall onto the table. His steel eyes found hers. "I don't want to accept this."

She fumbled with her napkin. "I appreciate that. But it doesn't change anything."

"Have I offended you that deeply?"

"Offended me?"

"By asking you out," he clarified, drawing his solid body up to its impressive height, even while sitting.

"No, you haven't offended me. This isn't about today."

"Then what is it about?"

"It's simply time for me to move on."

Mason's severe gaze held her, as it had so often in the past, but never on this personal a level. "I knew something was wrong when you came to my office this morning," he said, his voice softer than usual. "And I always knew you'd move on eventually. You were far too bright for this position the day you stepped into the building. I just thought I'd have some warning before you left. More than a few hours, anyway."

Well, that was more praise than he'd given her in...ever. "As it, um, as it says in, uh, the letter, I'll stay for four more weeks," she stumbled.

"That is when the West End County Club unveils the new conference center. David and I are supposed to be there."

"Yes, I know." Tess was fully aware of the high-profile situation for Field and Tramont. The company had put countless hours into design and construction for the West End Country Club's newest structure. The conference center was gorgeous, and the upcoming unveiling would be an event of monumental proportions here in Virginia, with old and new money as far as the eye could see. "I promise I will make sure everything goes smoothly on our end. I've already ordered your tuxedo for the gala that night, and..."

"And will you be there?"

"I was never going to be. You're supposed to bring a date."

Mason rested back in his seat. "I know. I want to bring you."

Tess arched an eyebrow. "You still think you want to date me? I just quit. Doesn't that change things?"

"No."

He said the word so simply, as if he'd predetermined the two of them together. While that option would normally curl her toes, right now it meant he wasn't taking her seriously. "Look, Mr. Tramont..."

"Mason."

She sighed. "Look, Mason, we need to hammer out some details about my departure. The newest structural engineers you hired are performing well, and the accounting department has finally gotten all the glitches out of their computer system, so things should flow pretty smoothly. You'll need a new secretary, but I'm willing to train my replacement. I'll even hire someone myself, if you prefer to be removed from the process." Tess would make sure he had the best secretary possible. She'd be sixty and toothless, of course, but damn efficient.

Mason's facial expression never wavered from overwhelming self-assurance. "What are you doing for dinner tonight, Tess?"

"Wow, really? Didn't you hear a word I said?"

"I heard everything you said. You've planned your departure with all the precision you're known for. I'm sure it will proceed as intended. But now, as I mentioned earlier, what I'm interested in is *you*."

She sat motionless, watching his lips produce the most incredible words ever. For a moment, Tess felt dazed by the idea. Her mind leapt into the fantasy world she'd kept hidden for so long, the one where Mason was madly in love with her and everything was perfectly perfect between them and they often ran together, hand-in-hand, through fields of wildflowers. It was a world she tried not to visit too often, since she understood how unrealistic it was.

But sitting here now, looking into his warm, sincere eyes, she didn't know what to think. Was this possible? Could she date Mason Tramont? Did he want her, even if she left the office? Even if she no longer did his daily bidding? Did he want her instead of his rich socialite? And where was that woman?

Tess steadied herself as best she could. "What about Malory Catskill?"

He didn't move at all, except for a twitch of his jaw. "What about her?"

"I'm familiar with your relationship." Hell, she'd watched that walking tornado drag Mason around – dumping, using, and re-dumping him – for years. "Where is she?"

"I have no idea. Nor do I want to. She's out of my life."

Tess bit into her lip, wondering how far she could push for information when they'd never before discussed such personal issues. "Can I ask what happened between the two of you?"

"It just wasn't a good relationship," he dismissed, even though his eyes darkened with countless emotions. Mason leaned closer, resting his arms on the table. "What about you? Are you over that Bryan person?"

"*Bryan*?" Tess was certain she'd never mentioned her ex's name to her boss. Also, that breakup was two years ago. "How do you know about Bryan?"

"I pay attention. You may not think so, but I see a lot of things."

"Yes, well, I see a lot of things, too. I know you're not done with Malory. You never will be."

The waitress came with their meals but Tess barely noticed the food...not with her daunting boss staring her down across the table.

"How are you so certain I'm not done with Malory?" Mason asked when the tattooed attendant exited again.

Tess took a bite of her salad, chewing on her lettuce and on his words. "Because that's how those relationships work," she explained between mouthfuls. "People who get trapped in situations like that – going back to someone over and over again even though they keep falling into the same toxic patterns – don't just break away with a few simple words. It's not that easy."

"It sounds like you're speaking from personal experience."

An olive lodged itself in her throat and she coughed hard. Copious amounts of ingested water later, Tess considered confiding in him. The freakish thought left her mind as quickly as it entered. She wasn't about to open *that* can of worms. "I just watch a lot of talk shows."

Mason shook his head. "He hurt you badly, didn't he?"

"Who?"

"Bryan."

She stabbed a crouton with her fork. "Why would you say that?"

"Other than you mutilating salad condiments at the mention of his name? I told you, I pay attention. You were different after your breakup with Bryan. You didn't laugh the way you normally do. You stopped tossing your ponytail around when you told a story. You even stopped rolling your eyes at me, like you do when you think I'm not watching. You just weren't yourself."

Heat crept into her face. Did Mason Tramont know her that well? Before today, she would have sworn he didn't even know she was female.

"I'm glad you're back to your normal self, Tess. I hope it means you're over him. I hope you can move on to someone new. Someone like me."

She set her fork down. "I can't believe you're doing this *now*," she thought aloud, her mind still grasping for some explanation. "After all this time, after everything I've done for you, after all the ways I've made myself the most indispensable employee…"

"Are you angry with me?" he asked, shifting subtly in his chair. "Do you feel I've taken advantage of you?"

"No, I don't." Maybe that wasn't entirely the truth, but Tess was much angrier with herself for everything she'd done to gain his attention.

"Well, I think you *should* be angry with me."

"Really? Why?"

"Because I did take advantage of you. You and your amazing organizational skills. In order to focus on my job, I let you oversee every part of my life that I didn't consider important. From my wardrobe to…"

"To your family."

He nodded, staring down at his untouched manicotti. "Yes, them."

"That reminds me, Ian called earlier. He wants to play golf with you this month. Oh, and I made sure Vanessa will get her birthday gift on Thursday."

Mason looked back to Tess. "I'll call my brother. And thank you for taking care of my sister's birthday, yet again. Can I ask what she'll get this year?"

"You're in a good mood this year. She'll get a hefty gift certificate to a lovely day spa."

"I am in a good mood, aren't I?" A smile tugged at his lips. "I must tell you, Vanessa will miss you very much when you leave. She's always known you're the one who picks out the presents."

"I know. She sends me thank you cards."

"Hmm. Then I can only imagine how it will buffer the shock of your resignation if I assure my little sister that you and I are dating now."

Tess caught herself grinning at the idea, the field-of-wildflowers fantasy creeping back inside her head. "I suppose that would make your sister happy. If only I could figure out why you chose *today* to ask me out, when we've really been together for the past six years." She stopped speaking immediately, her cheeks flaming with fire, as she realized what she'd insinuated. "And by *together*, I just mean *working* together, since I would certainly remember if we'd been *together* together. Not that I'm implying that being together with you is memorable, because that would mean I know what it's like to be with you, like *sexually*. Which I don't, and haven't imagined at all, of course, because that would be incredibly inappropriate, what with you being my boss and everything."

Tess's eyes got wider and wider as she spoke, but she couldn't stop the word vomit. *Damn it, damn it, damn it! I don't babble around Mason anymore! I don't!*

She peered at him, fully expecting a recriminating glare. But the look on his face wasn't judgmental, or condescending, or even mildly questioning. If she didn't know better, she would say he looked...smitten.

"*Tess*," he breathed, his deep voice drawing out the single syllable as his gaze drifted from her eyes to her mouth and back. "Does it matter why I chose today? Can we just say that I came out of a fog this morning and started seeing what's right in front of me? You're intelligent, charming, and beautiful."

Her lips parted while she stared at him. He looked so sincere. So certain. Tess had the overwhelming sensation that she was now standing on the winner's podium, being handed everything she ever wanted on a gold platter, and all she had to do was reach out and take it. At this moment, all those futile years – the years she'd spent pining over him, and watching him fall again and again into the arms of another woman, and sacrificing pieces of herself in order to be his indispensable servant – didn't matter. Right at this moment, Mason wanted her like she'd always wanted him.

She worked to hold back the tears of joy that threatened to spill from her eyes. But nothing could stop the melting of her heart.

"And maybe I should have asked you out long ago," Mason continued with a soft shake of his head, "but I just haven't thought about my personal happiness in so long. Not until I saw how happy David is."

Those words rang like a death toll in Tess's ears.

How happy David is.

She heard nothing but the tortured thumping of her own erratic heartbeat for stretched seconds. "Holy hell," she cursed.

David. David and Regina. That's why Mason chose today.

Tess understood now. She was not standing on the winner's podium. She was not being handed everything she ever wanted. Mason Tramont was just using her. Yet again.

"Oh my Lord!" she yelped. A second later, the tornado of realization hit her full-force and her mouth opened to a fury of words. "It's David and Regina! They just got back from their honeymoon today! I waited until they were back to give you my resignation so they could help you transition! But *you*! You waited until they got back to see if they were working out! You wanted to see if your business partner was happy with *his* secretary! That's it, isn't it? David gets back from his honeymoon all giddy and adorable, so you think, 'Hey, maybe Tess would be a passable option for me! Maybe my dependable, hard-working secretary could become my dependable, hard-working girlfriend!' And that sounded really wrong and I didn't mean hard-working in some weird sexual way! Oh...*damn it*! I guess I should be relieved David and Regina are happy! If they'd come back pissed off at each other, you probably would've fired me on the spot!"

Tess sat at the edge of her seat, eyes blazing. She knew the other restaurant patrons gawked at her, but she couldn't bring herself to care.

Mason looked genuinely confused. "Tess, if I've offended you..."

"Damn straight you've offended me," she stated, attempting to lower her voice out of range of onlookers. "I am not a high school science experiment for you to research, *Mister Tramont*. You can't test your boss-and-secretary coexistence theories on me. I'm worth more than that."

"Of course you are...that's not what..."

"Save it," she said, rising from her seat and grabbing her purse, thankful to the heavens that they drove separately. "I need to get back to the office. I have a lot of work to do before I'm out of there for good."

With one final glare, Tess stormed off, leaving a thoroughly baffled Mason Tramont in her wake.

～

TESS MANAGED to drive her car several blocks away and pull into an empty parking lot before bursting into tears. She dialed Annabelle's number on her cell and slobbered into the phone for several minutes before her friend could determine what had happened.

"Hold on, Tess, let me get this straight. Mason Tramont asked you out on a date and you said *no*?"

"You're damn right I said no! Didn't you hear me? He only asked me out because his business partner married *his* secretary! So, Mason and his emotion-less robot-brain thought it would make sense to ask out his own secretary! He wanted to use me as an experiment on love! Like a frickin' lab rat! And I started yelling in a restaurant full of people, Belle!"

"Tess, honey, do you think maybe you overreacted a little?"

"*A little*? Are you *kidding* me? I overreacted like the biggest idiot in the whole world! But that just proves my point!"

"And your point is?"

"He makes me *crazy*! Crazy, I tell you! How can he be so insensitive? How can he sit there like one of his stone columns and say he wants to *date* me, when he has no real interest in me whatsoever? How can he expect me to flip a switch and become his puppet-girlfriend, just because he'd like to see if it works? How can *anyone* be so damn cold?"

"But maybe..."

"I'm tired, Belle. Tired of being the steadfast, indispensable employee. I'm tired of blending into the wallpaper unless I serve some purpose. Mason Tramont has looked through me for the past six years. He needs to realize he can't treat people this way. He needs to be taught a lesson."

"Now, wait, Tess. Before you do anything stupid..."

Stupid? How could she do anything stupider than what she'd done since the day she walked into his building? All the feelings she'd harbored for him – the dreams of them being so happy together that they'd make everyone gag from their sugary sweetness – yet all she was to him now was an experiment. She was nothing more than a secondary thought, a passing whim to entertain him while he was separated from the person he really wanted: Malory Catskill.

Tess knew what it felt like to be second best. She wouldn't do that again.

With a steep breath, she settled herself before reassuring her friend. "I won't do anything stupid, Belle."

"Are you sure?"

Okay, no, I'm not sure. "Whatever I decide to do will be no more than the man deserves. Besides, even if it is stupid, I've only got four more weeks to work with him. He can't fire me when I've already quit. He could shorten my notice, but I'll pay that price if I must."

"Oh, honey, maybe you should come by the store for a bit."

"Why? Is something wrong? Do you need my help?"

"No, everything is fine here. I think *you* need *my* help."

Tess gripped her phone until her knuckles blanched. "Thank you, but this is something I have to do on my own."

"Please don't do anything rash."

She mulled over her friend's warning. "You're probably right. I'm too emotional. I'll give myself the afternoon to think it through."

"Or longer. Much longer. And call me back. I want to know your plan, since I'll probably need to talk you out of it."

"Don't worry. I'll get my head on straight before I make any decisions."

After all, revenge is a dish best served cold.

3

A SHOTGUN AND A SHOVEL

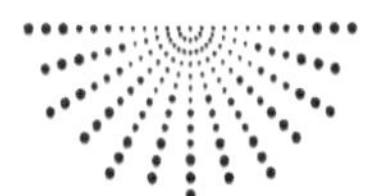

Mason sat behind his ebony desk, utterly confounded by the day's events. He'd gone from leaving his door open to losing the best secretary ever. Tess wasn't just an employee, either. He considered her a friend. Maybe she didn't see it that way. Maybe he never made her feel that way. But she was.

His door remained safely closed all afternoon, ever since he'd come back from lunch, passed her empty office, and walked into his. He wasn't sure if she'd even come back. He wouldn't blame her if she didn't. Apparently, he'd been a complete ass at the restaurant. He'd never seen her that angry. Not once in six years. He'd struck one hell of a nerve.

He ran a hand roughly through his hair as visions of his livid, fuming secretary rang in his mind. Was it so ludicrous, the thought of dating him? Enough to send her off the deep end? Admittedly, when David mentioned it this morning, Mason's first reaction was negative. He and Tess had an amazing professional relationship and he didn't want to screw it up. Yet, the more he thought about it, the more sense it made. She was the perfect secretary, so wouldn't she make the perfect girlfriend?

That, it seems, was where he'd gone wrong. According to Tess, he wasn't supposed to think things through so sensibly. But what was wrong with being practical about love?

Sighing as he leaned back in his chair, Mason stared at the clock on the wall. After six. Definitely time to go home, even though he hadn't gotten any work done today. He'd thought all morning about how to ask out his secretary. He'd thought all afternoon about how to apologize for asking her out. Basically, he'd thought about Tess all damn day.

"She has a right to be angry with me," he grumbled. "And not just for today."

After all, he'd used her, absolutely and without question, since the moment they'd met. A young college graduate, Tess was bright and bubbly and ridiculously over-qualified for what he needed at the time. Back then, Field and Tramont was just getting off the ground and he didn't have much for her to do. But she was eager to take on more and more duties – even personal ones – so he let her. He never said, "I don't need you to pick out my suits," or, "It's not your responsibility to buy birthday gifts for my family." He should have refused her countless offers, but Tess was just so good at everything. She made his life easier. Better.

Now, she might never speak to him again. She might even slap him. If she did, he would take it like a man. Lord knows he deserved it.

Mason shook his head, shut his laptop, and reached for his car keys. A small knock came from the other side of his closed door. He stopped and stared at the dark wood. "Yes?"

The door opened slowly and she stood there, just as beautiful as ever. She'd taken her ponytail out. Tess's freed curls were wild and wavy and everywhere. Her dark blue blouse hugged her breasts and highlighted the paler blue of her eyes.

He repressed a lustful grin as his eyes fell down her body to her snug black skirt, drawing his attention to the curve of her hips and the length of her legs. Forcing himself to look back to her face, he noticed she'd put on a new lip gloss. This one was a few shades darker, although no less inviting than any of the others.

"May I come in?" she asked, luring him from his reverie. Her voice sounded calm and soothing. Perhaps she didn't intend to slap him.

"Of course, Miss Troy, I need to…"

"Wait, please, Mr. Tramont. Mason. Before you say anything, I want to apologize."

"Apologize?"

"Yes. I was way out of line at lunch. My only excuse is that my resignation made me overly emotional. Still, I shouldn't have made such a scene. I'm sorry."

"I…I didn't expect an apology. I owe *you* one. I shouldn't have asked you out. That was a professional boundary I should never have crossed. You can file a sexual harassment complaint if you'd like."

Mason held his breath until he saw her smile.

"I don't think I'll be filing one of those," she said. "Actually, I hope you'll consider a different arrangement."

"Arrangement? What do you mean?"

Tess waved him toward her. "Come with me."

"Where?"

She laughed. "Just come."

He stared hard at her for a moment before placing his keys in the pocket of his suit coat and moving around his desk. Tess turned and exited down the hallway. He followed along, a puppy on a leash. She strolled past her office, past the employee lounge, out the front door, and down the steps. Her car sat curbside.

"I have to grab something," she said, popping the trunk of her red VW Bug and rummaging around. Briefly, Mason wondered if she had a shotgun and a shovel inside. The fleeting, ridiculous thought made him grin. After all, this was his sweet little Tess.

"Here we go." She stood, holding a green blanket in her arms.

He stepped forward and shut the trunk. "What is that for?"

"Over here," she encouraged, nodding her head toward the park. She eased across the empty street and he trailed behind, recalling his odd urge this morning to run over here and roll around in the grass. If he didn't know better, he would swear Tess had read his mind.

She stepped onto the lush lawn and kept going, past several trees and benches to an even, open area of grass polka-dotted with dandelions. Bending over and shaking out the blanket, she spread it on the ground. Mason tried not to stare at the reverse-heart shape of her bottom when she bent down.

He looked up instead, noting the golden glow of the slowly setting sun as it outlined a thousand spring leaves in the trees. He'd always loved living in Richmond, where he could surround himself with both traditional and modern architecture. Right this minute, he could surround himself with nature and with her. He couldn't recall a better moment in years.

"Come. Sit," she instructed, easing onto the blanket and kicking off her heels.

Mason obeyed, but kept his shoes on. He made sure his suit didn't touch the grass.

"You look uncomfortable," Tess noted, watching as he attempted to curl his large body onto his half of the blanket.

"Sorry. This suit doesn't give much wiggle room."

Tess laughed. "I've never heard you say *wiggle room* before."

She shifted onto her knees and crawled toward him. He swallowed hard at the sight of her down on all fours. Then her hands were on his chest, her palms flattening against his shirt before gliding upward to ease the jacket off his shoulders. The vanilla-and-flowers scent of her hair lulled him and he let her do whatever she wished. Yet, as distracted as he was, he still didn't miss the way her breath hitched while her fingers wandered over his body.

"There," she said, brushing her hands across his when she finally pulled the coat from his arms. She stood to lay it over a nearby tree branch. "How is your wiggle room now?"

He had to clear his throat. "Better."

Tess settled back down on the blanket beside him. She smiled, glancing up into the green leaves. "It's lovely today, isn't it?"

Mason watched her glossy lips move as she spoke. "Beautiful."

"I thought this would be a good place to talk."

"Talk?" *I can think of other things I'd much rather do.*

She met his intent gaze. "Yes, talk. Along with my apology, I wanted to tell you I've given a lot of thought to our conversation at lunch, and I realize your heart was in the right place."

"Well, I have to say that surprises me. After your...reaction."

She shrugged her slender shoulders. "I do get your reasoning. David is your best friend, and he and Regina are adorably in love. I can see how his happiness brought to light your unhappiness. I also understand why you want to fix it. The problem is, you chose the wrong person to fix it with."

"I don't think I chose the wrong person."

"Oh, but you did. I'm not the one you want."

Mason didn't believe that. Right now, seeing the sun sparkle off her gold hair, and the crinkles forming on her freckled nose while she squinted in the light, she looked pretty damn perfect. "Tell me, Tess. Since you have this all figured out, who is the one I want?"

"Malory Catskill, of course."

He choked on her words, coughing forcefully before he could respond. "You are *absolutely wrong* about that."

Tess stretched her legs out across the blanket. She eased down on her elbows and dropped her head back, her halo of curls soaking up the rays as if she were lying on a beach. He tried not to fantasize about her being naked and sandy. He failed.

"I'm absolutely right, actually. Do you remember what my bachelor's degree is in, Mason?"

"Hmm. I believe your résumé said psychology."

"Wow, you do remember. Brownie points." She awarded him with a wink and an electrifying smile. "I wish I'd understood the world better, back when I chose my college major. But my degree did prepare me to ask the universal question."

"Which is?"

"Do you want fries with that?"

He chuckled, shaking his head.

Tess grinned. "Let's just say my choice of majors didn't prepare me to conquer the job market. But it did prepare me for something else."

"What did it prepare you for?"

"Relationship counseling."

"Ah, I see. You think a few classes made you an expert on love?"

"A few classes and several years of experience with relationships," she corrected. "And don't forget the talk shows."

Mason couldn't help smiling at the playful look on her face.

She sat up, angling toward him, leaning in. He could smell her hair again, could see the exact shade of blue in her eyes. "So, what do you think?" she asked, exuberant and enticing.

"About what?"

"About me becoming your love coach."

"*Love coach*?"

"Okay, that sounds a little stupid. You can call it something else if you like, but you get my point. You need help and I'm here to help you."

He cocked his head. "What kind of help do you think I need?"

"Well, don't take this the wrong way, Mason, but you're a little bit stiff. You're missing the spark – or sparkle – that a woman wants from a man."

His chest tightened as he absorbed the reality of how Tess saw him. "What makes you think I don't sparkle?"

"I've been your secretary for six years. I know you."

"You know me at work. You don't know me personally."

"Don't I? I spend a ridiculous amount of time with you. I've been to your home. I've watched your interactions, with Malory and with your family. I have a better relationship with your sister than you do." Tess sighed. "I promise I'm not saying these things to hurt your feelings. You are an intelligent man and an exceptional boss. You deserve a good woman, but you're not going to get one until you loosen up. I'm sure even Malory realizes that. She loves you, but she can't commit because she's missing something. I'll teach you how to give it to her."

"*God*, how many times do I have to say it? I do *not* want Malory."

"Yes, you do. You just want her more vibrant and sparkly. Once you change, she'll change. Then your hundred-year, on-again-off-again relationship can be permanently on." Tess rested back entirely on the blanket, her eyelids drifting closed as she smiled into the sunshine. "Take a few minutes to think about my proposal, Mason. I'd like to help you and I'm not going anywhere. At least, not for four more weeks."

Take a few minutes to think about it? He could think about this for a year and still be confused...and more than a little offended. Did she really think he was an utter bore, or was she retaliating for his blundered attempt at dating her? He'd come across poorly at lunch, and for the last six years, but he wanted to change that now. Why couldn't she see it?

Mason stared at her, lying just out of his reach, looking more angel than earthly. He didn't know what kind of game she intended to play, but he was damn curious to find out. Maybe, if he played along, he could convince her he wasn't a lackluster, pigheaded curmudgeon who bored women so much that they couldn't bear to be in a relationship with him.

"So," he wondered aloud, "what exactly will your love coaching entail?"

Tess's eyelids popped open. She grinned wickedly, as if she'd already won the game. "Basically, it's me teaching you how to be freer and more exciting. I'll need you to do things that are outside of your everyday norm. Things that don't necessarily fit into your ordered life."

"You know, just because I'm a professional, and maybe a little picky, and a bit of a germaphobe, doesn't mean I'm not sparkly."

"If that's true, my job will be easy, won't it?"

"I guess. For clarification, if I agree to this, what will my job be?"

"That's simple. Just do everything I say, no questions asked."

He immediately shook his head. He trusted Tess to run certain parts of his life, but handing over complete control sounded insane. He hated being out of control. Yet here she was, asking him to let go of everything.

Grappling with whether or not he could play along with this particular game, Mason absorbed the vision of the little sprite lying beside him. Haloed by the sun and smiling in unfettered joy, Tess was officially the sexiest thing he'd ever seen. Why on earth hadn't he noticed before?

"Okay, I'll do it," he stated, thinking more with the organ below his belt than with the one inside his skull. "My life is in your hands."

Her responding grin nearly blinded him. She stood, motioning for him to join her. Mason rose and looked down to her, taken aback by their significant height difference when she wasn't wearing her heels.

She reached out to him and he thought she meant to shake his hand. But she grabbed onto him instead, arching up on her tiptoes to pull him in for a hug. Her arms wrapped around his neck as their bodies melded together. Mason placed his hands on the center of her back, unsure of how tightly or intimately he could hold her at this point.

Tess urged him down in order to press her lips to his ear. "I've got every-thing under control," she whispered.

She pulled away before he had the chance to fully enjoy the feel of her soft curves pressed against him. She smiled again, glowing and gorgeous. Then she grabbed the blanket from the ground and strolled away. "See you in the office tomorrow," she sang over her shoulder.

All he could do was watch her leave.

4

DANCES WITH ROBOTS

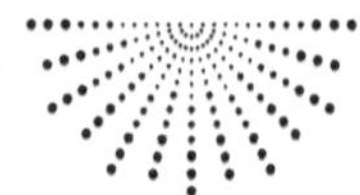

The next day, Tess worked hard to maintain normal appearances. She played the role of the dutiful secretary, addressing Mr. Tramont formally, as if nothing had changed. She couldn't afford a slip-up when her plan had started so well.

"It's after five, workaholic," Regina called to her from the hall. "You heading home soon?"

"Yeah, in a bit. Everyone else gone?"

"Everyone but your shut-in architect. David and I are going to Angelo's for some pizza and baseball on the big screen. You interested?"

"Thanks, but no. There's someplace I have to be."

Regina took a step into Tess's office. "You got a hot date or something? Please tell me it's a hot date."

Tess absorbed the eager look on her friend's face. "I wish," she said, laughing to conceal her nerves.

Regina frowned. "Oh, well. See you tomorrow?"

"Of course. Have fun."

"You, too."

Regina bounced off and Tess smiled to herself. She might not have a hot date this evening, but what she had planned *would* be fun. In a diabolical, evil-twin sort of way.

Grabbing her cell, she texted her boss: *Meet me at the park?*

A harrowing minute passed before he replied: *I'll be there.*

Tess's heart fluttered, part excitement, part guilt. She tamped down the guilt. This was no time to be delicate. Shutting down her computer and grabbing her bag, she stepped into the hall. She glanced at Mason's still-closed door before turning the opposite direction, striding out of the now-quiet building and down the stone steps to her waiting Bug.

Today, her car held more than just her fluffy blanket. She'd also packed a little cooler, a bottle of wine, and a picnic basket. Scooping everything up in her arms, she closed the trunk and crossed the street, finding her way to the same dandelion patch as yesterday. She spotted a few families in the park, throwing balls or lounging on benches, but they were far enough away that she and Mason would basically be alone here. After arranging the blanket on the grass, she grabbed her phone and dialed Annabelle's number.

"Hey, kiddo," Belle chimed in. "I was wondering when I'd hear from you. How's the dastardly deed coming along?"

"It's not *that* dastardly," Tess defended, opening the picnic basket with her free hand and arranging cheese and grapes on a platter. "And it's going swimmingly. He couldn't have responded better yesterday evening if I'd written a script and asked him to read it out loud. He fell for every word – hook, line and sinker. Now, I just have to reel him in."

"You do know he's not a fish, right?"

"Yes, I do know."

"So, what does today hold for Mason Tramont?"

"Today, I'll start extracting him from his cocooned comfort zone. This is only the beginning, so I'll be gentle. Just a little dancing."

"Just dancing?"

"For now. The challenges get worse as the week goes on."

"But nothing else today?"

Tess glanced up at the new leaves fluttering in the breeze. "Why do you ask?"

"Because I'll bet Mason thinks you're on a date, and a man on a date wants to get some."

Tess coughed against her suddenly dry throat. "No, no. I already told him I'm doing this to help him get back together with his ex-witch. Besides, he's not interested in me."

"Are you sure about that?"

"Yes, I'm very sure. I've spent six years as his office minion and he never even paid me a compliment until yesterday, when I resigned. Honestly, I wish he were interested in me, since it would make this whole plan a hell of a lot easier. As it is, I'm going to have to flirt my ass off just to get him where I want him. But he *will* be my manservant, Belle. My *manservant*, I tell you! Mu-wah-ha-ha!" Tess finished with her best maniacal laugh and started giggling.

The phone went silent.

"Annabelle? You still there?"

"Still here."

"That was supposed to be funny."

"I'm worried about you, Tess."

"Don't be. I'm giving myself five days to do this. I've already quit, so if everything turns out the way I've planned and Mason wants to kill me on Saturday, I just won't go back to the office."

"I'm not worried about your job."

"Do you think I've gone insane? I haven't. I'm doing this to increase my self-esteem. I'm not going to be that man's puppet anymore. It's female empowerment, really."

"Not worried about your mind, either. Although it's a bit haywire right now."

"You're not worried about my employment or my sanity? Okay, I'll bite. What are you worried about?"

Belle sighed. "Oh, honey, you know you're in love with him."

Tess grimaced. She hated hearing that out loud. It was too painful on too many levels. "I'm fine. Mason and I aren't meant to be. I've known that for years."

She glanced up, catching a glimpse of his dark navy suit as he stepped onto the grass at the far end of the park. A spark of nerves frizzled beneath her skin and she ran her trembling fingers through her hair. Her normally contained blond waves now lay draped against her shoulders. Her clingiest dress hugged every curve of her body. Her bare toes curled into the blanket beneath her. Her mouth ran dry.

"Just because you know it in your head doesn't mean your heart will listen," Belle's voice resounded in her ears. "You've held Mason Tramont up as the standard to every man you've dated since college, yet now you think you're going to use him and walk away unscathed?"

Tess watched her boss approach and reigned in her anxieties as quickly as they'd come. "I love you, Belle. I have since the day I met you our freshman year. But you're a worrywart and you're going to spoil the best fun I've had in years. He's coming. I've got to go."

"Don't kiss him, Tess."

Mason stopped a few feet from the blanket, his eyes fixed on hers.

"Thanks for calling, Belle. See you this weekend," Tess sang.

"I mean it. No kissing."

She smashed the off button on her phone and shoved the device in her purse before peering up at her prey. "Sorry, just talking to a friend."

"No problem." Mason glanced at the miniature party on the ground. "What's all this?"

"Picnic in the park. Kick off your shoes and join me."

Tess watched his deep brown eyes focus on her toes before drifting up her bare legs and onto her sleek red dress. Red like a sinner. Or a Sinister Secretary.

Harnessing all her confidence, she pressed her arms together to enhance the cleavage in her low-V neckline. "Come on, shoes off."

He didn't look away from her as he kicked his Italian loafers toward a nearby oak and eased off his jacket. She wet her lips while he laid the coat on a branch. Her eyes latched to the sight of his biceps shifting beneath his shirt.

Belle is a spoilsport! Look at the man! Would one kiss be so bad?

"What do you have planned for us today?" Mason asked while curling his body onto the blanket beside her.

Tess cleared her throat and her mind. "First, a snack and a drink. I hope you love wine as much as I do," she said, handing him the bottle.

"I do enjoy some wine now and then," he admitted, popping the cork and pouring the rich burgundy liquid into the two glasses she'd produced from her picnic basket. "Cheers."

"Cheers," Tess echoed, clinking her glass with his. She tipped her head back, downing the entire contents in one long, continuous gulp.

Mason looked mortified. "Wow. That's...wow."

She smiled. "What?"

"I've never seen anyone drink wine like that. Did you taste it?"

"Sure. It's an old college game: see who can drink the most, the fastest."

"You are an expert."

"I can drink a fraternity guy twice my size under the table, thank you. Not that I participate in those things anymore."

"I guess that's good."

Tess laughed and set her glass back in the basket before easing down on her side. She propped up on one elbow, resting her head in her hand while Mason continued sipping. "I take it Malory never did things like that in college?"

"Definitely not. Malory would never."

"I see. Are you disappointed in me, then?"

"Quite the opposite, actually."

"My goodness. Was that another compliment?"

His head tilted. "I'm not sure what you mean."

"Yesterday at lunch, you called me bright and pretty. Now, you approve of my parlor trick. You'd better slow down the wild praise or my head will swell."

Mason finished his wine and set his glass down beside hers. "Is my love coach informing me that I'm too sparse with my compliments?"

She caught his eyes. "Maybe."

He reached for the platter she'd fixed and pulled a grape from the stem. "Intelligent, charming, and beautiful," he corrected, reaching forward to place the grape against her lips. "That is what I called you at the restaurant."

Tess opened her mouth to allow him to push the tiny fruit inside. His thumb brushed against her lip, leaving a trail of fire in its wake. She chewed slowly and swallowed hard. "You sure do remember the details, don't you?"

"My life is all about details. I just happen to know which ones are important to me and which ones I can let someone else handle. And no, I don't give out compliments easily. When I do, I'm sincere."

She tried to decide if those words made up for six years of following him around like a dog waiting to be thrown a bone. They didn't. "Well, that's not good enough."

"It's not?" Mason stretched out beside her, mimicking her pose so they lay face to face, his legs reaching off the blanket and onto the grass. "Should I lie?"

"No, I'm not saying you should lie to people. But you can pleasantly overemphasize from time to time."

He pulled another grape from the plate and brought it to her mouth, running it slowly across her lips before allowing her to eat it. "Pleasantly overemphasize?"

Tess had to remind herself what their conversation was about. The obscenity of the situation wreaked havoc on her brain: Mason's body so blissfully close, his fingers feeding her, his words praising her. If she didn't know better, she would think he wanted her. But she did know better. "Let's talk about Malory," she reminded herself.

"Must we?"

"Yes, we must. She's the reason we're transforming you, after all. What would you compliment her on if she was here?"

He scrunched up his face, looked confounded for several moments, and then shook his head. "I've got nothing."

Tess giggled. "Seriously? You've been together forever. There must be some reason. What was she like when you first met?"

"Bossy."

"Hmm. That's a start. Change *bossy* into *self-assured* and you've got something. This is good. What else?"

"Well, when we fought, she often threw things."

"Ooh-kay. That one's a little tougher. But when that happens, you could say, 'Wow, you're such a strong woman,' or, 'Honey, you have the attitude of a real champion'."

Mason's brow cocked. "Good Lord. Do you really expect me to take Malory back so that when she's jumping around like a monkey and throwing dinner plates at me, I can tell her she has the attitude of a champion? Do you actually think that will make me sparkly?"

Tess tried to look serious but failed. She broke into hysterical laughter, so hard that she eventually snorted. "I'm sorry. I didn't mean to laugh," she managed to say through her giggles.

"Yes, you did." He reached out, pushing several curls over her shoulder. He ran his hand slowly down her arm before letting it fall away.

Her laughter caught in her throat.

"I have an idea," he said, looking straight into her eyes. "What if I practice my complimenting skills on you?"

"On me?"

"Sure. I'll say whatever comes to mind and you can grade me."

Oh, he's fallen into my web so nicely. "You can try, I suppose. But I must warn you: your love coach is a harsh judge."

"Then I'll have to do my very best."

"Good luck," she offered, forcing an indifferent smile. Inside, her nerves built. She'd waited for a Tramont Compliment for so long, she wasn't sure if she could handle the fallout.

Mason shifted his large body on the blanket and Tess held her breath. His eyes moved across her face, lingered on her lips, eased down to her hands. He became quiet, so much so that the cute, twittering birds in the trees began to annoy the hell out of her.

What on earth is taking so long? Is it that hard for him to drum up something he likes about me?

She stilled when his hand moved to hers, easing across her knuckles to trace the lines of her fingers. "I've watched these dainty, skilled hands do so many things over the past six years," he reflected, his voice so low she had to lean in to hear, "but I've never been able to touch them like this. And I've listened to your laugh a million times, but it never sounded more alive or contagious than it does now, when you're laughing just for me."

His eyes returned to hers, darker than before. "And your hair...damn, I love your hair," he continued, his fingers leaving her hand to push into the curls. "I love it in the ponytail. I love it down. You toss it around when you're happy, or when you want me to know how mad you are. It's even softer than I imagined it would be, now that I finally get to feel it, but it smells the same: like a field of flowers."

His eyes dropped to her mouth before he spoke again. "But I don't smell vanilla right now. I thought your hair smelled like flowers and vanilla, yet now I realize the vanilla scent must be from your lip gloss." His hand shifted, his thumb brushing across her lower lip. "You wear a different shade every day. I see it glimmer in the office lights and it's so damn sexy. Like you."

Mason stopped talking and stared at her mouth.

Tess was incapable of making her jaw close.

Oh, crap. I was wrong. He does want me. Almost as much as I want him. Belle's right. This is a mistake. A monstrous, hairy mistake.

He traced the side of her face. "So, love coach, how'd I do?"

She sat bolt upright, slamming the door on her traitorous heart. "Yeah, that was awful. I can tell you gave it your all, but I'm sorry to say you just can't do compliments. Hopeless, really. We'll have to move on."

Mason sat up to face her. "Seriously?"

Tess forced a laugh and stood from the blanket, disconnecting. She couldn't listen to his enticing words and keep on track. "We have a regimented schedule to follow, after all."

"You certainly are earnest about love coaching."

"Well, you deserve the best." She held her hand out to him. "Let's move on to dancing."

"I don't dance."

"I figured, but women love a man who can dance."

He grasped her fingers and stood to join her. The touch of his skin sent a shock of heat up her arm. She dropped his hand and leaned down, hitting the music button on her phone. One of her favorite electronic dance songs, loud and funky, filled the air.

Tess smiled at the unruly sounds and stepped back. "Okay, Mason, have at it."

"What do you mean? You want me to dance alone?"

"Of course. How can I evaluate you properly if I can't watch?"

Reaching out, he snaked his arm around her waist and pulled her against him. One large hand spread out on her back, the other took her fingers in his and held them to his chest. "I think you can evaluate me better this way," he suggested, beginning a slow, rhythmic sway.

Her breathing turned shallow with the feel of his strong, hard body pressed into her soft curves. Her hips moved with his against her will. She knew she should fight it, but couldn't muster the energy. Mason felt warm and solid and smelled like exotic spices wafting over the ocean on a clear, starry night. Or maybe she really was losing her mind.

Tess stared at her hand, resting on his chest. She eased her other hand up the back of his neck and into his hair. She sighed far too loudly.

He grinned, slow and devilish, before he pushed her away, twirled her in a circle, and reeled her back, clamping her to him once again. Then he dipped her low to the ground, her hair nearly touching the grass, before bringing her back up in that deliberate, agonizingly sexy way she'd only seen in movies. Face to face again, he stared into her eyes. Her footing faltered but he had it under control. He made sure she didn't miss a step.

Damn it. He dances, too. He's gorgeous, successful, brilliant, and gives the best compliments ever. Now he's awesome and romantic on the dance floor. Or at least in a patch of dandelions. It's just not fair!

Tess calmed her inner monologue. "I thought you said you couldn't dance."

"No, I said I *don't* dance, not that I couldn't. My mother put me in lessons when I was ten. Not a place a young boy wants to be, believe me. Now I only dance when forced. Or when gorgeous secretaries ask me."

"Do secretaries often ask you to dance?"

"Oh, all the time. It's quite odd, really."

He laughed and spun her again. Tess's world twisted. He wasn't doing anything the way she'd planned. She thought dancing might offer a humbling moment, but now he'd become the Fred Astaire Architect. He wasn't playing nice at all.

When he twirled her back against his chest, she forcibly stepped away, nearly toppling them both over.

"Whoa. You okay?" he asked, steadying her by the arms.

"Fine. Just a bit dizzy," she lied, struggling to ignore the electricity surging from his fingers into her skin. "Besides, I need you to do something else."

"I'm all ears."

Tess regained her footing once she backed away. "Well, your slow dancing is fine..."

"Just fine?"

She shrugged. "It's not in tune with the music."

His mouth pulled into a rakish grin. "There's music?"

Tess groaned. How dare he be so charming! "Yes, there's music. And only one dance that goes with it."

"Okay. Which one?"

"The Robot, of course."

The look on his face was worth everything.

"Are you telling me that women like men who can do The Robot?"

"Oh, yes," she answered with a smile. "It's female catnip."

"Female catnip. Really."

Tess folded her arms across her chest. She added a tapping of her foot. "I'm waiting."

He took a deep breath and stared her down.

Then he did it. Not that he didn't throw his arms up beforehand, or roll his eyes at her as he started, but he actually did it. Tess honestly wasn't sure he would. Yet here he was, arms at right angles, knees locked, head cocking this way and that, perfectly in tune to her frivolous music. Her boss, the most stoic man on the planet, the one who saw everything in practical terms – including love – was doing The Robot in a patch of dandelions in the middle of a public park. She'd never seen anything funnier in her entire life.

She started laughing. Uproariously. Uncontrollably. Until she begged him to stop, because her stomach hurt so much that she held it with both hands.

Mason ceased his mechanical gyrations and moved toward her, smiling wildly as her giggles slowed. He reached out to touch her cheek. "God, you're even more beautiful when you laugh."

She stilled entirely when he came even closer, his thick body heating all the surrounding air. His fingers wound into her curls, making her lips part on a moan. She nearly collapsed when he massaged her neck.

"Am I sparkly yet, Tess?"

Damn sparkly. Blinding, even. "Maybe. A little."

"You admit it?"

"Well, robots are generally made of metal, so that's often sparkly. Let's just say you have an exceptional teacher."

His gaze narrowed onto her mouth. "Mmm, yes. Exceptional."

Tess ached all over. She wanted him to kiss her. She needed a kiss. Just one. One couldn't hurt, right? But there had to be rules, otherwise she was screwed for sure. And not in a good way.

She watched in awed wonder as he leaned in, his breath blissfully warm against her lips. Her hand almost didn't reach his chest in time, but she managed to push away. He stopped instantly and looked to her eyes, searching for an explanation.

She stepped back before she lost the ability. "You're right, Mason."

"Right about what?"

"About kissing. We need to practice. We should definitely make sure you're doing it correctly."

"Doing it correctly?"

"Of course. Kissing is an important part of romance. Malory will appreciate you perfecting your technique."

"*Malory.*"

"Yes, Malory. This is all for her, remember?" Tess turned away before he could respond, reaching to the ground for her purse. "Now, since you seem to be fond of lip gloss, let me get some."

"Tess..."

The lowered tone of his voice heralded an impending speech – one she needed to avoid. "Just give me a second," she insisted, shutting off the music on her phone and rummaging through her bag for a little tube. "Ah, here's one. Vanilla flavored, no less. I'll put some on to make this interesting for you." She dabbed the shimmering liquid over her lips.

Mason watched her every movement. "Do you actually think I need you to wear lip gloss for this to be interesting?"

"Well, it couldn't hurt." She dropped the tube back in her purse before straightening in front of him. She willed herself to match his potent stare. "I mean, it's not like you've ever wanted to kiss me, not once in six whole years, so you could probably use some outside encourageme–"

"Oh, Tess." He cut off her speech by grabbing her face in both hands and pressing his mouth to hers.

The movement was quick, but the pressure of his lips was slow and warm and perfect. She grasped onto his forearms, needing the support. They stood still as they kissed, yet she swore Mason spun her in circles. She could do nothing but hold on.

With his mouth melded softly to hers, Tess questioned all her assumptions. Was it true he'd never wanted to kiss her before now? That wasn't how this felt. This felt both surreal and natural, like something years in the making. Surprising yet expected. Terrifying yet flawless.

When his lips eventually eased back, she gasped for air. He hovered there, his mouth a hair's width away, holding her steady as their breaths mingled for aching seconds. Her mind swam in a deep, contented haze. One of his hands moved across her cheek to push into her hair, his fingers threading into her curls. His other hand drifted around her back, banding her to him.

"Hmm...the vanilla does taste good," he murmured, "but I know you'll taste better." Her lips parted in surprise. This time when he kissed her, his mouth came down hard.

Tess had thought about being in this situation with Mason Tramont more times than was probably legal in the Commonwealth of Virginia. Consequently, a large part of her brain couldn't comprehend it. She'd always wanted her boss to take her in a fit of passion, but he'd been so reserved through the years that she never thought he could be this commanding. It seems she'd been wrong. About many, many things.

Mason knew exactly what he was doing. He was powerful and insistent and she had to grip his shoulders to maintain balance while his mouth moved faultlessly across hers. He pulled her even closer, supporting her as she trembled, his tongue tracing her lips before easing smoothly inside.

With the feel of him in her body, Tess finally snapped out of shock and became a full participant. She clamped her fingers into his hair while her lips and tongue returned his kiss with everything in her arsenal. Mason's large form engulfed her smaller one, yet she still felt powerful when he responded to her actions with groans of clear desperation.

Tess's head swam in the dream that her boss *did* want her, and had wanted her for much longer than either of them imagined. She forgot where she was, and what she was supposed to be doing, and allowed herself to sink into that fantasy. Nothing felt entirely real until his hand slipped down her back, coming dangerously close to the tightly outlined curve of her bottom. He used this new leverage to pull her harder against him, their hips coming flush together, with only a few flimsy layers of clothing keeping them separated.

A breathy mewl escaped her lips and Mason moaned in response. The sounds of their equally fierce desire rang in her ears, yanking Tess from her fantasy world. She had no choice but to stop this crazy ride.

Using every ounce of willpower she'd ever possessed in her entire life, she wrenched her body away from his. Stumbling backwards, she put as much distance between them as her wobbly legs would allow. She mumbled a filthy curse word. Or two.

For a long moment, neither of them spoke. They only worked to breathe. When she could, Tess chanted a livelier string of curses.

Mason cleared his throat. "What did you say?"

She stared at his chest. "Oh, um, just...yeah, that was...okay. A good start."

He stepped forward, one long stride closing the distance she'd put between them. "Maybe I need more practice."

"Nope," she said, holding up her hand. "We've got to put limits on that."

"Why?"

Tess glanced up to his eyes. It was a serious mistake. All her Mason-the-vampire fantasies looked silly compared to the hunger staring back at her. She pulled herself together, even if the mousy voice betrayed her. "B-because I'm your teacher. I have to stay professional. We can't forget we're doing this for Malory."

At the mention of his ex's name, Mason looked away. He raked a hand through his dark hair and stared at a nearby tree. A lifetime passed before his gaze returned to hers, as powerful as ever. "I'll play this however you like, Tess."

Nervous laughter bubbled from her throat. "Play? Who's playing? This is serious work we're doing. Speaking of which, what are your plans for the rest of the week?"

"As I told you yesterday, my life is in your hands."

"Well, good. That's the right answer. We'll be going out together every day after work."

"And what will we be doing?"

"Let's see…" She pretended to think as she turned away from him, busying herself with repacking the picnic basket. "Club dancing tomorrow, karaoke Thursday, bowling Friday, and Saturday…"

Tess fumbled with the wine glasses. Saturday this would all end. Badly. She hushed the voice of regret that screamed inside her head.

He took the picnic basket from her hands. "What's on Saturday?"

"Let's call that a secret," she quipped, bending over to grab the blanket. Her tight dress pulled across her hips, giving little room to move.

"Are you trying to pique my curiosity, Miss Troy?"

She heard a distinct rasp in his voice and her breath hitched. *Is he doing what I think he's doing?* From her bent position, she glanced over her shoulder. *Yup, he's staring at my ass.* Her pulse skipped while she gathered the fluffy fabric and stood. *I am in so much trouble.*

"That's it for today, then, Mason. Lesson completed."

"I'll walk you to your car."

"'Kay."

Tess felt like a toddler, gripping her blanket for dear life, while she trotted beside him. Just the movement of his shoulders beneath his shirt was enough to make her palms sweat. When they finally stepped out of the park, her fingers shook uncontrollably. She tried like hell to hide inside her car while he repacked her trunk, but she couldn't get the damn door handle to work.

"Here," his voice came from behind, his body far too close, his breath warm on her cheek. "Let me get that for you."

He encircled her waist to cover her hand. Tess glanced up.

Mason stared hard at her mouth. "I don't suppose you'd consider another kiss? Just to ensure I'm doing it correctly?"

She shook her head. "No. That's not a good idea. One kiss per day is plenty, and we've already covered that ground today, so..."

He opened her door. "Tomorrow, then," he promised.

"Um-hmm. Tomorrow," she agreed before falling into her seat.

Tess started the engine, unable to drive away fast enough.

When his ridiculously delicious body was a mere speck in her rearview mirror, she pulled onto a side street and parked her car. She fumbled with her phone, waiting impatiently for her best friend's voice to say, "Hey, Tess, how'd it go?"

"Holy crap, Belle! That man is...well, he's liquid testosterone! That's what he is! I can't see straight when I'm around him!"

"You kissed him, didn't you?"

"That's beside the point."

"You never listen to me."

"Also beside the point. I'm having a meltdown, here!"

Belle sighed. "Hey, I've got a nutty idea. Why don't you stop this little plan of yours and agree to date him?"

"You make it sound so easy."

"It is easy."

"No, it's not! I just have to recoup from today. I need to be stronger. Stoicer, or something."

"Tess, listen. I know you've been hurt, but Mason isn't Bryan."

"That's not what this is about. This is female empowerment."

"Damn, you're stubborn."

"And that's why you love me."

"No, that's actually not the reason at all."

She laughed while her thoughts ran wild. Belle could complain all day, but Tess knew exactly what this situation called for. If she wanted Mason Tramont, manservant extraordinaire, at her disposal, then she needed to do one thing.

Up. Her. Game.

5

POLYESTER NEVER LOOKED
SO GOOD

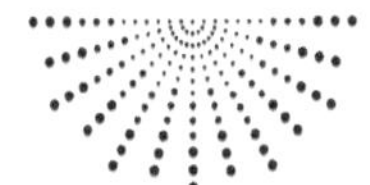

Friday came a lot sooner than Mason expected. He sat at his desk, eyeing the clock on the wall, waiting for it to say 5:30 so he could see her again. *Tess.* What he'd suspected on Monday was a certainty today: she matched him in every way. Even while doing her best to drive him insane.

Tuesday was difficult, when she made him dance The Robot in the park. He disliked it even more on Wednesday night, when she required him to perform in a club full of people. Then came the karaoke bar on Thursday. He could have gone his whole life without enduring that torment. And today, she would make him bowl. In public shoes, no less.

Still, the worst of her sublime tortures was by far the one-kiss rule. Now that he'd made up his mind about her, Mason didn't see the point in playing coy. While he thoroughly enjoyed every physical intimacy she'd allowed this week – holding her hand as they walked, wrapping his arm around her shoulders whenever the need struck him, pulling her close for a hug at the end of each night – the fact remained that one kiss per day wasn't anywhere near enough to quench his thirst.

But what did Tess want? What exactly did her love coach game entail? Maybe she wanted to be sure he truly desired her after six years of being stone-faced. Mason had made the effort to reassure her as much as possible during the past three days. He'd turned on every ounce of charm at his disposal, and she'd accepted his attentions with dazzlingly giddy smiles and deliciously indelicate whimpers. Still, the one-kiss rule remained in effect.

He would just have to try harder. She was worth every effort. Yes, Tess had started this game. But he intended to win.

A knock at the door made him jump. "Come in," he said, eager to see the bouncy blond ponytail and joyful blue eyes that would light the dark corners of his office.

"Hey, buddy," David greeted as he entered.

Mason tried not to look disappointed. "David. How are you?"

"Um, good. I guess."

"Anything wrong?"

David stepped further inside, concern etched on his face. "Man, I've got to tell you something. But first, I want to say how incredible the plans for the hospital wing look. You've been on fire all week."

Mason nodded his agreement. He'd never felt more creative, more driven, than during these days of Tess's blissful torture. "I've just been in a zone, I guess."

"Well, you being in a zone is damn good for business, so I really don't want to tell you this. I'm afraid it will end your zone forever."

"Now I'm worried. Just tell me."

David sighed. "Tess is quitting."

Mason stared blankly at him. Hearing his business partner say the words out loud made it sound so permanent. "How did you find out?"

"Tess told the whole office. Well, she told Regina, which is the same thing. Tess told Regina, Regina told Kathryn in Engineering, Kathryn told George in Accounting, and so on. I'd say it took all of two minutes for everyone to know."

"Then everyone knows."

"Yeah. And I'm guessing you already knew?"

Mason nodded.

David stepped closer. "Are you going to be okay?"

"I – I suppose I'll have to be."

"Oh, I'm sorry," Tess's voice came from the doorway. "I keep walking in on you two. I'll come back later."

"No," Mason insisted, unable to mask his relief at the sight of her. "Stay, Tess."

David's eyes darted between the two of them.

Mason straightened in his chair. "We, um, we have some things to discuss, Miss Troy."

Tess stiffened. "Only if you're finished speaking. Mr. Field?"

David observed them both for a moment before focusing on her. "Yeah, I think we're good," he replied, stepping out of the room. He glanced back once, his brow furrowed, as he cleared the long hallway leading to his office.

Tess eased inside the door and closed it behind her. She turned to Mason and smiled. "Hey."

"Hey. David just told me you broke the news of your resignation."

"I did." She shrugged as she moved toward him. Only then did he notice that she carried a box in her hand. "I figured I needed to let Regina know, so she can get used to the idea. I imagine David will have his hands full with her tonight."

"Probably. She'll miss you."

"Yeah, I know."

"I'll miss you, too."

Tess stopped short. Her eyes fastened on his. "I'm sorry."

Mason couldn't help feeling dejected by the fact that she wasn't going to stay, no matter what he said.

"Here," she offered, coming to stand before him. She handed him the box. "Maybe this will make you happy."

Only if this box contains an I'm-going-to-be-in-this-office-for-thirty-more-years letter. Although currently, I'll settle for a rescinding of the one-kiss rule.

He took the gift, yanked the lid off, and peered inside. "Wow," he remarked, pulling out a brown-on-brown short-sleeved polyester bowling shirt with his name embroidered on the pocket. "Tess, this is the ugliest shirt I've ever seen."

She laughed while closing the gap between them. Hiking up her formfitting skirt, she slid her bottom onto his desktop. "Come on, Mason! Unearth your sense of adventure! We're going to submerse ourselves deep into the world of bowling tonight. You need to look the part, or the natives will sense your fear instantly."

Good God. She looked so damn gorgeous, sitting on his desk as if she owned it. He clenched the armrests of his chair. He tried not to notice how far her legs went up. Or how short her skirt was. "Funny, I thought we were just going to throw some heavy balls as straight as possible."

"Eh. It's all about perspective."

Tess giggled again, tossing her ponytail over her shoulder. She shifted her legs, the movement pushing her skirt up to the top of her thighs. Mason stood from his chair without conscious thought, drawn by some bizarre magnetic force. He stepped toward her, his actions overtly eager, and her eyes widened.

She settled herself instantly. Her shoulders relaxed as she smiled and parted her knees further. Breathy wisps of air left her chest when his body came flush with the desk.

The floral scent of her hair drifted into his brain and he groaned deep in his chest. Reaching his hands to her hips, he dragged her perfect ass across the desktop to draw her even closer. He didn't stop pulling until her inner thighs cradled his hips. *Holy hell*, he loved the feeling of being between her legs for the first time.

Possessed by the overwhelming urge to kiss her, Mason leaned down to align his mouth with hers.

"You want your one kiss now?" Tess whispered against his lips. "It's fine with me if you do, but then there's nothing to look forward to later, is there?"

Well, that was wildly untrue. There was plenty to look forward to later. Like every moment she laughed, or jumped around with giddy fervor, or simply looked into his eyes and smiled.

But she was right. The anticipation was exquisite pain.

Mason sighed and dropped his forehead onto her shoulder. His fingers curled around her hipbones. Deep down, he knew it wasn't really a good idea to take her here and now, on his desktop, behind an unlocked door, at his place of work. Unfortunately, right at this moment, he couldn't quite comprehend why that would be so bad.

After several minutes spent breathing her in, he convinced himself to not use up his one kiss just yet. Instead, he relished the feel of her soft hands smoothing across his back while he regained his composure. Eventually, he straightened to stand before her.

"I guess we should go," she offered, her sweet smile brimming with innocence.

"I guess so."

Mason backed away slowly and painfully. He watched her jump down off his desk, straighten her skirt, and saunter out of his office, hips swaying seductively beneath the tight fabric. He grabbed his ugly-as-hell shirt and ran after her, intent on doing whatever she said.

~

THEY STEPPED out of the bowling alley hours later, into a cool, moonless night. "Ugh," Tess groaned, linking her arm in his, "I can't believe you're good at bowling, too."

Mason pulled her in closer to his side. He grinned as he led her behind the building to the otherwise empty parking lot where her Bug sat beside his Mercedes. "It's not that difficult. You just aim for the middle."

She stopped in the little space between their car doors and turned to him. He was instantly enraptured by the way her light blue eyes looked green when mixed with the yellow glow of the nearby streetlamp.

"You make it sound so easy. Just like everything you do."

He grasped her waist and pulled her to him. "Are you saying I'm good at everything?"

"Well, *everything* is a strong word." She licked her lips, refreshing the shimmer of her gloss, as his hands flattened on the small of her back.

"Tell me what else I'm good at doing. Please."

A playful smile lit her face. "Hmm," Tess considered, "now that I think about it, you're only good at bowling. Oh, and architecture."

"That's it, huh?"

She reached to his chest, her fingertip tracing the cursive *Mason* embroidered on the dull brown fabric. "Although, if architecture doesn't work out, you could definitely model bowling shirts. Admit it, you love this little fashion statement, don't you?"

"Sure. It's like mud and dirt started throwing excrement at each other and this shirt got caught in the middle."

"Come on, it's not that bad. And it goes perfectly with the shoes."

Mason cringed. "Yeah, about that – whatever else you have planned for me – please don't make me wear bowling shoes again."

"They're quite sanitary, I'm sure. I imagine they spray disinfectant in them at least once a day."

He moaned and shuddered.

Tess laughed, draping her arms over his shoulders. Her eyes glinted in the lamplight while she eased up on her tiptoes and pressed her mouth to his. She kissed him slowly, her tongue tentative, her lips soft and slippery. Then she pulled away and settled back on her heels.

Mason held her in place. "Mmm. What flavor is your lip gloss today?"

"Do you like it?"

"As much as Tuesday, better than Wednesday, not as much as yesterday."

"You and your attention to detail. It's grape soda."

"Grape soda and Tess. I can definitely get used to that," he said, knowing his words gave a veiled suggestion of a future between them. He looked to her, assessing her response.

She smiled, but it wasn't as giddy as it had been through the night. He even thought he saw a flicker of remorse in her eyes. "I can't believe tomorrow is Saturday already," she murmured.

"What's so special about Saturday?"

Her mouth pulled into a frown as she reached into the tiny pocket of her blouse. "I have something for you."

"Yeah? What is it?"

She pulled out a folded piece of paper. Mason took it in one hand, still keeping her body close with his other arm. He opened the paper and read. "It's an address."

"I want you to meet me there tomorrow. Does noon work?"

"Noon is fine. Can I know my destination, or is it still a secret?"

"A secret."

"How should I dress?"

"Very, very casual," Tess instructed, looking back up to him. She ran her fingers over his jaw before dropping her arms. With a sigh, she started to pull away.

He didn't let her get far. "Where do you think you're going?" he questioned, shoving the address into his pocket before returning both hands to her waist.

"I'm going home, Mason."

"But I haven't gotten my kiss yet."

"Is your memory faulty? We kissed a minute ago."

"No. *You* kissed *me*."

"That's still a kiss."

He stepped forward, walking her back until his Mercedes stopped their movement. He pinned her spine against the cool car door and leaned down until their mouths nearly touched. "You wouldn't deny me *my* kiss, would you, Tess? That would be going against the rules."

Her eyelids fell to half-mast. "I – I make the rules."

"Believe me, I know."

Mason pressed his lips to hers, eager for the taste, the wetness of her tongue. Part of him expected her to jerk away, or even slap him across the face, for taking liberties with her rules. He hesitated, not knowing what she might do.

But then her hands reached into his hair, her fingers curling greedily against the nape of his neck. Her breasts pushed into his chest. Her face tilted up higher. Her tongue eased out, gently at first and then more purposefully, as she urged him to her.

He breathed in deep, her heady mixture of wildflower hair and grape lips driving him insane. He wanted to savor her scents, to cherish the sensation of her willfully wrapped in his arms. But without warning, Tess threw her leg up onto his hip and knocked them both off balance. Mason had to wrap one arm tighter around her waist and slam his other hand against the car door to keep them from tumbling sideways.

She paid no attention to his struggles, fully engaged in exploring his mouth with her skilled, eager tongue. Her fevered whimpers made him wish like hell that his Mercedes was actually a Transformer that could convert into a gigantic bed. Did that one even exist? If not, it should.

The instant he regained his balance, Mason reached down to smooth one hand across her flawless backside, relishing the sound of her responding moans. Wanting more and more, he pushed his thigh between her knees, hitching her up higher on the side of his car so their bodies could meld together perfectly. Her breath caught in surprise when her feet lifted off the ground, but it didn't dampen her need. Quite the opposite.

They kissed in frantic desperation, his hand wandering across her hip before venturing higher, until he could trace the curve of her breast. Tess sighed into his mouth, her fingers gripping his hair to the point of pain. She rocked against him, grinding her bottom down on his thigh.

Her zealous actions caused his rapidly hardening erection to twitch into the softness of her belly. She gasped at the sensation and he shuddered in response, unable to muster any shame for his level of desire. God, he just wanted her, and he wanted her now.

Long moments later, in the haze of her body enveloping his, in the smooth wetness of her mouth and soft tickling of her hair, Mason vaguely realized she was trying to pull away. Subtly. Gently. But definitively.

Damn it, damn it, damn it.

Utilizing all of his energy, he forced himself to ease back from her lips and rest his forehead against hers. He thought to ask why they couldn't just keep going, but realized she wouldn't be able to answer. She panted far too hard to speak.

"*Tess,*" he breathed, not knowing how to ask her to come home with him without offending her. Splaying her out on his bed would be a blatant transgression of her one-kiss policy, but since they'd already demolished that rule tonight...

"Mason, I, um, I need to, uh, to go."

Exhaling hard, he grit his teeth together. "Okay. If you must." He released her slowly, keeping her steady until her feet touched the ground.

She tried to straighten out her clothes and hair but it didn't work. Her pink cheeks and pinker lips betrayed their actions and made her look sexy as hell. He worked his fingers together furiously to avoid touching her again. And again.

"So, I'll see you tomorrow?"

"Tomorrow," she agreed, but didn't look him in the eye. Instead, she ducked under his arm and opened her car door, easing inside without glancing back.

"Be safe, Tess."

She peered at him with a distinct sorrow in her eyes. "You, too."

Mason stood, utterly confused, as he watched her drive away. Why did she look so sad? And why in the hell couldn't he control himself around her?

For the last four days, he'd wanted nothing but Tess. This didn't make sense. He didn't obsess over women. Hell, Malory had been in and out of the picture for years, a whirlwind in her own right, but he'd never ached for her. Not like this. Nothing in his world had ever been like this.

Now, standing alone in the cool night air, he was left to wonder two things. What exactly did he feel for his secretary? And how long had he felt this way?

6

PUTTY IN YOUR HANDS

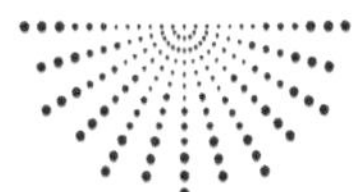

Saturday morning, Mason listened to the GPS in his Mercedes as the electronic voice instructed him to turn left off of Main Street. He'd considered researching the address Tess had given him, but she requested it be kept secret and he wanted to honor her wishes. Besides, he was much more focused on what happened yesterday than on what would happen today.

Last night, Tess climbed him like a mountain in the bowling alley parking lot. In turn, he'd been two seconds away from taking her on the hood of his car. He swore he could still smell her on his clothes, even though he'd showered this morning and no longer wore his ghastly shirt. She'd simply lodged herself inside him, taking up residence in some abandoned, cobweb-laden corner of his mind.

His leg bounced impatiently at a red light.

They'd only begun playing her little game on Monday, yet her every move since entranced him beyond belief. A connection like this didn't happen in five days. At least, not to him. Tess now occupied all of his waking thoughts – and a hell of a lot of his sleeping ones, too – so Mason could only assume he'd been in tune to her far longer than he thought. He just had no idea when or where that had happened.

The light turned green and he gunned the gas.

In truth, he hadn't been utterly oblivious to her these past six years, even if that's what his indomitable secretary believed. She'd just seemed so young and innocent at first, and then they formed a professional relationship that ran like a well-oiled machine, and then came her intermittent boyfriends. And there he was, grappling with Malory being in and out of his life, while struggling to build a company and a reputation from the ground up. There had never been time to relax and look at what might be walking around in front of his face.

He shook his head as he drove, fully aware that none of those issues concerned him right now. From the moment David said Tess's name on Monday morning, Mason became a snowball careening downhill. He didn't want to stop gathering momentum, no matter what might await him if he crashed at the bottom.

The only issue he currently cared about was the fact that his secretary was still playing a game with him. And in three weeks' time, she wouldn't even be doing that. She would be gone.

He cursed as he rounded another corner.

Tess not being in his life wasn't a fate he could fathom. But she was strong-willed and determined to leave, so what could he do? Maybe he could ask David what he thought – if he could tell David about him and Tess – if there *was* a him-and-Tess. Pretty big ifs, but Mason needed to make them happen. He needed to convince her to give him an actual chance. If she wanted him to dance bizarrely in public, sing loudly in bars, and wear insanely ugly shirts, he would do it all. Although he would have to put up a fight about those damn bowling shoes.

"Arriving at destination," the disembodied GPS voice announced.

Mason pulled his Mercedes against the curb, put the car in park, and looked out the window. He was in front of an older, well kept, single-story house on the edge of downtown Richmond. The house's siding was painted pink, the wrapped front porch white. He read the sign hanging above the entrance: *The Pooch Palace.*

Glancing back at the paper Tess had given him last night, he double-checked the address. *Yes, this is the place.*

After exiting the car, he stuffed his keys in the pocket of his jeans and walked up the short sidewalk. The lawn was lush green and weed-free. The steps didn't squeak under his weight as he climbed them. Unsure of what to expect from his mysterious secretary, he knocked on the front door with overwhelming curiosity, tempered by a healthy dose of fear.

A woman's singsong voice answered, "Come in."

Mason opened the door, setting off a gold bell over his head. As the bell jingled, several dog barks erupted from the back of the house. He stepped into the entry room and noticed a tall, simple, wood desk with a petite woman standing behind it. She was about Tess's age, had wavy, long brown hair, wore a pink T-shirt and blue jeans, and looked entranced by a computer screen.

"Welcome to Pooch Palace," she said, slow to turn away from the screen, "are you dropping off or…" Her prerecorded message faltered when she finally made eye contact with him. "Well, I'll be a monkey's uncle. It's you."

"I'm sorry," Mason replied, moving closer. "Do I know you?"

"Nope." She smiled and held out her hand. "Hi, I'm Annabelle."

"Hello, Annabelle, I'm…"

"Mason Tramont," she filled in, taking his hand in a firm shake. "Tess!" she hollered, releasing her grip on him when further dog barks resounded in the distance. "She'll just be a minute. Did you find the place okay?"

"I did. I take it you were expecting me?"

"Um-hmm." She sized him up like an artifact at a curiosity shop.

"Belle," he recalled. "Do you go by *Belle*?"

"Yep, that's me."

"Tess talks to you on the phone all the time."

"Yeah. She and I don't keep any secrets."

"Really?" He leaned over the desk. "Can you tell me why she…"

"Mason!" Tess announced her arrival, cutting an eye at Annabelle, who smirked in response. "I'm really glad you made it."

He turned to see his secretary step out of the back room. She glided toward him, a sight of beauty in a pink T-shirt and jeans, her wild hair contained by her usual ponytail and her blue eyes gleaming. Her lip gloss was also pink – probably cotton candy, his favorite flavor so far.

"I made it just fine. Can I ask where I am?"

Belle cleared her throat. "That's my cue to leave, I think." She came around the desk, stopping in front of Tess. "You need my help with anything else today?"

"Not right now. Thanks, Belle."

"Um-hmm." Annabelle turned back to him. "It was really nice to meet you, Mason. Really, really, really nice."

"You, too." He didn't miss the exchange of guarded glances between the women as Belle moved around them and headed out the front door. It clicked shut and more barking ensued.

"I'm sorry," he offered, "is my presence here upsetting Belle?"

"Of course not." Tess smiled. "So, what do you think?"

"About what?"

"About this," she said, spreading her arms wide. "I thought you might like to see where I'll be spending my time after I leave our office."

"Oh," Mason considered, looking around the sparsely furnished, mahogany-paneled room. "This is where you'll be working?"

"Not just working. I own it."

"You *own* it?"

"Yes, I co-own with Belle. Come on, I'll give you the grand tour."

She grabbed his hand, pulling him along as Mason absorbed her words. Funny, he hadn't thought to ask what she would do when she left. Probably because he still couldn't accept her resignation. "What kind of business is this?" he asked while she walked them through the back door, down a hallway, and into a large room filled with cages of varying sizes.

A chorus of barks broke out when she replied, "Doggy daycare."

He glanced at the dozens of crates filled with canines, both large and small. "People actually pay you to babysit their dogs?"

"Absolutely."

"Why don't they just leave them at home in their backyards?"

Tess laughed as if his question was ridiculous. "Because they love them and want them looked after by caring people. I'm sure you can understand. Didn't you have a pet growing up?"

Mason shook his head.

"Never?"

"Never."

"Not even a hamster or turtle or cricket or anything?"

"Nope. Not even a cricket."

"Hmm," she considered, nibbling her lower lip. "Then I guess forty dogs in a big room isn't what you're used to."

"Um, no," he conceded, taking in his surroundings. Dozens of little black and brown eyes stared him down. "Do you actually make money doing this?"

"You'd be surprised what people will pay to make sure their fluffy little balls of love are looked after."

"Fluffy little balls of love?"

Tess grinned as the doorbell tinkled in the distance. "Ooh, customer," she said, moving back to the hall. He followed on her heels.

"Hello, Ms. Travers!"

A small, grandmotherly woman, silver-haired with pale eyes, stood by the front desk. An intimidating Great Dane sat at her feet. "Hello, Tess dear. Just bringing Tug for a visit."

"Of course. How long will we have him today?"

"Oh, I just need to run a few errands, get my hair done. I'm seeing Mr. Wilks tonight."

Tess smiled, moving to the computer and punching in information. "How exciting! A hot date with Mr. Wilks?"

"As hot as it gets when you're eighty."

Tess laughed and Mason joined in, calling attention to his presence in the back doorway. Ms. Travers glanced at him. "Oh, hello, young man. Are you new here?"

"Um, yes."

Tess finished on the computer and caught his eye. "This is Mason. He's helping me out for the day."

"Wonderful," Ms. Travers replied, holding out the leash. "You can take my Tug. I always worry about Tess – she's such a slip of a thing."

"An adorable slip," Mason added. He stepped forward to take the leash, which was attached to a glittery rhinestone collar with a dangling heart charm. The Great Dane eyed him. "I assume he's a friendly dog?"

"A love," the older woman assured as she exited. "See you in a few hours."

"Goodbye," Tess called just before the door shut. She walked back to Mason's side. "It's so cute, her and Mr. Wilks. He dropped his Pekinese off an hour ago so he could go to the barber shop."

"Did the two of them meet here?"

"They did. See? I told you I was a good love coach."

"You are good at everything you do. Apparently, I've just got bowling and architecture."

Tess giggled as she stepped toward the back room. "Come take a look at the rest of the place. And watch out for Tug."

She spoke too late. The Dane jumped after her, nearly pulling Mason over on his face. "Holy crap, this thing is strong," he muttered.

Tess kept laughing. "Just let him know you're the boss." Moving down the hallway, she pointed to various doors, indifferent to Mason's struggles with the hairy beast. "This is the office, there's the bathroom, over here is the stock-room, and you've already seen the kennel."

They arrived again in the giant room of infinite dogs and Tess took Tug's leash. The canine instantly settled at her feet. "Good boy."

"Me or him?" Mason wondered.

"Um, both." She grinned as she unhooked Tug from his leash. "Stay," she instructed the Great Dane. "Come," she said to Mason.

He chuckled, following her out of the last door and into a large, open yard. Several caged sections surrounded the main area, half of which was paved, the other half a lush green turf. "Wow. This is a huge yard."

"It's the reason we bought this place. Belle and I have big plans."

Mason absorbed the twinkle in her eye. "What kind of plans?"

"Well, when we get the capital, we're going to have a dog gym built out here, so the pooches can play in style."

"Do you think you'll make that kind of money?"

"I'm certain we will. We've only been at this for nine months and already we're completely in the black on the books. Plus, I have so many other ideas."

"Like what?"

"Like I want to design my own line of dog collars, and maybe clothes. And homemade treats using organic ingredients. We can have portrait days and..."

She kept talking but Mason zoned out while watching her lips move. She thrummed with excitement, bouncing in place as she dreamed of her potential. He understood the thrill of starting his own business, of being his own boss. That's what Tess was now. She was her own boss. The student had become the master.

When she finished talking, she looked up to him.

"Tess, I'm impressed."

"Really?"

"Really. You've created something special here. You should be proud."

"I...I...wow. Thank you."

"You're welcome."

She smiled, as beautiful as he'd ever seen, and he had to kiss her right now – even if it was the only one she allowed him all day. He reached out and pulled her to him, lowering his mouth to hers. She didn't stop him or issue warnings about destroying the anticipation. She just kissed him back, responding the moment their lips touched.

Tess was all heat and cotton candy and sexy little sighs and he wanted her more than anything he'd ever wanted in his life. She didn't play coy. Her tongue wrapped around his, her body pressed close, her hands drifted over his back and into his hair. He would have happily thrown her in the grass and peeled off her jeans, if not for the extreme barking reverberating in his ears.

"Damn. Why are they so loud?" he grumbled against her lips.

"Mmm. They're getting antsy. It's exercise time." She eased away, putting her arms down to her sides.

He missed her. "What does exercise time entail?"

"I take them out in two groups and let them run the yard. The ones that don't play well with others go in the caged dog runs. The rest gallivant around out here. I have to supervise them all to make sure there's no unnecessary roughhousing."

"That sounds like a lot of work. Where did Belle go?"

"Belle runs the place all week while I'm at the office. I take my shifts on the weekends. When we started it was manageable, but now we're so busy. We're planning to hire someone else soon. Until then, I have to give her a break."

"But this is a lot for just you. Can I help with anything?"

Tess stilled, the sparkle in her eyes dimming. She glanced at the ground for a moment before looking back to him. "I'd hoped you would offer to help me, Mason. You're coming along splendidly."

"How so?"

"This is the next step in my love coaching plan. I call it, 'Doing whatever your woman asks you to do'. If you help out with her needs, afterwards she'll be putty in your hands."

He stared at her, painfully aware that she was still invested in her little game. But he'd already made up his mind to continue playing along, at least until he convinced her they could be so much more than coach and student. He *would* convince her, no matter what.

"Sounds good to me, Tess. Let's get started."

"You promise to do whatever I ask?"

"I will. Whatever you ask."

～

IT STARTED SIMPLY, with a little filing. He could do that – data entry of paper files into computer format and reorganizing the current digital files. When he finished, she seemed impressed with what he'd done. Still, she didn't miss a beat before she led him into the stockroom and asked him to rearrange all the dog food in order of manufacturer and type.

As Tess brought hounds of varying sizes and colors in and out of the kennel room, Mason put his back into organizing the stock. He never realized how many different kinds of dog food existed, or how heavy the bags were. There wasn't enough shelving to accommodate all the cans, so he eventually created can pyramids, although some remained on the floor.

She came in when he was nearly finished, said, "Good job," and asked him to help retrieve the feisty beasts from the runs while she tended to customers at the front desk.

This task was a bit worse. He didn't do well with animals, having never been around them, and would have been happier with some type of wrangler's gloves on. Thankfully, the pooches were just playful and the worst part was avoiding the steaming presents they'd left on the ground.

Until five o'clock, everything progressed rather smoothly. Mason's true moment of realization didn't come until he'd finished getting the last of the dogs inside while Tess ran back and forth between the kennel and front desk.

"Oh, thanks," she huffed, watching him drag in a Rottweiler named Goliath. "His owner is here." Tess took Goliath's leash and started moving up the hallway when she stopped and turned back. "Also, would you mind washing down the runs while I finish out front?"

Mason's brow arched. "Washing down the runs?"

"Yeah," she said as the bell tinkled again. "Just clean them up a bit, then the courtyard area, and whatever is left on the ground afterward you can get with the scoopers – they're resting against the back wall. I'd help, but it's the busiest time of day. Everyone comes for pickups now."

She turned and scurried up the hallway, Goliath in tow, leaving Mason standing alone in the kennel. He stared after her for a long minute before trudging out the back door to survey the hellish mess forty dogs left in a courtyard after five hours of play. Arming himself with a hose and a pooper-scooper, he headed into a germaphobe's nightmare.

That's when it hit him.

Somewhere between spraying water at dog patties and trying to scoop little logs out of the grass, he got it. Tess's game wasn't about love coaching. She didn't want to teach him to sparkle, or prepare him for a life with his ex, or fashion him into the perfect mate. The name of her game was *revenge*.

He remembered her wild eyes when she yelled at him in the restaurant Monday. He vividly recalled her outrage at being asked out with such practicality. She claimed she wasn't angry with him for using her as more than a secretary all these years, but obviously she lied. She was pissed as hell.

Mason finally understood. Tess set out five days ago to punish him. To make him do the things she knew would cause the most discomfort. Like dancing stupidly in the grass. Singing karaoke in front of drunk strangers. Bowling in a hideous shirt and rented shoes.

And shoveling dog crap.

It was genius, really. Evil genius. And he'd fallen into it with all the grace of a floundering teenage boy, panting after a luscious woman in full control of her world.

Mason picked up another steamy pile. He steadied his breath as he worked, making sure he didn't get any of the foul stuff on his clothes. As he shoveled, he imagined wringing his secretary's neck. Her slender, beautiful, perfect little neck.

∼

TESS STOOD at the back window, watching Mason's jerky movements while he picked up patties from the yard. All the dogs were gone, except Tug. Tess wasn't worried about Ms. Travers coming to pick up her pooch. But she *was* worried about her boss's thoughts.

Does he know now?

From his tense muscles and rigid scowl, Tess assumed he did. She wasn't sure why he was still here. He should have stormed off the instant he figured it out – after calling her a slew of nasty names and telling her not to come back to work, ever. She supposed Regina could clean out her desk for her.

The entryway bell jangled again. Tess took one last look at Mason's stiff back before grabbing Tug's leash and leading him up front. "Hey, Ms. Travers, you look so pretty!"

"You're sweet, dear. Do you think Mr. Wilks will like it?"

Tess smiled as she surveyed the fresh blue glow of the elderly woman's silver up-do and the rosy circles on her crinkly cheeks. "I think he'll love it. He was here today, too."

"Really?" Ms. Travers asked, reaching out to take Tug's leash. "Did he seem excited about tonight?"

"More than you, even."

"I can't imagine."

Tess leaned back on the tall desk. "I'm sure you'll have a wonderful time."

"And what about you? Do you have plans with that nice Mason?"

"Um, no. I don't think so."

"Oh, but he called you adorable. I'm sure he likes you."

Tess smiled halfheartedly. Maybe he did this morning. But definitely not now. "I like him too, Ms. Travers. I like him a whole lot."

"Well, he's behind you, so I think you should tell him that."

Tess stilled, now able to feel Mason's eyes boring into her back. Ms. Travers winked before leading Tug out the front door. It clicked behind her and the room fell silent. Tess was alone with her manservant. With no one to hear her scream.

She inhaled, forced a smile, and turned.

Mason stood in the doorway leading to the back hall, his rigid, muscled body consuming every inch of space inside the wood doorframe. He stared at her, the glare from his steel eyes erasing her artificial grin.

Tess grasped a hand onto the desktop. "Mason. There you are."

He moved toward her. Long, purposeful strides closed the distance between them instantly. She plastered her back to the desk, craning her neck to look him in the eyes. His heated body came flush with hers.

"I'm curious," he growled, towering above her, "as to what you'd like me to do next. If stocking shelves, wrangling dogs, and shoveling crap isn't enough for you, I imagine I could scrub the floor. Or maybe the toilet." He inched closer. "Tell me, Tess. Would that make you *happy*?"

Fire burned in his eyes. She'd never seen him like this, with anger seething from every pore. "I...I think we're done for today. Tomorrow, perhaps."

Mason drew himself up taller somehow, his fierce gaze keeping her pinned in place. Amazingly, he didn't smell like dog. He smelled incredible – like a powerful man after a hard day's work should smell.

He reached out and grabbed her hips, pulling her forward, fitting her body onto his. He stared hard at her mouth. Tess's breathing turned ragged, yet she still licked her lips in anticipation.

Good God, is it wrong for me to be this attracted to him right now?

She froze when his hands dragged up her arms and over her neck. His fingers ran across her cheeks before he steadied her face in both hands. His lips came down and she closed her eyes, trembling all over. The heat of his breath lit a raging wildfire under her skin.

She wanted to feel his mouth on hers. *Damn*, how she wanted it. She wanted *him*. To throw her against the desk and tear her clothes off and...

And then he was gone. Before she could pry her eyes open, she heard the tinkling of the bell and the slamming of the door. A second later, she heard his car engine rev. Then skidding tires. Then nothing.

Mason was gone.

Tess forced her wobbly legs around the desk and into a chair. She hung her head in one hand, dialing her phone with the other. She cringed while listening to the rings.

Within moments, Belle asked, "Well? How'd it go?"

"I did it. It's done."

"He's been knocked off his high and mighty throne?"

"You could say that. I made him shovel crap."

"Wow. From tyrant-boss to poop-wrangler in five short days. You play a skillful hand, my friend."

"I guess I do."

"Tell me, then. How does it feel to finally have your revenge?"

Tess sighed, acutely aware she may never see Mason again.

"It's awful, Belle. It's horribly, painfully, unbearably awful."

"I know, honey. And I love you so much, I'm not even going to say, 'I told you so.'"

7

REGRETS

If revenge is a dish best served cold, then regret is the slime left around the edge of the bowl the next day after you'd eaten all the revenge you could stomach but hadn't remembered to soak the bowl in water and dish soap overnight.

At least, that's what Tess concluded as she stared into the mirror Sunday morning. Priding herself on being a go-getter and a rose-colored-glasses girl, she wasn't used to this crushing emotion. She'd previously regretted only two things: wearing leg warmers in middle school and getting involved with Bryan. Now, she had another regret to deal with.

She focused hard on applying makeup, since the bags under her eyes weren't going anywhere after the little sleep she'd managed. Her only chance at not looking like a zombie was extra-curl mascara and thick eye shadow. At least the pooches wouldn't mind her hollow appearance.

Tess exhaled, wondering if Mason would throw her a bone by allowing her to clean out her desk in person. Would she hear from him again? Even for the purpose of yelling at her? Probably not. Ever.

Forcing a brush through her tousled hair, she winced. "It's a good thing he's out of my life now," she muttered to her reflection. "I couldn't hide behind love coaching and lip gloss much longer."

That fact was undeniably true. At some point, her boss would have started kissing her and she wouldn't have had the will to stop him. She'd practically mounted him in the parking lot of the bowling alley, for crying out loud. He was simply everything she'd ever wanted, and she would have succumbed to her unabated, overpowering lust for all things Mason. Even when she knew he would eventually leave her to return to Malory.

Tess shuddered. "You did the right thing, Troy. It was definitely better to push him out of your life now, before things went too far, than to have him rip your heart out later."

She believed that truth wholeheartedly, despite this devastating regret. Setting her brush on the sink, she pulled her hair up into a ponytail and practiced smiling at her reflection. She passed muster on the outside. Her insides, on the other hand, were little more than a murky heap of goo.

~

TESS ARRIVED at the Pooch Palace at eight, as she did every Sunday. Within minutes, customers rushed through the door. Shortly after, she stood alone in a house full of dogs. She concentrated on taking them in and out of the backyard, throwing balls and playing in the grass as they barked and jumped. They really were fluffy little balls of love, and her heart felt a smidge lighter when she came inside for lunch.

She returned Peaches the Poodle and Sugar the Yorkie to their crates before grabbing her sandwich. Wandering up the hall to the office, she slumped into her chair and took a bite of peanut butter and jelly. Before she finished chewing, the bell jingled over the entry door. "That figures," she grumbled. "Someone comes in just when you sit down."

Dislodging herself from the comfort of her chair, she trudged toward the hallway. She stopped cold when a man moved past her door, paying no attention to her. For a moment, she assumed her overwrought brain was causing hallucinations. Then she heard a thud.

Tess followed the sound down the hall to the stockroom. She halted in the doorway of the storage area, her mouth gaping in disbelief. Mason crouched down a few feet before her, setting several wood planks onto the ground. He wore a fitted black T-shirt and blue jeans, both of which strained against the muscles in his arms and legs. When he stood, she nearly fell over.

He turned to her and smiled. "Hello, Tess. Sorry I wasn't here sooner, but the lumberyard didn't open as early as I would have liked."

She had no idea what to say, so she settled for, "Lumberyard?"

"Yes." He moved toward her, stopping inches away. "My love coach told me I should help with my woman's needs, and you need more shelving in your stockroom. Now, if you'll excuse me, I have to get a few more things out of my truck."

Speechless, she moved aside. His arm brushed hers when he stepped into the hallway, the brief touch of his heated skin igniting her frigid body. Tess followed on his heels until he disappeared through the front door. Then she jumped to the window to peer outside.

Mason strode down the sidewalk to a huge green truck parked curbside. He reached into the back, hauling out a well-stocked tool belt and a large shopping bag. When he turned, Tess scrambled away from the window and attempted to stand casually in the middle of the room.

He met her gaze the moment he came inside. "I don't mean to disturb your workday, Tess. Please go about your business. Pretend I'm not even here."

Yeah, right. When monkeys fly out of my butt. "Don't you need my help?"

"Nope. I'm good." He nodded to her before moving down the hall and back into the stockroom.

She toddled after him, peering around the doorway to watch him cinch his tool belt around his waist. He took out a tape measure, using it to assess the far wall. Tess leaned against the doorframe, absorbing everything he did with utter curiosity and more than a little confusion.

"Since, um...since when do you build things by hand?"

"Since I learned to walk, pretty much," he explained while he measured. "It's the reason I became an architect."

"Oh."

"You sound surprised."

"I must admit, I think of you more as the brains, not the brawn."

He glanced back to her. "Can't I be both?"

No, you can't be both! You can't be perfect at everything! "I guess you can."

Mason began marking the wall at intervals. "You know, Tess, not everything has to fit into a category. Not everything needs rules. Sometimes you just go with what feels right."

Oh my Lord, did Mr. Everything-Has-A-Place-And-A-Purpose just tell me to loosen up? "Really? How long have you felt that way?"

He chuckled. "Since this past Monday, I suppose."

Monday. The day he'd decided to use her for his science experiment on love. Was he telling her now that asking her out felt right to him? She couldn't believe her ears. Or the bounding leaps of her pulse. "Well, I guess I'll let you get to work. I'll be around if you need me."

His eyes held hers. "If I do, you'll be the first to know."

∼

TESS KEPT POURING food in the water bowls and returning dogs to the wrong crates. Thankfully, her furry tenants didn't seem to care. They waited patiently for her to realize how badly she'd screwed things up.

Funny, she thought her biggest screw-up was yesterday, when she'd turned Mason into her manservant. Yet here he was, voluntarily doing her dirty work. What the hell did that mean? Did he forgive her for taking revenge? Or did he plot a punishment of his own? Lord, just the sight of him was agony, since she couldn't rightfully jump his bones.

Grateful whenever a client came in, Tess seized each opportunity to stroll past the stockroom and glance at his big, toned body performing manual labor. So strong, so intent, so sexy. She would gladly pay every last penny in her bank account in order to trade places with his tool belt.

Her final client came to collect his puppy just before five. Tess noticed Mason placing food cans on the newly constructed shelves when she passed by. She took Peaches out to Mr. Sully and chatted for a few minutes. Once they left, she closed the front door and turned around.

Mason stood inside the same doorframe as yesterday, only now he wasn't oozing anger from every pore. Today he looked absurdly adorable, with little bits of wood and plaster on his clothes and his tool belt hanging cocked to one side. Tess shifted her legs and clenched her fingers, working up the nerve to say something. All she managed was, "Hey."

"Hey."

"Hey," she repeated, biting her lip.

He smiled. "Was that your last client?"

"Yeah."

"I can finish up here if you're planning to head home."

"Oh, no. I've got some paperwork to catch up on, so you can stay. I mean, if you want. Although it looks like you're almost finished."

"I am finished in the stockroom. But I thought you could use a couple shelves in your office, too."

Tess couldn't believe how kind he was being. Did he really not despise her? "That sounds wonderful. Thank you."

"You're welcome."

She watched him turn and walk down the hallway, his carved backside sinfully outlined by tight jeans. She followed along, trying not to drool like a bulldog, before finding her way into the office. Sitting in her chair, she stared at the computer while straining her peripheral vision to watch him bring tools and planks inside the room.

Mason sized up the wall next to her desk, standing in silence for several moments. Then he turned toward her. She pretended she couldn't feel his eyes burning holes in her skin.

He rested against the wall. "Tess, I need to say something to you."

She rotated slowly in her chair, pinning her gaze to his. *Is he going to yell at me now? Tell me never to come back to work? Ask if I've lost my damn mind?* It was all she could do to sit still.

"Monday at the restaurant," he began, running a hand across the back of his neck, "I screwed things up pretty badly. Believe it or not, I was trying to apologize for the past six years, for letting you be more than my secretary. You took care of me in ways I shouldn't have allowed and I am truly sorry for my actions. I'm also sorry for the way I approached the topic of us dating. I realize now that I came across as cold and unfeeling. Honestly, when David suggested I ask you out..."

"David? David Field told you to ask me out?"

"Yes, he did."

"That's surprising."

"It shouldn't be. David is my best friend. He knows me better than anyone. He made the suggestion and I need to thank him. I may be good at architecture – and bowling – but I'll admit I'm rather obtuse when it comes to emotions. There are a lot of things I didn't see through the years. Mainly, I didn't see how much my actions at work hurt you. I also didn't see how asking you out the way I did might hurt you even more. Looking back on it all, I understand why you wanted to punish me."

As awed as Tess felt by his confessions, she still cringed with that last sentence. He'd said it out loud. Her revenge was on the table.

With her heart pounding against her ribcage, she leaned forward in her chair. "God, Mason, I'm so sorry. I really, truly am. I want you to know I regret that decision. I should never have tried to turn you into my manservant. I should never have even considered revenge as an option. In fact, I regret everything that happened this past week. Well, except for all the time we spent together. I don't regret that. Oh, and the kissing – I don't regret that at all. I mean, wow. After all these years, I really didn't think you wanted me. At least, not in any sexual sort of way. But, boy, did you prove me wrong, and I just..."

Tess watched his mouth pull into a slow grin as she spoke. She managed to stop herself before anything worse came out. Sitting back in her seat, she refocused on the problem at hand. "So, what happens now? Do you plan to get back at me? Do you want your own revenge?"

"Well, I must admit I considered it, last night around midnight. My thoughts were pretty upended at the time. But by two in the morning, I'd refocused. At that point, I decided on a different course of action."

"Wh-what course of action is that?"

"I want to be with you," Mason stated, as if it was the simplest and easiest thing on earth. "Whatever games you want to play, I'll play them. Although I'd prefer they didn't include bowling shoes or dog poop, if that's okay. And when you're done playing games, I'll still be here."

Her jaw dropped. "I...I..."

"Please don't feel like you have to make a decision right now. I'm just asking you to consider it." He turned and knelt, pulling a rolled-up sheet of paper out of the shopping bag at his feet. "In the meantime, I'd like to do something else for you. To make up for all my mistakes."

He stood and stepped forward, handing her the paper. Tess unrolled the sheet, glancing down at several sketches drawn in Mason's bold strokes. She'd know his designs anywhere, since she'd admired every building he'd ever imagined. Yet this was something she'd never seen before: a palatial structure filled with spirals and steps and slides.

"Mason, is this...?"

"It's a dog gym, for your backyard. I designed it like a palace, for the Pooch Palace, and I put in an obstacle course I thought would entertain them. There's also a special place toward the back where they can be trained to use the bathroom, so you don't have to treasure hunt every day."

Tess sat, altogether speechless.

He cleared his throat. "If there's anything you don't like, I'll be happy to change it. It's really just a rough..."

"I love it," she insisted, looking up to his eyes. "I absolutely love it. Thank you. Thank you so much. As soon as I'm able, I'll hire someone to start building."

"I already did. Actually, I just called in a favor to my brother, Ian. I'll get the supplies this week and he'll help me build next weekend."

"You mean Ian, the hotshot Washington, D.C. lawyer?"

"Well, he's not that much of a hotshot, but yes."

"Wow, I...I don't know what to say. I promise I'll pay you back."

"No, please. This is my idea, Tess. Let me do it. Field and Tramont wouldn't be where it is today if not for you. I just want to help your business the way you helped mine. I can't possibly do all the things you did for me over the years, but I would like to do this much, at least."

She absorbed the sincerity in his eyes before looking back to his drawings, her thoughts swimming in a thousand directions at once.

"Well, I'll get back to my work now," he offered in her silence. "I'll have these shelves up in no time."

Mason returned his attention to the wall. Tess wanted to watch him work, but couldn't see anything except his incredible sketches. She spread the paper out on her desk, staring in sheer amazement. The gym was exactly what she'd envisioned. He'd done everything just the way she would have, if she'd had the knowledge or expertise to put it down on paper. And he'd done it at two in the morning, and brought it to her here, now, after she'd made him organize her stockroom and shovel dog patties.

She didn't deserve his kindness. Not after how she'd treated him this week. She may have cursed him once or twice in the past six years, but she'd always known what an incredible man he was. Intelligent, caring, generous: these were the reasons she'd fallen in love with him.

Mason started drilling a hole in the wall and Tess glanced over. The definition of his bicep as he wielded his power tool was nearly her undoing. She loved her boss because he was an amazing person, but she wanted him because he was the hottest thing she'd ever seen. Angling her chair to get a more direct look, she leaned back and allowed herself to drink in every movement of his body.

How many fantasies had she had about this man? From Mason-in-a-vampire-cape to Mason-the-fireman to Mason-the-jewel-thief, Tess thought she'd imagined every possible way for him to take her in a rapturous fit of passion. Yet she'd never pictured him as a handyman putting up shelves in her office.

She would definitely have to move this scenario to the top of her lengthy list, since she absolutely loved what she saw. She loved the way his muscles flexed beneath his shirt, the way his large hands manipulated the tools. She loved the way he smelled, so clean and spicy. His scent filled her mind and made her want to bark or purr or make some other bizarre noise not intended for humans. She loved the way his jeans hugged his butt as he knelt to set the drill on the floor before standing up again. She almost wished he'd shown her a plumber's crack. Almost.

She also loved the telltale bulge in the front of his pants...the one not concealed by the dangling screwdrivers and hammers on his tool belt. Friday night, in the parking lot of the bowling alley, she'd wanted to grasp his swelling erection in her hand. She wondered what he would do right now if she actually fulfilled that desire, running her fingers over the thick, defined ridge she could plainly see outlined beneath his zipper. Would he grit his teeth together? Moan? Growl?

With her imagination in overdrive, Tess continued staring at the front of his pants. Until it occurred to her that Mason wasn't moving anymore. And, since she was staring at the *front* of his pants, he must be facing her. Which meant he'd been watching her stare at the front of his pants. For a while.

She dragged her gaze off of his delectable bulge, and up his rock hard chest, until her aching, desperate stare met his own. Heat flooded her face. *Damn, is there any way to pretend I wasn't gawking at his package?*

His penetrating eyes drilled into her and Tess knew there was no sense pretending. Her wicked thoughts lay open to his scrutiny.

Mason's sinful gaze fell down the length of her body before easing slowly back up again. He lingered on the curve of her hips and the swell of her breasts before his immoral stare settled on her lips. One of his brows arched while his mouth curled into a devilish grin.

She didn't know who moved first.

Maybe she sprung out of the chair, maybe he pulled her. She couldn't be sure. All she knew was that one second they were having eye sex, and the next second they became a tangled mess of lips and tongues and hands.

There were moans and groans. There was grasping and groping. She clawed at his shirt. He plastered her onto the desk. A straight rod stabbed her in the thigh.

Tess gasped against his lips. "Wow. That's really hard."

"What?" Mason glanced down. "Oh, sorry. Hammer."

"Oh. I see."

"I'll take that as a compliment."

She giggled as he fumbled to remove the tools. She tried to help, her trembling fingers pulling at his belt. Mason finally got it undone and let it fall, dropping it on his shoe. He cursed in pain but didn't miss a beat. His tongue tangled back with hers, hot and wet and demanding.

Tess leaned against the desktop when he fit himself between her thighs. Her hands roamed over his back and down to the waist of his jeans. She balled his shirt in her fists, raking her fingernails across his bared skin, relishing his sharp intake of breath. Her hands climbed farther up beneath the shirt fabric, tracing the line of his spine, urging him closer.

Mason pulled away, just enough to grab hold of her face. His eyes searched hers. "Tell me, Tess. Are you done punishing me?"

Working to catch her breath, she nodded.

"Say it. I want to hear you say it. Please."

"I'm done," she swore, desperate to have his lips on hers. "I'm done."

He smiled and kissed her again – even deeper this time, pressing her against the desktop until his sketches crumpled to the shape of her bottom. She continued working her hands under his shirt, fingers splayed against his back as he moved his mouth across her jaw and down her neck. He nuzzled into her shoulder and nipped at her skin.

Images of him in a Dracula cape popped into her head and Tess nearly had The Big One. She was incapable of controlling the odd squeal-moan that escaped her throat. Mason stilled at the sound while she tried fruitlessly to calm herself down. She felt his lips pull into a grin just before he bit back into the same spot.

The ridiculous sound sprang out of her again, but she decided she didn't care. Crazed with anticipation, she reached to his front, running her hand across the hard ridge in his jeans. Tess slid her fingers skillfully over his length, again and again, feeling him grow larger and thicker with her movements. He made an interesting noise of his own and she smiled.

He's a growler.

His mouth melded onto hers and she attacked him wholeheartedly. She tugged shamelessly on the button of his jeans. Her trembling fingers managed to get it undone but fumbled with the zipper.

The next instant, Mason backed away entirely. She nearly pitched forward off the desk. He steadied her by the arms, saving her from falling.

"Tess, I...I don't..."

"Don't what?"

"I don't have any..."

"Any what?"

He exhaled. "I don't have any protection with me."

"Oh. Right."

He didn't blink before asking, "My house?"

She nodded without a second thought.

Mason grabbed her by the hand and pulled her out of the building.

8

THE MARBLE COLUMN VS THE EMOTION PLANET

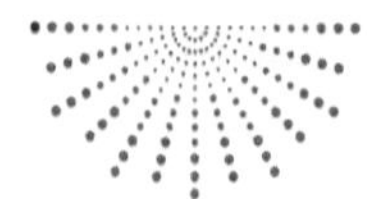

Tess watched Mason's hands grip the steering wheel and stick shift of his truck as he drove them through the streets of Richmond. Hands that would be on her again the moment they got to his house. *Damn*, how she wanted that. This was it. She was finally going to have the man of her multitudinous dreams.

If only he could have taken her on the desk in her office. If they'd been able to finish what they'd started right then and there, she wouldn't have had this time to think. Thinking was the worst. Since all she could think about was Malory.

Tess turned to look out the passenger side window, into the darkening night. She knew Malory wasn't out of Mason's life. If history had taught her anything, it was that those kinds of on-again, off-again relationships never really ended.

Maybe she could settle her fears somewhat if he just told her what had happened with his illustrious ex. But he wouldn't tell her, would he? She'd already asked him in the restaurant on Monday, yet he'd skirted the topic entirely. He simply never spoke about personal things. He'd even admitted, back in her office, how emotionally obtuse he was.

But Tess wasn't. She had enough emotions to form her own planet. She'd been in love with her boss forever, and what they were about to do – if they *ever* got to his house – would be a colossal mistake if she couldn't keep those rampant feelings in check. Bryan hurt her, but Mason? There was no end to the destruction he could wreak on her emotion-planet.

She peeked over at him and his eyes immediately met hers. He smiled before refocusing on the road, letting go of the stick shift so he could reach over to rest his hand on her thigh. The heat from his fingers melted through her jeans.

Tess stared at the spectacle of his large hand settled against her leg like it belonged there. She licked her lips, skin thrumming with the anticipation of feeling those fingers in places she hadn't been touched in a very long time. And never by a man she loved with all her heart.

She reconsidered her plight. Sure, emotional hell was a bad place to end up. When Mason left her to go back to his ex, Tess may as well tie herself up on a rack and slow-roast over flames for all eternity. But, even taking her inevitable demolition into account, wouldn't it be just as bad to deny herself the opportunity to have an affair with the man of her dreams? Wouldn't that horrifying denial do as much hellish harm, if not more?

He massaged her thigh slowly up and down, strong fingers kneading her rapidly heating flesh. Tess swallowed a moan and silently chanted a dozen curse words. Glancing at Mason's profile, her pulse skyrocketed.

Good Lord, look at him. He's gorgeous and wonderful and perfect and I have to have him, no matter what. But how can I do this? How can I be with him and not lose everything when he leaves me?

Tess had to figure out a way to keep things under control, and she had to figure it out fast. She needed to erect some serious emotional walls between the two of them. Walls and towers and ramparts and moats, with a bit of barbed wire thrown in for good measure. She needed another game plan – a *better* game plan – this one to protect herself from total annihilation. Otherwise, there was no question that Mason Tramont would utterly, irrevocably destroy her heart.

～

MASON WAS GETTING NERVOUS. Tess hadn't spoken a word since they got in his truck, and that wasn't like her. Tess talked. A lot. That much had never escaped his attention.

Being able to touch her here and now – to run his hand across her thigh in anticipation as they drove to his home – was heavenly. But would she allow anything else to happen tonight? She was obviously thinking, and her wild notions hadn't worked out well for him in the past. At least, not this past week.

Tess had set out to punish him on Monday. He knew that with certainty now. Yet what had amazed him last night – after he'd cursed and grumbled and bellyached to himself for hours – was *how* she'd chosen to punish him. After all, this woman had full control of his work computer and complete access to all his bank accounts and credit cards. If she'd wanted to, she could have made his life hell.

But that wasn't what she did. Tess's big plan of revenge wasn't to destroy his work, his finances, or his identity. Her plan was to take him to a park and a few bars. She danced and laughed and played with him. She held his hand and hugged and kissed him. Although she only allowed one kiss per day, since they could barely stop once they'd started.

He peered over at her, watching the side of her face while she stared pensively out the window. He wanted to have her tonight, but he also just wanted to be with her. He just wanted to be in her presence.

Mason knew exactly what it felt like to be with a cruel woman. This definitely wasn't it. The woman sitting beside him was kind and caring and warm, and bringing her home with him felt right on a hundred different levels. That truth settled peacefully into his chest. He squeezed onto her thigh, savoring this little taste of her body, smiling to himself as he drove.

Eventually, he turned his truck onto the familiar streets of his neighborhood and pulled into the driveway of the single-story house he'd constructed the moment his business began turning profits. A four-thousand-square-foot angular dream, situated on two acres of land in the West End, his home provided privacy and convenience and more than a little stately beauty, if he did say so himself. Tess had been here on several occasions, dropping off dry cleaning or picking up paperwork. She'd wholeheartedly admired his creation and her praise had pleased him to no end. He realized, right at this moment, that her approval always meant more to him than it should have. More than anyone else's ever had.

Now here he sat, suddenly anxious for her to see it again, hopeful she might look at it with different eyes. He wanted her to admire his home for a whole new set of reasons tonight. To possibly even picture herself living here one day.

Turning off the engine, Mason hopped out of his seat and walked around the front of the truck. He opened her door, holding his hand up to help her down. Her smaller fingers curled into his.

Once her feet hit the ground, he leaned in to kiss her. Tess turned her face up, eagerly smoothing her lips over his, and he took it as a good sign. He kept hold of her hand while they moved up the driveway.

When they arrived on the front porch, he released her to open the lock. Lagging behind as she walked through the door, Mason observed her reaction. She stepped silently into the living room, glancing over his sparse furnishings – the white leather couch and loveseat, the black stone coffee and end tables. He closed the door and threw his keys on the granite kitchen countertop while she looked out of the wide French doors into his backyard.

He watched her for long, quiet moments, savoring the sight of her in his home. She kept staring outside, looking utterly lost in thought. Eventually, he strode through the living room and stepped up behind her, careful not to startle her as he eased his hands across her bare arms.

"Tess," he hummed beside her cheek, loving the way her name rolled off his tongue. "Please tell me what you see."

She relaxed instantly into his embrace. "I see the big, beautiful yard and the bright stars in the sky. It's so peaceful here."

"I'm glad you like it."

He pulled her back against his chest, nestling his nose into her hair, breathing in. Wildflowers. Her scent. Soon, it would be all over his house, his bedroom, his sheets. He wanted that. He wanted to wake in the morning with her gold curls spread out on the pillow beside him, with that scent filling his mind before he could think about anything else.

Mason turned her around to face him. He needed to look into those sparkling baby-blues, needed to kiss her, to touch her. But when she glanced up at him, her eyes filled with unmistakable uncertainty.

Her obvious hesitance struck him. "Have you changed your mind about this?" he asked, wanting to give her a way out if she desired one. "If you've changed your mind about us being together tonight, I don't want you to worry about it. I'll understand if it's too soon."

"I haven't changed my mind," she stated with a firm headshake. "And we've known each other for six years, so I think we can forego the too-soon guilt."

He chuckled. "That works for me." He bent down to kiss her, but she pulled back.

Tess placed a hand on his chest, fiddling with his shirt pocket. "I haven't changed my mind, but we need to talk first."

"Yeah? About what?"

"About Malory."

Mason's shoulders dropped. "Seriously?"

"Yes, seriously. I need to know what happened between the two of you. I am asking you, right now, to please, *please* tell me."

"I...I..." he attempted to form words, without success. He couldn't believe Tess had even brought this up again. He didn't want to talk about his wretched ex, and he certainly wasn't about to revisit past relationship mistakes, especially ones that horrific. As far as he was concerned, those mistakes didn't need to be discussed at all – and definitely not now – when the only thing he wanted was to carry this woman to his bed and have the best sleepless night ever.

"Tess. What happened doesn't matter. It's over."

"It does matter. I know you still have feelings for her."

Mason inhaled sharply, reaching for her arms. He steadied his stubborn secretary with both hands. "I am going to say this one more time, and I *beg* you to hear me. I. Don't. Want. Malory. Not now and not ever again. That's all there is to it."

Tess stared into him, her gaze shifting, searching for something deep inside. He could tell she didn't believe him. But what the hell else could he do to convince her? He'd said the words, plain and simple. All he had left was to show her that she was the only woman on his mind.

Banding both arms around her waist, Mason pinned her to his chest before bending down to taste her bright pink lips. He half-expected her to reject him, but instead, she responded instantly. Her fingers threaded into his hair, her body shifting closer while they kissed.

"You're so beautiful," he whispered, easing his hands under her shirt to trace her spine. "So incredibly beautiful."

Her bra clasp came undone with a well-placed flick of his fingers. Unencumbered, he smoothed over the length of her back, from her soft shoulders to the perfect little indentations of her hips, again and again, until her breathing turned to short puffs against his neck. Then he hooked his fingers inside the waist of her jeans, eager to rid her of her clothing, as he kissed his way down her throat.

"Damn, I want you so much, Tess."

She trembled with his declaration. "I want you, too, Mason. I want this. But...but we need to put some boundaries on it."

He tasted her neck with his tongue, savoring the salt of her skin. "What boundaries do you need, sweet Tess?"

She gulped. "Three weeks. Three weeks and I'm leaving."

"I already know you're leaving work," he murmured beside her ear as he nibbled. "I promise I won't try to convince you otherwise."

"No, that's not what I mean. In three weeks, I'm walking away."

He ceased moving, ceased kissing, ceased nibbling. "Meaning?"

"Meaning we can have a good old-fashioned affair, but when I leave work, it's over."

Mason reared back, eyes wide as saucers. "Wait a minute. Did you just say what I think you said? You want us to have an *affair*?"

"Yes."

"And that's it?"

Tess blinked several times but held her ground. "Yes."

"You mean for now."

"No, not just for now. Three weeks and we're finished."

He stepped backwards, still staring her down. Was she serious? Was she actually serious? From the look on her face, he knew she was.

Holy shit, what do I have to do to get this woman to stop playing games? Yes, I did tell her earlier that I'd play anything she wanted. But I didn't think she'd actually take me up on it!

Mason forced a deep, cleansing breath into his lungs. "I thought you said you were done punishing me."

"I am done. I promise you, I'm done."

He huffed, since this certainly didn't feel like she was done. He rubbed his thumb and forefinger together, desperate to touch her again. *Damn it*, why wouldn't she just be with him? Why did she have to make this situation so absurdly complicated? He swore she could make Gandhi and Mother Teresa get into a fistfight over who won the privilege of yelling at her. But how could he possibly deny her demands when his entire being begged to have her?

"My God, Tess. You must realize this still feels like punishment."

She inched forward, closing the scant distance he'd put between them. "It's not. I swear it's not. I promise I won't punish you anymore, unless you like that sort of thing." She paused, her jaw unhinging. "I – I didn't mean that the way it came out, I..."

Her mouth clamped shut. A moment later, she exhaled. "Oh, who am I kidding right now? I meant that *exactly* the way it came out. If you like that sort of thing, I could totally be talked into it. I mean, I don't know about the whole handcuffs-and-whips scenario, and I'm not really sure about wearing one of those crotchless leather cat suits – they look like they might chafe a bit – but if that's what you imagine, I'm not going to judge. I actually have a very active imagination. And so many fantasies, I can't even begin to..."

"Tess!"

She ceased rambling and grimaced. "Sorry," she said, her shoulders bunched to her ears. "It's just that I want you. Obviously. And I think it's safe to say you want me, too."

A strangled groan left his throat.

"I just need you to agree to my limits, Mason. Please."

He stood in place, staring at her, desperate for answers. He knew there had to be some explanation for all this. Something, somewhere. Tess was not a cruel woman, so there must be a reason behind her ridiculous request to keep their relationship at affair-level.

Mason truly believed he could figure out that reason. He believed it because he'd been with Tess almost every day for six years, watching her movements, listening to everything she said and didn't say. He recalled the moment she'd stepped into his office Monday morning, when she'd been working up the courage to resign. At the time, he didn't know exactly what was going on in her mind, but he still knew she was a wreck.

He simply knew this woman, inside and out, so he knew her affair decision had to have a reason. Mason searched for it. He searched her clear blue eyes for what felt like an eternity.

Tess held her ground determinedly as the silent minutes stretched between them. She offered no further explanations, but she didn't need to speak. He found what he was looking for just the same.

Mason witnessed a distinct flicker of fear beneath her palpable desire. Subtle yet sharp. Tempered yet torturous. In that moment, he realized the truth. In that moment, he understood.

Tess is terrified.

Whatever pain she'd suffered in her past, whatever that damned ex-boyfriend had done to her, Mason was the one paying for it. Her huge heart – the one that had taken care of him in a million different ways over the six years they'd spent together – was still tender and aching. She was simply terrified of letting him too far inside.

With this newfound knowledge, Mason came to an unfortunate realization. No matter what he said or did, he couldn't change her mind about this three-week nonsense. Not tonight. And even though he was willing to work his ass off to prove that they could be perfect together, he wouldn't get the chance unless he gave in to her demands.

Tess's fingernails dug into her palms. "I need you to agree to this. Please. *Please*," she repeated, her entreating eyes fixed on his.

Part of him wanted to give in to her this instant. The other part knew they were both too strung-out after her last game to embark on a new one so soon.

As much as it pained him physically, Mason shook his head. "I don't think

I should. I'm not saying I won't agree at some point, but just not tonight. We can talk about it tomorrow or the next day, after you've had some time and distance."

"No," she said, reaching up to slip her hand over his jaw. "No more distance."

He tried to ignore the way his body leaned instinctively into her touch, the way his skin ignited beneath her fingertips.

She gave him the softest, sweetest smile, a direct contrast to the concern in her eyes. "No more waiting, Mason. Not for tomorrow or the next day. I'm positive I want this. All I need is for you to agree to my terms. Say we'll enjoy my last three weeks to their fullest, and then we'll walk away, no strings attached. Okay?"

He sighed with her words, his pitiful attempt at reason gone in a flash. Waiting wouldn't change her mind. She needed this new game, and honestly, he needed to start playing it as soon as possible. It was going to take every single second of the next three weeks to convince her they'd both win by being together.

Momentarily defeated, he nodded. "Okay. Okay. I'll do whatever you want."

"Oh, good," she breathed, her shoulders sagging in relief. "I mean, that's great. Really great. Although we should probably discuss..."

"Tess?"

"Yes?"

"I don't want you to take this the wrong way, but please stop talking. Just for a few minutes."

Her brow arched in defiance. She opened her mouth...then closed it again. She nodded her silent agreement.

For lengthy minutes, they just stood there, staring at each other. Mason feared moving. He feared he would startle her and she would run away screaming.

After forever, Tess reached to the hem of her shirt, preparing to pull it up over her head. "No, not yet," he said, halting her movements. "I need time to just look at you."

She released the material and let her arms drift back to her sides. Mason edged forward, reaching to her face with both hands. He held her steady inside his palms, his thumbs slipping gently across her soft cheeks. He looked at her in a way he'd never allowed himself before – with the knowledge that she was entirely his, right here and now. He allowed his eyes to wander over the contours of her face, the sprinkling of pale freckles on her nose, the perfect bow of her lips.

"Can I touch you?" she whispered.

Her question was as painful as it was absurd. "Always," he assured, even though he never wanted this moment to end.

She inched forward to place both her hands at his waist. Mason sucked in a breath. Grabbing hold of his shirt, she balled the fabric in her fingers and inched it upward. He tried to remain still during her excruciatingly slow task, but soon lost his patience. He grabbed the material and flipped it over his head, dropping it onto the floor.

Tess whimpered at the sight of his skin, her hips coming flush with his as she rested her palms on his bare chest. She splayed her fingers out, her hands soft and cool against the heat of his body. Bending her head, she trailed kisses across his collarbone and up his neck, finally ending at his lips. He leaned down to meet her and her tongue darted into his mouth. She giggled as shivers ran across his spine. He straightened just enough to look into her smiling eyes.

Fairly certain she didn't intend to dart away right this minute, Mason decided to fulfill the one fantasy he'd had many more times than he should this week. Reaching for her ponytail, he grasped the tie and slowly pulled it out, freeing her blond waves. Her hair draped against her back and he let the tie fall in order to push his fingers into the gold. She dropped her forehead onto his shoulder, humming in contentment.

He massaged her scalp, concentrating on the simple, perfect feel of her curls threaded through his fingers. Touching her like this felt intimate and sensual, more than he'd even imagined, flaming his already fierce desire. His body grew instantly thick and hard, every muscle taut with anticipation. He didn't know if it was the revelation of finally having her in his arms after six years in her orbit, or the knowledge that she only meant for this to be a brief affair between them, but the need to have his sweet Tess burned hotter and wilder than he ever thought possible.

She nestled further into his chest, the enticing sound of her responsive mewls threatening to finish him off way too prematurely. Mason didn't want to rush their first time together, but according to his body, he wasn't going to have much of a choice. He needed to see her, all of her, now.

Cupping her face again, he eased her head back. He waited until she opened her eyes and peered up at him. His little sprite looked blissful, almost drugged, as she rewarded him with a leisurely, seductive grin. He groaned when he reached down to grab the hem of her shirt in both fists, edging the pink tee upward.

Tess did her best to stare him in the eyes while raising her arms above her head. The curve of her lips was an invitation and a dare and he didn't recall exactly how he got her shirt and bra off simultaneously. He only knew that his mouth was meant to be at her breast, his tongue wrapped around her nipple, his ears filled with the sounds of her soft whimpers. He paid proper attention to each breast in turn, until her fingernails dug into his shoulders and her legs swayed.

Wrapping his arms around her waist, he pulled her closer, keeping her upright while moving his mouth up to her collarbone. Unable to resist, he nipped at the skin over her shoulder, curious to see if she would make the same crazy-sexy noise she did when they were in her office earlier today. As expected, a strangled, impassioned scream left her throat.

Mmm. My Tess certainly enjoys being bitten.

Mason smiled against her skin, loving the secret knowledge he'd gained. He just hadn't counted on the frenzy his bite would create.

One minute he was happily discovering her little secrets, the next minute she attacked him like a rabid animal. She kicked off her shoes and wriggled free of her jeans and pink lace panties before he had the ability to devour the sight. He couldn't even properly appreciate the fact that she stood naked in his living room before her mouth fixed to his and her fingers frantically popped the button on his jeans.

Tess yanked down his zipper, her hand curling around his jutting erection so fast that he barely registered what had happened. But the coolness of her skillful fingers against his hot, tight flesh made it very clear that he needed to take immediate action. He needed to get to his damn nightstand and grab a condom before he lost it like an untried teenager.

He dragged her body closer, agonizingly aware of all the ways her bare skin touched his. Without warning, Tess jumped up on him. She wrapped her legs around his waist and her arms around his neck, her teeth nipping his jaw. He caught her without thought, his fingers digging into both cheeks of her ass, clamping her in place as she moaned her approval.

Mason took off running. Well, if fumbling through his living room, pants half-off, balancing her against his chest, with the hardest erection he'd ever had in his life poking her in the stomach, could be called "running". More thankful than ever that he'd built a single-story house, he made it into the master bedroom and tossed her onto his high-backed, four-poster bed. She went down on the mattress in a heap of arms and legs and laughter. He'd never seen anything sexier than his sweet Tess, naked as a jaybird, giddily sprawled out on his steel grey bedspread.

He kicked his shoes, socks, jeans, and boxers into a pile. He jerked the handle on his nightstand so fast that the drawer popped out and crashed on the floor. She laughed harder while he cursed and fumbled for a precious gold packet. Getting the damn thing open and on was the pinnacle of his life's achievements.

Mason turned back to the bed, expecting her to be lying in wait. He should have known she would never be the expected.

Tess stood on the mattress, pacing back and forth. "Come and get me," she said, her voice husky and entrancing.

"Are we wrestling?" he questioned as he climbed up to stand in front of her, wondering if his king-sized bed allowed enough room.

"Oh, I don't think you'd want to wrestle me. I'd take you down pretty hard and I would hate to burst your ego."

"Something's going to burst. I don't think it's my ego, though."

She grinned as she edged over to the tall mahogany headboard and flattened her spine against it. Her body stilled while his advanced.

Mason aligned himself with her, pressing her onto the polished wood. He groaned when her tight nipples eased into his heated chest. "That certainly was easy, Tess. I thought you'd put up more of a fight."

"Who's fighting?" she purred. "I just want you the way I want you. Now get down on your knees."

Mason stared into her eyes. He'd never seen them brighter – mischief and seduction wrapped into one. He didn't argue. He dropped to his knees before her.

Tess smiled, simultaneously wicked and gleeful. The next instant, she slid down the headboard and lodged herself on him, his erection gliding into her slick sheath with delicious ease. She moaned blissfully as she settled in place. Then she wrapped her legs around his waist, taking him in farther still.

She was hot and tight and wet and perfect and Mason bit into her shoulder to keep from losing his mind. He heard her make that insane, yes-please-bite-me noise as her head flattened back against the wood. Her gold hair splayed out in every direction, a stark contrast to the dark bedframe, driving him mad with need.

He couldn't wait another second. He thrust himself deep inside her, over and over, pounding her body into his headboard. He gripped onto her hips as he watched her hair shake around her face and shoulders, saw her eyes roll back in her head, and listened to the wild growls and groans escaping her throat.

Mason held on for dear life until she whimpered in time to each and every lunge. She babbled words he couldn't quite discern, since his hammering heart pulsed like a freight train in his ears. His whole body contracted around hers, desperate for her pleasure while fighting back his own. Moments later, they both came so hard that he didn't know where her screams ended and his began.

Instantly spent, Tess devolved into a boneless mass of damp skin. She slumped forward against his chest, her sudden dead weight forcing him to collapse back onto the mattress. She jostled on top of him when they landed together on the bedspread, but she didn't bother to move.

Her hair covered his face, tickling his nose with every inhale. Mason reached out to gather the gold waves in his hands, brushing them down her back as he traced the line of her spine. He loved having her bare breasts crushed to his chest, her arms and legs draped across him, her rapid breaths warming his shoulder.

He waited several minutes, working to catch his own breath, before he spoke. "Tess, you're absolutely amazing."

She sighed. "I always wanted to be nailed against that headboard."

"You mean...this particular headboard?"

Her floppy hands balled up tightly. "Um, no, not *this* headboard. I just, I mean, uh, headboards in general. Got a thing for headboards."

"When was the last time you were in my bedroom, exactly?"

Her entire body stiffened. "A few months ago, maybe? I can't remember. I was probably bringing in your dry cleaning." She sat up.

"Hey, wait," Mason complained, reaching for her arms. "Where are you going? I like it when you lay on me."

"I – I need to go to the bathroom. Clean up a bit."

"Oh. Of course. You can use the one in here and I'll go to the one in the hall. But then you'll come back to bed, right?"

Tess nodded. "Yes, I'll come back."

"Good. Because I'm nowhere near done with you."

9

PRISONERS AND PROMISES

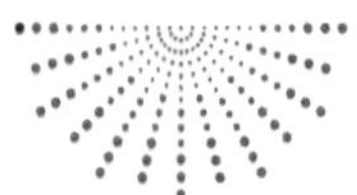

My God, what have you done? Tess glared at her reflection in Mason's bathroom mirror. *Have you lost your mind utterly, completely, and without reserve?*

"Gee, Mason, I always wanted to be nailed against your headboard," she mocked herself in a low whisper. "Why don't you just tell him you've wanted to jump his bones daily for the last six years? I bet that'll go over nicely."

And, as if that verbal gaff wasn't bad enough, she was pretty sure she'd babbled that she loved him while he pounded her mercilessly into his wood bed frame. Thank goodness she'd been unable to form any clear pattern of words he could have possibly understood.

Holy hell, why don't you just cut out your heart, wrap it in a bow, and hand it over to him? It'll save you all the worry!

Brushing disheveled hair back from her face, Tess continued looking into his mirror. But she didn't see her current reflection anymore. She saw a younger, much more innocent version of herself, staring longingly into Bryan's earnest eyes. She knew in her head that Mason wasn't Bryan, but the connection was too strong for her heart to sever.

Years ago, after watching Mason take Malory back for the fourth time since Tess had known him, she gave up on the dream of having a relationship with her boss. Within weeks, she'd met Bryan. He was the perfect substitute – smart and successful – the complete Mason-package. He even came equipped with his own Malory, a beautiful ex named Kendra. The only difference was that Kendra and Bryan had been on-again off-again for only a few years, as opposed to the decade Mason and Malory had. Bryan swore on his soul that he was over Kendra, and Tess believed him because she wanted to. She thought Bryan was The One.

Kendra and Bryan were married now. The afternoon Tess came home early from work and found them in her bed was one of the worst days of her life. It certainly didn't help that it reminded her of the other worst day of her life, when her parents' marriage had ended the same way. Megan Troy had come home to find her husband in bed with their next-door neighbor. Tess and her sister, Emma, were just kids at the time, but they were old enough to realize their lives would never be the same. And definitely old enough to watch their mother struggle afterwards, working 60-hour weeks to put food on the table after their father left.

When Bryan devastated Tess so similarly to the way her mother had nearly been destroyed, she knew she had to become a stronger, more independent woman. Going back to school, starting a business, becoming her own boss... those accomplishments got her on track. She couldn't repeat her mistakes now. She couldn't hand her heart to another man who already belonged to someone else.

Tess shook her head. She didn't want to feel this way. She didn't want to let fear rule her life, and Mason had said on multiple occasions that he didn't want Malory anymore. But when she'd asked him point blank – both Monday at the restaurant and again here tonight – to tell her what had happened between them, he wouldn't. He refused to confide in her, refused to let her inside. Honestly, he felt as closed off as ever.

Of course, Mason had behaved differently in the past week. During her days of revenge, he'd laughed with her and played with her and said all the right words. Yet underneath it all, she feared he was still the same marble column she'd worked beside for six long years.

Tess shut her eyes against the tight pain in her chest. She wished her boss had changed. She wanted so badly for him to be open with her, to be willing to love her. But she couldn't retreat again into dreams of them running together through fields of wildflowers. She needed to embrace a future in her Pooch Palace – to give herself a chance at happiness – to give herself a chance at love. *Real* love, with a man who was willing to love her back with all his heart.

Unfortunately, devastatingly, her stoic architect just wasn't capable of giving her that. No matter how much she wished otherwise.

Leaning over the sink, Tess rested her forehead against the mirror. She inhaled steeply. Mason's scent lingered all over her. She could still feel him, his hot skin, his slick tongue, his sculpted fingers. She wanted him again. And again.

She willed her heart to stop longing for him, even though she had no intention of willing her body to stop. After all, she was here now, post-coitally naked, with the man she'd wanted forever. Was it too much to ask for some physical enjoyment after all this time? Didn't six years as his faithful servant mean she deserved a bit of fantasy-fulfillment?

Pangs of guilt over her actions tonight seeped into her skin, but she forced them away. After all, this sexual attraction was definitely not one-sided. Mason wanted her nearly as much as she wanted him. And she'd been upfront about her intentions – he'd agreed to the option of a limited, no-strings-attached affair – so didn't that make it okay for both of them?

Pulling back, Tess focused on her reflection. "The three-week agreement is good. You're both adults, and you both know where you stand. You can do this, Troy. Just fulfill all the fantasies you can, and don't fall in love with him any more than you already are, and then walk away with your heart still intact. That's all possible. It really is."

Her reflection didn't look as certain as she wanted, but it would have to be. Mason waited for her on the other side of the door – waited to do wonderful, horrible things to her – and a pack of wild dogs couldn't drag her away. Not when the man she'd wanted for six years currently wanted her back.

Turning away from the mirror, she took another deep, calming breath. She pictured her boss's face as he'd stalked her across the mattress earlier. Getting nailed by him against that headboard was only one of her countless fantasies. Tess was ready to fulfill more. A lot more.

With her nerves mostly settled, she cracked open the bathroom door. She wondered what Mason had occupied himself with while she'd been busy panicking in his bathroom. Neat freak that he was, he might have made the bed or sorted their clothes into lights and darks.

The room was shadowed, illuminated only by the light coming from behind her. When her eyes accustomed to the dimness, she spotted him lying in wait on the mattress. His clothes still lay strewn about the floor. Bed sheets still sat rumpled beneath his body. And by "his body" she meant his perfectly hard, definitively muscled, strikingly naked body, with abs worthy of any self-respecting Greek god.

Mason's head sat propped on a pillow, his eyes pinned on her. Tess bit into her lip and he watched the movement with harrowing intensity. He looked like he would attack her at any moment, yet despite the transparency of his desire, she couldn't help the frizzle of shyness that crept into her bones. She shut off the bathroom light before heading back to bed.

His voice came, deep and certain, out of the darkness. "Wait." He clicked on his bedside lamp. "I want to see you."

She stopped halfway to him.

Mason sat up, his gaze roaming over her bare form. She tried not to fidget as he lingered on each and every curve. He cleared his throat. "Turn around, please."

Tess didn't hesitate. She pivoted, staring at the wall until she couldn't stand the wait anymore. She peeked over her shoulder to see his reaction. If devouring her with his eyes were actually possible, she would have huge chunks missing from her backside. Laughter bubbled up from her chest as she turned and walked to the bed.

He caught her eyes when she reached the edge of the mattress. "Damn, Tess. You're gorgeous."

"Thank you. But don't ask me to dance naked, because then you'll see where all my jiggly parts are."

A smile curved his lips. "I like your jiggly parts. Feel free to dance anytime."

"Hmm. I don't think so." She matched his grin while crawling into bed beside him. He dropped back on the mattress and she seized the opportunity to turn on her side, snuggling into the crook of his arm to lay her head on his shoulder. His body was perfectly heated, his scrumptious scent renewed with his closeness. "Well, maybe," she reconsidered.

"You'll dance naked for me?"

"Maybe. Someday."

"I'll take that as a promise."

Tess couldn't wipe the smile from her lips as she wriggled closer, curling her leg around one of his and resting her arm on his chest. He took hold of her hand, playing with her fingers, lacing them together. "I wish we'd done this a long time ago," he lamented, the deep timber of his voice reverberating through his body and into hers. "It's too bad the office setting doesn't provide much romance."

Her brow quirked. "Are you joking, Mason? You must know office romances are the norm. If you and I had been laid out on your desk every day for the past six years, it would be par for the course."

"Really?"

"Yes, really. Right now, Kathryn from Engineering and George from Accounting are going at it like rabbits. Chad walked in on them in the copy room the other day and then hollered about it for an hour. Didn't you hear about that?"

"In the *copy room*? No, I didn't hear. But I'm sure David handled the situation appropriately. He takes care of all the staff issues."

"Well, I imagine he didn't feel justified giving Kathryn and George too much grief for their behavior. Not when David and Regina have defiled that office in every possible way."

Mason arched back, the look in his eyes akin to terror. "No. They wouldn't. David wouldn't do that in our office."

"Good Lord, are you utterly innocent? Or just not adventurous?"

"Adventurous? How about sanitary?"

"You're right. It's not sanitary at all."

Mason's head shook before settling back on their shared pillow. "That does it. Tomorrow I'm hiring one of those crime scene cleaning crews to come in and wash down the entire building. Using special equipment and black lights."

Tess giggled. "You're such a germaphobe."

"Yes, and I also don't see how having sex in an office is normal. That's supposed to be a place of work. *My* work."

She smoothed her fingers across his. "Funny, I don't remember that being an issue for you earlier today. When we were on *my* desk."

"Well, I...I think that was different."

"Yeah? How so?"

"Because it was the heat of the moment. And because you and I were the only people there. And, in case you didn't notice, I did stop us. Office sex simply isn't appropriate."

She rolled her eyes. "Appropriate-shmopriate. It's fun and sexy and dangerous. It's the allure of maybe getting caught at any minute but wanting that person so much you'd risk anything to have them right there. It's completely inappropriate and utterly wonderful."

"Hmm," he considered, running his free hand through her hair. "It sounds like something you're particularly interested in."

Tess opened her mouth but then closed it. She buried her face in his neck.

"Wait, unless...have you already had sex in our office, Tess?"

She maintained her hiding place, recalling a thousand fantasies of Mason taking her in various and sundry places in their office. Including on the copy machine, which honestly didn't sound comfortable at all.

He gave her a gentle shake. "Come on, you have to tell me."

She mumbled into his shoulder.

"What was that?"

Tess raised her head. "I said, 'Never.'"

Relief washed over his face. "Never, huh? Well, who's the non-adventurous one now?"

"Hey, I'm adventurous. At least, in my mind. Maybe I haven't actually done it in the office, but I've had some awesome daydreams."

"I see. Any in the past few days? Any involving me?"

She pressed her lips shut as heat crept into her cheeks.

Mason ran his hand down her arm. "I'm going to take your silence, and that beautiful blush of yours, as admissions of guilt. Unless you care to divulge some of your fantasies?"

No way in hell. Stretching, she faked a yawn. "Wow, look at the time. I should get some shuteye. I have to be at the office early. My boss is a real stickler about work hours."

He chuckled. "Don't I know it."

Tess tried not to look overly relieved by the change of topic. No matter how much she wanted her Mason-fantasies fulfilled, she couldn't imagine confessing to any of them. She couldn't fathom the humiliation of admitting to the magnitude or duration of her elaborate dream world.

In his silence, she settled back into the space between his arm and his chest. Honestly, this space felt made to fit her. Content to lounge in her new happy place indefinitely, Tess startled with a simple realization.

"Oh, crap. I don't have my car here, Mason. It's back at the Palace." She propped up on her elbow, staring him down.

He looked utterly unconcerned. "Um-hmm."

"That means we have to go now."

"Why does it mean that?"

"Because I need my car to drive back to my apartment, so I can get dressed for work in the morning. I can't exactly wear my Pooch tee and jeans to the office."

"Why not? You'd look adorable."

"Yeah, not so much. I need to go home before work."

He smiled, pushing a curl behind her ear. "Then you can take my car home. In the morning."

"I can't take your car. I don't drive stick."

"The truck is stick. The car is automatic."

"Good Lord. Are you suggesting I drive your Mercedes to work?"

"Sure. I can drive the truck."

"You're missing the point here, Mason. Can you imagine what would happen if I rolled up to the office in your Mercedes – in front of all our coworkers?"

His eyes brightened like the sun. "Tell me what would happen."

"Well, for starters, no one would get any work done all day. Including me, since I wouldn't be able to hear myself think above the roar of gossip. Then I'd spend half the day in the Emergency Room, because Regina would have had a heart attack."

"She's young and healthy. They'd revive her."

"Mason!"

"Seriously, Tess, just tell them it's none of their business."

"Easy for you to say, Mr. I-Sit-In-My-Office-Behind-A-Closed-Door-All-Day. People talk to me. A lot. I've managed to work there for six years without being the brunt of any major gossip. I'd like to leave with that accomplishment intact."

He exhaled. "Fine. If you won't take my car to work, you can leave here in the morning, drive to the Palace, drop off the Mercedes, take your Bug home so you can change, and drive that to the office. Then tomorrow evening, after everyone has left the building, we'll swing by the Palace in your car to pick up mine."

"That is incredibly complicated."

"It'll work out."

"Or you could just drive me back now."

"No."

Tess smiled despite herself. "Let me get this straight. Am I to understand that I'm being held prisoner in your bed until morning?"

"Yes, that's correct. Not that I have any handcuffs or whips lying around to enforce it. Also, oddly enough, I'm fresh out of crotchless leather cat suits."

She hung her head. "Oh, God. I was hoping you didn't remember me saying any of that."

"Didn't remember? It was barely an hour ago. And even if it was a year ago, I'm pretty sure I'd still remember that one."

"I know. I know it was bad. I just...I always hoped you zoned out whenever I went into babble-mode."

Mason reached to her chin, drawing her gaze back to his. "I would never zone out during babble-mode. It's one of my favorite Tess modes. I was actually sad, since you seemed to overcome it in the last few years. I thought you'd completely stopped babbling around me. At least, until this past Monday at the restaurant. Then it all came back with a vengeance."

"Yeah, I'm sorry about that. Again. That was a bad day."

He shrugged. "Or a good day, depending on how you look at it. Either way, you should stop apologizing, since I'm not making any apologies for keeping you here tonight."

"You can't actually be serious about holding me prisoner in bed."

"I am absolutely serious."

"Mason..."

Before she could finish that thought, he arched up, flipped her over onto her back, and propped himself above her. "Tess. You've given me three weeks. I'm taking them. Every second of them. Deal with it."

She tried not to grin like a six-year-old with a brand new puppy. "Did I ever tell you that you're pushy?"

"I prefer authoritative."

"Okay. You're authoritative. In a pushy kind of way."

"You really need to work on your complimenting skills."

"Ugh! You're aggravating, too."

"Then go to sleep and you won't have to deal with me."

"That's just what I'll do," she insisted, fighting back her laughter. Lying stiffly beneath him, she clamped her eyelids shut and worked to calm the giddy smile overtaking her face.

Tess could hear his deep breathing as he hovered above her, could feel his wicked gaze perusing her naked form. She felt his head dip down, lips settling against her shoulder. She fought to remain motionless as his tongue traced hot little circles on her skin.

When her pulse began racing, she whispered, "Um, Mason?"

"Hmm?"

"May I ask what you're doing?"

"I thought you were sleeping."

"Oh, I am. I was just curious."

"Well, I promised myself that if I ever got you in my bed, I would kiss every inch of your body. Literally. So, here I am."

She peeked out of one eye to watch the top of his head while his lips roamed across her shoulder and down to her chest. "When did you promise yourself that, exactly?"

"Tuesday," he murmured against her breast, "when you wore that tight red dress in the park. It revealed too much and not enough, all at the same time. Amazing."

His mouth hovered over one nipple, teasing her before he sucked the tight bud inside. Tess arched her back and shoved her hands in his hair. Her fists balled against his scalp.

"Mmm...I don't mean to disturb you, Miss Troy." His breath cooled her wet skin, sending shivers across her entire body. "Feel free to sleep, as long as you understand I have important business to attend and cannot possibly stop."

He blazed a heated trail to her other breast, grasping the nipple between his teeth. Tess inhaled sharply. "I understand, Mr. Tramont. It's like you always say: business first."

"Precisely, Miss Troy."

She shut her eyes again, attempting to minimize her wriggling as his mouth discovered every inch of her skin. His lips moved farther down, circling across her tummy and over her belly button. He explored the curve of each hip in turn, taking his torturous time, until he finally edged between her knees. The stubble of his jaw scraped deliciously against her inner thigh and she had to fight back a scream because, *holy hell*, how many times had she fantasized about this?

Tess spread her legs, panting with anticipation. His tongue was hotter than she imagined as it slipped into her wet folds. Her hips bucked wildly in response. Mason pressed one strong hand against her stomach, holding her steady while his other hand joined his tongue in a delirious assault on her senses. His fingers pushed inside her, first one and then another, finding an ethereal rhythm almost instantly. He hummed against her skin as his mouth performed some sort of sexual miracle on her tight little bundle of nerves.

She squealed in utter, luscious pleasure.

Oh, well. So much for sleep.

TESS HAD NEVER BEEN this nervous driving before. But she'd also never navigated Richmond, pre-dawn and completely exhausted, in her boss's Mercedes. She sighed in relief when she finally reached Pooch Palace. Transferring over to her Bug, she hopped inside and dialed her phone.

A full minute later, a sleepy Annabelle answered. "Um-hmm?"

"Hey, Belle. Did I wake you up?"

"Tess, it's not even six in the morning."

"Oh, sorry. I can call back later. I just didn't want you to worry about the car."

"What car?"

Tess started the engine and pulled onto the street. "Mason's Mercedes. It's parked in front of the Palace. He's going to pick it up tonight. So, that's it. Go back to sleep."

A rustling sound came over the receiver.

"Belle? You still there?"

"Sorry...dropped the phone. Why is Mason's car at the Palace?"

"Well, um, yesterday I was there, doing work, and he came back. He wasn't mad anymore, and he put up shelves in the stockroom, and..."

"Holy crap! You slept with him, didn't you?"

"Hey! I'm not a tramp."

"Then you didn't sleep with him?"

"No, I slept with him. But you didn't have to assume I did. All I said was he put up some shelves, and you just went right there."

"Tess, don't make me hurt you. Details. Now."

She stopped at a light, leg wiggling against the brake. "I can't remember *all* the details. We went to his house and one thing led to another. The first time was against his headboard, then there was a him-on-top thing, then the floor – I don't remember exactly how we ended up there, except he kept telling me I couldn't leave the bed and I was determined to prove that I could, but then he proved a few things to me, let me tell you, and, yeah, sorry, that was probably more detail than you really wanted – and then an hour ago, I was trying to leave and I went into the living room to get my clothes and he pinned me down on the couch. So, I didn't really get much sleep."

"Hot damn! Four times?"

"Yeah."

"Wow. I haven't done it four times in a row since Scott Peters on prom night."

"That's a teenager for you."

"And architects, apparently. I may have to get one of those."

Tess sighed. "He's definitely one of a kind."

"Oh, honey. I'm so happy for you. You're finally dating the man of your dreams."

"No, we're...we're not dating."

"What? What do you mean? Isn't your revenge thing finished?"

"It is finished, but I can't date him."

"Why on earth not?"

She gripped the steering wheel, her knuckles whitening. "Because I can't. I can't hurt like that again. Mason is still hung up on Malory."

"Did he say that?"

"No, of course not. But I've spent the last six years watching them together. I've seen the way he takes her back, time and time again. He says he's over her now, but I can tell he isn't. I see it in the raw reaction he has whenever I mention her name. He still has feelings for her and he won't talk about them. I can't fight that. I won't. I know I'll lose."

Tess's eyes brimmed with tears. "I tried, Belle. I swear I did. I asked him to tell me what happened with her. I practically begged him to open up to me, but he just wouldn't. And that feels like an insurmountable obstacle. I mean, even if by some miracle he truly has put Malory behind him, how am I supposed to build a relationship with someone who simply refuses to let me inside? I want more than that. I want to be loved by a man who is willing to give me his whole, entire heart. I'd like to think it's what I deserve."

"It is," Belle assured. "You deserve to be loved completely."

"Thank you for that."

"Of course. So...what are you going to do now?"

Tess watched the yellow blobs of streetlamps flash against her windshield as she drove. "I'm going to have a hot, torrid affair with a man I've wanted for six years. I'm going to fulfill as many of my fantasies as humanly possible. And in three weeks, I'm going to walk away from that office – and from him – with my head held high."

"I'm still not worried about your head."

"I know, Belle. I know. Thanks for always looking out for me."

"Someone's got to do it."

"Love you, kiddo."

"You, too. Call if you need more support. Just not before seven."

"Will do. Bye."

"Bye."

Tess hung up the phone. A tear fell onto her cheek. She brushed it away, attempting to concentrate on the well-worn roads between the Palace and her apartment.

"Don't get all sentimental," she chastised her weary heart. "You have to look at this positively. How many people get to live out their fantasies for one night, let alone three weeks? Count yourself lucky."

She rounded several more corners before her apartment complex came into view. After exiting the car, she climbed the stairs. An instant later, she stood in the shower with water pouring down her bare skin.

Tess hugged her arms as the welcoming heat infused her. She did consider herself lucky for the three weeks to come. She just had no idea if Mason would see it the same way in the cold, somber, fluorescent glow of their office lights.

10

BUSINESS FIRST

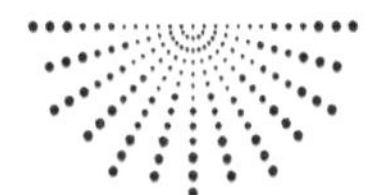

When Tess pulled her Bug to a stop in front of Field and Tramont later that morning, Mason's truck was already parked curbside. Part of her hoped to see him in the driver's seat, but the other part was relieved the truck sat empty. It was probably best she walked into work alone, went straight to her office, and pretended nothing was different about today.

After all, no one needed to know she'd spent her night under, over, and around a gorgeous man's naked body. No one needed to know anything about it. Except for Mason, who owned said body, and may or may not be rethinking all the things that transpired between them last night...and this morning.

Tess swallowed against the lump in her throat as she walked up the stairs and into the building. She managed to slip inside, scurry to her chair, and start her work, all without seeing a soul. In fact, she remained blissfully incognito until noon, when Regina ambled into her office and perched one butt cheek on the edge of her desk.

"Hey, Tess. How was your weekend?"

She took a deep breath, reminding herself that no one suspected anything untoward. And she needed to keep it that way. Forever. "It was okay. I was working at my other job."

"You mean the one you're ditching us for?"

Tess gave her a sheepish smile. "I'm sorry, Regina. I promise to keep in touch after I leave. Who knows, maybe I can charm you into working for me."

"Wouldn't that be a riot? I'd love to see the look on David's face if I told him I was going to help you babysit dogs…"

She tried to focus on Regina's rapidly moving lips, but her mind floated down the hall to her boss's perpetually closed door. Tess's eyes shifted to the clock. She'd spent all morning in avoidance and denial, but now she had to face facts. She'd arrived here nearly four hours ago, yet she hadn't heard a word from Mason. Not a call. Not a text. Nothing.

Regina paused, staring at her, obviously waiting for an answer to a question. "Um, we have forty dogs right now," Tess replied, hoping the response made sense.

"Forty! I can't even imagine…" The perky brunette continued talking, her arms as animated as her voice.

Tess managed to smile even though her heart raced. What was Mason thinking behind that thick black door of his? He'd agreed to a lot last night, in the heat of the moment. Did he regret his late-night decisions? Was he worried that their habitual boss-secretary relationship would now be agonizingly uncomfortable? Would their first post-coital office encounter be more awkward than either of them could bear?

Business first. They'd joked about it in bed, but she knew it was absolutely true. Business did come first for Mason. In fact, she'd bet he wasn't nearly as disturbed by the unsanitary practices of his over-sexed staff as he was about the missed hours of work such cavorting entailed. Was he sitting at his desk now, worrying about her jumping all over him during office hours? Was he trying to decide the best way to tell her to keep her paws to herself while they were here in this building?

Until she knew what he wanted, she would have to remain professional above all else. She would have to act perfectly normal, as if nothing had changed between them. She would have to pretend that she did *not* want the copy machine to take pictures of her bare ass while he plowed into her.

Her phone buzzed and she nearly flew out of her seat.

"Wow, what's up with you?" Regina asked mid-sentence.

"Sorry. Didn't get much sleep. Guess I'm a bit edgy." Tess pulled her phone from her purse and stared at the message. From Mason.

Meet me in my office ASAP.

"Anything important, Tess?"

She looked up at Regina and forced her stiff shoulders to shrug. "Just the boss. He wants me for something."

"Ugh. Always work, work, work with that one. It's no wonder you're leaving. If he was my boss, I'd have left a long time ago."

"Well, I guess I'd better go see what he needs."

"You look worried, doll. Is he giving you a hard time about resigning? He can't do that, you know. I could have David talk to him."

"No, no. It's okay. I can handle it."

"You sure? You should be able to spend your last weeks here in peace."

Tess held back a groan. "Yes, I'm sure. Thanks, though."

"Anytime. You just let me know." Regina winked as she stood, fluttering out of the door, leaving Tess to her disconcerting thoughts.

She reached into her purse and grabbed her compact to check her makeup. She applied a little blush and added some lip gloss, attempting to enliven her sleepy features. But nothing hid the apprehension in her eyes.

Standing from her chair, Tess smoothed the thin wrinkles from her ivory pencil skirt and fiddled with the cuffs of her peach silk blouse. Satisfied with her professional appearance, she tossed her ponytail over her shoulder, walked around her desk, and strode down the hall. The ominous black door glared at her for a long minute before she mustered the nerve to knock.

His deep voice came clearly from the other side. "Yes?"

With trembling fingers, she turned the knob and entered.

Mason sat behind his desk, distinguished and stately in a perfectly tailored navy suit, his unyielding eyes business-only.

"You wanted to see me, Mr. Tramont?"

"Yes, Miss Troy. I need to discuss something of importance with you. Shut the door, please."

Mason didn't smile at all. Not even after she closed the door.

He straightened in his chair. "I'd like you to come over here."

"Certainly," Tess replied, keeping her tone as formal as possible. She moved to the massive block of wood he called a desk and then eased around it, her fingers touching the shiny black surface as a small means of support. Her fist balled when Mason swiveled his chair to face her.

She came to a halt a foot in front of him. "Yes, Mr. Tramont?"

He stared at her, his features unmoving. "I've taken the time this morning to think about our...situation. I need to make a few things perfectly clear."

"Very well."

"This is a place of business, Miss Troy. It is imperative that we maintain a professional work relationship while here at this office."

Tess grimaced. "Of course, Mr. Tramont. I would never..."

"Certain things would be wrong for us to do," he interrupted.

She didn't know what to say. She looked to his face, searching for clues. For a long while, he didn't move at all. Then Tess watched in wonder as his gaze shifted down to peruse her body, slowly and sinfully. He took his time, focusing on the way her clothes hugged her hips, her breasts. His eyes eventually returned to her face, now dark with desire.

"For instance, Miss Troy, it would be wrong for me to ask you to pull your skirt up now. While I watch."

Tess's breath caught on a gasp. *Is he serious*? Her eyes darted to the closed-but-not-locked door...then back to her boss. He wasn't moving, wasn't grinning, wasn't turning away. He stared in expectation.

She wet her lips. How many times had she wished for something like this to happen? How many times had she dreamed of him looking at her the way he was at this very moment, in this very room? With his piercing stare fixated entirely on her, Tess ignored the reality of the unlocked door. Heart pounding in her throat, she reached down to the hem of her skirt and curled her fingers into the fabric, inching it upward.

Mason tracked every miniscule movement she made, until the skirt sat bunched entirely at her waist. He walked his chair forward, the leather squeaking beneath his solid body as he reached out to grasp her hips in both hands. With one finger, he traced the laced curve of her panties beneath her belly button. Then he hooked the sides and eased the tiny scrap of fabric down, until it fell at her feet.

He looked back up to her face, his expression sheer hunger. The chair creaked when he stood. He circled her body to come up behind her, his chest pressed to her back, the fabric of his suit pants rubbing against her exposed flesh. His hands found her hair, his fingers running the length of her ponytail before brushing it forward over her shoulder.

Tess whimpered as he traced her silk-covered spine with his fingertips, starting at her neck and stopping when he encountered the crumpled skirt bunched at her waist. He paused for a moment before flattening both large palms against her bare ass cheeks. She pressed her lips together hard to keep from moaning.

Mason cupped her flesh as he nuzzled his face beside her ear, hot breaths rapid against her neck. His fingers kneaded her bottom, moving farther and farther down. When he found the slick entrance to her sex and pushed two fingers inside from behind, Tess used all her willpower to suppress a scream.

She writhed against his hand while he enticed her eager flesh with his fingers, caressing her both inside and out. His other arm wrapped around her front, pulling her against his chest, his thick erection prodding the seam of her ass through the fabric of his pants. Nimble fingers flipped open several buttons on her blouse, pushed the silk aside, tugged her bra down, and rolled her nipple.

Her spine arched with the consuming sensations, her head lolling back onto his shoulder. He continued his sinful work for long, drawn minutes. By the time he nibbled up her neck to her ear, Tess stood crazed with desire.

"No matter what, Miss Troy, I should never ask you to bend over on this desk for me. That would be very, very wrong."

A groan escaped her throat. She twisted out of his arms to pin her upper body onto his desktop, flattening her hands on the smooth, black surface. "Mason," she murmured, barely recognizing the husky sound of her voice, "there's no lock on your door. Anyone could walk in."

"I know. But sometimes you want someone so much, you'll risk anything to have them."

Tess closed her eyes, vividly recalling the words she'd said to him last night in bed. She remained bent over, hearing him unfasten his zipper and open a foil packet. Then it hit her. His ever-present computer wasn't on his desk. He had a condom in his pocket. He'd planned all of this.

The tip of his erection nudged her from behind. Tess spread her legs wider on instinct, arching up on her tiptoes inside her patent leather heels. She tilted her ass up as high as she could, offering him easy entry. A feral growl slipped from Mason's throat. He grabbed hold of her exposed flesh, one cheek in each hand, spreading her open as he sunk into her wet sex in one swift motion.

The force of his thrust pushed her entire body forward, rubbing her nipples against the desktop, adding infinite height to her senses. Mason withdrew slowly before driving back in even harder. He leaned forward, his chest against her back, and whispered, "Don't scream, Miss Troy."

She shook her head. "I can't promise anything, Mr. Tramont."

He huffed out a laugh as he stood and moved his hands to her hips. His fingers squeezed into her flesh, pulling her to him while he thrust deeper still. Tess nearly came undone in an instant, struggling to cope with this fantasy surging to life.

Her fingers slipped back and forth against the dark wood surface as he lunged into her over and over again, the moisture on her palms leaving slick handprints behind. She stifled her groans while her breaths came faster and faster, mimicking his carnal movements. She ground her bottom into his thighs with every thrust, amazed by how deep and thick he felt inside her.

Tess knew she couldn't scream. She knew the entire staff would come running into his office and find her, bare-assed and boobs-out, being pummeled against the desk by her boss. But when her orgasm hit, she couldn't remember her own name, let alone where she was.

The need to scream overtook her sensibilities, yet Mason reacted soundly in an instant. He dropped forward, clamping his hand around her mouth to press his fingers into her lips. She bit down on his flesh as her body convulsed in pure bliss. The moment her teeth met his skin, he came hard inside her. His head collapsed onto her back, his fitful groans muffled against her shirt.

Tess's muscles twitched uncontrollably as her release continued, as he continued pumping in and out, milking every last sensation from both their bodies. Her roaming hands steadied on the cool desk surface while her thwarted cries of lust transformed into contented little moans. She kissed the fingers still covering her mouth.

Eventually, his hand dropped to the desk. She took the opportunity to apologize. "I'm sorry, Mason. I didn't mean to bite you that hard."

"You bit me?"

She grinned. "I imagine you'll feel it later."

He stood and slid out of her. Slower to rise, Tess heard him fumble through his briefcase and turned to see him grab a pack of tissues he'd apparently brought in from home. He offered her one, but she shook her head. Averting her eyes, she repaired the state of her bra and blouse.

He's come prepared for everything – even the aftermath cleanup. And here I was, worried he'd changed his mind about our affair.

Tess searched the floor for her discarded panties, slipping them on and pushing her skirt down. By the time her clothes were in place, Mason sat in his leather chair, leaning back, looking as if nothing had happened.

She stared at him in astonishment. "You're really something."

"You think so?"

"I cannot believe you planned this entire thing."

He gave her a roguish grin. "Tell me, did I get close?"

"Close to what?"

"Any of your erotic daydreams?"

At a loss for words, she shook her head.

"No? Then I'll just have to try again."

"Mason! You know perfectly well that your door doesn't lock!"

He shrugged. "You and David give me hell for keeping my door closed all the time, but really, who would dare enter unannounced? I'd say my shut-in behavior is coming in handy right about now."

Tess tried to look appalled but failed. "Well, you do have a point."

"Then come back later and we'll go again. Perhaps I'll discover your fantasy next time."

"Excuse me, Mr. One-Track-Mind, but I actually have work to do."

"Yeah? Like what? Maybe I could talk to your boss."

"Please do! Tell him I'm a very busy woman. I mean, on top of all my regular work, I have to hire a new secretary to replace me."

Mason pinned her eyes. "You're irreplaceable, Tess."

She couldn't ignore the warmth that shot through her veins. "My thoughts exactly. So, you can see what a tough job that'll be. I also need to make sure everything is on track for the West End Country Club opening. And we still have to pick up your car at the end of the day."

"I liked having you in my bed last night."

"You're not listening to me at all, are you?"

"Will you come home with me again?"

Tess tossed her ponytail over one shoulder and blew out a breath. She struggled to not look directly at him, at the charming grin curving his lips or the devilish hunger in his eyes that made her want to strip naked right here and now. "That depends. Will I get any sleep tonight?"

"I can't guarantee it."

"Okay, then."

～

MASON COULDN'T STAND the wait – the grueling hours between having Tess on his desk and the moment he would see her again. But he forged through, making up for lost work time by delving into ideas for ingenious new structures. Tess made all his juices flow, creative and otherwise.

At 5:20 he stared at his clock, clenching his jaw as his mind leapt again to the amazing woman he'd only begun to truly discover. He already knew one thing for certain...the few moments they'd actually been *together* together were nowhere near enough for him to learn everything he needed to know about the spirited Miss Troy. He was starting to believe an entire lifetime wouldn't be long enough for what he wanted to experience with her.

Yet she only intended to give him three weeks.

Scrubbing a hand across the back of his neck, Mason sighed. Tess had obviously been hurt in the past. She'd had her heart broken and it hadn't mended properly. She was scared witless to offer him a future, and he was just as terrified that she would leave him in a few short weeks.

But how on earth am I supposed to change her mind?

He hoped the more fantasies of hers he fulfilled, the more she'd want to stay. That's why he'd taken her on his desk a few hours ago. He intended to work on every sexual daydream she'd ever had. But there had to be more he could do. He needed to keep her in his life indefinitely...maybe permanently.

Permanently? Good Lord, when did that thought enter my mind?

Mason shook his head. He didn't know when he'd first thought it. He just knew it made perfect sense. They'd only truly been together for a few days, but it was as if a light had been switched on. He couldn't imagine turning it off.

He knew Tess would be outraged over his current thought process. He was thinking this through logically again and he knew how much she hated that. But it wasn't all logic. That much was certain. There was something different about her. There was something different about *them*. Mason wanted nothing more than to figure out what that something was.

When the clock struck 5:30, he rose from his desk and stepped into the hall, the silence making him acutely aware that the rest of the staff had already left. He walked toward her office, his mind still heavy with thoughts of this affair she wanted. When he arrived in Tess's doorway, his sweet sprite smiled up at him from her chair. He saw the twinkle in her eyes, watched the light from the window catch the gold of her hair, and his heart immediately eased.

"Hey there, Mr. Sunshine," she sang. "Ready to go get your car?"

Mason could only stare and nod.

Tess gathered her things and walked over to him, pushing up on her tiptoes for a quick kiss before brushing past him into the hallway.

Damn it. He wished *someone* were still here. If any employee had witnessed that kiss, they would know he and Tess were together.

He realized he needed that moment to happen. Such a gossip-worthy revelation was a necessity, since the more people knew about them being a couple, the more real their relationship would seem. And the more real it seemed, the harder it would be for Tess to simply walk away when the time came.

Mason followed on her heels, down the deserted hall, past the empty lounge, out the front door, and to her Bug. He opened the driver's door for her before walking around to slide into the passenger's side.

Tess grinned at him while he folded onto the seat. "You look awfully adorable all curled up in my little car."

He fumbled with the seatbelt in the cramped space. "How adorable am I?"

"Pretty darn," she said as she pulled into the street.

Mason studied her profile while she drove, absorbing the almond shape of her eyes, lingering on the little upturn at the tip of her nose, admiring the determined set of her full lips. He hated the ticking clock she'd set on their time together. He had to figure out how to change her mind – her wondrous, brilliant, stubborn-as-hell mind.

If their coworkers knew about them, it would be helpful. But it wouldn't be enough. Tess had to feel so entrenched in his life that she couldn't imagine leaving. She had to realize they fit together, in every possible way, and that she wanted to stay with him. And he had to start making her realize it right now, because there was no time to waste.

Mason cleared his throat. "You know, we're still going to have to drive to work together one of these days."

Her nose crinkled. "Why's that?"

"Well, I'm picking up my Mercedes today, but my truck is still at the office. I need to drive to work with you sometime so I can take the truck home."

"Hmm," she considered at a stop sign. "I guess you're right."

"Of course, I'm right."

She rolled her eyes as she turned the corner. "Okay, I'll drive you to work tomorrow. But we're going to have to leave your house super-early in the morning, so no one sees us arrive together."

"Fair enough. Let's go to your place, then. You'll need to pack."

"Pack? What are you talking about?"

"If we're leaving from my house in the morning, you'll need a change of clothes for tomorrow. You'll also need a hairdryer and a toothbrush. While you're at it, you may as well gather everything else you need."

"Huh. You make it sound like I'm moving in with you."

"For the next three weeks you are."

Tess whipped her head toward him, her face contorted in disbelief, before she refocused on the road. "Um, no, I'm not."

"Yes, you are. You said yourself that we're having an affair."

"I did say that, but..."

"But nothing. People live together while they're having affairs."

"Really? In what world?"

"In the little world in my head. Also, I'm pretty sure they did it in England during the reign of the Tudors."

Her lips trembled to suppress a laugh. "Mason..."

"No. Don't say anything else. Three weeks, Tess. They're mine. For the next three weeks, I want you in my life and in my bed. All night. Every night."

She shifted in her seat. "At some point, I will need to sleep."

"You can sleep anytime I'm not having my way with you."

"If we keep up this pace, I'm going to start walking funny."

"Is that a complaint? Do you need me to curb my appetite for you?"

Her slender fingers curled around the steering wheel. "Nope. I don't need that." With a shake of her head, she pulled the car into the left lane to make a U-turn. "I guess we're going to my place to pack."

Mason looked out of the window and smiled.

11

OFFICE DISTRACTIONS

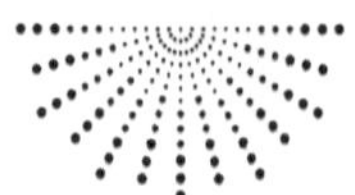

David Field sat behind his antique Colonial desk, peering over the piles of paperwork, down the long hallway, to his partner's closed office door. It was Friday – an entire week after Tess announced her resignation – and guilt ate him up inside. He had to know if he was the reason she'd quit.

Mason was his oldest friend. Sixteen years they'd known each other: through college, years of architectural study, various girlfriends, and the creation of their amazingly successful business. David never questioned the decision to enter into a partnership with his best friend. After all, Mason Tramont was the most levelheaded, practical person he'd ever met. Even now, his partner's designs were more brilliant than ever. Yet David still worried about him.

The first time he'd met the Tramont family was at the end of their college sophomore year, when he and Mason took a road trip to visit them. The Tramont house was more like a mansion. Graham Tramont donned a coat and tie. Louise Tramont wore a tailored skirt set and exquisite jewelry, even though it was a random Wednesday. Mason hadn't seen his folks in nearly nine months, hadn't even been home for Christmas that year, yet all Mr. and Mrs. Tramont said was, "Hello." They asked about the drive. They shook David's hand. Nothing else.

David couldn't comprehend living in such a sterile environment. He'd been home over Christmas break and his mother slobbered on him so much that it took seven tissues to get her lipstick off his cheeks. Yet Mason's parents didn't even touch their son. David remembered Mason confessing once that he'd never heard his parents say, "I love you."

In a strange way, understanding his upbringing made David feel responsible for his friend's happiness. He wanted to make sure Mason made the right decisions – that he followed his heart, even if he had no idea what it told him. Malory Catskill was never the right decision. She was cold, hard, and demanding. David believed Mason only stayed with her because she felt familiar, and because he didn't know any better.

But Tess...she was a different story. She had been from day one.

David knew Mason had feelings for his vivacious secretary. He also knew Mason didn't have a clue what those feelings were. He didn't blame his friend; with that emotionless upbringing, it was amazing he functioned around humans at all. Honestly, the day David suggested that Mason date Tess, he'd only been looking out for his partner's best interests. He had no idea he would start a chain of events leading to this: Tess's resignation, and the possibility of Mason crumpling without her.

Unable to wait another moment, David stood from his desk and marched down the hallway. He had to know if he was the one who screwed all this up. If so, he fully intended to apologize for falling down on his self-appointed Mason-heart-protection duty.

When David arrived at his friend's perpetually closed door, he knocked and waited for a response. None came. He figured the man was so wrapped up in work that he hadn't heard a thing. He waited another moment before knocking harder.

"Come in," Mason finally offered.

David opened the thick door to his partner's vast, sparsely decorated office. "Hi, buddy."

Mason sat in his chair, elbows on his desk. He smiled. "Hi."

"Have you seen Tess?" David asked as he entered. "Regina wants to talk to her. As always, but I think she actually has a question for her."

"I'm sure Tess is around here somewhere."

"Well, I guess I'll let Regina know."

"'Kay."

David stood motionless. By the clipped answer, he could tell his friend wasn't in the mood to chat. But he couldn't walk away, not without getting a few things off his chest. "Listen, Mason, are you doing okay?"

"I'm fine. Better than fine, actually."

"Really? Because you've been acting funny."

"Have I?"

"You have. And I think I know why. It's Tess, isn't it?"

"Hmm. I suppose you could say that."

"I knew it. It's because she's leaving, isn't it?" David hung his head. "Buddy, there's something I have to ask you."

"What?"

"Is it my fault Tess is leaving?"

"Why on earth would it be your fault?"

"Because I told you to ask her out."

"Oh. That."

"Yes, that. Did you ask her out?"

"I did."

"Well, damn. Did it piss her off?"

"Yes. Significantly," Mason confirmed.

"Aw, man, I'm sorry. Truly. Do you want me to talk to her? To apologize? I can tell her it was just me playing stupid matchmaker and it wasn't even your idea."

"David, you may have planted the seed in my mind, but it was absolutely my idea to ask Tess out. Please don't feel bad. Her resignation had nothing to do with you. She said it didn't even have anything to do with me. She would have left anyway."

"Really? Huh. Well, I'm glad, in a way. I didn't want to be the cause. But I'm also sad to hear she's really leaving. Do you think I could convince her to stay? Or maybe you could?"

"Unfortunately, I don't think that's possible. When Tess makes up her mind about something, she can be quite pigheaded."

David heard a thud and saw Mason wince. "You okay, buddy?"

"Yeah, I just hit my knee on the desk. Will you please excuse me now? I have something I need to do."

"Sure, I'll let you get back to work," David agreed, already turning away. He knew how protective Mason got over office hours. "So, you and me, we're good?"

"Of course, David."

"Good. And will you tell Tess that Regina is looking for her?"

"As soon as I lay eyes on her."

"Thanks."

"Anytime."

David stepped out of the room and shut the door.

∼

MASON WATCHED the door close behind his friend. He smiled wildly. Pushing his executive chair back, he peered under his desk. "Regina is looking for you."

Tess exhaled inside the cramped quarters, bare shoulders falling. "Crap, that was close. Do you think he knew I was under here?"

"No, but it would help if you didn't smack my leg while I'm trying to act nonchalant."

"You called me pigheaded! You deserved worse!"

Mason laughed as he watched her crawl out, discarded blouse in hand. He didn't know anyone else in the world who could display such fiery indignation while half-naked on all fours. She was unlike anything he'd ever seen. "Well, Miss Troy, maybe you shouldn't have been eavesdropping on our conversation."

She cleared the desk and sat back on her heels, glaring up at him. "Eavesdropping! I can't believe you were talking about me when I was right here!"

"I was well aware of your location, believe me. But I'm not the one who stuck you under the desk. I don't care if David knows about us."

"Mason, my shirt was off!"

"He does have terrible timing. Another minute and I could have had that lacy bra off, too. Did I mention I love it when you wear blue lingerie? It goes perfectly with your sensational eyes."

She attempted to look mad as she knelt in front of him. Her feigned anger didn't last long. She broke into her gorgeous smile, the one that buttered his insides.

Tess leaned forward, bouncy blond hair tumbling over the cleavage peeking out from her bra. "Okay, then. I'll admit you've mastered complimenting," she offered, her words dripping with honey. "But that's beside the point. David can't know about us."

"Why can't David know about us?"

The momentary calm ended when she threw her bare arms up in the air. "Because! We've already gone over this!"

Mason bent toward her, easing his fingers up her flushed cheek. "I'd be happy if everyone knew. Honestly, I'd like to walk into the hall right this minute and shout it out loud. In fact...here I go."

Grinning ear to ear, he started to stand from his chair.

Two dainty hands landed on his thighs, pushing him back down.

"Not so fast, Mr. Tramont."

He settled into his warmed leather seat again, enjoying himself way too much. "I'm going to do this, Tess. It's been five days since we started defiling my office on a daily, often twice-daily, basis. I'd like to start defiling yours."

"You can't just start coming into my office! People will know something is going on! They'll want to know what it is!"

"That's why I plan to announce our intentions ahead of time, so they'll leave us in peace."

She huffed at him and he couldn't help chuckling. Tess looked so damn enchanting, kneeling on the floor and rolling her eyes. God, he loved watching her. And he especially loved living with her.

It had only been a few days of them being together at his house, but he already knew how she liked her breakfast. He also knew she refused to eat anything until she'd had exactly three sips of coffee – *because three is my favorite number and that makes it a good start to the morning, Mason* – and she brushed her teeth for ten minutes before bed. She actually brushed for ten entire minutes, during which time she wandered about the house, humming a little tune in the back of her throat, working up a toothpaste lather so thick that it made her look like a freakishly adorable pirate with a frothy goatee.

He smiled with that image as he watched her now, blowing a disheveled hair out of her face and staring up at the ceiling. He could see the gears in her brain turning and wondered what she was plotting. When her gaze drifted back to his, an enticing smile spread her lips – so beautiful it caused him physical pain.

"Why tell people?" she purred, shifting closer. "You've already got me. And you've already had me, countless times."

"I can count them."

"Yes, well. I have ways of keeping you silent."

She crawled over to him, still kneeling when she fit her waist between his knees. She splayed her hands on his thighs before running them upward to the button on his suit pants. With a quick flick, she undid the closure and eased down the zipper. Her eyes darted to his while she ran her tongue across her glistening pink lips.

"You can't possibly distract me from my mission, Miss Troy."

"Can't I?" she questioned, freeing his rapidly stiffening erection to her exploring fingers.

He hissed, focusing on the sexy-as-hell sight of this impeccable woman staring innocently up at him as she grasped his thick shaft in her hand. Damn, he'd already had her this morning at home and again first thing at work. It still wasn't enough.

Her fingers slid up and down. "Are you distracted yet?"

"No. Not a bit," he lied.

She smiled before bending over to suck his length into her mouth.

Mason inhaled sharply. He forced himself to stare at the wall as her tongue moved in delicious circles across his overly heated flesh. He couldn't look down. He couldn't watch her. If he caught sight of her glossed lips wrapped around him, of her gold hair spread out on his thighs, of her lithe body wriggling on her knees, he was going to lose it before he had the chance to be inside her again.

He gripped the chair's armrests until his knuckles whitened. "This...this doesn't change a-anything. I am completely focused."

She sucked harder, more rhythmically, her fingers fitting around the base of his shaft, tightening while she moaned. Closing his eyes, he swore under his breath. The head of his cock hit the back of her throat and he nearly emptied himself entirely. But he didn't. He had to maintain control. He couldn't give in to her demands right now. If he did, they would spend the rest of their lives together with her thinking that when she wanted to win an argument, all she had to do was unbutton his pants.

On second thought, maybe that wasn't necessarily a bad thing...

Tess pulled back and Mason finally risked opening his eyes. Pushing off of his thighs with both hands, she rose slowly to stand before him. With a charming smile, she reached around the back of her skirt and undid the zipper, letting the fabric fall to the ground. Her panties came next, followed by her bra. Wearing nothing but black high heels with little bows on them, she stared shamelessly down at his state of arousal.

She didn't say another word. She just took a step forward, parted her legs, and climbed into the chair with him. Tess slid herself onto his raging erection in one seamless motion. A soft whimper escaped her lips when she settled fully down. Mason had to focus hard on getting air in and out of his lungs. He tried not the think about how she was 99% naked and the only unclothed part of him was currently buried deep inside her.

Her perfectly tapered fingers ran across his face, tracing the rough shadow of stubble on his jaw. She rose up and glided back down, once, twice. "How about now?" she whispered. "Have I distracted you yet?"

"That's...um...not." He wasn't sure what he'd said.

Nuzzling against his cheek, her tongue darted out to taste his skin. "I see." She bit into his earlobe, licked the little indentations she'd made, then straightened to see his face.

Tess pinned his eyes as she reached down to grasp her breasts with both hands. She ran her thumbs across her stiff nipples before leaning forward to present them to his mouth. "How about now, Mr. Tramont?"

"Holy fuck," he cursed, sitting bolt upright in his seat. He wrapped an arm around her back, fastening her to him. He feasted on one taut bud, sucking it hard into his mouth. His other hand clamped onto hers, overlapping her fingers, squeezing and pulling on the erect peak of her other breast until she moaned as frantically as he did.

She rose up and down again within his tight embrace, surrounding him in slick wetness, contracting her inner muscles to milk his erection. He let go of her breast to pull her head down, slamming his mouth against hers, desperate to taste. Her hips ground into his and she groaned.

"Tell me you're distracted," she murmured against his lips.

He couldn't see straight. "Yes. God, yes. But I will tell everyone. Eventually."

"But not now. Not yet," she encouraged, kissing him deeper.

She arched up before landing back onto him with full force, the flesh of her ass pounding harder against his thighs as she worked them both into a delirious frenzy. The chair grumbled in protest, but Mason couldn't understand why. He couldn't think of a single thing in the whole world to protest at this moment.

"Anything you say, Tess. Anything."

She smiled...and finished what she'd started.

TESS STEPPED out of Mason's office sometime later, only after triple-checking her outfit. After all, she couldn't afford to have anything on backwards or ridiculously wrinkled. She closed his door behind her and peered down the hallway, thankful David didn't see her exit. Side-stepping to the left, she scurried toward her own office.

Regina popped out of the doorway. "Tess!"

She skidded to a halt, hand flying to her chest. "Yikes, Regina!"

"Did I scare you? Sorry."

Tess straightened, forcing a smile. "I – I just wasn't expecting you there." She moved around the vivacious brunette and into her office.

Regina's brow arched. "Is everything okay with you?"

Tess sat stiffly in her chair. "Yes, of course. Why?"

"Because you look really flushed."

She touched her heated face with the back of her hand. "Do I? Maybe I'm, uh, coming down with a cold or something."

Regina's arms folded across her chest. She stared her down. Tess tried not to shift under the scrutiny.

Regina pursed her lips. "Don't even think about calling in sick for the next two weeks, Tess Troy."

"No, no. I wouldn't do that to you." She let out a sigh of relief.

"Well, good. Did Tramont tell you I was looking for you? David told him to tell you."

"Um, yeah. I do remember that."

"Well, I wanted to know what you're doing next Friday."

I'll probably be doing my boss. "Why do you ask?"

Regina danced around the desk. "Can you say *party*?"

"A party? For what?"

"For you, silly! A going-away party. I've got a boatload of tables reserved over at Angelo's. Everyone in the whole office wants to come."

Tess swallowed hard. "You mean *everyone* in the office?"

"Oh, I didn't tell your boss. I know that's probably wrong, but it's my party and I don't want him to know about it. I mean, he wouldn't come anyway, and if he did – can you imagine? Mr. Stone-Heart would make everyone freak out."

"I can only imagine."

"So, next Friday at Angelo's. Right after work. Sound good?"

"Sure."

"Awesome!" Regina sang as she spun on her heels and left.

Tess made sure her friend was gone. She made sure she was entirely alone. Then she dropped her head into both hands and groaned.

She already dreaded this party. First, because she would miss this place, and everyone in it, so she didn't see any reason to celebrate. Second, because she would have to keep this a secret from Mason all week and she didn't want to do that. Third, because if he did actually come, she wasn't sure what he would do.

For some reason, her boss wanted to tell everyone that they were a couple. And if he did? She couldn't even imagine. She was barely handling things as they were. They'd only been cohabitating for a few days – she refused to say *living together* because...well, because – and yet they'd already struck up a weirdly perfect routine.

They took turns cooking. They took turns setting the table. They took turns doing dishes. She knew which drawer his can opener was in. *His can opener*. She knew he vacuumed his house every day – *seriously, who does that?* – and he sometimes babbled in his sleep, and he always wanted to cuddle first thing in the morning. Also, she'd had to accept the fact that he woke up looking just as gorgeous as he did when he went to bed, which was so unacceptably unfair, since she woke up looking like Medusa's eviler twin.

Tess wasn't even sure how any of this had happened. One minute, she'd been sitting beside Mason in her Bug, still wrestling with the fact that he'd blown off his no-sex-in-the-office rule and bent her over his desk – okay, technically she was the one who'd bent over, but still, it was totally his idea – and the next minute, he insisted she move in with him.

At that moment, she'd just been coming to terms with him being in her car. Frankly, she was amazed his huge body even fit in the seat. She'd felt the heat of his skin radiating directly at her, as if he'd specifically told it to do that, and the next thing she knew, Mason started talking about cars being in the wrong places and people living together during affairs and some mention of King Henry. Then she found herself agreeing to pack up her things and walk into his house with a suitcase.

Except she didn't actually walk into his house with a suitcase. Mason carried it inside for her. He put her clothes in a couple of drawers he'd cleared out in his bedroom, stuck her toiletries next to his in the bathroom, and put her suitcase so high up on the back shelf of his immense walk-in closet that she couldn't possibly reach it without a ladder. Immediately after that, he cooked dinner and she set the table and they spent the evening laughing over candlelight and a few glasses of wine and – *holy hell* – what was happening here?

Still holding onto her throbbing head, Tess tried to ignore the blissful domestic images roaming in her brain. She concentrated on her immediate dilemma. No one could find out what was taking place at Mason's house. She couldn't fathom her coworkers knowing any of this. It was bad enough that her pillow had taken up residence on his bed.

Her. Pillow. Was. On. His. Bed.

And, as if all of that wasn't overwhelming enough, tomorrow she would meet Mason's brother for dog gym building day. That felt like a massive thing, to be introduced to family, and she didn't know what to think of it. Her nerves were already shot, and if she had to deal with her coworkers hounding her about their relationship on top of everything else, she would probably have a complete breakdown. People knowing they were a couple would make everything so much more real and raw. It would make leaving Mason akin to *Mission: Impossible*.

As it was, Tess didn't want to imagine another day without him.

12

GRUMPY BEAR

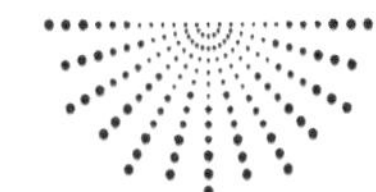

Tess woke on Saturday morning to a large, warm body snuggling up beside her. Mason's hands eased under his puffy comforter, finding their way to her bare hips and pulling her closer, pressing her breasts into his solid chest. Her nipples tightened against his hot skin as he nuzzled his face in her tousled hair.

"Mornin'," she whispered, giggling when his scratchy chin rubbed against her shoulder.

"Mmm," he murmured, warm breath heating her neck. "This is my favorite time of day, when I reach out and you're right here beside me."

Tess peeled an eyelid open to see a pale stream of light peeking through the gap in the window curtains. "What time is it?"

"I already told you. It's favorite-time."

She smiled against his cheek. "This is my favorite time of day, too, you know. Although, I must say, last night was pretty damn amazing. Seriously, you were on fire. That move you did with your fingers and tongue at the same time? Priceless. Really, there's just no price to put on that, and yeah, I'll stop babbling about your sexual achievements now."

He chuckled beside her ear while running his hand up and down her spine. "Please don't stop; that's another reason why this is my favorite time of day. You always wake up in babble-mode."

"Well, as much as I enjoy favorite-time, can we attach some numbers to it this morning? We actually have things to do today."

Mason raised his head, eyes locking with hers. "I know, but I would be crazy happy just lying in bed with you for the next forty-eight hours. I have so many more finger-tongue moves to share."

"Wow. It would be difficult to put into words how much I want that. But I think your brother would be pretty pissed if he had to build my dog gym alone."

"Eh, he'd get over it."

Tess laughed, running her fingertip across his lip. "I can't believe I finally get to meet Ian today. What exactly did you tell him about us?"

Mason nipped at her finger. "You sound nervous."

"Well, he's part of your family, so...yeah, I'm a little nervous. I'll bet he's curious about why you're taking a weekend off to help me with my business. He must be wondering what kind of relationship you and I really have. Did you tell him you just decided to do something super heroic for your secretary today?"

Mason smiled into her eyes, but he didn't answer right away. Tess held his gaze, waiting patiently for a response to her question, while he grabbed her by the hips and tucked her beneath him. He arranged her naked body under his own, situating their chests, arms, and legs together, pinning her to the mattress. His massive form engulfed her and she worked to focus against the onslaught of sensations. No matter how often she found herself in this position, gazing up into his beautiful brown eyes while she lay underneath him, she still felt awed by it all.

He dipped down for a kiss before finally answering. "Come to think of it, I may have told Ian that you and I are living together."

"You...*what!*" Tess tried like hell to sit up, to no avail. She pushed against the wall of his chest for several seconds before noticing the devious grin spread across his lips. "Mason! Did you pin me to the bed on purpose before you told me that?"

"Yes, that's exactly what I did."

She glared up into his twinkling eyes. "Damn, you are...you're so..." *Adorable. Frustrating. Dreamy. Irritating. Completely, utterly perfect.*

"I'm so...what?"

Tess bit into her lip. "Did you really tell Ian I'm living with you?"

"Yes."

"Can I ask why?"

"Because it's true." He traced a finger down the side of her face. "And because I wanted to tell someone. I didn't tell him everything about us. I just said we'd decided to move in together, to see how we liked it."

"But I don't understand. It's only for two more weeks. You'll have a lot to explain to him later."

"I'll deal with that when the time comes. For now, I needed to talk to someone. I can't say anything to David, or anyone at the office, per your request. It felt good to tell my brother. I think you can understand, since you have Belle. You talk to her all the time about...things."

"That is true. I just never imagined Mason Tramont needed to talk to anyone."

"Wow. Do I really come across as that much of a loner?"

"Um..."

"Wait. Don't answer that."

She gave him a soft smile.

"I'm not a robot, Tess. I swear. Even though I can do the dance."

The memory of him doing his best Artificial Intelligence impersonation in a field of dandelions made her sigh. "I know you're not a robot. I just don't want your brother to have preconceived notions about me. Is Ian going to think I'm a tramp for living with you?"

"No, he's going to think you're a saint for living with me."

Tess laughed. The motion shifted Mason's body on top of hers, hard and soft rubbing together. Arching her head off the pillow, she pressed her lips to his and whispered, "But I'm not a saint right now."

He grinned. "I was really hoping you'd say that."

She returned his grin, her pulse quickening as she anticipated another vigorous round of spirited sex with plenty of finger-tongue moves. Except Mason didn't budge an inch from his current position. He didn't rush any movement. Instead, he eased both hands into her hair, holding her still while he kissed her again.

His tongue was slow and languorous, dancing with hers. Tess could feel his length hardening against her thigh and she tried to wriggle beneath him, to encourage some quick friction. But he wouldn't allow it. He just continued his deliberate actions, steadying her face in his hands as he traced her lips with his tongue, as he rubbed his nose against hers and smiled into her eyes.

She reached her arms around his waist and lowered her hands to his ass, grabbing hold of both cheeks and giggling. She tried to wrap her legs around the backs of his thighs and rock her hips upward, to force him to go faster, but he wouldn't take her bait. Mason kept her fastened securely to the bed as he gazed on her face.

Slowly, one at a time, he reached down to her arms and drew them away from his body and up over her head. He wrapped both her hands in his, entwining their fingers and sinking them into the pillow beside her hair. He held her like that for lingering minutes, peppering tiny kisses over her lips and nose. Tess's breath stuttered in her chest as she watched his eyes grow darker, not only with desire, but with something...more.

Forever passed before he finally started to move, rocking his hips against hers. His thick erection slid between her slick folds, over and over, until it found home. But he didn't enter her quickly. He moved slowly, so slowly that Tess wanted to scream from the torture of waiting. She tried to buck into him, yet the faster she attempted to go, the steadier he became. When she finally surrendered to his desire to take his sweet time – when she finally acquiesced and settled down against the mattress – he withdrew himself all the way to the tip before restarting his precise descent into the heat of her body.

Several moments later, Mason allowed himself to sink entirely inside her. She moaned out loud, the intense feeling of fullness overpowering all her conscious thoughts. He held her hands beside her head and she grasped onto him, clinging in sheer desperation.

Mason stared into her, unflinching. Her heart pounded in her chest as she stared back. His gaze was raw and potent and harrowing in its honesty. It hurt to look at him like this. It was too close, too intimate. It made her want so much more. It made her want too much.

"Tess," he whispered, pressing more gentle, devoted kisses to her cheeks and lips. "Tess...Tess," he echoed her name over and over. Like a plea. Or perhaps an understanding. He nudged her nose with his and rested their foreheads together, closing his eyes as his body stilled inside hers. He surrounded her, consumed her, filled her, and for these precious moments she felt truly safe and blissfully secure and absolutely cherished.

Until the emotion of the moment overcame her. Tess's chest squeezed in pain. A pressure built in her lungs, a pressure that had nothing to do with the heaviness of his body, and she found it difficult to breathe. "Mason, please. *Please*."

He opened his eyes and raised his head. He looked inside her, deep inside, and Tess wanted nothing more than to look away. But she didn't. She stayed just like that, staring into him for drawn minutes, while he filled her completely. Time stopped as his fingers eased across hers, as his warmth infused her skin, as his body anchored hers to the earth.

Finally, he gave her a tender smile and a little nod and started to move. He still went slowly, spending leisurely time easing in and out. Their hips rocked together in perfect, subtle synchronicity, the measured movements generating more heat than she could have imagined.

The soft skin of her breasts and belly pressed into the taut muscles of his chest and abdomen. The sunshine grew brighter through the gap in the curtains, cocooning them in light. Mason kept gazing into her, never tearing his eyes from her face as their bodies melded together.

Her orgasm built, small and tenuous at first, but then stronger and stronger. His perfectly controlled thrusts continued, mercilessly assailing her with a depth of emotion she simply wasn't prepared for. Gratefully, when the ache in her chest became damn near unbearable, his breathing changed. He pressed deep inside her, then deeper still, the tenuous friction hurtling them both so close to the edge.

Tess fell over that edge, still staring into his eyes as her mouth dropped open. He followed her without hesitation, both of them crying out wildly from the intensity. Their hands gripped hard together, their fingers wrapped tight, until he finally broke their stare to drop his head into her shoulder, gasping into her neck.

Tears fell from her eyes, purely against her will, but she couldn't stop them. When Mason felt the wetness, he pulled back just enough to kiss the drops from her cheeks. He pressed his lips fully to hers, drinking her in, as he released his fierce grasp on her hands to cradle her face in his fingertips. All she could do at that moment was wrap her arms around him and hold on for dear life.

~

AN HOUR LATER, Mason drove Tess to the Pooch Palace in his truck. She sat quietly in the passenger seat, trying not to look at him, since she could barely control her nerves as it was. It wasn't just the prospect of meeting his brother that made her hands tremble and her pulse race. It was the realization of what they'd done this morning.

That never should have taken place. They were having an affair, plain and simple, and everything between them was supposed to be airy and amusing. But airy and amusing wasn't what existed in that cocoon of early morning sunlight. They'd made love, and there was nothing plain or simple about it. She knew it. And she knew he knew it. And she knew he knew she knew it. And...well, they both knew it.

Even though Tess knew what had happened, she still struggled to understand it. After all, their lovemaking hadn't been her choice. Mason chose it. He directed it all. He didn't allow her to play like she usually did. Instead, he ensured those moments were impassioned and intense and overflowing with the emotions she'd tried so desperately to keep buried.

The whole thing scrambled her brain, turning her insides out. She reminded herself again that this situation wasn't permanent, no matter how much she wanted it to be. No matter how her heart fought to reach out of her chest, to reach for his heart, and hold on forever.

"Hey," he said.

His deep voice made Tess jump in her seat. She clasped her hands together, laughing at her own skittishness. "Hey."

Mason lowered his voice. "Are you doing okay over there?"

"Um, yeah. I'm okay."

His hand eased onto her thigh, the heat of his skin seeping through her jeans. "You don't need to be nervous, Tess. I'm right here with you. Everything is going to be fine."

She looked up to see him smile at her and found herself smiling back. He was probably telling her not to be nervous about meeting his brother. Then again, maybe he was telling her something else entirely.

Mason refocused on the road and Tess closed her eyes. Something had changed between them this morning. Something big. It gave her hope, which scared the living hell out of her.

She shook her head. She really couldn't think about this. Not today. And probably not tomorrow. Or the next day, either. In fact, it would be best to not think about making love to Mason ever again. Because that wasn't something she ever wanted to walk away from.

When they finally arrived at the Palace, the house was still empty. But only for a few minutes. Customers soon came through the door in droves and Tess tended to them while Mason prepped the backyard. An hour later, she watched out of the front window as a giant red pickup, loaded with building supplies, pulled up to the curb.

"Is that Ian?" Mason asked, walking up from the back hall.

"I think so."

"Yup, that's his monster truck. I'll go help him."

He smiled at her before leaving. Tess returned to the window to watch a baby-faced, adorably cute guy hop out of the red pickup. Mason approached his brother with an outstretched hand but Ian ignored it, pulling him into a bear hug instead.

They started talking and Tess eased away from the window. She moved to stand by the tall desk, waiting until she heard their heavy footsteps on the front porch. Mason came in first.

"Hey, honey," he greeted in a deep drawl while setting a few bags on the ground. Ian came in on his heels, but Tess didn't have the chance to say hello. Not before Mason strode over to her, pulled her into his arms, and kissed her hard.

She half-wanted to slap him for being rude and half-wanted to ask Ian to excuse them for a few minutes. Or hours. She stood, stunned and wobbly, when Mason finally released her.

Ian cleared his throat as he walked over. "Okay, okay, big brother. Quit marking your territory."

Mason shook his head despite the distinct glimmer of guilt in his eyes. "Tess, this is my brother, Ian – lawyer, goofball, slave to fashion."

"Ha, ha." Ian snorted before turning to her with a cheesy smile. He reached to take her hand. "Hi, Tess. It's lovely to finally meet you."

"You, too, Ian."

"Thanks for all the gifts you've bought me over the years." He shot Mason a dirty look.

Mason rolled his eyes.

She laughed. "You're very welcome. Thanks for coming to help today. I know how busy you are. This is really wonderful of you."

Ian still held her hand and Mason stole it away, winding his fingers with hers. Ian grinned wildly. "Glad to be here. I'm happy to pay tribute to the person who recognizes my monumental birth each year, since my brother's too big of a dork to do it."

"Gee, thanks, Ian." Mason chuckled, turning to her. "I'm going to get him out of your hair now. We'll be out back if you need us."

Tess nodded. "Just let me know if I can help. I can order Chinese for lunch."

"You're talking my language," Ian said, lifting bags off the floor.

Mason gave her a quick kiss before turning to help.

TESS STOOD in the kennel for much of the day, playing with the dogs in turn as she watched the two brothers through the back window. By the time they'd brought out the supplies, dug holes, poured cement, and placed the support beams, it was well past noon. She ordered the food and called them in to eat.

"It's a damn beautiful day out," Ian declared when they stepped inside. "Sorry the pooches can't enjoy it."

Tess smiled. "They'll understand when they see the end result."

Mason brushed sawdust off his shirt. "I managed to get cement on my hands. Guess I should wash up before lunch."

She followed him with her eyes while he exited down the hallway, loving the way his body moved in a T-shirt and jeans. A vision of the two of them this morning, wrapped so tightly around one another, heated her skin. She turned away as quickly as she could, but knew she'd been staring too long when she saw the look on Ian's face. "Um, the food should be here soon," she offered, averting her gaze.

"Sounds great."

"Let me just refill a couple more dog dishes."

"Can I help?"

"Oh, no, you've been so great already. I'm really thankful for all you're doing."

Ian shrugged. "Well, I'm really thankful for all you're doing."

Tess laughed while lifting a bag of food. "Is this about your birthday gifts?"

"In a way. Did you know we never gave gifts before you?"

She stilled midway through feeding Tug. "Never?"

"No, never. Our parents didn't believe in that sort of thing. No Christmas gifts, either. Not for Mason, Vanessa, or me."

The Great Dane barked and Tess startled, dumping a mound of kibble in his bowl and closing his crate. She stood, leaning back on her work counter, staring at Ian. "You guys never got any presents? I didn't know that. I always thought Mason was too caught up in work to do it."

Ian rested against the counter beside her. "Oh, I'm sure he was too caught up in work. The first time we got birthday gifts from him, even though we knew they were from you, was amazing. Vanessa and I talked about it a lot over the years. It made us feel like there was still a chance to have him in our lives."

"But if you never gave gifts before, why did he let me? He could have said no or stopped me. When I suggested it, he just let me do it."

"Well, I like to think he wanted to do something, but just didn't know how to start. Not until you came along."

"Wow," she said, unable to stop a smile from curving her lips. "I'm glad I could help him, then. He's helped me a lot through the years. He's an amazing boss and I've learned so much about business from watching him. He's truly the reason I had the courage to open this place."

"Ah. I see." Ian glanced to the ground before looking back to her. "Tess, this is none of my business, so feel free to tell me to put a sock in it. But I have to ask...how long have you been in love with my brother?"

"What?" She gripped the counter. "What makes you think that?"

He shrugged. "It's nothing big. You just smile a certain way when you talk about him, like you have a million dreams floating in your head. And there's that sparkle in your eyes when you look at him. To be brutally honest, you wear it like a second skin. But please don't worry, if you're keeping your feelings to yourself for now. I get paid to notice things about people. Mason gets paid to notice things about buildings. He's clueless, I'm sure, and I won't say anything."

Unable to deny a word, Tess stared at the dog crates.

"You're right," Ian said. "It's none of my business. But can I ask you a favor?"

She forced herself to meet his eyes again. "What's that?"

"If he ever drives you crazy and you decide to leave, will you please think about giving him another chance? Will you consider that his emotional underdevelopment isn't entirely his fault, and maybe stick around a little while longer?"

Tess grinned. "Did you just call your brother underdeveloped?"

"Yeah, please don't tell him I said that. He'll be pissed as hell."

"Rest assured, your secret is safe with me."

Ian matched her grin. "Damn, he's lucky to have you, Tess. So are we. Vanessa and I couldn't be happier about the two of you. I talked to her yesterday and she said how much she liked the birthday gift you sent and how she wished you and Mason were dating. When I told her you guys are living together, she screamed so loud my ears were ringing."

"Really? She was that happy about it?"

"Truly. You've made us feel like he's closer to us. Like we haven't lost him."

"I don't understand. Didn't Malory ever do anything with you?"

Ian's entire body stiffened. "Malory the coldhearted bitch? Do anything unselfish? That woman is a *fucking cancer*."

Tess's eyes widened. "Wow, Ian, don't hold back. It's not good to bottle things up inside. Tell me how you really feel."

He glanced at her and they both started giggling.

"Man, you do have an awesome laugh, just like Mason always says." Ian nudged her with his elbow. "You know, if you ever do get fed up with my brother, remember I'm single."

"Okay, thanks."

Mason's footsteps approached.

Ian waggled his eyebrows at her. "Did I mention I'm a lawyer?"

Mason stalked up to him, flaming arrows shooting from his eyes. "Damn, little brother. I leave for five minutes and you move in on me?"

"Well, big brother, I don't see a ring on her finger."

Mason stepped over to take Tess's hand in his. "You don't need to look at her finger. Or anything else, for that matter."

Ian grinned mischievously. "Aw, who's being a grumpy bear?"

Mason huffed.

"I'll just clean up and meet you two over lunch," Ian said, chuckling as he walked out.

The moment he left, Tess looked up to Mason. "Grumpy bear?"

He shook his head. "It's from a book I read to him when we were kids. It's about a bear who's always cold and grumpy, until one day his brother gives him a bunch of blankets, and then he's warm and happy. It's silly. Just a bedtime story."

She watched the emotion move through Mason's deep brown eyes while he spoke. "I think that's sweet. And Ian is really something."

"Do I need to apologize for him? He's always been a flirt."

"He's the flirt, and you're the stern older brother?"

"You mean the more intelligent, handsomer, stern older brother?"

"Yeah," she agreed with a laugh. "That's exactly what I mean."

"We're a little competitive, in case you hadn't noticed."

"No. Really?"

"I sense sarcasm."

"You are one intuitive man, Mason Tramont."

He reached out to cup her cheek, staring longingly at her mouth. "You're pretty intuitive, too. Can you sense what I'm feeling, Tess?"

"Um, are you hungry?"

"Um-hmm."

"For Chinese food?"

"Oh, no. You missed that completely."

"I guess I'll have to work on it. Maybe tonight I'll figure out what you're really hungry for."

"Keep teasing me and I won't wait. Ian will get quite a show."

She grinned, taking him by the hand and pulling him down the hall. "Come on, Grumpy Bear. It's time to eat."

Mason groaned and followed.

~

THE MEN WORKED ALL DAY, until well after the dogs had gone. When Ian finally left for his hotel, promising to see them bright and early tomorrow, Tess knew Mason was exhausted. "Hey, you want to grab a bite to eat?" she asked as she locked the front door of the Palace behind them.

"Would you mind if we just pick up pizza on the way home?"

A shiver went down her spine when he said *home*, as if his house belonged to both of them. As if she belonged there with him. "Yeah, pizza sounds good."

Mason fell silent inside the truck, so Tess filled the quiet by babbling about the amazing job they'd done. She loved the progress they'd made in just one day, loved how the clients who came to pick up their pooches were as excited as she was. He simply listened, and nodded, and held her hand.

It wasn't until they'd made it home, eaten dinner, and flopped onto the couch, that Mason spoke up.

"You know, Tess, we spent all day with Ian, and it made me realize I don't really know anything about your family."

She slumped against the cushioned armrest of the sofa and pulled out her ponytail holder, letting her hair fall to her shoulders. She didn't miss the sexy little groan that escaped his lips as he watched. A second later, Mason pulled her legs onto his lap and began massaging her feet.

"Mmm," she hummed while his fingers worked their magic. "What do you want to know?"

"Everything."

She couldn't help giggling at such a Mason-answer. "Well, *everything* is a tall order, but let's see. I have a mom and a sister, Emma, who's three years older than me. We grew up here in Richmond. Emma got married the year before I went to college and had two kids pretty quickly. Her husband got transferred to California for his job and Mom wanted to be near her grandkids, so they asked me if I would be okay if they all moved there. I was halfway through college here in Richmond, so I said sure."

"Your family lives all the way across the country?"

"Yup."

"And what about your father?"

Tess stiffened and Mason's eyes darted to hers. "I'm sorry," he amended. "You don't have to talk about it if you don't want to."

She gave him a tender smile, relaxing into the cushions while he continued soothing her sole. "It's okay. I just don't think about him much anymore. He left when I was young. The only good memory I have of him is Donut."

"Donut?"

"She was my dog. Dad gave her to me when I was six years old and she grew up with me. When he left, she was my lifeline. I love my mother and sister, but they always had more in common with each other. I felt like I had more in common with my dog." Tess quieted to peek at her boss, wondering if he would find the concept strange. He only nodded. "Donut is the reason I love dogs, the reason I love my business now."

"Then I'm glad you had her."

"Me, too. I had her for the longest time, right up until Mom and Emma and the kids left for California. Donut died that same month."

Mason's forehead creased. "And then you were all alone?"

"Well, I was twenty and could take care of myself. I cried a lot about Donut, and I missed my family, but it's not like they abandoned me. Belle's the one that really got me through it. She's like my other sister."

"Ah, yes. Annabelle, your business partner and best friend. Like I have David."

"Yeah, we do have that in common, don't we?"

"We do. I guess she's a good business partner?"

"She's great. We manage really well together."

"Still, if you need help, I would be happy to do more for you. What about bookkeeping? I could find you a decent accountant. Maybe even lend you Chad or George for a while."

Tess smiled, both from the feel of his strong hands and from his desire to help. "Thanks. I really appreciate the offer, but I can do it myself. I have my MBA now."

Mason stilled. "Your MBA? When did you get that?"

"I took night classes for the past two years."

He stared blankly at her. "Good Lord, Tess. Are you telling me you worked with me every day, took Master's courses at night, and started a successful business on the weekends, all in the last two years?"

"Yes. That is exactly what I did."

"That's...that's incredible. You're incredible."

God, those were the best words she'd ever heard. "Thank you."

He grew silent before resuming his attentions on her tired feet. "You know, I wish you'd told me about earning your degree. I would have bought you a graduation gift."

"You would have?"

"Of course."

"But Ian told me…"

"Told you what?"

"That your family doesn't believe in giving gifts."

Mason grimaced. "I wish he hadn't said that."

"Why?"

"Because it makes my upbringing sound freakish, which it wasn't."

"Most people celebrate birthdays."

"My parents gave us every advantage. They instilled us with a strong work ethic and moral code. When we performed well, we were rewarded – not because another year elapsed, but because we earned it."

Tess saw the muscle in his jaw twitch. "Ian seems different than you, though."

"More sparkly?"

"No. Just different."

Mason focused on her feet. "I was the oldest. The example. They were a little gentler when Vanessa came along, and then Ian…he was such a bubbly kid, you had no choice but to love him. Plus, they're all lawyers. Ian is a criminal attorney, Vanessa practices real estate law, and Mom and Dad are corporate lawyers."

"And you chose architecture."

"That's right." Mason's eyes found hers and he sighed. "So, there it is. You've discovered my deep, dark secret."

"Which is?"

"I'm the black sheep of the family."

Tess burst out laughing. "The black sheep? Yeah, right! You're a brilliant, creative, successful entrepreneur, your designs are fantastic, and people jump to do whatever you say. Don't even try to pretend you're a disappointment to anyone, let alone your own parents."

"I'm still not a lawyer."

Tess sat up, wiggling closer to rest her hand on his arm. She pinned his gaze. "Mason, you are fantastic at everything you do. Architecture, bowling, compliments, dancing, kissing, sex…everything. If you wanted to be a lawyer, you'd kill that, too. But I'm glad you're not, because I think you're doing just what you want to be doing, which is building things. And you're incredible at it."

He reached for her, slipping his hand into her hair, drawing her closer. "You know, sometimes you look at me like I can do no wrong."

Her stomach flipped. "I do?"

"Yes. Not very often, only when you let your guard down. But when it happens, it's amazing. No one's ever looked at me that way."

"No one?"

"No one. And I love it, even if I don't deserve it."

"Why wouldn't you deserve it?"

"Because I'm not perfect, sweet Tess."

She stilled beside him, mulling over his words. The only wrong she could ever imagine him doing to her was if he left her to be with Malory. Of course, that would be the ultimate destruction. But why would he leave her for Malory if that shrew never looked at him like he was the best thing since sliced bread?

He is the best thing since sliced bread. Hell, he's the best thing since bread. If he would just confide in me...if he'd just open his heart...

Mason curled his fingers into her hair. "What's going on in that wonderful mind of yours?"

Tess smiled softly. "Just something Ian and I talked about."

"Yeah? What else did my brother have to say?"

"He, um, he mentioned he doesn't like Malory."

"Well, that's putting it mildly. Are you sure he didn't use any foul language?"

"Oh, he may have thrown out a curse word or two. Do you know why he feels that way?"

"Ian is just...overly protective."

Tess's heart lodged in her throat as she held his eyes. "Mason, I know you say you don't want Malory anymore..."

"Wait. You actually heard me say that?"

"Yes, I heard the words."

"I must admit, I wasn't sure. You tend to ignore them a lot."

She swallowed hard. "Please tell me what happened between the two of you. Please. If you really are over her, tell me why."

Tess stayed close to him, holding onto his arm. She watched all the deep, raw emotions move across his face at the mere mention of his ex. Her pulse threaded through her veins while she waited.

Eventually, Mason's shoulders fell. "I realized she wasn't the person for me. It took forever, but I realized it. We're over. That's all."

There was a little part of Tess that really thought this would be the moment he would truly open up to her. There was an ache inside her chest, so fathomless and wrenching, begging to have that emotional intimacy with him. But when he spoke, all her hopes were dashed and all her dreams shriveled back up. He wasn't going to share himself the way she needed. Ian asked her to give him another chance, but she didn't know if that was possible.

She forced a smile onto her lips, knowing all she could do was make the best of their last two weeks together.

Mason pushed a wayward hair behind her ear. "You look tired. I know I am. You want to go to sleep? It's another long day tomorrow."

"I am tired," she admitted. "I could use a shower, though."

"Okay. You go shower; I'll straighten up and meet you in bed."

"Yeah, you could do that. Or you could take a shower with me."

His eyes met hers. "Suddenly, I'm not tired anymore."

Tess grinned, determined to live out her fantasies for as long as she could. "I plan to do things to you that'll make the soap bar embarrassed."

She squealed when Mason threw her over his shoulder and ran them to the bathroom.

13

FRENCH FRIES AND FIRECRACKERS

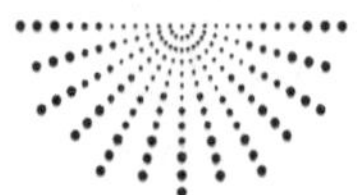

Mason took great care to refasten each of the delicate buttons on her lavender blouse. Tess sat on his office desk, absorbing his intent expression while he focused on the task. Considering how animalistic he'd been a few moments ago, it amused her to see him so gentle now, assuring the clothes he'd thrown to the ground were perfectly replaced.

She leaned forward, pressing a kiss to his forehead. Mason sighed at the touch of her lips. Finished with the buttons, he reached for her hips and pulled her body flush with his. Tess rested her hands on his chest.

"Thank you," she whispered.

He searched her eyes. "For what?"

"For putting my clothes back on."

"It was the least I could do, since I took them off."

"Well, I still appreciate it. And thank you again for my dog gym."

"I'm sorry I spent the whole week finishing it. I thought Ian and I could do it in one weekend, but it took longer than expected."

"I'm amazed it's done. Thank you for working on it every night."

"Wow. You certainly are in a grateful mood."

"What's not to be grateful for? We've had two wonderful weeks of nonstop sex and I have a brand new dog gym. I'd be insane if I wasn't utterly appreciative."

He nodded before focusing on her loose hair, curling a strand around his finger. Tess left the blond waves out of her normal ponytail today, trying to look less formal for her going away party tonight. The party she'd never told him about, despite a whole week of opportunity.

Mason dropped his hand onto her shoulder, easing his heated palm slowly down her arm. "Are you sure you have to go out with Regina tonight? If you come home with me instead, I'll give you a lot more things to be thankful for."

Tess smiled in spite of her guilty conscience. "You know how Regina is. If I don't keep my promise, she'll go all crazy on me. I don't think I could live with that, even if I do have only one week left here."

With those words, Mason stopped moving. Every muscle froze for aching moments until he wrapped her in his arms and banded her to his body. "Only one week left," he repeated, his voice somber when it rumbled through his chest and into hers. The next second, he pressed their lips together. His kiss was firm and insistent, but also incredibly soft and invasively warm.

As she melted back into him, Tess told herself she could exist without this. She didn't need his closeness. Or his heat. Or his strength.

One more week is plenty. You don't need to keep living in his home, going to sleep beside him every night and waking in his arms every morning. You don't need to keep eating every meal together, laughing and playing, and sharing all the random thoughts that pop into your head. You don't need to keep making love, over and over again, until you're exhausted and thrilled and blissfully content, all at the same time. You don't need any of that. Just act out your remaining fantasies and move on.

The problem was, the more time they spent together, the more fantasies she created. Only these involved marriage. And babies. And growing old together. They were the best dreams she'd ever had.

His kiss went on and on, his body solid and strong, his arms encasing her entirely. Tess's chest grew heavier while the moments passed, until she finally tore her lips away out of self-preservation. She rested her forehead against his, attempting to steady her breathing. "I really do have to leave, Mason. Regina's waiting for me."

"I know. It's just...when I have you in my arms, I don't want to let go."

Her whole being ached as she looked into his eyes. "I promise I'll be home in a few hours. We can pick up right where we left off."

"I'll see you at home, then."

Tess jumped down off the desk, trying not to dwell on the intimacy of his words. She placed a quick peck on his cheek before straightening her skirt and slipping away. As soon as she stepped into the hallway and closed his door, Regina found her.

"There you are, Tess! I've been waiting for you forever! What does that man make you do that takes so much time? It's your going away party, damn it!"

"I'm here, I'm here."

Regina hooked arms with her. "No more thinking about work, baby cakes. Tonight we're gonna party and drink and have a good old time. I don't want you worrying about that grumpy boss of yours."

Grumpy bear, Tess corrected silently. "Okay. Let's go party."

∼

ANGELO'S RESTAURANT was a lovely place. Quaint wooden tables strewn here and there, along with plenty of chairs, enabled the entire staff of Field and Tramont to chat and laugh and drink together, telling stories to make the rest laugh harder. Tess enjoyed looking at all the faces: the people she'd known for so long, each accompanied by their own set of memories.

Regina and David sat in the middle of the group, fawning over one another like the adorable newlyweds they were. Beside them, Chad joked with tiny blond Becca from Marketing. To their side, George whispered to Kathryn as he dipped a french fry in ketchup and fed it to her. Tess watched the couple exchange Cheshire-cat grins. She wasn't sure if they were trying to keep their affair a secret, but if so, they'd failed miserably.

George and Kathryn could definitely take covert-op lessons from her and Mason, although Tess knew the only reason nobody caught on to her own torrid affair was because no one believed Mason had a pulse. She smiled with that thought. *How wrong they are.*

She raised her glass and sipped; she wasn't crazy about beer but she would make do. She wanted to blend in, just for this night, before saying goodbye to the people she felt like she'd grown up with. In truth, she had grown up here – from the wide-eyed grad she'd been, to the businesswoman who would now make her own company flourish.

"Hey, Tess!" Regina hollered above the raucous din of their coworkers. "Remember the time Chad bet you that George couldn't eat an entire box of glazed donuts in one sitting?"

Tess nodded. "Yes. And I remember Chad did an amazing blindfolded Chicken Dance when he lost, too."

Chad grinned even as he shook his head. "You know, Becca posted that video online. My family still makes fun of me."

Becca elbowed him. "But you never bet against Tess again, did you?"

"Nope, learned my lesson," he confirmed, giving Tess a salute.

Everyone laughed and Tess rested her elbows on the table with a contented sigh. Conversations continued, the decibel level climbing as the level of beer in the pitchers decreased. Her ears grew accustomed to the riotous noise. But then everything changed.

Everyone stopped talking. Everyone stopped laughing. Everyone stared.

At Mason Tramont, who'd walked through the front door.

Mason paused, looking around the crowded restaurant, before locating their cluster of tables. Tess's breath hitched when his eyes caught hers. The other restaurant patrons cleared a path as he strode toward their group, stern and purposeful in his tailored suit. A moment later, he arrived at his secretary's side. Her heart raced while he grabbed a chair and placed it directly next to her. Mason sat and surveyed his staff.

For anxious seconds, no one said a word. No one dropped a pin either, although Tess knew she could have heard it hit the floor. David finally broke the tension. "Hey, Mason, I wondered when you'd get here. Want a beer?"

"No, thanks. You all continue with whatever you were doing."

It didn't sound like a command, but people instantly started talking again, even if their voices were lower and their laughter nonexistent. Tess fingered the rim of her glass and stared straight ahead. Nerves coiled in her stomach. What was Mason doing here? How did he know? Was he mad at her? Could anyone tell her entire body hummed with his presence?

She tried to pretend he was just her boss – someone who'd come to wish her well – but knowing she'd been splayed out on his desk a few hours ago made it difficult. She hoped the fresh redness in her cheeks would be attributed to alcohol alone.

Mason leaned over to whisper in her ear. "Why is everyone so quiet now?"

Tess shook her head at his innocent question. "They're probably afraid you're going to fire somebody."

"Why would they be afraid of that?"

"Because you never leave your office, so they figure if they see you, they're goners."

He appeared utterly confused by her statement.

Tess resisted the urge to reach for his hand. She looked away, needing to not dwell solely on him. She met Regina's concerned gaze across the table. Tess nodded to her friend in reassurance. Regina's shoulders slumped before she resumed talking to Becca.

Mason cleared his throat. "Excuse me, everyone," he announced. All eyes fastened on him. "This is a celebration for Miss Troy. She has made a huge difference in this company, and I appreciate all her efforts through the years. Therefore, tonight's bar tab is on me."

Tess had never seen a group mood change so quickly. The promise of free booze apparently meant Mason was no longer their boss and no one had to censor a word. George and Chad started high-fiving while Kathryn giggled. Even Regina raised her glass to acknowledge the kind gesture. By the time the waitress brought several more pitchers to the tables, the noise level had returned to earsplitting.

With everyone else agreeably occupied, Tess angled toward him. "I'm impressed, Mr. Tramont. Look at you, playing nice with others."

"I can play nice," he defended, his voice lowered for her alone. "Is that why you didn't invite me? Because you thought I couldn't blend in?"

Her heart sank with the sadness in his eyes. "I'm truly sorry I didn't invite you. I swear I never meant to hurt your feelings. I didn't arrange the thing, so it didn't seem like my place to invite anyone."

"Let me guess...Regina doesn't want me here?"

"Well, she did make the plans. But I wasn't sure you'd want to come, since you don't hang out with anyone at the office, except David. I also didn't want you to feel like you had to be here if you preferred not to. Then there's the celebrating-me-leaving thing, which I wasn't sure you'd want to do, either."

"I'm not celebrating you leaving, Tess. I'm celebrating the six years you were with me. I'm very happy David mentioned the party."

"Ah, it was David. I should have figured. When did you know?"

"Earlier today."

"So, you knew when we were...um..."

"Together in my office at the end of the day? Yes, I knew."

"You didn't say anything."

"I kept waiting for you to say something to me."

She cringed. "Are you angry with me?"

"Just, perhaps, a little disappointed."

"I'm really, really sorry, Mason."

His somber expression morphed into a devilish grin as he leaned toward her. "You know, I could probably punish you for it later."

Her eyes flew wide. "Mmm," she hummed, shivering in anticipation. "I think I'd like that."

Mason chuckled, draping his arm across the back of her chair. Enticing warmth radiated from his body. Tess stiffened, just now remembering where they were. She glanced around, wondering if anyone heard what they'd just said to each other, or noticed how close they sat.

They didn't. The entire staff looked three-sheets-to-the-wind, all watching as dainty Becca downed an entire beer, slammed the glass on the table, and emitted the biggest belch in the history of mankind. Chad fell on the floor laughing and Tess giggled despite herself. She settled back in her chair, resting against her boss's arm.

~

MASON SURVEYED the faces of the people he'd hired over the years. He recognized everyone at this party, but he didn't really know them. He left the day-to-day staff situations to David, preferring to concentrate on what he did best: sitting alone at his computer screen. But he had to admit, lounging here in this rickety wooden chair, with everyone drinking and talking and laughing, was significantly enjoyable.

People took turns telling tales – some he believed, some that sounded like outright lies. He found himself smiling, especially as he watched the Field newlyweds. David played with Regina's fingers while she rested her head on his shoulder. He looked so happy. Happier than Mason ever remembered him being. Happy being a married man.

Mason turned to look at Tess. She listened avidly to a story one of the marketing people told an engineer he'd hired a few months ago. Mason couldn't remember their names, but he could barely remember his own. Without a drop of alcohol, he still felt drunk.

Tess was simply stunning. Not just because of her intuitive eyes and captivating smile, but because of the way she engaged with the people around her, the way her laugh made the entire room feel brighter. He paid rapt attention as she attempted to push a blond curl behind her ear, to no avail. Her hair fell back over her shoulder and he reached out without thinking. Mason angled toward her as he tucked the strand around the curve of her ear.

Tess turned to meet his eyes. Her laughter died in her throat.

He was too close to her. That much he knew for certain. His arm curved around her shoulder. His hand shifted over her hair. This wasn't boss-secretary behavior. But he didn't care.

Mason looked down at her lips, at the dark, sparkling gloss. Probably grape soda. He wanted to taste, wanted it so badly that he could hardly see straight.

His fingers moved to her face, cupping her cheek. The roar of people around him dimmed in his ears. He could only see her, could only hear the shallow, rapid breaths coming from her lips. He watched her eyes as he leaned forward. The dazzling light blue stared into him, questioning his intentions.

He fully expected her to stop him – to place her hand on his chest and push away, or stand and excuse herself. He took forever to close the distance between them. He gave her every opportunity for retreat.

Tess never shook her head. She never withdrew. She sat completely still, focused on his eyes, until his mouth came down on hers. Just before he tasted her grape lips, Mason swore she smiled.

Then he kissed her the way he always did, as hard as he did when they were alone, and she responded. Her hands moved to his hair, curling against the nape of his neck. Her tongue darted out to tease and tangle with his. He forgot where he was when she made that soft little whimpering noise, the one he'd heard a thousand times, the one he would never get enough of. He reached for her hips, knowing he just had to pull forward and she would be in his lap, curled up on him, his to explore.

But then it occurred to him that they were in a public place. Surrounded by his employees. And it was...completely silent. Mason pulled back slowly, noting the amused expression on Tess's face before he looked over at his staff.

Everyone stared, dumbfounded. Their mouths hung open. A french fry dangled from George's lower lip. Regina's eyebrows lodged into her hairline, her full lips pursed.

The brunette's shrill screech broke the silence. "Shut up! You two are...? Holy crap!"

Insane chatter burst around them, like firecrackers exploding in the night. Tess started laughing. Mason turned back to her, watching his sweet sprite grin wildly while a jumble of conversations from different voices filled his ears.

"When the hell did *that* happen?"

"You think that's why she's leaving?"

"They sure do spend a lot of time in his office..."

"I thought he was gay."

"Naw, don't you remember his bitchy ex-girlfriend?"

"I thought that was a dude."

Mason chuckled as he focused on Tess's bright eyes. "I guess I didn't think this all the way through."

"I warned you," she said, still grinning.

Conversations continued, but he tuned them all out until someone shouted, "Kiss her again!" He thought it was Chad, but he wasn't sure. In truth, he didn't care. Mason pulled Tess close and pressed his lips to hers.

He realized just now that he'd never had anyone whistle and clap for him while he kissed a woman. And definitely never an entire bar full of wild, whooping, hollering, drunken people.

～

Several hours passed, yet Tess and Mason were still the first to leave the party. Tess glanced over her shoulder to see Regina and David walk out behind them, grinning and giddy. David set his hand on Mason's arm when they reached the sidewalk. "Double date – you guys and us."

"Yeah, we'll talk," Mason replied.

Regina pulled Tess in for a hug. "You're leaving work, but at least you're not leaving us."

Tess smiled at her long-time coworker, a knot of pain in her chest. "I was never leaving you, Regina. We'll always be friends."

"Yes. Definitely."

David pulled his wife to his side. "Come on, babe, let's leave them in peace. One of these cabs has our name on it."

Tess turned to see the curb-filling line of taxis Mason had called to get his staff home safely. The only non-yellow vehicle in sight was Mason's Mercedes, centered in front of Angelo's entrance. Tess waved to her friend while David opened a cab door. Mason moved up beside her, banding his arm around her waist. She rested her hand on his.

"I never thought I'd say this," Regina remarked as she slumped into her seat, "but you two look really adorable together."

David waved to both of them before edging in beside his wife.

When their taxi drove away, Tess leaned into the man at her side. "I think Regina's a bit tipsy."

"She's a lot tipsy. But at least she didn't have a heart attack."

Mason shifted to stand in front of Tess as she gazed up at him. A mixture of moonlight and streetlamp lit his face, showcasing the desire in his eyes. She would never tire of witnessing how much he wanted her.

Pushing up on her tiptoes, she planted her mouth on his. He took over eagerly. His lips didn't leave hers, even when he stepped her backward until she bumped into the door of his car. She rested against the cool surface, wrapping her arms around his neck, blissfully contented to kiss him out in the open.

"'Night, Tess," a female voice called. "You too, Mr. Tramont."

Tess peeked around Mason's shoulder to see Kathryn and George stumble out of the restaurant together. "Goodnight," she answered.

Kathryn waved while slipping into a cab with George at her side.

As that taxi left, Tess looked back to her boss.

Mason pinned her eyes. "So, everybody knows about us now."

"Yup, everybody knows."

"Is that okay?"

She shrugged. "Well, it'll make my last week in the office a lot more interesting, that's for sure. And you certainly took the go-big-or-go-home approach, picking the most public forum possible to spill the beans."

"Are you angry with me?"

"Maybe. A little. I could probably punish you for it later."

Mason grinned. "Mmm. I think I'd like that." He dipped his head down, his voice dropping even lower. "Perhaps I can make it up to you right now."

"Yeah? How so?"

Tess fully expected him to open the car door, shove her inside, and find new and exotic ways to pleasure her in the back seat. He didn't. Mason straightened instead, reaching for the inner pocket of his suit coat. She noticed a slight tremble in his fingers as he eased them beneath the fabric. When he pulled out a long, thin jewelry box, her throat went completely dry.

"Here," he said, grasping the box in both hands. "This, um, this is for you."

"For *me*?"

"Yes. I couldn't very well come to your party empty-handed."

"What – what is it?"

"It's just...will you...just please open it and see."

She eased the box out of his steel grip and pried open the top. A platinum necklace lay inside, situated on a white velvet backdrop. The biggest diamond she'd ever seen in real life hung from the chain, with countless facets reflecting a fiery brilliance in the lamplight. "Oh, my goodness," she breathed. "This is the most beautiful..."

"You like it?"

Tess looked up to his face, watching his eyes brighten with puppy-like expectancy. "Mason, this is a *huge* diamond."

"I did a good job, then?"

"You did an amazing job, but..."

"Oh, thank God. I'm so glad. It's my first time."

"First time what?"

"First time giving a gift."

"You mean ever?"

He nodded, giddy as a schoolboy.

A band wrapped around Tess's heart, squeezing so hard it stole the air from her lungs. "I'm so grateful, Mason, and you did a wonderful job picking this out, but I – I can't accept it."

"You most certainly can."

"No, I can't. This is far too extravagant."

"Too extravagant? Are you kidding me? This is the least I can do, to tell you what you've meant to me all these years."

"You mean, what I've meant to the *business*, right?"

"Well, of course the business would never have done as well without you." He ran his fingers into her hair. "But this gift is from me, Mason. Not your boss. Just Mason."

Tess gulped, gawking at the perfectly round solitaire that shone like the North Star on a moonless night. "Will you please put it on me?"

"I would love to."

She lifted her hair while he wrapped the intricate strand around her neck. "You know, I could get used to this gift-giving thing," he said, his breath tickling the side of her face. "It's really a lot of fun."

Mason finished with the clasp and situated the diamond against her skin, his finger tracing the gem before he refocused on her eyes. "There you go, Tess. Just a little something to remind you that I can be sparkly."

Fighting back tears, she slipped her fingers over the curve of his jaw. "You know you're sparkly, right?"

"Wow. I never thought I'd hear you say that."

"Well, just for the record, you sparkle more brilliantly than anyone else, ever. You always have, Mason. Since the day I met you."

She arched up to kiss the crooked grin from his lips, arms snaking around his shoulders. Without hesitation, he pinned her to the door of his car and wound their tongues together. Tess would have been perfectly content for him to take her here and now, thrown haphazardly onto the hood of his Mercedes, if not for the catcalls in the distance.

"Woo-hoo! Troy and Tramont – going at it! Dude! Get a room!"

Mason paused. His eyes found hers. "Was that Chad from Accounting?"

Tess laughed. "I'm pretty sure."

"I'm so firing him."

"No, you're not."

Mason sighed. "No, I'm not. Besides, a room is a good idea. We have a room. We have a whole house full of rooms."

She pressed her breasts into his chest. "Mr. Tramont, I'm going to ride you like a cowgirl on the back of a wild stallion galloping across a desert plain with nothing but the hot sun bearing down on their backs."

"Get in the car. Now, Tess."

How they got to his house without getting a speeding ticket or thrown in jail for indecent exposure would forever be a mystery to her.

14

COWBOY HATS, BEAR BLANKETS, LOVE BITES, AND ASS VAMPIRES

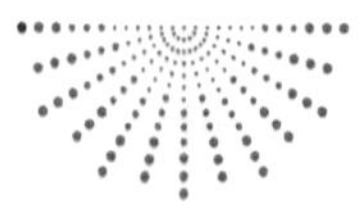

"Yee-haw!" Tess yelled, pushing up on her thighs before landing back down on Mason's gigantic erection. She wore nothing but her diamond necklace and a cowboy hat. Mason savored the sight, relishing this fantasy fulfillment even more than he imagined. Lord, he was so damn hard inside her, he felt legitimately concerned he might hurt her.

She didn't seem to mind his feral state. In fact, his little sprite looked positively delirious as she rode him, screaming with every thrust. He knew she hated being quiet when they were together at work. Here in his bedroom, she could let him know how much she loved feeling every part of his body as they devoured each other on his silky bed sheets.

Tess whooped again when she pulled the hat off, circling it in the air before setting it back on her head. She gazed down to his face and giggled, her half-lidded eyes sparkling with joy, mischief, and wonder. She picked up her pace, slamming down over and over, the soft cheeks of her ass pounding against the hard muscle of his thighs. Mason could only stare up at her while drinking in the intoxicating sounds of flesh on flesh.

He watched her every movement, hungry and desperate for each touch, each moan, each smile. Her breasts danced as she worked their bodies together, the sight stealing the air from his lungs. He'd been struggling for a while now to maintain his position beneath her, to let her ride him the way she'd so giddily promised earlier tonight. But when Tess dragged her hands across his chest and down farther still – tracing over the ridges of his abdomen while licking her lips – Mason couldn't remain passive any longer. He sat up, his mouth instantly at her breast.

Sucking one nipple onto his tongue, he rolled it between his teeth before licking his way up to her neck. His hands grabbed hold of her ass of their own volition. He couldn't prevent his fingers from roaming, teasing their way gently down into the soft seam between her cheeks. Tess moaned deep in the back of her throat, tightening her severe grip on his shoulders. His erection jerked fiercely inside her. Mason clenched his jaw to keep from finishing without her.

Forcing his hands back to her hips, he dug into her skin, using the leverage to pull her to him again and again. The slickness of their flesh enabled them to slide together with rapid, blissful ease. Her arms and legs trembled around him and he knew she was close to the edge. He ached to hear the breathy little mewls she always made before she let herself go.

Mason held his breath as he waited for those perfect sounds, yet they didn't come. Instead, he watched in awe as she released her hold on him, allowing her upper body to lean farther and farther away, until her shoulder blades touched back against the mattress and her arms fell to her sides. The hat tumbled off her head, but she didn't seem to notice. She'd simply given herself over to him completely.

He supported her that instant, steady and strong, with one arm banded around her low back. His eyes feasted on her – the golden hair spread across his sheets, the peaceful expression on her softened face – and he ceased moving. He stopped everything they'd been doing, just for a moment, to worship the beauty before him. Placing his hand at her base of her neck, he stared, captivated, as the diamond on her necklace fell into the hollow of her throat. In this moment, he was acutely, painfully aware that the brilliance of the costly gem simply paled in comparison to the soft shimmer of sweat on her skin.

Mason slowly traced her curves, skimming over her breasts, her ribs, her belly, memorizing every inch. Tess whimpered with his actions. He clearly heard the ache inside her, and as much as he wished this moment could last forever, he knew she needed him. He gave in to his desperate desire for both their sakes. Resuming their pounding pace, he drove himself into her body with the most deliberate and intense precision he was capable of at this point.

Sliding his fingers down her stomach, he sought the hot, wet juncture of her thighs. He pressed into her folds at the same instant he lost himself and exploded inside her. Tess screamed out in lush release, all her muscles convulsing at once. She arched back up, banding her arms and legs around him, cocooning him inside her embrace as she ground down against his hand. "Mason! Oh, God, Mason," she gasped into his neck.

He pulled back just enough to find her lips with his, tasting her tongue and swallowing her moans while the force of her orgasm continued to clamp their bodies together. "My sweet, beautiful Tess," he whispered, humming the mantra over and over until he felt her inner muscles relax. He pressed his forehead onto hers, refusing to let go until every last tremor left her body. He needed to stay right here until the moment she flopped onto his chest, a boneless, spent mass. That was the moment she felt complete. That was the moment she allowed herself to be one with him, the moment she allowed herself to be at peace.

Once her dainty hands dropped to her thighs, and a soft sigh left her pink lips, and her damp cheek fell onto his shoulder, Mason smiled. With his heart and arms full, he let his mind go blank. He eased back onto the sheets, taking her with him.

~

SEVERAL MINUTES after collapsing on top of Mason, Tess managed to flop over onto her back, resting her head against her pillow while waiting for the air to return to her chest. Mason lay beside her, having just as much trouble breathing. As her conscious thoughts slowly emerged from the fog of pleasure, she grinned wildly at the unusual events of the night.

Tess couldn't quite believe everything her boss had done this evening: crashing her going away party, kissing her in front of the entire staff, giving her the amazing gift that now rested against her neck, and staring at her with savage hunger as she promised him an unforgettable night of rugged, Wild West lovemaking. She felt fairly certain she'd come through on that promise.

Raising her head off the pillow, her eyes wandered around the bedroom until they fixated on the huge pile of clothing, shoes, and miscellaneous junk spilling out of Mason's walk-in closet. When they'd been standing in front of Angelo's restaurant earlier, she'd never expected all that would transpire between them after they left for home. But now, lying here beside this magnificent man, she felt giddy about every damn thing they'd done.

It had all started out fairly normally. They'd been kissing in front of his car when Tess promised to ride him like a cowgirl and Mason demanded she get inside. He opened her door and closed it behind her. He ran around his Mercedes, peeling off his suit coat and tossing it into the back, before sinking into the driver's seat. They'd both buckled in, and he'd pulled into traffic, and everything was quite innocent between them. Right up until they started touching each other.

Mason drove with one hand on the steering wheel while she pulled his other hand into her lap. She took the time to unbutton the cuff of his sleeve and roll the material up, so she could trace the hardened muscles of his forearm. His hand latched onto her knee, his fingers easing upward, massaging her skin as he inched her skirt higher. Tess loosened the strap of her seatbelt to lean closer, to press her face into the side of his neck and breathe in his spicy-hot scent. She nibbled her way up to his earlobe, licking it and giggling.

At that moment, Mason's hand clenched around her thigh and the most interesting thing popped out of his mouth.

"I own a cowboy hat," he said.

She stared at the side of his face. "You own a cowboy hat?"

"Yes. I have it and I want you to wear it. God, I really want you to wear it."

Tess couldn't help smiling. "You mean, while I *ride* you?" she purred, straining against her seatbelt to press her face back into his neck. She slipped her hand onto his leg, smoothing her fingers up his inner thigh and over his bulging zipper.

"Hell, yes. I want you to wear it while you fucking *ride* me."

His sharply edged words made her entire body throb. She mewled into his ear. With that sound, his hand finally released its grip on her thigh to move up under her bunched skirt. When he discovered the wetness already soaking her panties, Mason groaned in the back of his throat, pulled the material aside, and shoved two fingers deep inside her.

The ferocity of the action caught her off guard and Tess gasped.

"Sorry. Sorry," he apologized, easing his fingers back.

She clamped her trembling legs around his hand, preventing his retreat. "No, it's good," she panted. "Don't stop. It's so good."

He didn't waste a second before sinking his fingers back into her. Tess squirmed beyond control. She sucked onto his neck before licking her way to the rough stubble on his jaw. Her tongue tingled with the salt of his skin as his erection jerked obscenely beneath her hand. Her entire body shook, and her fingers were too uncoordinated to get the zipper of his pants undone, so she did the only thing she could do. She worked the steel length of him beneath her palm, again and again over his clothing, while he strained against the unforgiving material.

Mason moaned in time to her movements. He dipped his fingers farther inside her wet heat, sliding into her over and over, escalating her already fevered sensations. It took mere moments for Tess to come undone. Her head dropped onto his shoulder. Her teeth bit into his shirt as she attempted to stifle the screams bursting from her throat. The force of her orgasm clamped her hand around his erection, gripping onto him for dear life while he twitched into her hot, moist palm.

Then Mason growled at her. He actually *growled* at her. "You need to stop touching me right now, Tess, or I'm going to come in my pants like a goddamn teenager and probably crash this fucking car."

She whimpered, not from his ferocity, but from her thwarted desire to feel him inside her hand. Yet she still obeyed, releasing her vicious grip and curling her fist up on his thigh. He seemed relieved when she withdrew her fingers, but apparently, he had no intention of withdrawing his own. He kept them buried inside her body, as if he had every right to do whatever he desired, since he simply belonged here.

The knuckles of his other hand strained white against the steering wheel while he drove them home. Tess was vaguely aware of stop signs and red lights along the way, but at this moment she couldn't see any of it. She could only see him, could only feel the strength of his body, could only hear the strained, rasping breaths leaving his chest. And she felt grateful beyond belief that Mason took them where they needed to go.

Sighing in utter contentment, she snuggled her cheek into his shoulder. That was the moment he chose to start moving his fingers again. Slowly at first. Softly. He eased them across her swollen flesh, reigniting the sparks running from her tight little bundle of nerves to her entire body.

Tess honestly didn't think she could be ready for him again so quickly, especially not after such a mind-shattering orgasm. Yet he worked her slick flesh with such expertise, enticing every possible sensation from her body, that she was drenched in need within minutes. By the time they reached home, Tess wasn't entirely sure where she was. She just knew she was with him.

He only removed his hand so he could leap out of the car and scurry around to open her door, pulling her from her seat. Mad with desire, Tess jumped onto him immediately, banding her arms around his shoulders and her legs around his waist. Mason pulled her hard to his chest as he rushed them across the driveway.

When they reached the front door, he supported her with one arm while fumbling his key into the lock. He cursed when she bit into his earlobe, but the jerk of his rock hard shaft against her stomach assured her he wasn't opposed to her actions. Once inside, he kicked the door shut behind them. Her mouth clamped onto his and he sucked on her tongue as he staggered through the living room and into the bedroom, only releasing her when he could deposit her body beside the bed.

"Wait right here," Mason demanded, staring hard into her eyes. "Don't you dare move a fucking muscle."

Goose bumps rose all across her flesh. She nodded beneath his intense scrutiny, standing stunned when he left her to stalk into his closet. Tess watched him with her heart in her throat, actually nervous for his return yet still aching for it. He'd wound her body as tight as a bowstring, making it hurt to even breathe.

She didn't think she was capable of laughter at this moment. But he just looked so damn adorable – rummaging through shelf after shelf inside the giant walk-in cubbyhole, sporting a ridiculously huge, tenting erection that could very well pop his zipper open – while searching fruitlessly for his cowboy hat.

"Y-you don't need to do this," she assured through her giggles.

"Yes, I do. You want this fantasy and I'm sure as hell going to give it to you."

"But I've already got my fantasy. I don't need the hat, baby."

His movements stilled, his eyes fixing on hers. "Damn it, Tess. Did you just call me *baby*?"

"I did."

"Good God, that's incredible. Never in my life did I think I would want anyone to call me *baby*, and yet here it is coming from your lips, and I can't even..."

"Just forget about the hat."

"No. I can't. I won't give up, no matter what. I own the thing and I'm giving it to you. I want you to have every little thing your heart desires."

The air rushed from her lungs when she heard the emotion infusing his words. She could see, so plainly, his aching desire to please her. Tess relented without a second thought, fidgeting with her fingers while she waited, standing exactly where he'd placed her.

Mason returned to his task, apparently content now to throw things on the ground while he searched. He cursed ferociously when a shoe dropped off a shelf, landing on his toe. Tess thought to help him, but he'd told her not to move a fucking muscle.

Eventually, the wait proved more excruciating than she could bear. Rather than stand here and do nothing, she decided she would happily deal with whatever consequences her defiance might bring. Reaching for the top button of her blouse, she quickly peeled every last inch of clothing from her body.

When Mason finally shouted in triumph, turning to show her his find, she was buck-naked and down on all fours on the mattress.

His eyes narrowed that instant, glaring ferociously at her once he realized she'd disobeyed his command. Tess couldn't know the potential consequences of her actions, but her nipples tightened in anticipation. A slow smile curved her lips.

"Mason, baby, come get me. And bring the fucking hat."

He groaned, crushing the stiff brown brim within his fingers. She feared he might actually break his neck leaping over the pile of assorted crap on the floor in order to tackle her. Thank God he didn't.

So began one of their most energetic rounds of lovemaking ever.

Now that it was over, Tess was having one hell of a time wiping the ridiculous grin from her face. She sat up to reach to the end of the mattress, grasping onto her boss's odd little treasure. Flopping back down on their bed, she rotated the hat in the air.

"You know, Mason, no matter how I look at this, I just can't picture it on your head. Why on earth do you own a cowboy hat?"

"Don't I seem like the cowboy type?"

"Not really."

He smiled. "Ian got it for me one year as a birthday gift."

"Ian bought you a cowboy hat? Your brother, Ian?"

"Yes. He always buys me weird things I don't need because he says I have everything. Also, he says you're the one who buys the gifts, so he should really get you something instead of me."

"Well, thinking about it now, I suppose this gift *was* for me."

Mason's body rumbled with laughter. "Mmm. I suppose so."

"What other silly things has your brother bought you?"

He rolled on his side to face her. "Once, he got me a plastic animatronic fish that hangs on the wall and sings oldies tunes. Another time, he got me a helmet that holds a beer can on each side, with tubing going into your mouth so you can drink out of both cans at once."

"Wow, that's handy. I'm surprised I haven't seen you wear it."

"Maybe I'll wear it to work Monday."

Giggling, Tess set the cowboy hat on the nightstand before turning toward him. "Didn't he ever get you anything useful?"

Mason reached out to run his fingers across her collarbone, just beneath the necklace. "A few years ago, he did buy me some blankets."

"Blankets? Like the grumpy bear from your bedtime story?"

"According to that story, once the bear's brother gives him blankets, he's not supposed to be grumpy anymore."

"Yeah? How's that working out for you?"

He met her soft gaze. "I don't know, what do you think?"

"Hmm. I think now, since we're not being so physically active anymore, I'm a little chilly. Where do you keep those blankets?"

"In the hall closet."

"Ooh, I am getting one right now," Tess squealed with excitement as she slid out of bed, padding across the floor and into the hallway. Opening the closet door, she stared at the stacks and stacks of blankets filling shelf after shelf – all colors, all sizes, all materials. "My goodness, how many did Ian buy you?"

Mason's voice sounded funny when he answered. "Um, five?"

"Five? There must be at least thirty in here."

"Yeah, I kinda collected them over the years."

She peered around the corner to see him. "You *collected* them?"

"Just from time to time, if I was out and I saw a nice one, I'd buy it." He shook his head. "Please don't tell Ian. I'll never live it down."

Tess absorbed the adorably fragile look in Mason's eyes. "Don't worry. I won't say a word. Which is your favorite?"

"The green one with the bears on it."

She grabbed said blanket from the top of one stack and ran her fingers over the little brown bears embroidered into the fuzzy surface. Hugging it to her chest, Tess skipped back to the bed and climbed in beside him, spreading the fabric over them both. Mason snuggled into her that instant, wrapping his arm around her shoulder and burying his face in her hair.

She breathed in his scent, currently a mix of spice and sex, a heady combination that made her want to be even closer, to melt into him in their cocoon of green. She could hardly believe the blanket-hoarder beside her was the same practical, commanding boss she'd worked under for the last six years. He was just such a...puppy dog.

Tess smiled almost painfully. She'd finally burrowed inside him, inside the hard shell he'd wrapped himself in for so long. She wanted to stay here forever, where it was soft and warm and safe.

He leaned in to press a tender kiss to her mouth and she hummed against his lips, blissful beyond belief. When he pulled back, she searched his eyes. Her heart stuttered with the emotion staring back at her.

"I have to be honest, Mason. The first day I stepped in your office, I would never have guessed you were a grumpy bear in need of blankets."

He ran his fingers up and down her arm. "No? What did you think of me that first day?"

"Well, it was my first real job interview out of school, so I was super-nervous to meet you. I remember pacing around my apartment that morning, not knowing what to wear. But I had this sweater my grandma knitted for me when I went to college, and it always made me happy. Even though it probably wasn't very professional, and I really should have worn something else, I just put it on."

"I remember it. The color was blue. Like your eyes."

Tess sighed and nodded.

He looked down to her hand, playing with her fingers. "And what did you think when you first saw me?"

"Well, of course, I thought you were cute."

"Cute?"

"Yes, Mason, you're cute."

He grinned, all toothy and dimply and sparkly-eyed.

Tess laughed. "But even though I thought you were cute, I also thought you were scary."

"Me? Scary?"

"Yes, you, scary – but in an exciting sort of way. Then, when I got past being afraid of you, I realized very quickly that you were brilliant. And that you were kind and helpful, even if you were a shut-in."

"You always saw the best in me."

"It was pretty easy, once I looked past your crusty outer shell."

His head arched off the pillow. "My crusty shell?"

"Oh, yes," she answered with a smile. "Hard and burnt and crusty. Like a marshmallow left on the campfire too long."

"Hmm," he considered, propping his head in one hand. "Thank goodness you had a crush on me. Otherwise, you'd never have bothered to look past all that."

Her heart stopped. "A crush? Wh-what on earth are you talking about?"

Mason traced the side of her face before returning his hand to her shoulder. "There's no need to deny it, Tess. I always knew you had a crush on me. Hell, you were so innocent and sweet, straight out of college. Eager and excited and so damn beautiful. You used to get flustered around me and you would babble nonstop, dropping these incredibly inappropriate sexual innuendos before you even realized what you'd said. And you used to look at me with your eyes so wide, like you were amazed by every word out of my mouth."

She swallowed against her dry throat. "I, um, uh..."

"I've known for six years. I always tried to stay professional back then, to pretend I wasn't aware of your feelings. Still, no matter how stone-faced I forced myself to be, I couldn't help thinking about you. I couldn't help wondering why you latched onto me the way you did. I never found an answer. Not until this week. You may have learned that I was a grumpy bear in need of blankets, but I've learned that you were a huge-hearted young woman who'd lost her dad, and her dog, and whose entire family had moved across the country, leaving her alone and basically homeless. You were looking for someone to fill that void, because your huge, generous heart needed someone to take care of. I just thank the heavens that I was in the right place at the right time."

Tess stared at him with her lips parted, having no clue what to say. She could barely believe the words she'd just heard. Mason Tramont knew her. And she'd always known things about this man in her arms, but she never *really* knew him. Not until this moment. She wished it had happened so much sooner. But now here she lay, wrapped in his warm embrace, unable to deny a word he'd said.

She smiled with her whole body, giddy with the joy of it all, and inched a little closer. "Well, then. I guess I have to admit I had a crush."

Mason inhaled sharply. "Please say it again," he begged, although the look in his eyes was positively demanding. "Say it like you *mean* it."

Tess's pulse surged. "Very well. I had a crush on you the moment I met you, Mason Tramont. A terrific, awful, fantastic, overwhelming crush. Full of impure, dangerous, beastly, lustful thoughts."

"God, yes," he sighed, his fingers easing down her chest and across her stomach, his eyes drinking in the sight of her bared skin as if he'd never seen it before. "Well, well, well. It turns out my sweet little secretary wanted her big, bad boss."

His voice lowered while he drew lazy circles around her belly button. "What did you want me to do to you, Tess? Bend you over on my desk? Or maybe your desk? Take you up against the wall, or on the copy machine? Did you want me to make love to you, or did you want me to fuck you? Or both? I prefer doing both, especially at the same time."

He looked back to her eyes, his deep brown brimming with both desire and regret. "It's too bad it never happened. It's too bad you got over your crush."

She pressed her lips together on a moan.

"When did you stop wanting me?" he wondered aloud, tracing the edge of her hip. "Was it when you dated that guy the year after you started? What was his name – Bob?"

"Rob."

"Oh, yeah, I remember. Well, not really. I thought it was Bob."

"It was Rob."

"Hmm. Tell me, is he the reason you stopped wanting me?"

Tess tried to think straight as Mason's hand slipped lower, easing across her thighs. She propped up on her elbow to look him in the eye. "If you knew I had a crush, why didn't you do anything about it? If you'd even looked sideways at me, I would have fallen into your arms, very dramatic and swoon-like. We could have been doing this for the last six years."

He dragged his hand slowly back up to her belly, then up further still, smoothing across the underside of her breast. "Looking back now, it seems ridiculous that I didn't do anything. But at the time, you were one of my first employees and I was focused on running the business. Also, there was the age issue. You were so much younger than me."

"We're not that many years apart."

"It felt like we were."

"Mason, I was 22 and you were 28. Now I'm 28 and you're..." Tess paused, grinning wickedly. "Oh, wait, I see what you mean. You are older than dirt. Maybe we should stop having sex. We need to respect your brittle bones."

In the blink of an eye, he flipped her onto her back and crawled on top of her. "I'll show you brittle," he growled.

"And you'll give me a bone?"

Mason burst out laughing, his head falling against her shoulder. He nipped at the skin across her collarbone, teeth razing her flesh. She made a garbled groaning sound and shivered.

"Mmm. I've learned something else about you, my sweet Tess."

"What's that?"

He raised his head to pin her eyes. "You like it when I bite you."

"Maybe. A little."

"A *lot*."

"Okay, a lot," she admitted, reaching up to trace his widow's peak. "It's just that I have a fantasy about you wearing a cape like Dracula."

"Dracula? Really?"

"Yeah."

"I see. Did you think about that when you had your crush?"

"Perhaps."

Mason shifted against her, his growing erection pressing into her thigh. "Do you want me to bite you more, then?"

"Well, you don't need to gnaw on me like Hannibal Lector or anything, but a few love bites here and there might be nice."

Tess expected him to laugh again, but he froze. "*Love* bites?"

She didn't miss the inflection in his echoed whisper. She didn't miss the way the word *love* made her body shudder, lighting a warm glow inside her chest. She threaded her fingers into his hair, keeping him close.

"Okay, Mason, I'll admit you've figured me out. I do enjoy a good bite. But I've got you figured out, too."

"You do?"

"Oh, yes. I know your dirty little secret."

"What would that be?"

"You totally love butts."

He chuckled. "Your butt in particular, actually. It's fucking magnificent. Anyway, that's not a secret. All men love butts. Baby got back, junk in the trunk. It's a universal understanding."

"So, you admit you are an Ass Man?"

"I prefer Ass Vampire, thank you."

Her instantaneous fit of giggles was interrupted as he arched up, grabbed her around the waist, and spun her over onto her stomach, all in one swift motion. Tess thought to put up a fight, but he had both her arms pinned above her head before she could form conscious thought. He leaned over, his chest pressed to her spine, nibbling on her neck and growling into her ear. "Now sit still, cowgirl. I have work to do."

Tess squeaked when he nipped his way across her shoulder blades, then farther and farther down, until he reached one butt cheek and tugged a good bit of flesh between his teeth. She hummed in the back of her throat, taken by the deep pleasure inherent in that tiny bit of pain. "Damn, baby," she mumbled against the mattress, "I'm not gonna be able to sit down for the rest of the week."

Mason smiled against her skin and continued.

15

THE HUMAN SHIELD AND THE HUMAN TORNADO

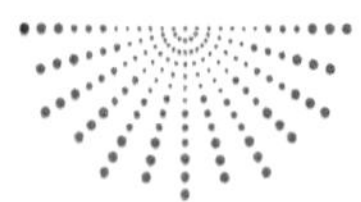

Tess grinned at the grandmotherly woman by her side. "I can't tell you how glad I am that you're here today, Janice."

Janice's eyes twinkled like Santa's while the two women walked down the hall from Tess's office to the employee lounge. "It seems like a nice workplace."

"Oh, it is," Tess assured, thrilled to have a warm body beside her as she faced her coworkers for the first time since The Great Revelation at Angelo's. Tess stepped into the lounge and spotted George and Chad sitting at a table, sharing donuts. Their eyes lit with devious joy the moment they caught sight of her. Chad's lecherous grin consumed his face, but as he opened his mouth to say something Tess knew would be terribly lewd, she cut him off. "George Caldwell, Chad Rivers, I'd like you to meet Mrs. Janice Barton, Mr. Tramont's new secretary. She'll shadow me all week and take over next Monday."

One look at the cherubic older lady made the men straighten in their chairs. "Nice to meet you, Mrs. Barton," they chimed.

"You too, boys. Are those donuts you're eating?"

"Yes, Ma'am."

"Hmm. Have you had a *proper* breakfast?"

George hung his head, staring at the sugary glaze coating his fingers. Chad cleared his throat, fidgeting.

Tess smiled so hard it hurt. "Okay, well, this is the lounge, Janice. George and Chad work in Accounting; you can talk more later. Let's move on with the tour, shall we?"

Janice managed to smile at the two men and look disappointed in them simultaneously. As the women exited, Chad and George remained speechless. It was a beautiful sound.

Leading Janice back through the hallway, Tess realized she'd never had a human shield before. She liked it very much. She'd dreaded this day for so many reasons: the first Monday of her last week at Field and Tramont; the first day in the office after the entire staff found out about her affair; the first time she would look at her distinguished, amazing, grumpy-bear boss in his thick leather chair and know, without a doubt, that she'd made a complete mess of everything.

Tess *enjoyed* having a human shield against her gossip-mongering coworkers, but she *required* protection from Mason. She needed some sort of armor to keep her chest from imploding every time he looked at her. If she busied herself teaching Janice the ropes, then she wouldn't be able to think about the sweetness of his smile, or the brightness of his eyes, or the warmth of his heart. She wouldn't be able to think about how her entire body and soul reached for him, begging to stay in the cocoon of his arms forever and ever. And she wouldn't be able to think about how there was no conceivable way she could leave him this Friday without being reduced to a quivering mass of Jell-O.

Her feet stopped automatically when they arrived at his door. "It's time for me to introduce you to Mr. Tramont," she announced over her anxiously grumbling stomach. She'd avoided this moment as long as possible, had lingered unnecessarily in every other room of the building. Standing at the solid black entrance to his boss-cave, Tess stiffened her spine and pushed her loose curls back over her shoulders.

"Why is his door the only one closed?" Janice asked.

"Mr. Tramont is a very structured worker. He prefers solitude, but will be there if you need him for anything. Don't let him intimidate you. His bark is definitely worse than his bite."

Janice took a step backwards when Tess knocked.

"Come in." Mason's deep voice sent shivers down her spine.

Tess opened the door. He looked up from his chair, fastening his eyes on hers. He smiled, slow and sexy.

"I missed you," he said. "It's only been hours since we were together, but I can't think about anything else."

"Mason, I..."

"Damn, I want you, Tess. I'm going to spread you out on this desk and..."

"Mr. Tramont! I'm here to introduce your new secretary." Tess side-stepped and pulled the older woman up next to her. "This is Janice Barton. She'll be replacing me."

Mason bounded out of his seat, raking his fingers through his hair. He flew around the desk, clearing the distance of the room to stand in front of them. "It's a pleasure, Ms. Barton," he offered, reaching out to shake her hand.

Tess stared at the floor, trying to compose herself.

"It's *Mrs.* Barton," Janice corrected when the handshake ended. "Been married almost forty years now."

"Wow, that...sounds amazing." Mason glanced at Tess, smiling briefly before turning back to his new secretary. "I take it Miss Troy is getting you acquainted with the office?"

"Oh, yes. She's wonderful. I have some big shoes to fill."

"Yes," he agreed. "That is an understatement."

Tess's mouth went dry. She cleared her throat, redirecting her attention to her protégé. "So, um, we should probably go back to my office now and get you started on the computer system."

"That sounds good. Nice meeting you, Mr. Tramont."

"You, too. Please let me know if you need anything, although I'm sure Miss Troy has it all under control."

Tess grimaced. *Good Lord, Mason has never been so wrong. I have nothing under control. Nothing at all.* Reaching out, she patted her human shield on the arm. "Come on, Janice, let's head back."

The kind woman nodded and started down the hall. Tess began following, until she felt Mason's large hand slip over her back. He stepped up behind her, his body hot and full against hers, making her footing falter. "I'll see you later, Miss Troy," he whispered into her hair.

Having difficulty looking at him, and even more difficulty breathing normally, she nodded and followed Janice into her office.

Mason's new secretary stood inside the door as Tess rounded the corner. "So, where were we, Janice? Oh, yes, the computer."

The woman gave her a soft smile. "Mr. Tramont seems nice."

"Yes, he is. He's..." *Incredible. Intelligent. Gorgeous. Giving. And I am more in love with him now than I ever thought possible.*

"I take it you two are together?"

"Well, we are, in a way, although Friday's my last day." Tess paused, her mind swimming. "You know what? Let's dive into the computer now and then I'll introduce you to Regina. She's David Field's secretary, so she'll be your best resource person. If you have any questions after I'm gone, you can always go to her."

"Wonderful."

Tess stepped forward, forcing her mind away from the man down the hall.

∼

Hours later, Tess sat alone in her office. Shifting side to side in her office chair, she realized for the first time today just how sore she was. She attempted to focus on her computer while the leather seat creaked in conjunction with her uneven movements.

Honestly, she didn't want this time to herself. Janice was with Regina right now, probably being assaulted with more office tales than she could bear, and Tess missed her human shield. The older woman had provided hours of much-needed distraction from her tumultuous thoughts. Like how her apartment no longer felt like home, how her bed seemed way too small and cold to sleep in again, and how the prospect of life without the man she desperately loved sounded like the worst kind of hell.

"Hey." Mason's voice came from her doorway.

Tess looked up to where he stood, shoulder resting easily against the doorframe. Her heart melted a little more. "Hey."

"You're fidgety today."

"How long have you been standing there?"

"Long enough to see you wriggling in your chair."

She leaned back, shifting the weight of her body once again. "That would be your fault, you know."

"Yeah? How so?" he questioned, pushing away from the door.

"Well, your ass-vampirism tendencies, while desirable, are accompanied by some soreness. In order to sit, I have to keep moving from cheek to cheek."

Mason walked around the desk to stand in front of her, so close that she had to crane her neck to see his face. Sparks lit his dark eyes. "I'm sorry about that. Being an Ass Vampire was a new experience for me. I may have become overzealous in my fantasy-fulfillment duties."

"Oh, you don't need to apologize. I certainly wouldn't have stopped you, even if I knew this chair would become my mortal enemy."

He chuckled, yet his laughter dissipated quickly. A second later, he crossed his arms over his chest and stared her down. "Well, then, Miss Troy. Let's consider that soreness as preemptive punishment."

"Punishment? What on earth am I being punished for?"

"Seriously? Did you hire the oldest secretary you could find?"

"Oh, that. Honestly, you're lucky she still has all her teeth."

"Hmm. Am I to conclude from this that my Tess is jealous?"

She huffed out a laugh, attempting to sit still and look him squarely in the eye. "For your information, Mr. Tramont, Janice had the best qualifications. She's a professional, a mother of four, and a grandmother of six, so she'll be able to handle this odd conglomeration of characters you call a staff. She also has tremendous organizational skills."

Mason unfolded his arms and took a step forward, leaning down to place one hand on each armrest of her chair. He nudged the tip of her nose with his. "I think you're jealous," he whispered, "and I love it."

"That's ridiculous. I'm not jel..."

He silenced her with a warm, smooth kiss. He nipped at her lips and stole her breath and Tess wanted to forget everything in the world except for them. She wanted to get crazy with him in her chair for once, if it weren't for the irritating voice of reason in her head. "We – we can't do this now," she mumbled against his lips. "Someone might walk in."

"I don't care if anyone walks in. As of Friday night, the whole staff knows about us. And as of this morning, I think Janice knows, too."

"I'd say it was pretty hard to miss. You're lucky I interrupted your little speech before you embarrassed us both to death."

Mason straightened to full height. "I'm not embarrassed, Tess."

"Well, I am! She's a grandmother!"

"Yes, and I'm sure she knows all about the birds and the bees."

"It's one thing to know about them, it's another thing to have rabid swarms unleashed in your face."

He gave her a roguish smile.

Tess licked her lips, tasting him on her skin. "You know I hate to say this, Mason, but now that Janice is here, we're going to have to slow down."

"What do you mean?"

"I mean I'm going to be training her this entire week. I can't disappear into your office for an hour without arousing suspicion, especially after that display this morning. She'll know exactly what we're doing and that is wrong on way too many levels. You and I are simply going to have to ease up on the conjugal visits."

His eyes darkened. "Hell, no. That is wholly unacceptable. I only have five days left with you in this office. I will need you more, not less."

"Mason..."

"No, Tess. No protests, no discussions. I will need you *more*. Why do you even think I'm here right now?"

"Um, why are you here?"

"I'm here because I grew tired of waiting for you to be done with your work. I grew tired of waiting for you to come back to my office alone. Therefore, I took matters into my own hands and came to you."

Tess edged forward in her seat. "Oh, wow. I can see this all so clearly now. What you're telling me is that you just made a booty call."

"Good God. Did you just say the words *booty call* to me?"

"Yes," she answered with a giddy grin. "Yes, I did."

"I'll have you know I've never made a booty call in my life."

"You mean, until ten minutes ago, when you left your office to walk down the hallway and into my office, for the express purpose of having sex with me."

Mason's eyes narrowed. "I do not make booty calls."

"I realize it's not the most elegant terminology, Mr. Tramont, but I'm just calling a spade a spade. Did you or did you not travel down the hall and into my office in order to have your way with me?"

His steely glare never wavered as he loomed over her chair. "Hmm. I think I see the point you're making, Miss Troy. You're saying that because I left my office with the complete intention of coming in here to get you – to lift you up from that chair, spread you out on this desk, push your skirt up to your waist, pull your panties off with my teeth, bury my face between your thighs, and lick and suck on you until you scream my name while coming on my tongue – then those intentions would indicate that this is actually a booty call?"

Her mouth hung open. All she could do was nod.

Mason smiled wickedly in her silence. He leaned down again, placing his hands back on her armrests. "Well, then. I stand corrected. This is definitely a booty call."

Tess's fingers trembled in her lap. *Damn it! Why is he so much better at this than I am?* "You know, Mason, we, um...we can't do any of that in here."

"Why not? I do own the building."

"Because Janice or Regina or anybody could literally walk through that door at any moment."

"Then come back to my office with me. No one dares enter there."

"I already told you we can't spend all our time in your office."

He exhaled slowly. "You're making this difficult, Tess. But I'm not taking *no* for an answer. If we can't be in here, and we can't be in my office, we'll have to find another place. What about the copy room?"

"The copy room?"

Mason slid his hands from her armrests onto her thighs, his warm fingers tightening over the thin material of her skirt. "Yes, the copy room. Are you going to tell me you've never fantasized about us in there?"

His thumbs shifted slowly across her legs and Tess swore she could feel his skin on hers, even without the contact of flesh on flesh. She wanted nothing more than for him reach under her skirt now, to touch her the way he did in his car Friday night. "I...um..."

Mason's fingers drifted down, dangerously close to her skirt's hem. "I need you to do something for me, Tess. I need you to think back to the past. Back to when you had your overwhelming, beastly, lustful crush on me. Can you remember when you were the sweet little secretary who wanted her big, bad boss? Can you remember how much you *hungered* for me?"

She nodded. Violently.

The gleam in his eyes was pure sin. "That's good. So good. Now, I want you to think about how you felt back then, back when your desires overtook your logic. I want you to remember when I was everything you wanted. When I was *all* you wanted." He paused, letting the words sink into her skin. "Do you remember it? Do you remember it well?"

"Y-yes."

"Perfect. Now please tell me, in all honesty...did you fantasize about the two of us – naked and hot and sweaty – in that room together?"

Her lips parted, but no sound came out.

Mason stared into her. "I see the gears in your mind turning. Are you going to deny it? Are you going to tell me you never wished that I would take you in the copy room? That you never longed for it? That you never ached for me to fuck you senseless on one of those machines?"

Tess grasped onto her armrests, her damp palms sliding across the leather. "Uh...no...of course I didn't..."

"God, you're gorgeous. But you're a terrible liar."

She only managed to hold her tongue for a second. "Damn you, Mason! You and all your crazy sexy! The answer is yes! I thought about it all the time back then. Hell, I thought about it last week. I even thought about it an hour ago, which made it really hard to look Janice in the eyes, let me tell you. I desperately want you to take me in there. I want you to plow right into me while that copier takes pictures of my bare ass. So, there! Are you happy now?"

He smiled so deeply that little dimples puckered his cheeks.

The beauty of it caused her physical pain.

"I don't think *happy* can begin to describe what I feel with you, Tess. All I know is we're going to the copy room. Right now."

"But...there's no lock on that door."

"Do you honestly think there is any world in which that will stop me from doing what I want to do to you?"

"Good Lord! You're temptation incarnate, aren't you?"

He answered her with a silly smirk and a kiss on the tip of her nose. She nearly grabbed him by the hair and dragged him to the copy room herself. But it just wasn't possible.

"Mr. Tramont. I know it feels like we're safe in this office because we've done a lot of things in the past few weeks and haven't been caught. But the copy room? People go in there. All the time."

"Hmm. If it makes you feel better, I promise I will close the door firmly behind us and jam a chair up under the handle. No one will be in there. No one but you and me...and the copy machine." He leaned in, pressing heated kisses to her neck. "I swear I'll turn that room into a fortress, just for us. But you should be aware that it won't even matter to you, because I'm going to fuck you so hard you're not going to know where you are, let alone care."

She moaned in the back of her throat, her knuckles turning white against the armrests. "Mason. Do you know how much one of those machines costs?"

"I don't know. A grand, maybe?"

"Try several grand."

"So?"

"So we could break it."

"It'll be worth it."

"Mr. Tramont!"

He pressed his mouth hard to hers, pulling her lower lip between his teeth before the kiss ended. He captured her with his eyes, their dark brown nearly black. "Miss Troy, does that machine make color copies?"

"Y-yes."

"Do we have any poster paper we could use?"

"Why do you need poster paper?"

"Because I want a full-color poster of your ass, of course."

Her jaw fell open. "I...uh...I don't know. About having poster board, I mean. But even if we did, it wouldn't fit in that copier. I'm pretty sure that machine only takes 11 by 14 inches, at most. We do have some nice paper in 11 by 14 – it's my favorite, which is 24-pound, 97 brightness – and it would do a fair job. But we may also have some actual photo paper, although it will just be your standard 8 ½ by 11 inches. I think it's 5-star glossy photo paper, which is really nice, unless you're more interested in a matte finish. They're both smudge-proof, though, so either will do well for what you have in mind..."

Her rambles trailed off as a glow of amusement lit his face. Deep chuckles emanated from his chest, skittering across her skin. Tess hung her head. "Oh,

God. I'm so sorry, Mason. You probably didn't want that much information, did you? I'm terrible at this dirty-talking thing."

"No, no, it's good information. Very helpful. I like it." He reached out to cup her cheek in his palm, drawing her eyes back to his. "I love it, actually."

Her heart pounded. She watched in awe as he eased forward, the heat of his body enveloping her like a soft, fuzzy blanket. "Do you know what I'm going to do after I take a photo of your glorious backside with that smudge-proof, 8 ½ by 11 inch, 5-star glossy photo paper, Tess?"

"You've...you've already thought about it?"

"I've thought about little else all day, to be honest."

Her mouth ran dry. "What are you going to do with it?"

"I'm going to plaster that picture inside my desk drawer. That way, anytime I desire, I can open the drawer to see my beautiful photo. After all, you know how boring some of our client meetings can get. But I don't ever have to worry about that anymore. I'll just pretend I need a pen, and reach into my desk, and that client will have no idea I'm staring at the most magnificent ass the world has ever seen – the one I've had my hands and mouth all over – the one I've had in my teeth."

Flames of red shot into Tess's face. She shifted in her chair, trying like hell to relieve the ache he'd created between her legs.

Mason eased back to look her over. "Damn, that's amazing."

"Wh-what's amazing?"

"It's amazing that you can blush, so innocently and beautifully, from a few mere words. When at the same time, you're squirming in your seat from the bite marks I left on your skin."

The depth of wonder she witnessed in his eyes set fire to the pile of kindling that was currently her body. Tess sat bolt upright in her chair. "That's not why I'm squirming in my seat right now, Mr. Tramont."

She grabbed hold of his tie and yanked him down to her. Their lips crashed together and she pushed her tongue into his mouth, seeking some small taste of everything her body begged for. He responded instantly, gripping the armrests for support as her chair bent backward beneath their weight.

After eager, messy minutes, Tess pulled back just enough to catch her breath. "Wow, Mason. You have a fantastically filthy mind."

"Mmm. That is entirely your fault."

"It is?"

"Hell, yes. We both know I wasn't like this a few weeks ago. But now..."

"But now?" she echoed, wanting – needing – to hear the end of that sentence.

He gave her the softest smile. "Now I just can't imagine living my life any other way."

Her lips quivered as she smiled back. Mason lunged for her, erasing her grin with his mouth, their teeth clashing in his frenzy. She whimpered when he pushed her back farther, ignoring her chair's protests.

"Tess?"

She tugged on one of his shirt buttons. "Yes?"

"Tell me I can take pictures of your ass. Tell me you want me to do it. *Insist* on it. Also, if you would be so kind, I need you to call me *baby* while making your demands."

She hummed against his lips before matching his dark gaze. "Mason, will you please take me into the copy room? Because I can't even begin to tell you how many times your sweet little secretary wished her big, bad boss would fuck her senseless on one of those machines."

He growled and Tess gripped harder onto his tie. "Oh, and baby," she whispered, "I definitely need you to take full-color, glossy pictures of my bare ass and put them in your desk drawer. That way, wherever I am in this world, and whatever fantasies I'm having about you, I'll know you're fantasizing about me, too."

Mason froze with her words. He stopped everything and stared her down. "You must realize," he said, his voice aching with need and hope, "that it's not fantasizing if you actually get to do it. If you make the decision to live the dream, then it becomes real. As real as you want it to be. As real as we *both* want it to be."

Tess's heart thudded painfully but she didn't look away. "I – I suppose you're right."

He blinked several times. "I am right. Please tell me you know I'm right."

She didn't have a chance to answer before he kissed her again, consuming her thoughts. She didn't fight it. She just let herself live with him, here and now, since there was nowhere else she could imagine being. There was nowhere else she could imagine ever wanting to be.

The chair complained again as he urged her back, his hands clenching the armrests. Tess threaded the fabric of his tie more intricately between her fingers, binding him to her, refusing to let go. She pressed her eyelids shut and swam in the sensations of Mason's body.

She never heard the approaching footsteps that came to a halt in front of her office door. But there was a little part of her brain that registered the disapproving clucking noise coming from the hallway. And she definitely heard the second, decidedly louder, throat clearing.

Mason didn't care. He just kept kissing her, either entirely oblivious or utterly unconcerned. But Tess couldn't help wondering who waited impatiently at her door. Was it Chad, revving up to yell at them about getting a room? Was it Regina, already rolling her eyes? Was it Janice, wondering what kind of place she'd agreed to work in?

Tess managed to pull her lips from Mason's, turning her head toward the hall as he nuzzled his face into her hair. He pressed his mouth to her neck, nipping and sucking against her skin. In any other situation, she would have squealed in sheer bliss. But all she could do right now was stare at the person in her doorway.

It wasn't Chad. Or Regina. Or Janice.

It was Malory.

Malory Catskill.

The wiry brunette sized them up with sharp eyes, her thin lips pulled into a straight line. Tess's breath caught. The shivers coursing down her straightened spine had nothing to do with the love bites Mason blazed across her skin.

"Excuse me, the two of you," Malory said with crisp, enunciated words.

Tess felt Mason's muscles stiffen instantly at the sound of his ex's voice. She felt his entire being change, turning hard and unyielding against her. He lifted his head to stare at the woman in the doorway.

Malory crossed her slender arms over her sapphire dress. "I was just on my way to your office, Mason...when I noticed you were in here."

He attempted to stand but Tess restrained him unconsciously, holding him in place with her ferocious grip on his tie. She kept staring at Malory, not realizing she'd restricted his movement, until his fingers covered hers. Mason rubbed his palm over the back of her hand, but Tess still couldn't accept what was happening. He took his time to gently pry her fist open before the material fell from her clenched fingers.

She felt the loss of that touch immediately and turned to see his face. He looked a million miles away now, even though he stood inches before her. Tess's cheeks were on fire. Mason's eyes were on fire, too, but she couldn't tell which emotions churned inside them. She only knew there were so, so many.

"I need to speak with you, Mason," Malory asserted with several taps of her toe against the hard floor. "I only need a moment. I'm sure your *secretary* can be without you for that long."

Tess didn't miss the disdain in the shrew's voice. She also didn't miss the board-like rigidity of Mason's spine, or the telltale twitch of his jaw muscle. "Will you excuse me please, Tess?"

She nodded mechanically.

He smiled stiffly before turning away, stepping around her desk, and brushing past his ex into the long hallway.

Malory watched his movements hungrily, only looking back to Tess when Mason was out of view. With a single glance, she made Tess feel like a bug on the bottom of her designer heels. Then she turned and was gone, and Mason with her. In a whirlwind.

Malory just breezed into the office, said a few words, and swept him away. Leaving Tess alone.

The memories came instantly. Uninvited. Unwelcome. Memories of the day she'd found Bryan in bed with Kendra.

Tess still remembered the excitement she felt, thinking she would surprise her loving boyfriend with her early exit from work that day. She could still hear the moans and giggles filling her ears when she'd walked down her hallway toward the bedroom. She could still see their bare legs twisted up in her bed sheets, could envision the bliss on Bryan's face while he lay on top of another woman.

Pain tore through Tess's body now, just as it had then. She knew, from the moment she'd suggested this affair with Mason, the danger she put herself in. She knew the only thing worse than watching Bryan leave her for Kendra would be watching Mason leave her for Malory.

She was absolutely right.

Slumping onto her desktop, Tess clutched at her chest. She tried to physically hold her heart together, to prevent it from shattering into a billion pieces. But all her grasping fingers could find was the diamond dangling from her neck. A reminder that Mason could be sparkly. That he was the most sparkly thing in her life. And that she couldn't fathom the devastation of losing him.

She blinked against the salt burning her eyes. Mason and Malory were together, right now, in his office. He was back with the woman he'd been with for over a decade. The thought of all the times he must have touched her coiled like a snake in Tess's gut. Knowing what it felt like to be held in his arms, she just couldn't imagine him holding Malory the same way. It was absolutely unthinkable. It was simply unbearable.

How long have they been apart now? Two months? This was about the time they usually found their way back together. Tess shook her head, over and over again, the horror of her thoughts shoving her below the surface. She knew she would drown – sinking like dead weight beneath this hideous pain – if she didn't fight like hell to survive.

She forced herself to sit up in her chair. She straightened, releasing her grip on the diamond. She pushed her hair back over her shoulders, brushed the tears from her eyes, and stared at her computer.

"This is a good thing," she muttered. After all, she knew this was coming. She'd always known. "You needed to be reminded, Tess."

She'd simply become too attached. To his home, to his bed, to his life. To him. She had to remember this was all over on Friday.

Tess heard Mason's office door open in the distance. A blur of sapphire rushed through the hallway without a glance in her direction. A moment later, her boss appeared in her doorway.

His eyes found hers. "Tess."

She cleared her throat. "Mason."

"I'm sorry about that," he offered, motioning to the spot in the hall recently occupied by his ex-tornado. "I assure you, it was only business. A few matters dealing with the West End Country Club opening."

"Of course. Her father owns the place, doesn't he?"

"Yes."

Tess swallowed hard. "She's worth millions, I suppose."

"None of that matters to me," he stated, stepping forward until he reached her desk. His broad body encompassed her field of vision. "Tess, I want you to come to the Country Club gala with me."

She shifted in her seat. "You mean...on *Saturday*?"

"Yes, on Saturday. The event you've been preparing us for. The one I asked you to that first Monday in the restaurant."

"No. I can't. Friday is my last day. That's three weeks. That's the end. We both have lives to get on with."

She expected him to be angry, to glare at her or loom even more ominously. He didn't. Mason softened instead, smiling gently into her eyes. "It's just one more day. What can one more day hurt?"

Shivers flitted over her skin. "Wh-why do you want me to go?"

He rested his hands on the desktop, his entire body focused on hers. "I want you there because I worked day and night on that project, and you were right beside me, and I couldn't have done it without you. I want you there so I can show it to you properly, and celebrate it with you, for all you did to help it become a reality. And I want you there...just because I want you there. Having you on my arm will make me the happiest person in the place. The happiest person in the world."

Tess clutched at the diamond again, heart pounding against her fingertips. She didn't miss the sincerity in his eyes. She didn't miss the intimacy of his words. She couldn't ignore the aching, eager response of her body, even when her brain screamed at her to leave while she still had a miniscule chance at self-preservation.

∼

MASON HELD his breath as he waited for an answer. He wished like hell Malory hadn't shown up just now. That woman always did have terrible timing. But today, in front of Tess, was the worst. His sweet sprite was skittish enough. She didn't need another reason to run away from him.

Back when Mason had agreed to Tess's ludicrous idea of a no-strings-attached affair, he understood what it meant. He understood he would have obstacles to overcome. Tess had constructed so many barriers and erected so many walls, there were times he thought he'd never be able to see over them. But he was close to the top now. He was so damn close.

He just had to keep climbing, persistent and unfailing. Saturday may only be one more night, but it meant a future between them, one that extended past her three-week time frame. That was a wall he desperately needed to hurdle, a barricade he had to break through. If he didn't, she would leave him – and that just wasn't an option.

He rubbed his thumb and forefinger together, growing impatient. "Please, Tess. Tell me you'll come to the gala Saturday. Tell me you'll spend one more night with me." *And then another. And another.*

Her eyes locked onto his, their light blue swimming with more emotion than he knew what to do with. After forever, she finally nodded. "Okay, Mason. I'll come with you."

The kempt air left his lungs in a rush. "Yes. Perfect." He reached out his hand. "Come on. It's time to get out of this building."

"Get out? It's only three o'clock. Where are we going?"

"We're going shopping. I'm into this gift-giving thing now, and I want to buy you a dress for the gala. Anything your heart desires."

"What about Janice? I can't leave her alone on her first day."

"Regina will take good care of her, I'm sure."

"But you never leave work this early."

"Well, today I am. I want us to go on a date like normal people. Everyone knows about us, so we don't have to hide. I want to take you shopping, and to dinner, and maybe to a movie, if you like."

Mason waited as patiently as possible with his arm outstretched. He watched in wonder when she finally grasped his hand, allowing him to pull her from her seat and draw her to him. Having her back in his arms was a moment of triumph, quelling the panic that set into his bones the second Malory's shrill voice rang in his ears. When he'd felt Tess stiffen at that sound, it nearly broke something inside him. He instantly dreaded the things Malory might say and what Tess might think of him then.

For that terrifying moment, he feared never getting to hold his sprite again. He feared never getting to watch her lips move as she babbled into his ear before the sun had fully risen through the curtains in their bedroom. He feared never getting to see her eyes light with mischief and seduction and oh-so-beautiful contentment as they made love. More than anything, he feared spending a single day of his life without her. That was absolutely unthinkable. It was simply unbearable.

With his Tess back in his arms where she belonged, Mason knew he couldn't waste a second. He banded her against his chest, clamping them together. She sighed and sank into him, her body responding in a way her heart couldn't just yet.

Resting his forehead against hers, he rubbed their noses together. She giggled softly, trembling inside their cocoon. "Then, sweet Tess, after our date is completed to your utter satisfaction, I have other plans for us."

"Yeah? What plans?"

"First, I'm going to bring you back to our home."

"Mmm...what will we do there?"

"We're going to take a bubble bath, to soak your sore cheeks."

"I take it you don't mean the cheeks on my face?"

"Not exactly. But don't worry; the bath will help. And when you're feeling entirely relaxed, I'm going to wash your hair." He paused, his brow furrowing. "God, is that creepy? Please tell me it's not, because I really want to do that."

Tess hummed as his fingers wound into her curls. "Not creepy," she sighed. "Blissful."

"Wonderful. And after I wash your hair, I will dry you off, lay you on our bed, and massage you until you feel all better." His hand moved from her scalp down to her neck, tracing across her collarbone. "That is, until I start biting you again."

She smiled briefly before her gaze fell. "Mmm. Promises, promises, Mr. Tramont. Just so you know, I make it a point to never trust Ass Vampires."

"Well, that is definitely a good policy." He eased his fingers to her chin, raising her eyes to his. "But you can trust *me*, Tess. I hope you know that."

Her light blue didn't reflect the certainty he wanted. But she still pressed her lips to his, wrapping him in the warm blanket of her body. For now, it was all he could ask for.

16

LONG-OVERDUE REALIZATIONS

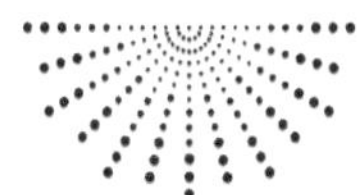

Friday. Tess's last day.

Mason never thought it would arrive this quickly.

He sat in his office chair, staring at his closed door, waiting for her. She promised she'd be here as soon as possible and he could do nothing else until he had her in his arms again. So, he waited. Impatiently.

It had become common knowledge among the staff this week that he and Tess had "alone time" together in his office each morning and were not to be disturbed for any reason. At first, his little sprite had been quite flustered by that particular information being open for public consumption. Now, she simply embraced it. As for Mason, he honestly didn't care what anyone else thought. He just needed her with him.

The doorknob shifted across the distance of his office. His focus narrowed when she entered and closed the door behind her. Tess turned to him, her blue eyes bright. He held his breath as she walked forward, across the room and around his desk, stopping in front of his chair. She didn't say anything. She just plopped down in his lap, giggling while wrapping her arms around his neck.

Her luscious pink lips pressed against his mouth and he grabbed hold of her body, crushing her chest to his. The air left her lungs with a whoosh. The next second, he lifted her, standing from the chair with his Tess in his arms and setting her on his desk. She balanced on the edge, held in place by the wall of his body.

He cupped her face in his hands. "You're going to be here for a while," he said, since every other morning visit to his office this week had a thirty-minute time limit – *because that's how long I told Janice to take for breakfast, Mason* – and that wasn't going to be enough today.

Tess didn't argue. She only whispered, "Okay."

"And I want every piece of clothing off," he added, knowing she wouldn't normally allow them both to be entirely naked in his office. She would say there was too much to cover up if anyone knocked on the door.

Once again, she didn't put up a fight. She only nodded. Mason appreciated the current understanding between them. After all, this was their last morning here. These were their last minutes to spend together in the place where they'd lived so much of their lives for the past six years.

When he began peeling her clothes off, kissing every inch of revealed skin, Tess remained calm and pliant. She hummed in synchronicity with the pressure of his lips. He took time and care with every movement, until she sat completely bared.

Tess smiled at him then, reaching up to remove her hair tie.

His hands grasped hers. "No. Do *not* pull your ponytail out."

Mason didn't know what she would think of his demand. He just wanted her to look like she did the first day she'd ever stepped into this room, when she'd changed both of their lives irrevocably. Still, he knew his words were forceful. As an afterthought, he added, "Please."

Tess didn't look upset in the least. She simply nodded again. She'd apparently decided to acquiesce to all of his desires today, which somehow made this worse. He just couldn't get enough of her, no matter how hard he tried.

Mason's voice shook as he said, "Thank you."

He ran his hands over her entire body, exploring every curve, while Tess whimpered and purred. He stilled when she eventually worked her fingers into the knot of his tie, taking her sweet time undressing him, as if they had forever together. After several minutes, she finally got the knot undone and started tugging, rather ineffectively, at his shirt. As much as he enjoyed the site of her painted fingernails fumbling with his buttons, he couldn't stand being this far away from her bare skin for a single second more. He took over, ridding himself of every stitch of clothing with harrowing speed.

He was probably too frustrated at this point. His nerves were probably too heightened by the realization that this was the last time he would ever have her in his office. He probably should have tried to calm down, but he simply couldn't bear the thought of never being here with her again. It made him crazy, and he thrust himself inside her, deep and full, in an instant. Tess's eyes widened and her breath caught, her pink lips pursing with the softest little, "Oh."

Before he had the chance to feel guilty about his coarse actions, before he had the chance to apologize or withdraw, she wrapped her arms around his neck and pulled him closer. She pressed her lips to his ear and whispered, "This is perfect, baby. Just perfect."

He shuddered with the tickling of her breath against his skin. Tess banded her legs around his hips, linking her feet over his back, bringing him further into her body. When Mason felt her fingertips easing through his hair, and her mouth placing tiny kisses against his jaw, he finally got himself under control. He began making love to her slowly, with the smallest of movements, because he wanted this to actually last forever.

Dropping his head, he nipped at her shoulder so he could listen to the strangled groans emanating from her throat. The expected sounds soothed him now, since he knew this woman inside and out. He knew his Tess just as well as she knew him.

Mason couldn't help but wonder how these last few days would have progressed if his ex-tornado hadn't shown up here on Monday. Would he have already finished scaling Tess's thickly constructed walls? Would she have already agreed to keep living with him, and to give this relationship an actual chance, if she hadn't been spooked by Malory's untimely arrival?

He supposed he would never know the answers to those questions, even though the week had gone better than expected after that unfortunate incident. Once Tess agreed to leave work early with him Monday, they'd spent every possible waking and sleeping moment together. Leaving work early became their custom each day. Except for Wednesday, when they stayed extra-late because she refused to go into the copy room with him until everyone else had gone for the day.

That evening, despite the office being utterly empty, she'd still made him jam a chair under the doorknob before allowing him to come anywhere near her. Mason had been more than happy to oblige, since the magnificent photo now plastered inside his desk drawer – which was, ironically enough, currently beneath her lovely bare bottom – had become his most prized possession. He didn't even mind the hefty fee he had to fork over to the copy machine repairman to come in during off hours in order to get the copier back to functionality before morning. Although, when "Big Mike" asked him what the hell happened to that machine, Mason found himself at quite a loss for words.

The past few days had flown by in a blur. Honestly, the last four weeks felt like a blur, but he couldn't stop time from moving. And now it was Tess's last day, and he would stay late with her in the office again. He wanted every last second he could get with her being just one room over, and having just one wall separating them. Since he would give anything for that to be the only wall between them.

"You're thinking really loudly," Tess said, pressing her breasts into his chest.

The sound of her gentle words redirected his wandering thoughts. Mason ran his fingers across her neck and over her hair, grasping her ponytail inside his hand. "Sorry about that."

"You know, you can pull my hair if you want to."

"Excuse me?"

"Well, you've got quite a hold on it. If that's something you'd enjoy, I promise I won't mind."

He wound his fingers further into her curls. Part of him wanted to flip her over and take her from behind, pulling her ponytail back with his fist and driving into her furiously, until she screamed in utter pleasure. But the other part of him, the one that loved taking his time and savoring every minute, wanted to see her face when she sighed in release.

Mason freed her gold mane from his grasp. "Thank you, but no. I don't want that now. I want you just like this."

"Okay," she said, shifting herself on the desk.

"Are you uncomfortable?"

She shook her head and pressed a kiss to his lips. He withdrew himself from her body so he could push slowly back in. She shivered with the movement, burying her face in his neck.

"Are you cold, Tess?"

"No. I'm never cold when I'm with you. You're like a furnace. It's amazing."

He smiled, smoothing his hands over the goose bumps on her skin.

"It's been nice, not being cold these past few weeks," she mumbled against his chest. "I'm grateful it's almost summertime now. Sometimes, in the winter, my fingers feel like icicles."

"They are icicles in the winter," he agreed, reaching for her hand to thread their fingers together. "I've always watched you warm them up on your coffee mug and some days they would turn nearly blue. Whenever that happened, I'd ask you to get me more coffee, even if I didn't want it. I just knew you were busy, and paying more attention to everyone else than to yourself, and I wanted you to hold onto the mug to get warm."

Her fingers clamped onto his as he spoke. He could feel her pulse surge through her skin into his. He always wanted to keep her hands warm. He always wanted to be able to count her heartbeats like he could right now, through his fingertips. Tess was softness and love and compassion and just... happiness. He hadn't had much experience with any of those things, so he assumed they would feel foreign and unnatural. But they didn't. Not with her.

"I'm warm now, Mason."

He eased back and her eyes dragged up to his. She looked as drunk as he felt. "I'm warm now, too, Tess."

She smiled then, the most beautiful smile he'd ever seen, ever. He knew, right at this moment, he was happy. God, this was true *happiness*, and he honestly wasn't sure if he'd ever felt it before these past weeks.

Her arms encircled his neck, pulling him down to press her lips to his. He let himself melt into her. He loved being buried deep inside her, feeling the heat and softness of her body as it tightened around him. He loved running his hand down the length of her spine, from the nape of her neck to the little indentations of her hipbones against her low back. He loved feeling her arch into his chest and shiver beneath his touch. But what he loved most was how open she was with him in these moments, how raw and perfect her emotions were, written here on her face.

Mason stared into her for a long minute, looking into her beautiful blues, loving the way they looked back at him. Tess tightened her hold on him using all available limbs. He shifted inside her, eliciting a tiny gasp from her lips. That tender sound was all it took to break him. As much as he didn't want this moment to end, he started moving again, taking her with him into their own sweet heaven.

～

HOURS LATER, Mason sat alone in his office chair, staring out of the arched window to the park across the street. Four Mondays ago, he'd been doing this exact same thing. David and Regina had just returned from their honeymoon, and all Mason wanted to do was run out of the building and roll around in the grass.

That was the day he realized he needed a change. He needed something out of the ordinary, someone to help him feel alive. He just had no idea she'd been walking around in front of him for six years.

Tess.

She'd been here, naked and wrapped around him on this desk, mere hours ago. But it still wasn't enough. It would never be enough.

Mason inhaled deeply, renewing her scent of wildflowers and vanilla. He loved that he could smell her on his clothes. He loved that her hairbrush was in his bathroom, that her pillow rested beside his on their bed, and that she called his house "home". He loved being able to reach out and take her whenever he felt like it, and he loved how she always responded the same way: like it was the first time she'd ever felt his touch, like it was the best thing she could imagine.

It couldn't end tomorrow night after the gala.

He couldn't lose her.

He wouldn't.

His mind grasped for solutions, but instead of his usual logic and reason, he found only panic and desperation. He shook his head, not knowing what to do with these emotions. He'd never experienced anything like this. He was a practical person, and these were the most impractical feelings ever. They were magnificent, overwhelming, and insane. And they sure as hell hadn't happened in four weeks.

A knock came at his door, catching him off guard. "Yes?" he asked, hoping Tess had come to visit his office one last time.

A long moment passed before David poked his head around the corner. "Is it all clear in here? Safe for entry?"

Mason rolled his eyes.

David chuckled as he stepped inside. "Hi, buddy."

"Hi."

"So, it's Tess's last day."

"Yeah."

"Good thing you two are together, otherwise this would be tough."

"Yes. It would definitely be tough."

"Well, you *are* together, so it'll be okay. Right?"

Turning back to the window, Mason stared at the bright green grass in the distance. He needed answers, and he knew the person who had them stood right here. "David, you're my best friend."

"Right back at you."

Mason looked to him. "Do you remember, a few years ago, when you told me I didn't love Malory and we would never work out?"

"Um, yeah. Sorry about that. I shouldn't have stuck my nose in."

"Don't be sorry. You were absolutely right. Which brings me to the sad realization that you know my emotional state better than I do."

David grinned. "You're the best at a lot of things. Emotions just aren't one."

"You're right about that, too. And since you *are* good with emotions, I need to know something. A month ago, when you told me I should date Tess, was that just on a whim?"

"God, no, Mason. It was absolutely not on a whim."

"Hmm. I didn't think so." Reality dawned, slow and dim but getting brighter. "I need you to answer one more question for me, to the best of your knowledge."

"Okay."

Mason sighed. "Can you please tell me how long I've been in love with my secretary?"

David glanced down, chuckling, before looking back. "At least two years."

"Hell, that long?"

"It happened right after she broke up with her last boyfriend."

"Bryan?"

"I believe that was his name. Regina hollered about him a lot. She was royally pissed over how the bastard mistreated Tess and how Tess was so sad all the time. But then the strangest thing happened."

"What happened?"

"You just zeroed in on her. It was amazing to watch, because you always seemed oblivious to how beautiful she was and how she stared at you constantly and how she laughed at your jokes, even when nobody else did. After that breakup, though, you saw how deeply she'd been hurt. You saw her in real pain, and you couldn't stand it. It awakened some kind of sleeping giant in you.

"Things were different after that. You talked more and more about her. You paid more attention to everything she did. You found reasons to keep her late in the office and gave her unusual tasks – ones that kept her close to you – even though they really weren't her responsibility. But she still did them, because you asked her. Regina would get all nuts about it, complaining that you were an ogre and you were committing secretary-abuse and if I acted that way she would leave me and not look back."

Mason cringed. "Sorry."

"It's okay. I kinda love it when she goes crazy like that. She gets really feisty, in a good way."

"Still, I owe Regina an apology. And Tess...I owe her a thousand apologies."

"Mason, if I ever thought Tess felt abused, I would have intervened. But she never complained. God, I think she enjoyed it. She always wanted to do things for you, from the day she arrived in this office. It just took you four years – and her having a bad breakup – to notice."

"And when I started noticing Tess, then you told me I didn't love Malory?"

"Yeah."

"But you didn't tell me I loved Tess."

"Sorry, buddy. You needed to figure that one out for yourself."

Mason leaned back in his chair, exhaling. "I've figured it out."

"I can see that."

He stared blankly at his desk. "David, what you said to me back then, about not loving Malory, didn't fall on deaf ears. I was planning to break up with her for good, but then she brought us the West End Country Club project and I didn't. I should have, but I didn't. That's *my* fault."

"Well, shit. I always suspected she used that project to keep her hold on you. I didn't know you were trying to get away. You should have told me. We wouldn't have taken the job."

"It was good for business."

"Yes, but it shouldn't have kept you with that woman. You should have felt like you could leave her without jeopardizing our work."

Mason rubbed a hand across the back of his neck. "I've made so many mistakes. I don't want to make more. Especially not with Tess."

David gave a promising smile. "You won't. You and Tess are great together."

Mason returned the smile, but didn't say a word. How could he tell David that Tess intended to run away, as fast as her lovely legs would carry her, the minute the gala was over? He didn't want to admit that to himself, let alone to his best friend.

"Anyway," David said, "I guess I should go check on Regina. She's going to be a mess after Tess leaves today. I know we'll see you at the Country Club thing tomorrow night, but we'll also need to do that double date soon. Otherwise, my life will be pretty miserable for a while."

"I'm looking forward to many double dates," Mason assured. "And I promise I'll do everything I can to make them happen."

～

TESS STARED at her near-empty desktop. There was only a computer left now. There were no photos of her family, no vacation trinkets, no lists of things to be done. It felt as blank as the day she'd arrived.

"I think we've got it all now, doll," Regina said, placing a photo frame into Tess's oversized bag. "You are officially packed up."

Tess saw the tears welling in her friend's eyes. "Oh, please don't start crying," she begged, grabbing onto her. "Or I'll start, too."

Regina sniffled as they hugged. "I know, I know; I'll be good. We've got the gala tomorrow, after all. And now that you and Mason are dating, we'll see each other all the time, right?"

Tess pulled back, forcing a smile. "We'll talk soon. I promise."

David appeared in the doorway. "Hon, you doing okay?"

Regina looked to her husband. "I'm okay."

"You ready?"

"Yeah." Regina gave her one last hug. "Janice is really nice, but that doesn't make this any easier."

"I know you'll take good care of her." Tess smiled, watching her friend disappear around the corner before waving goodbye to David.

Alone again, she turned to look at the empty walls. Tess never imagined, the day she stepped foot in this room, that she would still be here six years later. She'd never imagined how attached she would get to the people around her, or how hard it would be to leave. But then again, she hadn't known how madly she would fall in love with her boss.

Images of the past four weeks swirled through her mind – from the moment Mason told her he was interested in her and she insisted he wasn't – right up until this morning, when they'd made love on his desk one last time. This past month with him was her favorite. But she would also miss the six years before that, when she'd absorbed everything he taught her and grew into a successful businessperson in her own right.

Damn, damn, damn! Why is there another woman in his life? Am I cursed to only fall in love with men who already love someone else? Is that my special gift?

"Hey. You doing okay?"

Mason's voice came from behind her, deep with concern. Tess pivoted on her heels to see him standing in her doorway. "I guess I'll have to be," she said, heart clenching as he moved toward her.

He reached for her the moment he could, winding their fingers together. "How is this room ever going to be anything but Tess's office?"

"You be nice to Janice. Don't try to scare her."

"I didn't try to scare you, you know."

"But you did."

"And yet you still wanted your big, bad boss."

"Yes, well, I obviously wasn't thinking straight."

His eyes fastened on hers. "And now you are?"

Tess studied him for a long moment with her lips pressed together. She remembered sitting with him on her blanket in the dandelion field, just four weeks ago. She remembered tossing back a glass of wine as she plotted ways to punish him. Yet that moment seemed like it took place years ago, with a different her and a different him, because what she felt between them now was unlike anything she could have imagined then.

Mason ran his hand down her arm, a distinct sadness permeating his normally strong features. "Do you need help taking your things out?"

"No, I'll manage," she said, afraid to acknowledge just how much this moment hurt them both. She picked her bag off the floor and pulled it onto her shoulder. "Regina helped me earlier and I already made one trip to my car. I'm all set."

"Can I at least walk with you?"

"Sure."

She moved awkwardly past him, a step ahead as she exited her office and strode down the hall, never looking back. He held the front door open for her while she stepped out onto the ivory stone staircase. The door closed behind them and he came to stand beside her on the top step. They both looked down to their cars parked against the curb.

Tess felt the heat radiating from his body as she fiddled with her keys. "Well, I guess I'll see you tomorrow at the gala. I'll just, um, meet you by the entrance."

"I can come by your apartment to pick you up instead."

"No, no, that's not necessary. I think I should drive myself."

"Okay."

Their voices trailed off and they stood together, neither moving nor saying a word. Then Mason turned toward her, taking a step closer. She held her breath as his hand eased to her face, fingers drawing softly across her cheek. He waited patiently for her to have the courage to look at him. When she did, she nearly came unglued from the pain in his eyes.

"Tess, I know you're leaving here today and there's nothing I can do about it. But the thing is, I don't want to come back into this building without you. And that is crazy, because this has meant everything to me for as long as I remember."

She stared at him, grief-stricken. If only two things would happen simultaneously – Mason screaming out his love for her at the top of his lungs, and someone throwing a bucket of water on Malory Catskill to melt her into a puddle – then maybe they would have a chance. But neither of those things would happen.

"You're going to be okay," Tess attempted to reassure them both. "It's time for us to move on. We'll have the gala tomorrow and then we'll walk away, just like we planned."

"I'm aware of the plan. But I need you to tell me something first."

"What's that?"

"I need you to tell me what happens when I refuse to walk away."

Her body froze solid. "Well, that's...that's not going to happen. We made a deal, Mason. We set limits."

"No. *We* didn't set limits. *You* set limits."

She shook her head, wanting desperately to deny the words.

He took her by the shoulders, angling her toward him. "Listen to me. Please. I know I pissed you off that first day at the restaurant. You accused me of making an intellectual decision to date you, not an emotional one. You accused me of looking at love too practically and you were right. That's exactly what I did." His fingers tightened on her arms. "But don't you see how it's changed? Now, *you're* the one who won't allow yourself to let go. You're the one making the rules that keep us separated. Can't you just be with me? Because I want that. I want you. *All* of you. Damn, you've got to know that by now."

She stood, flabbergasted.

Mason released her arms, keeping her immobile now with only his unwavering gaze. "I was going to wait until after the gala tomorrow to say this. But I can't wait anymore, Tess. I've realized a lot in the last four weeks, and I am absolutely certain that you and I will be fantastic together...if you just give us a chance. Will you do that? Will you give us a chance?"

The air rushed from her lungs.

He stepped closer and pressed forward. "There's no reason not to, is there? Everyone knows we're a couple now. We have infinite double dates on hold with David and Regina. Ian and Vanessa adore you. They already think we're living together and they're both asking for family dinners." Mason took hold of her hand, pulling it onto his chest. "And you could move right into the house, as soon as you want. So many of your things are there already, in our home."

Tess stared at his large fingers interlaced with her smaller ones. She whimpered, blinking hard against her tears. "That...that is true."

"Yes. It *is* true."

She smiled at the sound of his voice, filled with such hope and promise. She closed her eyes, overwhelmed by everything he'd said. Her mind swam, fierce and tumultuous. Yet her heart felt perfectly at peace.

Mason placed a kiss into her hair. Nuzzling his lips beside her ear, he whispered, "You won't even have to change your initials."

She arched back, gripping hard to his hand. "*What*?"

"Tess Troy, Tess Tramont. Your initials are the same either way."

Her mouth fell open, eyebrows flown to her hairline.

He smiled softly, easing the tip of her ponytail over her shoulder. "I'm sorry, sweetheart. I don't mean to get ahead of myself. I just...I see such a future for us. I want you to see it, too. It would mean everything to me if you took tonight to think about our future. Will you do that for me? Will you do that for *us*?"

Feeling like she'd been Tasered, Tess nodded mechanically.

"Good. And you'll meet me tomorrow at the Country Club?"

She managed to squeak out the word, "Y-yes."

"I'll see you tomorrow, then."

Mason leaned forward, pressing a firm kiss to her still-parted lips. He inhaled deeply before turning, walking to his car, and driving away. Tess crumpled instantly onto the staircase. She sat, staring out into space.

THE NEXT EVENING, Tess sat on the edge of her bed, staring out into space. She'd been doing a lot of that lately. It was just her and her emotion-planet, drifting along in the Milky Way.

The dress Mason bought her for the gala dangled from a hanger on her closet door. She surveyed it, admiring the way the sewn-in clear crystals accented the bodice and swirled down the long, draping length of bright red fabric. She remembered the look on his face – like he wanted to swallow her whole – when she'd first modeled the luxurious gown for him in the exclusive boutique he'd taken her to on Monday afternoon. Would he look at her like that again tonight? Could she endure it if he did?

Tess pressed her lips together, refreshing the scent of cotton candy gloss – his favorite flavor. Her hair was freshly washed and pulled up on the sides, held by tiny pins adorned with more crystals. The rest of her hair lay in long curls down her bare back, which would remain bared by the deep drape of her gown. Her silver heels rested on the floor. All she had to do was stand up and put everything on. But she still sat on the bed.

The phone rang and she glanced at the picture on the screen.

Annabelle.

Tess answered. "Do you have ESPN or what?"

"Just wanted to see if you'd left for the ball yet."

"No. Not yet."

"Why not?"

Tess stared into the mirror hanging beside the gown. "I don't know if I can do this, Belle. Maybe I need to leave well enough alone and just be done with him."

"Why?"

"Because I waited my whole life for Prince Charming from the palace to sweep me off my feet, and there was never any sweeping. Even when I thought I'd found a prince here and there, I just got hurt again and again. Then I accepted that there was no prince, and I put on my big girl panties, and made my own damn palace."

"But it's a Pooch Palace."

"Yes, but it's *my* palace and I don't *need* Prince Charming. I don't even need Prince Grumpy Shut-in Architect."

Belle sighed. "I know you're strong, Tess. I won't argue that. And I know you've been hurt and you've come through it and made yourself even better. I commend you, okay? You get gold stars for all you've accomplished. I also verify the fact that you don't need Mason. But tell me this...what do you want?"

A tear slid down her cheek. "I want *him*. Good Lord, I can't even put into words how much. I want to spend every moment of every day of the rest of my life loving Mason Tramont. But how can I do that? Do I just trust what he says about Malory? He still won't tell me what happened between them."

"Hasn't he told you about fifty times that he doesn't want her?"

"Yes."

"And isn't he a pretty trustworthy guy?"

"Don't go getting all logical on me, Belle. That's Mason's problem, too. He doesn't talk about feelings. Yesterday, he basically told me he wants to marry me, yet he's never even said he loves me."

"That's probably because you've only been dating for a month. If you can even call what you've been doing *dating*. Just because you've been in love with him for six years doesn't mean he's on your timeline."

"But what if he doesn't love me? Maybe he thinks that me being a good secretary – and us having super-fantastic sex – is all it takes for a lifetime of happiness."

"Or maybe he thinks that's the beginning of something even deeper. Maybe he's going to be the best husband in the world. Maybe he will love you more than any man's loved any woman ever. But you'll never know unless you go to that *damn ball* and give him a *chance*."

Tess exhaled, trying to wrap her brain around those words.

"Stop thinking about it," Belle said, confirming that she could read minds. "Just let everything go and see where this takes you. You owe it to both of you. And you'll regret it like crazy if you don't."

"Man, you sure are old and wise."

"We're the same age."

"Yet you're older and wiser."

"Just wiser. Are you going to the ball, Cinderella?"

"Yes, I'm going." Tess watched her reflection in the mirror, witnessing the joy that lit her eyes when she made her decision. "You're absolutely right. I need to set all my fears aside and give us a real chance. I need to go to Mason tonight with an open mind and an open heart, and just love him in every way I can."

"If you do that, Tess, I know he'll love you, too."

"God, Belle, he's been trying to love me. I know he has. He's been trying in every way he can, but I've been so scared that I've just pushed away. I couldn't accept that he would actually want this, that he would actually want *me*. But no matter what stupid rules I set, he stayed. He's still here, and he's still trying, and I don't want to push away anymore. I want to love him and I want to learn to let him love me back."

"That's my girl," Belle whispered, her voice trembling. "You know, honey, Mason could very well be your happy ending."

Tess brushed a tear from her cheek. "I really do believe he is."

17

THE MARBLE COLUMN

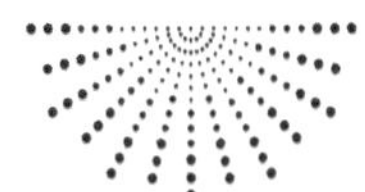

Tess parked her Bug a short distance from the entrance to the West End Country Club. Her fingers trembled when she pulled the key from the ignition. She took a deep, steadying breath. "Belle's right. I have to let everything go. I love Mason, and I know he's trying to love me, and I need to walk in here tonight with an open mind and an open heart."

Open mind, open heart. The mantra echoed in her head as she stepped out of the car and onto the cobblestone sidewalk. Tess smoothed the sparkling, clingy fabric of her dress across her hips before moving forward. The sky was dark and magnetized, holding a million stars in place. Elegant old-fashioned streetlamps lit her steps, allowing her to observe the magnificent couples making their way toward the elaborate entry. She felt a little out of place among the opulence, but no one seemed to notice. The other patrons nodded and smiled at her, confirming that Mason had amazing taste in ballgowns.

She'd almost reached the end of the sidewalk when she saw him. He stood to the right of the entrance, near a bed of red roses that glowed crimson in the lamplight. His eyes searched the oncoming crowd. Tess knew he looked for her, but she couldn't say anything to catch his attention. She was simply speechless.

She had never seen Mason in a tuxedo before. She'd ordered them for him, and even delivered a few to his home, but she'd never witnessed how the deep black material accentuated his dark hair and eyes, or how the cut of the jacket highlighted his broad shoulders and chest. The sight made her fingers tremble again, for entirely different reasons.

Tess could have stood here and stared at him indefinitely, but then he saw her. His first reaction was a sigh of relief. His next reaction forced the air from her lungs. To say he looked hungered would be far too mild. Ravenous was more like it, or fork-and-knife-in-hand salivating at the mouth. She'd never felt more beautiful or desired than now, as he devoured her with his eyes in the dark night.

Her wobbling gait managed to carry her to him, and for a long moment Mason didn't say a word. He watched her, his gaze drifting across every shimmery-red covered curve of her body, until his eyes settled on hers. "You're here," he said, his voice sending shivering waves across her skin.

"I'm here."

He reached out, tracing the edge of her diamond necklace. "You look more stunning than ever, which is unbelievable, since you always take my breath away."

"Thank you, Mason. For the dress and for the necklace."

"Please don't thank me. I should be thanking you for even showing up."

"You don't need to thank me for that."

"I do, actually. After I thought about what I said to you on the steps yesterday, after how forceful and presumptive I was, I knew there was a chance you wouldn't come. But I'm so grateful you did, because you've given me the opportunity to correct my mistake."

"What mistake?"

He stepped closer, one hand moving to cradle her face. "The fact that I never asked you the most important question. I spent all night thinking about you – I absolutely hated being alone in our home – and as I tossed and turned in that big, cold bed, I realized I never asked how you feel about me."

Tess clutched at his chest, fingers curling into the lapels of his jacket. She wanted to shout out the emotions she'd bottled up for so long, to just scream it all at the top of her lungs. But nothing came out, because she didn't know where to start. She didn't know how to express everything inside her, since no words seemed enough to do it justice.

His hand brushed her cheek and she melted into his touch. "You know, Tess, the only reason I tried asking you on a date a month ago was because I knew you'd had a crush on me, once upon a time. And even though it's been six years, I hoped some of that emotion was still inside you somewhere, in a cobweb-filled corner."

She opened her mouth to respond.

Mason touched his finger to her parted lips and shook his head. "Wait. Let me finish, please. I know I've been unfeeling in the past, and I know I've made you angry, but I promise I'll work like hell to be better. I swear to you, I am going to sparkle so brightly that it will hurt just to look at me. And I will do everything in my power to make you happy."

His eyes drifted down along with his fingers, to run across her shoulder. "I also need you to understand how sorry I am that my ex is going to be here tonight. I can assure you, with complete sincerity, that I have absolutely no desire to see her." His rapt gaze returned to Tess's face. "You are the only woman I see. You are the only woman I want."

She whimpered, holding tighter to his jacket.

He leaned forward, pressing his lips to her ear. "Come home with me tonight, sweet Tess. Come home and let's start over. Give yourself a chance to feel something for me again. That's all I want, all I hope for."

Her heart thudded hard in her chest. She needed to tell him just how much love she held for him. She needed to explode in a rambling fit of confessions that would surely knock him to the ground. "Mason, I…"

"Hey, there you guys are," David greeted as he walked up.

Tess quieted instantly, pulling back to meet Mason's intense stare. The ferocity of his blatant need stunned her. It took a long moment to tear her eyes away. "Hi, David. You look very handsome tonight."

David shrugged. "Yeah, it just happens, no matter what I do."

Tess laughed and Mason's fingers curled possessively into her hip.

David glanced at Mason's hand and grinned. "Sorry to interrupt you two, but I wanted to touch bases before we got lost in this crowd."

"Yes, of course," Tess agreed. She took a step toward the staircase but Mason banded his arm around her waist, keeping her at his side.

"Where's Regina?" he asked his friend.

"At home, unfortunately. She's not feeling well. She said to tell you how sorry she is that she can't be here."

Tess eased her hand up Mason's back, smoothing over his taut muscles. "That's too bad. I hope she feels better soon."

"I hope she will, too. Frankly, I'd rather be home with her, but I guess we have to rub elbows and all. You guys ready to go hobnob with the rich and glamorous?"

"If we must," Mason answered.

David walked toward the front entryway and Mason followed behind him, guiding Tess's steps. He bent his head to hers and whispered, "Will you think about what I said?"

Holding onto him for dear life, she gazed into his eyes and nodded. Mason gave her a brilliant smile. Then he swept her into the vast room, letting the world swim around them.

The night passed in a weird and wonderful fog.

Mason stared at her constantly, as if she might disappear if he looked away too long. He didn't miss an opportunity to touch her bare back or entwine their fingers. They met hundreds of people, heard a thousand compliments on the expert design of the conference center. Guests questioned him repeatedly about where he got his ideas and how he shaped his work. He answered by pulling Tess to his side and introducing her as his inspiration. At first, she didn't know what to think of the ease of his praise. But the more she heard it, the more she believed.

They lost David at some point; Tess wasn't sure when. Her mind moved so rapidly, from person to person and conversation to conversation, all while contemplating what to do when the clock struck midnight. Her prince wanted her to come home with him. If she let herself, if she embraced the open mind and open heart she'd set out to have tonight, then she could forget about Malory and be with the man she'd loved forever.

"May I call your office for a consultation on a summer home?"

Tess emerged from her haze to reply to the intensely manicured woman now questioning Mason. "Of course, Mrs. Newport. I'll be more than happy to take your information and have someone get in touch with you right away."

Mrs. Newport reached into her handbag and grabbed a business card, giving it to Tess. "I look forward to it."

The woman pivoted away and Tess handed the card to Mason. "You've had a million inquiries."

He tucked the card inside his pocket. "You're not my secretary anymore, you know. You're my date."

"I know, but I like to see the firm doing well. How could it not? The conference center is amazing. Everything you touch is magnificent."

Mason eased his fingers over her low back. "You're magnificent."

Tess had to look away from him for a moment. The feelings contained inside her heart for so long had reached maniacal proportions and the way he looked at her made her incapable of breathing. Her eyes drifted to the dance floor, where couples twirled to the orchestral band music she'd been hearing all night. The image of dancing with Mason in a field of dandelions a month ago brought a beaming grin to her face.

His fingers curled around her hip. "Are you having fun tonight, sweetheart?"

Tess shifted her gaze back to his. "Sweetheart," she echoed. "You called me sweetheart yesterday, too."

"Do you like it?"

"I love it, actually."

He placed a kiss on the tip of her nose. "Good. I love it, too."

She stared up at him, smiling with her entire body.

"God, you're beautiful, Tess."

She felt fairly certain that chunks of her heart melted off and slid down into her stomach.

"Would you like to dance, sweetheart?"

Her brow rose. "I thought you didn't dance."

Mason pulled her closer. "Only for you."

"Well, then...I would love to dance, baby."

His eyes narrowed and he leaned down to growl in her ear. She giggled as he grabbed her by the hand, leading her onto the dance floor, into the throngs of elegantly attired patrons. She expected him to assume a properly framed ballroom hold – worthy of the lessons he'd been forced to take as a boy – but he didn't. Mason reached around her instead, banding her body to his with one hand pressed to her bare back. With his other hand he grasped her fingers, winding them inside his own and resting them against his chest. She grasped his shoulder as he started swaying, guiding her in time with the band's sweet music. Then he pressed his cheek against hers and started humming in her ear.

Tess closed her eyes to listen. She found herself smiling again, since Mason's hums were nowhere near in tune to the music. She thought he might be tone deaf, which would mean she'd discovered the only thing in the world he wasn't good at doing. But after she listened a while, she realized he hummed his own song. A song just for them. In that moment, Tess understood that they were the only two souls in this palatial, packed, preened, and perfumed room of people. They were the only ones here, because Mason created an entire world for her inside his arms.

Dear Lord, she loved him. She loved everything about him. She even loved the things she didn't love about him. All of that emotion made her feel full and heavy and she leaned into him for support, squeezing his fingers as he swayed them. His body heated her skin, his humming filled her ears, and his hand traced tempting circles on her lower back. Before Tess even realized it, she panted with need.

Mason must have felt the change in her body. He must have sensed the shift in her breathing or noticed the way she'd curled her greedy fingers in his hair. His mouth found hers in an instant, their tongues tangling and teasing and exploring. It was an obscene kiss to share in the middle of an elegant society gathering, but Tess couldn't bring herself to care. She would have been thrilled to let that shameless act go on forever. Until she realized the music had come to a swelling and glorious conclusion, and everyone around them now clapped in appreciation.

"I think they're clapping for us," Mason whispered against her lips.

"Mmm. I'm sure they are. That was one hell of a kiss."

He raised his head to meet her eyes.

She gasped at the desire raging inside his deep, dark brown. "You know, Mason, this *is* a conference center."

"Yes, I actually do know. I kinda built it."

"Then you must know what that means."

"What does it mean?"

"It means they definitely have a copy room here somewhere."

A sinful grin lit his face. "Why, my dear Miss Troy, what are you suggesting?"

"Oh, my darling Mr. Tramont, I'm suggesting that we...ugh."

"Ugh?"

She ducked her face into his chest. "Sorry, I just saw Malory. She's over in the corner with some guy."

Mason exhaled harshly. "Damn, I really don't want to deal with that now. Let's just walk the other way. Maybe they won't notice us."

Tess looked back to his eyes, plainly witnessing his sincerity. He didn't want his ex. At this moment, she knew without doubt that Mason wanted her and her alone. It lifted the weight of the world off her chest.

He took her by the hand, pulling her from the dance floor toward the back of the spacious room, winding them around other couples as he headed toward the multitudinous glass doors overlooking the darkened golf green. Drawing her in close, he whispered, "Let's go outside."

Tess nodded.

They'd nearly escaped when a throat cleared forcefully behind them. "Excuse me. Don't be *rude*, Mason. Say *hello*."

He cursed under his breath, obviously aggravated by the sound of his ex's voice, and Tess couldn't help smiling. He grabbed hold of her waist, turning them both as one unit to face the brunette. "Hello, Malory."

The woman stared straight ahead, never looking at Tess directly despite the fact that Mason's hip stayed glued to hers. Malory motioned to the man beside her, who looked as though he might pass a stick from his colon at any moment. "You remember Brenton?"

"Of course," Mason replied. "And this is Tess, my date."

Malory's etched brows furrowed. "Don't you mean *secretary*?"

"No. I mean *date*."

"Hmm."

She still didn't acknowledge Tess, but her escort showed far more interest. "I'm Brenton Clearwater," he stated, reaching for Tess's hand.

Feeling the need to be polite, she took it. "Tess Troy."

Brenton gripped her hand tightly and leaned down to kiss the back, his wet lips lingering against her skin. Mason's arm tightened around her as Tess wrenched her fingers away. Brenton grinned at her, in a decidedly highbrow yet disgustingly lecherous way, and she was amazed he could do both at the same time.

"So...nice job on the design of this place, Tramont."

"Why, thank you, Clearwater," Mason replied through tight lips. Tess could feel his back muscles strain beneath her hand.

Brenton shrugged. "Of course, the Country Club in Charlottesville is much better. My family prefers our membership there, but I'll admit there are some interesting sights here tonight." Brenton's eyes drifted back to Tess. She suddenly felt itchy all over. She gripped the back of Mason's coat as Brenton looked to her chest. "Nice necklace," he said.

She reached for the diamond. "Thank you. It was a gift."

Malory's sharp gaze descended on her then. "A gift? From *Mason*?"

Tess wasn't sure what happened inside her brain, but something about his ex's haughty indignation, the disdain with which she spit out his name, and the tension in Mason's muscles, made her mad as hell. Tess felt furious with this woman – who'd been with him for so long yet never looked at him like he was the best thing since sliced bread – and her next words popped out before she could stop them. "Yes, Mason did give me this. The diamond sparkles so brilliantly, it reminds me of him all the time. He has impeccable taste in gifts, don't you think?"

She felt guilty almost immediately, when she saw the look on Malory's face. The woman masked her pain as best she could, but Tess still witnessed her fury. She stiffened inside Mason's grasp.

Malory snorted and wrapped her hand around her escort's upper arm. "Come, Brenton. We need to mingle with other people."

"Sure, sure," Brenton agreed. He glanced down at the cleavage beneath Tess's necklace before winking at her. "Nice seeing you, Tess."

She encouraged her esophagus to control her stomach contents.

As the dynamic duo turned away, Mason clamped her harder to his side.

He started walking again, leading Tess to the back of the crowded room. She moved with him wordlessly. His body felt so rigid beside hers, she wasn't even sure if he breathed. When they crossed through a set of glass doors, exiting down the stone staircase into the warm night, he finally dragged air into his lungs. But he didn't stop walking.

"I'm sorry about that," he apologized, guiding her farther away.

"About what?"

"Malory and Brenton. I really wanted to avoid them."

Tess held tight to the back of Mason's coat, thankful for his solidity as she maneuvered the landscaped golf course in her heels. "It was a noble thought. But probably not reasonable, since the Catskills own the place."

"Yeah, I suppose." He kept walking, supporting her when her footing faltered.

"Where are we going, Mason?"

"There's a gazebo out here I want to show you. It's well built."

"Well built?"

"Yes."

She saw the gazebo in the distance. The sounds from the party quieted as they approached the sizeable octagonal structure. When they finally reached the gazebo steps, he released her. Tess's eyes drifted up the thick, smooth marble columns, extending up to the glass roof. "You're right," she told him. "This is well built."

He walked several feet away before turning to face her, staring in silence. She couldn't help noticing how the cut of the tuxedo framed his body in angles against the dark green backdrop of plush lawn. She'd come to know his body so well...the feel, the heat, the taste. She wished there was more light now, enough to see the subtle nuances of his face. But she could still see his eyes, how they fixed on hers, piercing even in the darkness. She felt each beat of her heart as he watched her.

The commotions of the ongoing gala were no more than gentle murmurs at this distance. Tess heard the chirping of frogs from the nearby lake, their soothing songs lending a soft soundtrack to the night. She drew her fingers to her necklace, running the diamond back and forth on the chain. "Mason, can I ask you something rather personal?"

The muscle in his jaw twitched. From the look in his eyes, she wasn't sure if he would answer. After several tense moments, he nodded.

"Why didn't you ever buy gifts for Malory?"

He didn't reply at all this time. He just kept staring at her.

Tess stilled, her fingers gripping the sparkly gem. "I guess I don't really understand it, since I know you're such a generous person."

"Generous? I've never been called that before."

"But you are generous in so many ways. Especially with your ideas and time. You always answered my business questions, always listened to my suggestions, and always paid attention to my ideas." Her arms fell to her sides. "Is it because your family didn't give gifts, so you thought it was unimportant for her?"

Mason ran a hand through his hair. "That would be the easy thing to say, wouldn't it? I could just blame it on my parents. But truthfully, I was an adult and I understood what I was doing. Giving gifts would have been appropriate, especially since we'd been together for so long."

"Yet you never gave her anything."

"No, I didn't. I just didn't care enough. I realize that now."

He took a step forward – with a positively predatory, devouring look in his eyes – and Tess felt a shiver run down her spine. She wasn't sure if people were allowed to look at other people like this. The only thing she knew for certain was that no one had ever looked at her the way he did right now. It both exhilarated and terrified her, and she stepped back on instinct, reaching behind her for support. Her hands found one of the gazebo's thick marble columns and she leaned against it, letting her bare spine touch the cool, smooth surface.

"Can I ask you something else?" she questioned, breathy with anticipation.

Still stalking silently forward, Mason nodded again.

"Why did you let me start buying gifts for your family?"

He stopped directly in front of her, the muscled wall of his chest mere inches away. She bit her lip as she met his eyes. He fixed her with a piercing stare while his deep voice moved across her skin. "I let you buy them gifts because I knew you were doing it for the right reasons. Malory hated my family. She didn't want us to have anything to do with them, and I had just let that happen. I hadn't been in contact with my brother or sister in years. I didn't want it to be that way."

Mason paused, reaching to her mouth to trace his thumb across her lower lip. He watched the movement intently as he continued. "Then one day, not long after you'd started working with me, you came bouncing into my office – with your ponytail bobbing around your shoulders and a beautiful smile curving these perfect pink lips – and you asked me about my family. I remember that moment like it was yesterday. I remember staring at you, not really sure where you'd come from, or how you'd come to be in my life, but knowing with absolutely certainty that you could fix everything. I *wanted* you to fix it, and you did. I started talking to Vanessa and Ian again right after you sent the first gift for her birthday."

Tess listened in awe. His voracious gaze held her in place, his body so close that she sweltered beneath his furnace-like heat. When he moved his hand to her face, drawing his fingers across her jaw, she locked her knees to keep from swaying.

"My sweet, beautiful Tess. I have a confession to make."

"Wh-what confession?"

"I don't give a damn about this gazebo. I just wanted to get you alone. I wanted to touch you with no one else watching." Mason traced the length of her neck, fingertips easing across the diamond before smoothing over the hint of her cleavage highlighted in shimmering red. "I missed you so much last night – the smell of your hair, the sound of your voice, the feel of your skin on mine. I wanted to get my hands on you the minute you arrived here tonight, to have you all to myself, to get this gorgeous dress crumpled onto the floor. It's been excruciating, not being able to touch you the way I want to."

His fingers slipped beneath the neckline of her gown, running just inside the edge. "But then, I got a taste of you on that dance floor," he groaned. "I got to hold you against me, to listen to your soft, panting breaths in my ear, to feel your body respond to mine. I damn near took you right there, in front of all those people. It was all I could do to restrain myself. And I'm not in the mood to practice restraint any longer."

Tess sighed as she gave in. Her hands pulled against his shoulders, urging his mouth down to hers. She traced her tongue across his lips, teasing him until he took control. His fingers slid across her arms and down her sides, settling on her hips, the heat of his flesh branding her through the thin material of her dress.

When his mouth dragged across her neck, nipping and suckling her sensitive skin, she could barely catch her breath. She clutched him to her, basking in every incredible sensation. Her eyes rolled upward to the dark sky. She saw the stars twinkling overhead, sparkling just for them. The beauty of it overwhelmed her, filling her heart with sheer happiness, reminding her to thank the heavens that she'd been given this moment – and every moment of the last few weeks – to live her dreams.

Giddy with joy, Tess whispered, "Baby?"

He growled against her throat. "Yes?"

"Since we're making confessions tonight, I should make one, too."

Mason raised his head to pin her eyes. "What's your confession?"

"It's about the crush I had on you when we first met."

"What about it?"

"Do you still want to know when it ended?"

"I thought it ended when you started dating Bob."

Tess shook her head. "No. Not then."

His brow rose. "When you were with Bryan?"

"No. Not even then."

Mason inched closer, his body pressing hers against the marble. "When did it end?"

"It didn't end. Not ever."

He stopped moving, stopped breathing.

Her entire body froze as she waited for him to respond.

Mason grabbed hold of her, his hands on either side of her face, grounding her to him. "Dear God, Tess. Are you telling me you've wanted me for *six solid years*?"

She swallowed hard. "Y-yes."

"But...why? Why didn't you say anything?"

"What was I supposed to say? It's not like I could have you. You were terminally unavailable."

Mason exhaled slowly before his forehead collapsed onto her shoulder. "Damn it. *Damn it.* So much time wasted. So much time. I don't want to waste another second." He looked back to her eyes. "Being without you last night killed me. I never want to be without you again. Never."

His mouth returned to hers, only harder this time, leaving no question that she belonged to him. Tess didn't have any desire to question it. She opened to the exploration of his eager tongue, threading her fingers into his hair as his fiery body imprinted itself on her skin. She lost herself in the moment, in the fantasy of *her* Mason, wrapped inside her arms, telling her in no uncertain terms that this was her home.

His hand trailed downward, across her hip and onto her thigh, but she paid little attention. She was too caught up in the heady desire of his kiss, in the decadent pleasure of their entwined tongues. When he pulled up her skirt, bunching the fabric in his fingers, she took the opportunity to wrap her freed leg around him. Mason grabbed her bare thigh and hitched it higher around his waist. He pushed the fingers of his other hand between them, tracing the laced edge of her exposed panties.

Tess moaned, clinging to him in utter desperation.

"I want to touch you. I want to feel you," he growled against her lips. His hand dipped beneath the lace, slipping lower. A moment later he delved into the hot sheath of her sex, first with one finger, then two.

She gasped and writhed against his palm.

Mason pressed the side of his face into hers, his rapid breaths tickling her ear. "Tell me about your crush," he demanded. "Tell me everything. Tell me how much you've wanted me."

"I wanted you...from the first moment...I saw you," she panted, focused on the sensation of his fingers moving in and out, back and forth.

"You wanted me to touch you like this?"

"Yes. *Yes.*"

"I love touching you." His skilled hand worked faster, sliding across her slick flesh. "I love how wet you always are for me. How your entire body begs to have me inside you."

She groaned, clinging to his shoulders while her hips rocked beyond control.

"Tell me how long you've wanted me, Tess."

She forced air into her lungs. "Every. Damn. Day. For. Six. Fucking. Years."

Mason smiled against her neck. "That's a long time." He sucked her earlobe into his mouth and bit down. "How many fantasies have you had about me? Over a hundred?"

"Over a thousand."

"A *thousand*? You've been busy."

"Yes," she admitted, too aroused to be ashamed.

He breathed in the scent of her hair. "I'll make them all come true. I swear I will." Pushing two fingers deep inside her, Mason pressed his thumb against her throbbing little circle of nerves.

Tess lost it. She cried out, her screams muffled by his mouth when his lips captured hers. She ground down onto his hand, her inner muscles contracting around his fingers. Grasping at his neck, she kissed him over and over while waiting for the thrumming of her body to stop. But it wouldn't. It just wouldn't.

Somehow, the insane orgasm he'd given her hadn't brought her any relief. It only made things worse. He'd simply set her on fire, making her quake and tremble and ache and burn. "Damn, I want you," she murmured, frantic hands running down his shoulders to his chest.

His gave her a roguish grin. "Later tonight. In our bed."

"Now."

"Tess..."

"Now, Mason! I want you *now*."

Her eager fingers found the waist of his pants and quickly freed his taut, straining erection. She pulled her dress higher, pushing her panties to the ground. Tess stopped moving and stared into his eyes. Her silence was both an invitation and a dare. He didn't say another word. He lifted her, pinned her against the marble column, and brought her down hard against him, filling her completely.

His sharp inhale echoed her own when he surged inside. Tess held his piercing gaze as he edged slowly out and back in again. "Now, you're right where you should be," she breathed, wrapping her legs fully around him, fisting her hands in his hair. "And by you, I mean *all* of you."

"That's entirely true. Tell me, does this count as a fantasy?"

"Absolutely."

"Only nine hundred ninety-nine to go."

"I beg your pardon. I said *over* a thousand."

Mason thrust in again, even deeper this time, the smooth, gliding sensation of flesh on flesh sending jolts of electricity throughout her body. "I'm so sorry I misspoke," he offered, lifting her knees higher, pushing up to hit the perfect spot inside her.

"*Oh*," she moaned. "You're forgiven."

Tess watched him as long as she could, while he took his sweet time moving in and out, rocking her hips against the cool stone at her back. She held onto his arms, feeling his biceps strain against the tuxedo material, feeling his strong fingers dig into the bared flesh of her thighs. She watched him as the astonishing sensations swelled higher and higher, until the blissful waves prepared to overtake her once again. Then she closed her eyes, leaning her head against the marble.

Mason grabbed her face in one hand, pulling her back. "Look at me, Tess. I want to see you."

She met his deep brown eyes. In the dark haze, in the starlit night, his focus on her was more powerful than ever before. Nothing compared to the desire she witnessed inside him.

He held her rapt gaze as he drove into her again and again, until he thrust one last time, pulling her hips down hard and emptying himself entirely. She watched the pleasure move over his face, watched the emotion in his eyes go deeper still. Knowing he'd found his release in the warmth of her body brought her to the edge so fast that she fell before she even thought to catch herself. She screamed, her body shuddering beyond control. Mason growled as he clamped her to him, arms banded around her like steel.

He held her against the stone, their bodies still entwined while they panted in synchronicity. He pressed his lips to her nose, her cheek, her neck. Tess sighed, spent and sated and warm and happy. She collapsed against him, her head rolling onto his shoulder.

The cool touch of the marble to her bare back made her smile. There was a time, not long ago, when she would have thought she was trapped between two marble columns. She used to think of Mason as a pillar of stone – handsome, hardened, structural perfection. But now she realized how wrong she'd been.

This incredible man holding onto her was strong and solid, but he wasn't cold or inanimate. He was deeply loving and intensely passionate. He wasn't a marble column, and she could snuggle up to him just fine.

When he finally released her, letting her toes touch the ground, Tess felt drunk with pleasure. After pulling up his zipper, Mason knelt down to find her panties and draw them back up to her hips. He straightened her dress, running his hands over her stomach and legs, smoothing out the fabric until everything was back in place. Then he knelt down, collecting her heels and easing them back onto her feet.

Tess laughed. "Did my shoes actually fall off?"

He peered up at her and smiled. "They did."

"I don't even remember that."

Mason stood, aligning their bodies. "I remember everything."

She pressed her chest to his. "I already want you again."

"Such an appetite, Miss Troy."

"Only for you, Mr. Tramont."

He cupped her face, holding her steady. "This is the beginning for us, Tess. We're starting over fresh. Right now. No rules. No limits. Just tell me you'll come home with me. Please tell me you'll come home."

She stared into him, knowing what she wanted to say. Knowing how tired she was of hiding her insane feelings for this wondrous man. But she was also painfully aware of another couple stumbling toward the gazebo, touching and talking and giggling as they came.

Mason noticed the intruders at the same time. He grabbed her hand, pulling her around the side of the large octagon. They circled back toward the party as the new couple reached the gazebo stairs and started kissing.

Tess tiptoed beside him as best she could in her heels. "Yikes, that was close. Do you think they saw us?"

He shook his head. "No, we're okay."

She exhaled as noises from the party escalated. "Thank goodness. I wouldn't want to ruin your good reputation, not with so many new clients here tonight."

"Are you kidding? I barely kept myself from attacking you on the dance floor. I would have taken you against the bar in the main banquet hall if I thought I'd have enough time to satisfy you properly before security threw us out."

She leaned into him as she laughed, only straightening when they reached the back doors to the main room. An elderly gentleman stood on the staircase, puffing a cigar. She nodded at the distinguished-looking man, attempting formality. When she eased one foot onto the steps, Mason tugged on her hand. She pivoted to meet his earnest eyes.

"Tess. I promise I'm not going to hound you about us anymore tonight. You know what I want. You know the future I see, with the two of us together. So now, I'm going to go to the bar and get us drinks. I'm going to spend the rest of the evening enjoying your lovely company. And when I drive home later, I hope you'll be in the seat beside me."

She didn't have time to respond before Mason gave her a tender smile, pressed a gentle kiss to her lips, and walked up the steps. She stood still for a moment, watching him disappear into the crowd. Her legs swayed as she climbed the stairs, entering the main room in a daze.

She'd come here alone tonight. But she didn't have to be alone anymore. Tonight, she would go home with Mason. She never had to be without him again.

Tess smiled as she strolled, a secret smile of joy and contentment and love, her entire body floating. She wasn't paying enough attention to her surroundings, and floated right into a severely Botoxed woman who reeked of scotch. "I'm so sorry," Tess offered.

The woman eyed her while attempting to frown.

Tess flushed, wondering how disheveled she must look after her recent columnar encounter. "Excuse me, please," she said, moving past the woman to look for the restroom.

She found it, although the ladies' lounge was more of a living room, nearly as big as the Pooch Palace. She felt dwarfed the moment she stepped inside, but the space did offer refuge from the sights and sounds of the ongoing gala. After using the facilities and tending to her appearance, she stood alone in the huge room.

Tess allowed herself a moment's respite by flopping on one of the over-stuffed sofas, resting her head back and closing her eyes. She could still smell Mason's spicy scent on her dress, could still feel his arm around her waist where it had been most of the night. Her feet throbbed inside her heels, but she knew he would rub them for her when they got home.

Home.

Their home, together.

"So, you're Mason's secretary."

Her eyes popped open. She stared up into Malory Catskill's angular face. Tess looked around the still-empty room, wondering where the stealthy creature had come from. She swallowed against the sudden dryness in her throat. "No, I'm not his secretary anymore."

"Hmm. Did he fire you?"

Tess stood from the couch, hands shaking as she backed toward the door. "Not that it's any of your business, but I resigned."

"You quit? Why? Did he lie to you? Use you?"

Tess shook her head, disgusted that this woman – who had been in Mason's arms just two short months ago – could stand here and speak so foully about him. "Mason would never lie to me. He would never use me. I know him. He's an incredible person, and I don't care to listen to this, so..."

"Did he tell you about the pregnancy?"

Tess's feet stilled. "Pregnancy? What pregnancy?"

"*Our* pregnancy." Malory's hand fluttered to her abdomen, bony fingers stroking her still-flat belly.

Tess stared at the movement for a long minute. Then she looked back to Malory's face, watching a smile spread her thin lips. The shrew nodded in confirmation. Tess stood in a stupor, unable to believe what was happening. Somehow, some way, Malory had managed to tell her something even worse than her worst fears.

Her heart sank. It sank so far that Tess wasn't sure she would ever find it again.

"Mason's not very forthcoming, is he?" Malory asked with a distinct note of satisfaction. "He never is. Plays things very close to the vest, that one. But you know him *so well*, so I'm sure everything will turn out just fine between you two." With those words, Malory brushed past her and out the door, heels clicking brusquely on the polished floors.

Tess stood in the empty room, stunned. Beyond stunned.

Malory is going to have Mason's baby.

That's it.

He will be connected to her forever.

Tess's heartbeat thrummed in her ears, pounding so fast she thought it would burst from her skin. Nausea swept over her, roiling through her gut, and she couldn't think anymore. She got the hell out of there. Out of the bathroom, through the crowd, and toward the front doors, as fast as her legs could move in her form-fitting gown.

She nearly made it outside when a hand caught hers. David stood beside her, concern etched on his face. "Tess? What are you doing?"

"Leaving."

"Why?"

She shook her head. "I just...I have to go. Please let me go."

She attempted escape but David urged her back. "Damn, Tess. What did Mason do?"

The tears came, hot and salty, to her eyes. She couldn't cry here. She wouldn't. "Goodbye, David." Pulling away, she ran for her car.

AN HOUR LATER, Annabelle's pants were soaked through to her skin. Tess had apologized a hundred times for it. But she still couldn't stop crying as she lay on the couch in her friend's apartment with her head in Belle's lap.

"Quit saying sorry, Tess. I have other pants. Just get it all out."

She let more tears fall. She couldn't have stopped them anyway.

Belle petted her hair. "Are you absolutely sure the witch didn't just make up the pregnancy?"

"Why would she? That wouldn't make any sense, not when Mason was so close by. All I had to do was ask him about it."

"But you didn't ask him."

"No! What would be the point? To watch him go back to her in front of my eyes?"

"You know that is a completely irrational thought, right? He wouldn't do that, he..."

Tess's phone rang, buzzing against the coffee table and cutting off Belle's words. She glanced over to see the picture of Mason's face on the screen.

"That's ten times in the past hour, Tess. He's not going to leave you alone."

"I know. I know I have to talk to him, just...not right now."

"Maybe he wants to apologize."

"And what would I say? Oh, that's okay, Mason. It's no big deal that you didn't tell me your ex is pregnant with your baby. Holy hell. I mean, maybe I could actually forgive him for keeping something this monumental a secret. Maybe I could chalk it up to the fact that his parents were cold and emotionless and never taught him to open his heart, so he's spent his whole life collecting blankets to make himself warm. Maybe I could reason all of that out and be fine with it. But how on earth am I supposed to compete with a Millionaire Baby Mama?"

Tess sat up, brushing away the melted mascara on her cheeks. "I don't think I can do it. I can't compete with that."

"Yes, you can – if that was even an issue. But it's not, because there is no competition," Belle insisted, staring into Tess's red-rimmed eyes. "You're not exactly thinking clearly right now, honey. I know this is a lot to absorb and I know you're in a tailspin. But you've got to realize, deep down, that Mason doesn't want her. He only wants you."

"It doesn't matter. He's going to be a dad. Eventually, that reality is going to sink in. And Malory will always be there. Forever."

Belle sighed and grabbed her hand. "What are you going to do?"

"I don't know. I just...I feel so lost, Belle."

"Do you want to know what I think?"

"God, yes. Please tell me. I'll do anything you say."

"I say you need to get out of town for a few days."

Tess sniffled. "Really? You want me to leave? What about you? I'm supposed to start helping you at the Palace. That was the whole purpose of me quitting my other job."

Belle shrugged. "You haven't had a vacation in a long time. You've worked every single day for two straight years – during the week with Mason and on the weekends at the Palace – and every night you took classes and studied. Then, after two years of complete and utter stress, you chose to enter into a bizarre, highly emotional affair with your boss that you had no chance of coming away from unscathed. Now, you simply need to leave. I'll manage another week on my own. You need this time to get away and get your head on straight."

"But I don't know if it will ever be straight again."

"It will be. You just have some thinking to do."

Tess stared at her dearest friend, her mind working to wrap around this new plan. It was brilliant, really. A few days alone. A few days to breathe, all by herself. Without Mason.

On cue, her phone rang again. She glanced over to see his face on the screen. With quivering fingers, she grasped the phone and took a deep breath in. "Hello?"

Mason exhaled roughly on the other end. "Oh, *thank God*. Where are you, Tess? Are you okay?"

"D-didn't David tell you I was leaving the gala?"

"He did, I just...I don't understand it."

More tears streamed down her face. "I'm sorry I left so abruptly. Something came up."

"What is it?"

"I, um, I have to leave town. For a few days."

"*Leave town*? Where are you going? Is everything okay?"

"I – I hope it'll be fine. It'll just take some time. I'll call you when I get back."

"Tess..."

"I'll talk to you soon, Mason."

She shut the phone off and set it back on the table. The fear and panic in his voice still rang in her ears. That may have been the worst conversation she'd ever had in her life. Other than the one she'd had with Malory earlier. And the next one she would have to have with Mason.

Belle patted her hand. "You did good, kiddo. Do you want to stay the night?"

"No. Thank you, but I think I should leave right away."

"You know you can call me anytime. I'd go with you if I could."

"I wish you could come. You're always the voice of reason. Not an emotional wreck like me."

"A very lovely emotional wreck."

Tess laughed through her tears.

18

LIFE DOESN'T ALWAYS TAKE YOU WHERE YOU THINK IT WILL

Mason pulled his Mercedes up to the Pooch Palace first thing Monday morning. He was supposed to be at work, but he couldn't imagine entering that building without Tess. He'd spent yesterday walking around like a zombie, wondering why in the hell she'd run out of the gala the night before. She'd told him on the phone that she needed to leave town for a few days, but nothing about that made any sense.

He just couldn't figure out what went wrong. Things felt so perfect between them Saturday night and he truly believed she would be in the car with him when he drove home. She'd admitted she still had her crush; she'd had it all six years they'd worked together. And even though it wasn't love, Mason hoped it might be, one day.

But then she left, and he hadn't had a moment's peace since. He couldn't have any peace again. Not until he had her back in his arms.

Pulling his keys from the ignition, Mason stepped out of the car and walked up the sidewalk to the porch-wrapped pink house. He climbed the stairs, holding his breath as he opened the front door, wanting her to simply appear before him. She didn't.

Annabelle stood behind the tall front desk, turning when she heard the overhead bell jingle. She met his eyes and stilled.

"Hi, Belle."

"Hi, Mason."

He exhaled, grateful the woman spoke to him. "I don't suppose she's back yet? From wherever she went?"

"No. Sorry."

He shook his head, moving forward until he arrived at the other side of the desk. "It was worth a shot."

Belle studied him. "I am glad you came by, though."

"Yeah? Why's that?"

"I wanted to thank you for building us the dog gym. It's brought in lots of new clients and the pooches love it. It's just what we wanted."

"I'm glad I could help your business. Tess has done so much for mine."

"Well, I still wanted to say thanks."

Mason couldn't keep up this charade of formality any longer. He leaned forward on the desktop. "God, Belle, please help me. I'm worried as hell about her. She ran out of the gala Saturday without saying anything to me, and she was so cryptic over the phone that night. I know she left town but she didn't say why. I've got the worst scenarios running around in my head, and I've tried calling again and again, but she won't answer. Please tell me she's really okay."

"She's really okay. I promise."

His shoulders dropped on a sigh. "Thank you for that."

"Sure thing," Belle answered, chewing on her lip. "Now, what about you? Are you okay?"

Mason clenched his hands together on the tall desk, his knuckles whitening. "I'm...I'm miserable."

She gave him a sympathetic smile. "I can see that."

"It's that obvious?"

"Yeah."

"Hell, I know it is. It's just...I need her here with me. I have to get her back. Do you know why she left?"

"I do."

"Does it have something to do with me? With us?"

Belle grimaced as she nodded.

He leaned closer. "Will you please tell me what it is?"

"I can't. You guys have to work that out on your own."

"But don't you see? We can't work anything out if I can't talk to her. Will you at least tell me where she is?"

"I can't do that, either."

Mason raked a hand through his hair and blew out a harsh breath.

"Look, I'm sorry. I truly am," Belle offered. "I've been your advocate through all of this, and believe me, I know what a mess Tess can be. I want you guys to work out, for my own sanity as much as yours. She loves you more than life itself, and if you don't end up together, she'll be miserable forever."

His jaw unhinged. "What did you just say?"

"Um, which part?"

"The part where you said she loves me."

"What about it?"

"You said she loves me more than *life itself*."

"Yup. I did say that."

"And you're sure?"

"Pretty damn sure. I just figured you already knew, since it's so obvious."

"Good Lord. How long has she been in love with me?"

"I don't know; what day did she start working for you, exactly?"

Mason glanced down to his clasped hands. "Damn, I'm slow."

"Excuse me?"

He looked back to her. "Nothing."

Belle grinned. "You know, that was a huge mistake I just made, when I *accidentally* told you that Tess is head-over-heels, insatiably, ridiculously, desperately in love with you, and has been for six solid years. I mean, I shouldn't have said that at all, and obviously it was just a slip of the tongue, so I'm thinking it could be our little secret."

"Sure, Belle. It'll be our secret. Can you just tell me when she'll be back?"

"Saturday. She'll be working here all day."

Mason straightened. "Saturday. Okay. Thank you. For everything."

"You're welcome. I take it you'll be around?"

"Absolutely."

"Even though Tess is stubborn as hell and flies off the handle periodically and becomes irrational at the most inopportune moments?"

He chuckled. "Yes."

"You're going to have your hands full with her. You know that, right?"

"I look forward to it."

An air of satisfaction lit Belle's face. "Good."

He nodded, turned, and walked out of the door. When his feet hit the front steps, Mason stared down at his Mercedes. He didn't want to go back to work without Tess. He didn't want to do anything without her. He missed her like crazy and it hurt like hell.

At least he knew for certain that she loved him. Hopefully, it would be enough to fix whatever was wrong. Now he just had to figure out how to get through the next five days without her.

~

WHEN TESS LEFT Richmond Saturday night after the gala, Belle had given her simple instructions: don't talk to anyone, just be alone and think.

The first thing Tess did, after checking into her hotel room in Washington, D.C., was collapse on the bed and start crying again. She cried non-stop for nearly a day, then passed out cold and slept for twelve hours. When she woke up, she forced herself to leave the hotel. Over the next couple of days, she went to the monuments and visited the art galleries. She found the cutest little coffee shop, where she could sit by herself at a tall table and drink a latte with extra sugar.

Usually, she loved it up here. She'd visited D.C. many times before, and the springtime trees and flowers were her favorites. She thought she had the chance to be happy on this little vacation. Yet she couldn't be, since the only thing she wanted was to be with Mason.

When she strolled through the museums, she wished she could hold his hand and ask what he thought of the displays. When she lounged at the coffee shop, she imagined him sitting across from her. She dreamed of inviting Ian to meet them, so they could all talk and laugh and spend time together. When she lay on the big, cold bed in her hotel room, she wanted to leave, to go back to Richmond and walk straight into Mason's house, knowing it was actually home. Their home, together.

He'd asked her to do just that, during the gala. He'd asked her to come home with him and she'd wanted nothing more. That night had been magical and perfect, showing her the life she'd always hoped for.

Now, after everything that happened, Tess knew two things for certain. The first thing was that Mason wanted to be with her. He'd made it perfectly clear at the gala, and honestly, over the entire last month. She knew he wanted her and no one else. The second thing was that she loved him with her whole heart. She would always love him, no matter what.

Knowing these two things forced her to acknowledge that the reason she'd been alone here all week wasn't because of Mason.

It was because of her.

On Friday evening, after six days wandering the city, Tess found herself back at the hotel. She sat on her bed, staring out the window. Tomorrow was Saturday, and she would return to the real world first thing in the morning. Part of her felt excited go home, even with the messy thoughts still occupying her mind. The other part knew she needed to resolve this muddle of emotions before she could go anywhere.

She'd tried to think in fits and spurts all week, yet every time she tried, she felt even more emotionally overwhelmed than usual. She figured it must be because of what had happened at the party. Everything before Malory found her in the ladies' room had been akin to utopia. Everything after Malory's toilet speech left Tess spinning out of control. She'd panicked and done the exact wrong thing. She'd run away.

Now, one emotion usurped all her others. *Guilt*. She felt guilty as hell for running away from her problems, from her fears, and from the man she loved.

The puzzling thing was that Annabelle was the one who'd told her to run. Belle – who'd encouraged Tess to be with Mason all along – had, in the end, told her to leave. And after taking her advice, and spending the past six days so miserably alone and physically drained that she'd actually woken up sick to her stomach for the last two, Tess realized her friend had played her perfectly.

"You're a genius, Belle," she whispered to herself. "You told me to run so I would understand that it was wrong thing to do."

Tess shook her head at her friend's brilliance. Then her stomach grumbled again. She rubbed her belly to calm it down. Her body was finally revolting against her after all the stress she'd put it through in the last two years. Not to mention the emotional overload of the last month.

But her stomach would just have to relax right now, because she had serious work to do. Tomorrow, she would return to Richmond, to the Pooch Palace, and to real life. Consequently, she only had this one night to find some sense of peace with her life.

As she stared out of her hotel window, watching the sun sink between two skyscrapers, she returned to the two things she knew with absolute certainty: Mason wanted to be with her, and she loved him no matter what. Her shoulders fell from her ears, those two thoughts making her mind clearer now than it had been in over a month.

She forced herself to think back to that night at the gala, to the moment when Malory told her she was pregnant. Tess's gut roiled again, just as it had then. She could still feel that pain and panic, but she pushed it down, working to keep her emotions at bay.

"Come on, Troy," she urged aloud. "Use your brain and figure this out. Start at the beginning, first things first. Possible life outcome number one: Malory could have been lying about the pregnancy."

Tess paused to consider that thought. It would certainly be the happiest scenario, but it didn't make sense. All she would have had to do was walk up to Mason and ask if Malory was pregnant. He would have denied it, and said his ex was crazy and vindictive, and that would have driven an even bigger wedge between him and the shrew.

Tess wished it could have happened that way. But she'd seen how Malory looked at him in the office, with such hunger in her eyes. She'd witnessed the pain on Malory's face at the gala when she saw Tess's necklace. The shrew definitely still had feelings for Mason. She wouldn't do anything to widen the rift between them.

"Okay, then. Scenario number two is that Malory is pregnant, but she never told Mason about the baby, so he never knew to tell me."

As comforting as that sounded, it didn't make sense, either. Being pregnant would help Malory's cause. She would definitely share that information.

Tess stilled, hesitant to move on. "That brings me to possibility number three," she forced herself to say. "Which is that Mason knew Malory was pregnant and chose not to tell me."

This was the possibility that hurt the most when Tess heard the news. But now, after taking time to clear her head, she acknowledged something she'd truly always known: Mason would never hurt her. Not on purpose. If anything, he would protect her at all costs.

There had to be a reason he didn't tell her about the pregnancy. She just needed to put herself in his shoes and figure out what that was.

Tess continued staring out of the now-dark window to the city below. The sun had fallen and she could see all the lights stretching into the night. Her mind drifted back to the day she'd sat with Mason at the restaurant, when she'd given him her resignation. They'd been staring at each other across the table, with him insisting he wanted to date her. She couldn't believe her ears at the time, so she'd asked him what had happened between him and Malory.

He probably didn't think he could afford to tell her then. After all, Tess hadn't agreed to date him yet, and he had no idea if their relationship would ever get far enough, or last long enough, for the pregnancy to matter. On top of that, she never actually offered him a relationship.

"I offered to be his love coach instead. I spent a week acting out my stupid revenge, and then I put the icing on the cake by making him shovel dog crap. That should have ended any possibility of a relationship between us."

Her heart squeezed with that horrifying thought. She wasn't entirely sure why he came back to her after what she'd done. Any logical man would have turned and run screaming in the opposite direction. But her normally robotic boss wasn't being logical at that moment. Something emotional already existed between them. He may not have understood it completely, but it was enough to bring him back.

Tess recalled their first night together, when she'd stood in Mason's living room and looked out into his backyard. She remembered how he'd come up behind her, wrapped his arms around her, and breathed in deep, like he wanted to inhale her into his body. He was so sweet and kind, worrying that their physical intimacy was progressing too fast, even though he obviously wanted her just as much as she wanted him.

She cringed, recalling his frustration when she'd begged him to confide in her about Malory that night. Tess realized now that he couldn't have told her then. Not when they'd only just said their apologies to each other for the mess they'd made the week before.

"I thought his refusal to confide in me meant he still had feelings for Malory, so I freaked out and told him I only wanted an affair." Tess huffed out a breath. "My Lord, it's amazing the two of us managed to get together at all."

It was almost funny, how badly they'd messed things up. Once she'd insisted on them having an affair, Mason couldn't risk telling her the truth. She'd made it clear she would only be with him for three weeks, and if he'd tried to tell her the truth during those few precious days, he would never have been able to convince her of the possibility of a future between them – a future he desperately wanted.

Tess's eyes brimmed with moisture. "He tried so hard to show me how good our life could be together. He worked and worked at it, but I was so caught up in my own anxieties. I never looked past my fears to see that Mason was scared, too."

Brushing at her tears, she considered his life: how cold and sterile his parents were; how he'd never really known what it was like to be deeply loved and cared for; how he'd chosen to stay with a woman who gave him no warmth and then wandered through the world collecting blankets; how he'd spent all his time proving his strength through marble and stone; and how Malory had taken the last bit of human connection away from him when she'd separated him from his brother and sister.

"Mason was terrified," Tess whispered, her voice trembling as much as her body. "Terrified of losing what we'd found in each other, of what he'd found in me. He told me I was the only person who'd ever looked at him like he could do no wrong, and that he didn't deserve it, since he wasn't perfect. I didn't know why he said that at the time, but I see now. He was too scared to tell me the truth about Malory. Which made me too scared to let him any further into my heart."

Tess laughed through her tears. "But I did let him further into my heart, since there was no way to stop it. Mason is my soulmate. I know that. I just never imagined there would come a day when he would know it, too. But I think he does, or he could. If only he can find it in his heart to forgive me for running away."

She straightened on the bed, pushing her loose curls behind her shoulders. "I don't know how we're going to handle this situation with Malory. But I do know, as long as we're together, we can do anything."

Right at this moment, the peace that wound its arms around her was unlike anything Tess had ever known. Her entire body relaxed. She could practically feel Mason's warmth against her skin.

When her phone rang on the bed beside her, she startled. She grasped for it, hoping it was Mason. The face on the screen wasn't his, but that was okay. Tess still looked forward to the human contact.

She pressed the phone to her ear. "Regina? Is that you?"

"Hey, Tess! You *are* alive."

"Yes, I'm alive. Man, it's good to hear your voice."

"Yours, too. I called a few days ago, but you didn't answer."

"I'm sorry about that. It's been a really weird week. I'm also sorry I didn't get to see you at the Country Club gala last Saturday."

"I really wanted to be there, believe me. I wish I'd felt better. David wanted to stay home with me, but I told him he had to go. I knew how important it was to the business and I didn't feel up to it."

"Why? Are you sick?"

Regina laughed. "No. I'm pregnant."

"You're *pregnant*? Oh, my goodness! I'm so happy for you!"

"Thanks. David and I are thrilled. I just found out very recently. It's way early, but those pregnancy tests work so fast these days. And not that you really want to know this, but morning sickness blows. I hug my toilet bowl so much, we've developed a relationship."

"Wow. That's disgusting and cool at the same time. You have to call me constantly. I want to know everything."

"I will. But where will I be able to reach you? At Mason's house, maybe?"

Tess stilled. "H-how much do you know about us?"

"Not much, really. I just know you left him at the gala and then left town. I'm thinking something pretty bad happened."

"I...I can't say anything about it yet. I'm sorry."

"I understand. Just tell me – did Mason hurt you?"

"No! God, no. He would never hurt me. I left because of *me*, because I needed time to come to terms with a few things."

"Okay. I'm not going to bug you to talk about it if you don't want to. But there are things happening here that I think you should know."

"Yeah? Like what?"

"Like Mason's changed, Tess. He's completely different now."

"Different? How so?"

"Well, he left his office door open this whole week, and yesterday he walked around to people's desks to ask how they're doing. I didn't even know Mason Tramont could carry on a conversation, and there he was, making people smile and laugh. Also, he and Janice have been getting along famously. It's like she's his long-lost mother. He came into the office late Monday morning, looking like something the cat dragged in, and Janice started fussing all over him. I expected him to pull away, but he didn't. Now, she gives him advice and he just listens. I swear I'm waiting for the moment when she licks her thumb and uses it to wipe something off of his face. I think he'd let her do it. It's kind of creepy, really."

Tess giggled. "I'd like to see that."

"Yeah, well...on top of all that, there's the gifts."

"Gifts?"

"He gave everyone at the office a bonus – a share of profit for the success of the business. He also had Janice send out a memo saying everyone would get birthday and holiday bonuses, too. And that's not even the most amazing thing. You won't believe this, but he actually *apologized* to me."

"He apologized?"

"Yes. He said he was sorry if he ever made me uncomfortable, or did anything to make me doubt his respect for me or you. He said you and I have always been the backbone of the office and he never wanted me to forget that. And I just stared at him, with my mouth hanging open, while he smiled at me. I swear, I don't know what you did to him, but he really has changed. He's become...human."

Tess shook her head, knowing Mason hadn't changed at all. He'd just finally decided to show people his true self – the mushy marshmallow beneath the crusty shell. She smiled wildly, aching to throw her arms around him.

"I've got to admit, I actually like him now," Regina confessed. "And I never thought in a million years that I would do this, but I'm going to plead his case. I can see he's nuts about you, and I think you two will be great together. I just have to ask one thing: how do *you* feel about *him*?"

Tess gripped tight to the phone. "Honestly?"

"Please."

"I love him like crazy."

"Well, thank God! I definitely need double dates with you guys! This baby growing inside me is making me insanely emotional. If I don't get double dates, I may throw an honest-to-goodness hissy fit."

"I want double dates, too. I swear. And I promise I'll do everything I can to make them happen."

"Perfect. Now come home soon."

"I will, Regina."

"Okay. I love you, you know."

"I do know. I love you, too. Thanks for everything."

"Anytime. Bye, Tess."

"Bye."

Tess turned off the phone and flopped back on the bed. The diamond on her neck fell into the hollow of her throat and she reached for it. She remembered the night Mason gave her the sparkly gem. She remembered lying in bed with him afterwards, spent and giddy after fulfilling her Wild West fantasy. Four weeks ago, she'd started an affair with her boss in order to fulfill as many fantasies as she could. But what she truly wanted wasn't a fantasy at all.

What Tess wanted, what she desired most, was a home. A home with Mason. Not a fantasy home where everything was perfect – because he wasn't perfect and she certainly wasn't perfect – but a real home, with two people who tried to love each other the best they could.

God, she wanted to run to him right now. She wanted to talk to him and apologize to him and hold him and love him. But she was so far away, and she was so damn tired. Her eyes closed for just a moment and the exhaustion of her body took over. She fell asleep instantly.

Tess woke at three in the morning with her stomach roiling again. Pressing her lips together, she shot out of the bed and into the bathroom, having just enough time to kneel and raise the toilet seat before heaving. When she swore her toes had come up through her throat, and there could be nothing left for her to expel, she collapsed back against the side of the bathtub and groaned. She hadn't eaten much and couldn't understand what would cause her body's unseemly behavior.

Regina's words bombarded her mind then, bringing a flood of understanding with them.

Morning sickness blows.

All the air rushed from Tess's lungs.

"Oh, holy hell," she croaked.

~

TESS MADE it to the Pooch Palace later that morning without smashing into any other cars. No small miracle, considering all the times she'd caught herself staring at the pharmacy bag in her front seat – the one that carried a three-pack of pregnancy tests. Hopping out of her Bug, she grabbed the bag and sprinted inside the building and into her office. She opened her desk drawer and tossed everything inside. She couldn't go through with that whole pee-on-a-stick thing. Not yet. She had a business to run.

In mere moments, customers filled the house, surrounding her with dogs. Tess did her best to concentrate, working with determination all morning. She didn't drum up the nerve to take the first test until after lunch. She followed the directions on the box to the letter. When she finally looked down at the little telltale window after the specified amount of time had passed, the pink sign had gone from a minus to a plus.

"Well, that could be a mistake," she considered, understanding it was necessary to be very sure about things before freaking out.

She set the stick on her desk and took the dogs out to the gym. She concentrated wholly on watching them play. Two hours later, she forced herself to pee on the second stick. It did the same thing as the first one.

"Hmm," she pondered, setting the sticks side-by-side. "It is possible they could both be wrong." She put on a smiley face and tended to her customers until the end of the day, when all the pooches were gone except for Tug. Ms. Travers had asked Tess to keep Tug a few minutes extra because she was going to an early dinner with Mr. Wilks, so Tess had some time to herself.

Leading Tug into her office, she patted the Great Dane on the head and told him to stay. After all, she needed his support. She went into the bathroom with stick number three. When she returned, she didn't look at the test. She set it on the desk and sat down in her chair. She stared at Tug and he stared back. Several moments later, Tess took a deep breath. "Third time's a charm," she assured the pup before turning to glance at the little window.

A pink plus sign.

She threw her arms up and started yelling. "Well doesn't that figure! He's good at everything he does! I should have known he would be ultra-virile too!"

Tug barked.

Tess refocused on him. "Sorry, boy. I didn't mean to scare you. It's just... he's got two women pregnant at the same time! And I'm one of them!"

The Dane's big, soulful eyes stared into her.

"What am I going to do now, Tug?"

He woofed.

"You're right. I should call Annabelle."

Tess picked up her cell and dialed the number.

Belle's voice was bright and cheery. "Hey, honey, how are you?"

"Fertile."

"Excuse me?"

"I'm knocked up. Got a bun in the oven. Totally, utterly pregnant."

No answer came from the other end.

"Belle? You there?"

"Oh...my...great...googly-moogly."

"I don't think those are real words."

"Tess! You're *pregnant*? Holy crap!"

"How did this even happen, Belle? I thought Mason and I were careful. Well, I mean, we were kinda careful. In the beginning. Sort of. Sometimes." Tess pinched her eyelids shut and cringed. "Oh my Lord, we were almost never careful! We were terrible! Really, really terrible!"

"If it helps, I don't think it would matter if he wore condoms of steel. As much as you guys went at it, they were bound to fail. It's the law of averages."

"Yeah, but now he has *two* baby mamas."

"Try not to think of it that way."

"Damn it! When did my life become a reality TV show?"

"I'd say right when you decided to take revenge on your boss."

Tess shook her head, trying to concentrate on breathing. *Inhale. Exhale. Mason's baby needs oxygen. You're going to be a mom.*

"Um, Tess...you and I are best friends, right?"

"God, yes. We're family, Belle. I honestly don't think I'd make it through life without you."

"Then can I ask you a ridiculously personal question?"

"I don't see why not."

"When did you have your last period?"

"Why? Do you think I should have realized this sooner?"

"No, not at all. I'm just curious."

"Well, I remember it started a few days before I gave Mason my resignation, and finished sometime during that whole revenge-week, and then I had so much on my mind that I just didn't think about it anymore. I didn't even realize I was late, I mean, sometimes I'm a little late and it doesn't mean anything and..." Tess's words trailed off as she listened to her friend's muffled giggles. "Annabelle! Are you *laughing* at me?"

"I'm – I'm sorry. It's just that I was watching one of those baby shows the other day and they were talking about how they decide on a woman's due date and how they start counting the pregnancy from the first day of her last period, even though conception is later…"

"Dude! I'm dying here. Please get to the point."

"The point, my dear friend, is that the day you started your revenge plan against Mason, you were technically already pregnant with his baby."

Tess's mouth fell open. "Well…that doesn't sound right at all."

"I know! But you've got to admit it's a little funny."

"Belle!"

"Sorry. I'm not going to laugh anymore, I swear. I'm just overwhelmed."

"*You're* overwhelmed?"

"Oh, honey, I don't know what to say. I wish I could give you a hug right now, because I can't imagine what you're going through. Are you okay?"

Tess's hand drifted down to her stomach. She stilled, feeling her heart pound inside her chest, instantly amazed by the thought of a new little heartbeat pulsing inside her. "You know what? I am okay. I know this pregnancy is probably way too much, way too soon. I know it probably never should have happened, and I know it adds a whole new level of complicated, but…"

"But what?"

She leaned back in her chair. A soft smile found its way to her lips. "But I already love this baby. I love this baby so much."

"Are you going to tell the father?"

"I can just see our little boy now, Belle. He'll be charming and adorable, with dark hair and gorgeous brown eyes, just like his dad." She sighed, her shoulders dropping. "But I bet Malory's baby will be gorgeous, too. She's got that whole leggy model thing going on…"

"Tess, I don't care if Malory's baby comes out wearing a tiara and your baby looks like Shrek. Mason needs to know you're pregnant. And he damn well needs to hear from your own lips how much you love him."

"I know. Don't worry. I'm going to tell him everything. I had a lot of time to think while I was on that little vacation you sent me to."

"Yeah? Aside from finding out you're pregnant, how did your week go?"

"Really, really good. That was some serious voodoo reverse psychology you pulled, telling me to run away."

"Well, unfortunately, sometimes you have to do a thing in order to realize it's the wrong thing to do."

"You're amazing. You should have been a psychiatrist."

"I don't know about that. But I'd love to hear what you realized while you were gone."

"I just…I finally realized all the mistakes I'd made these past weeks, and especially the night of the gala. Mason is my home and I shouldn't have run away from him. Instead of trying to work on our problems, I took off at the first sign of trouble. I shouldn't have done that. I don't know if he'll be able to forgive me for it."

"Tess, Mason loves you."

"I think he does, but he's never actually said it."

"Dear Lord, have you even *looked* at the man? He came here this past Monday, trying to find you. And no, I didn't tell him anything about where you'd gone or why, but I did get a good look at his lovesick face. There's no way anyone could see him and *not* know how much he loves you. He's practically wearing a sign around his neck."

Tess grinned as a tear wandered down her cheek. "Then do you think he can forgive me for running away?"

"The last time I checked, love was as much about forgiveness as anything."

"Thank you, Belle. For standing by me through all of this."

"I'll stand by you through everything. You know that."

"Even the mess that will be Mason, Malory, me, and two babies?"

"Absolutely. People do this stuff nowadays. Families are messy. There's yours and mine and ours, and Mason will love both kids. But he'll only love one woman. *You.*"

Tess closed her eyes, allowing another tear to fall. "You know, when Malory told me she was pregnant, it was worse than my worst nightmare. But now, I can finally accept that he'll always have some feelings for her. They were together for so long, and they're going to have a child, and it's unrealistic to expect him to not feel anything. But I don't think that means he'll go back to her, and I don't think the feelings he has for her will be anything like what he feels for me. I believe I can let those fears go now and concentrate on the future. If Mason loves me even half as much as I love him…"

"He loves you maniacally."

"…then this is all going to be okay."

Belle sighed across the phone. "Oh, thank goodness. I love it when you see reason. And it only took you one week."

"Thanks for making me run."

"No problem. Now will you please run toward Mason, instead of away?"

"I will. I'm going to go find him now."

"Do that. Please, please do that."

"I love you, kiddo."

"Love you, too."

"Thank you, Belle. Really, thank you for everything."

"That's nice. Now stop talking to me and go! Go find him!"

"Okay! Don't you know it's bad luck to yell at a pregnant lady?"

"You totally just made that up."

"Yes, I did. I'm going."

"Good luck, honey. You know I'm rooting for you."

"I do. Bye, Belle."

"Bye."

Tess turned off her phone and stood, watching Tug's big brown eyes follow her every move. "Come on, sweet boy," she said, grabbing his leash.

She made it out of her office and into the front room before the bell above the door rang. Ms. Travers walked in, grinning as she looked around. "Oh, hello Tess. Hope I'm not too late."

"It's no problem. I really enjoyed having Tug's company."

Ms. Travers kept smiling wildly, her tiny body quivering.

Tess tilted her head, staring at the blue-and-silver-haired beauty. "What are you so happy about, Ms. Travers?"

"Oh, Tess! Mr. Wilks asked me to marry him!"

"Wow! That's fantastic! Good for you – good for both of you!"

"Thank you, dear. I'm thrilled!"

"And to think you met here. How wonderful."

"It is wonderful. Love is still so wonderful, even after all these years." Ms. Travers reached out to pat her on the arm. "What about you? Is that nice Mason fellow with you?"

Tess's hand shifted to her stomach. She glanced down at her flat belly, imagining how it would look in a few months. A part of Mason would always be with her, from here on out.

"Ah, I see," the older woman said. "I have three myself."

Tess looked up. "Three?"

"Three children, all boys. They look just like their father. If you'd told me when my dear Harold passed away that I would ever get married again, I would have said you were crazy. But you know, life doesn't always take you where you think it will."

Tess focused on the woman's kind, bright eyes. "No, it doesn't."

"But I can assure you of one thing: there are no mistakes, dear. It all happens for a reason." Ms. Travers took Tug's leash and gave her another smile. "You take care of yourself and that baby."

"Thank you. I will."

The godmotherly sprite winked at her as she exited.

Tess ran to her office, grabbed her car keys, and headed out to find Mason.

19

EMPLOYEE OF THE MONTH

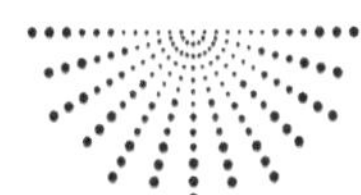

Tess didn't get far in her quest for Mason. As she locked the front door of the Palace, she heard a car pull up to the curb behind her. Dropping the keys in the pocket of her jeans, she turned to see his Mercedes ease to a stop behind her Bug.

Her feet continued to move down the stairs, but her heart froze the instant Mason exited the driver's side. Tess nearly fell over. She hadn't seen him in a week – it was probably the longest she'd gone without him in six years – and her entire body reacted to the heartrending sight. She didn't understand how he could manage to be any more attractive to her, but he was. Even while wearing a rather bizarre outfit.

His eyes locked onto her as he stepped around the back of his car, his long strides carrying him quickly up the sidewalk. When Tess reached the bottom step of the Palace, Mason stopped walking. Only a few feet of space remained between them. She bit her lip while they stood and stared at each other.

"Hey," she said.

"Hey," he echoed.

"You're here."

"Of course I'm here." His head tilted. "Where are you going?"

"I'm going to find you."

"Oh." Mason inched closer, his thumb and forefinger rubbing together. "I would have come earlier, but I wanted to wait until everyone was gone, since I know this is the time of day you normally clean up."

"Clean up?" she questioned, her gaze shifting over his unusual clothing.

"Do you like the outfit?" he asked, spreading his arms wide.

Tess perused his *Mason*-embroidered polyester bowling shirt, jeans, and rubber boots, as well as the thick rubber gloves in his hands. "It's certainly interesting, but I'm not sure why you're wearing it."

"Well, obviously, this is my favorite shirt."

She couldn't help smiling. "I think that might be stretching the truth."

"No, really. You gave it to me, so I love it. I've worn it a few times this week, actually. And as for the rubber boots and gloves, I thought they'd be helpful for cleaning up dog patties."

"Why would you need to clean up dog patties?"

He took another step forward. "Because I don't want a life without you, Tess. So, if shoveling dog poop is the only way I get to spend time with you, then that's what I'll do."

She shook her head violently. "Oh, no, Mason. You don't owe me anything. I'm the one who owes you. I owe you honesty, and I owe you apologies, and I – I have so many things I want to tell you."

"What do you want to tell me?"

"First, I want to tell you that I understand about Malory."

"Malory? What about her?"

"I just, I understand you'll always have feelings for her, and..."

His face contorted. "Seriously, Tess? You *still* think I have feelings for Malory? Even after everything I said to you at the gala? How in the hell can I convince you that *I don't want her*?"

"No, no. That's not what I meant. I'm not saying this well. What I want to say is that I understand your connection to her."

Mason threw his arms up. "Connection? There is no connection! I *don't* have feelings for her! Good Lord, you make me *nuts* sometimes! If I didn't love you so damn much, I swear I would just...*Gaah!*"

Tess's knees wobbled. She collapsed onto the step behind her, sitting and looking up to his wild, vibrant eyes. "You love me?"

His arms fell. "Yes. God, yes. So much that I'm crazy with it. I barely eat. I hardly sleep. I just think about you. I just need you. So damn much."

She sniffled and smiled. "You...you never said it before."

"Didn't I? I actually thought I did."

Taking a step forward, Mason turned to sit. He eased down onto the same stair she'd collapsed on, setting his gloves beside him and folding his hands in his lap. He released a slow breath, his elbow brushing against hers while he settled in.

"I'll say it now, Tess. I'll say it as much as you want. I'm in love with you. I've been in love with you for years."

She pinned his eyes. "Did you say *years?*"

"I did. At least two years. Probably six. I don't know for sure. I'm not exactly an expert when it comes to the organ in my chest that pumps blood around. But I can fix it. I'll do anything you want to fix it. Just please don't make me go back to that house alone again. I haven't been able to sleep in our bed since you left. And the couch isn't comfortable at all, no matter how many blankets I put on it."

"You missed me that much?"

Mason angled toward her, slipping his fingers onto her cheek. "Yesterday, when I couldn't smell you in the house anymore, I took your shampoo bottle into the living room and set it on the coffee table like a damn air freshener." His hand fell back onto his thigh. "If you don't come home soon, I might lose my mind. Or start shampooing with wildflowers. I'm not sure which."

"I'm so sorry I was gone. I'm so sorry I left. I went to D.C. to clear my head, and once I did, I realized I never should have run away in the first place. I should never have run away from you. From *us.*"

"I wish you hadn't left, either. But if you needed that time to find your way back, then I'm glad you took it. It's just overwhelming to learn how empty my life is without you." He paused, his eyes drinking in the curves of her face. "You see, during all those years I dated Malory, it was really like being alone. I always thought I managed fine by myself. But now I see I was never truly alone, because you were right there with me. You're a part of everything I do, Tess. You have been since the day you first walked into my life."

"Wow," she said, amazed by his revelations. "Well, then. I know it's a little late, but maybe you could make me retroactive Employee of the Month."

Mason chuckled. "Especially for that last month, right? I mean, you were phenomenal the whole six years, but the last month deserves special recognition. Definitely an award or something."

She smiled with her whole body as she watched him. She reached out to touch his hand where it lay on his thigh. "Thank you for telling me you love me. It means everything to hear you say it."

He curled his fingers into hers. "Then I'll say it constantly. I love you, Tess. I love you, I love you, I love you. Now please tell me how to reassure you that I want absolutely nothing to do with my ex."

Her hand trembled in his. "Mason, I...I know about Malory."

"What do you mean?"

Tess forced herself to maintain his penetrating gaze. "She told me. Malory told me she's pregnant."

A flash of pain shifted across his face, tensing his entire body. Mason sighed as he looked to his feet. "Let me guess. She told you at the gala."

"Yes."

He raised his head to stare out into the street. "Well, that explains why you left." He sat quietly for long moments, his fingers moving slow and steady over hers. Eventually, he turned back. "Wait a minute. She told you at the gala that she's pregnant, and you still came home to me?"

"I shouldn't have left in the first place. I should've stayed and..."

"But, Tess, I have to tell you..."

"No, wait, please," she begged, pivoting on the step to truly face him. "I need to apologize. I'm so sorry I ran away. That night at the Country Club was perfect between us. It was everything I ever wanted. But when she told me that, it was like a bomb exploded and I..." Tess's voice left her as she gasped in air, fighting to get her words out. "I totally panicked, and that is completely my fault. It just felt like the walls were caving in and I was being crushed and I couldn't breathe and..."

"Hey, hey," he stopped her, reaching for her face, brushing his thumb across her cheek. "It's okay. I'm right here."

She settled immediately with the warmth of his skin. "I know you're here, and all I want is to be with you. I've always wanted to be with you. I should have stayed that night – stayed and fought for us. But I'm here now, if you'll have me, and I want to work this out. It's going to be crazy complicated, yet as much as I want sunshine and rainbows and running hand-in-hand through fields of wildflowers, what I really want is us. I want us working together to figure everything out. And I think we *can* figure it out, because you told me once that I have a huge heart."

"You have the biggest heart ever, Tess."

"Then I don't see any reason why I can't love Malory's baby. After all, it'll be your baby, too."

Mason stared into her. He just sat and stared for the longest time. She could see him fighting to hold back his tears. He slid his hand into her hair, pulling her closer to touch his forehead to hers. "Have I told you in the last five seconds how much I love you?"

"Not in the last five seconds, no."

"Then I'm falling down on my job." He placed a lingering kiss on her forehead. "I think we can still find fields of wildflowers to run through, sweetheart. But first, I need to tell you what happened between me and Malory."

Tess raised her head, hope swelling in her chest. "If you'll share that with me, I will truly appreciate it."

He nodded, recapturing her hand in his. Engrossed in the sight of their intertwined fingers, Mason sucked in a deep breath. "Okay, here goes. I screwed up with Malory. I screwed up really, really badly."

"How did you screw up?"

"Oh, in so many ways. The worst of which was staying with her for so long. I'd known for years that we didn't belong together. Hell, I probably knew as soon as I started dating her, but I didn't do anything about it. I guess I thought we would eventually work out. On paper, we seemed like a good fit. And she certainly didn't put any demands on me emotionally, since she's a bit of an ice princess."

"Malory? An ice princess? *No.*"

He chuckled. "Yeah, well, I didn't do anything to change that. You were absolutely right, love coach. I didn't sparkle for her. I didn't try. I put school first and then business first. Through the years, she grew to resent everything I did. Yet, even after she threw fits and stormed off, she always came back. I don't know why. Maybe she didn't want to admit we'd failed. Maybe she thought I would change. All I know is I really started to pull away two years ago. She knew I had one foot out of the door and she would have to do something big to keep me. So she did."

"What did she do?"

"She brought me the West End Country Club project."

"Oh."

Mason hung his head, his fingers working across hers. "I know. I should have refused. But it was good for business, so I took the job and I stayed with her. She was happy at first. But after a while, she could tell I wasn't there for the right reasons. The closer I came to completing the conference center, the angrier she got. We fought like crazy. I barely ever touched her. When I'd finally had enough of her ranting and raving at me, when I finally said I was leaving for good, that's when she told me she was pregnant."

He paused to rake a hand through his hair. "I'm sure she thought I would stay. I'm sure she thought I would ask her to marry me. We'd been together for so long, and the pregnancy changed things, of course. I wracked my brain with every possibility. I knew I would take care of the baby, but no matter how I envisioned the future, the prospect of marrying her wasn't appealing at all. I couldn't make myself want that."

Tess reached for him, smoothing her free hand across his thigh.

Mason sighed with her touch. "I needed someone to talk to, so I called Ian.

As you know, my brother doesn't like Malory. He didn't even believe she was pregnant. He made me get evidence. I can tell you she wasn't very happy when I insisted on seeing ultrasound photos."

"Yikes. I'll bet that went over well."

"I'm lucky to still be alive, actually. But she produced the pictures, and I showed Ian. He still wasn't satisfied. He hired a private investigator to make sure she hadn't forged the photos. Instead, we found out something else entirely. She was cheating on me."

"What? No way! She was cheating on you? On *you*?"

"Remember Brenton Clearwater from the gala?"

"Yes."

"That's who she was with."

"Ew. Why would she want *that* when she could have *you*?"

"But she couldn't have me. I was done with her and she knew it. She was just trying to keep her hold on me, for whatever screwed-up reason. And I need you to know something else – as much as I'm sure you don't want to hear about her and me together – I was always very careful to use protection with her. I never slipped up, not once in all those years. There was never a time when I decided not to use a condom, or forgot in the heat of the moment. That *never* happened, so the baby probably wasn't mine."

Tess stared blankly, trying to wrap her mind around everything. "Wow. So...when? When will you know if the baby is yours?"

"I won't," Mason said, his voice trembling. "She miscarried."

Tess's fingers curled hard inside his. "Oh, my heavens. I'm so sorry. I can't imagine anything worse. That must have been horrible for you."

The muscles in his clenched jaw worked furiously. "You know, she didn't even tell me when it happened. She kept pretending to be pregnant, demanding to get married. But I'd had enough. I told her I would be the best father I could be, if the baby turned out to be mine, but I wouldn't marry someone I didn't love. That's when she told me she'd lost the pregnancy, that she'd actually lost it weeks earlier. And she told me with such cruelty in her eyes – like she was thrilled to get one last punch in."

He shook his head. "At least, I thought that was her last punch. Apparently, she left the knockout for later, when she told *you* she was pregnant. For that, I got to spend one more week in sheer misery."

Tess sat motionless, gripping tight to his hand. "I don't even know what to say. That is so awful. When...when did this all happen?"

"Right before David and Regina's wedding."

"Good Lord, you must have been hurting so badly."

"Well, it certainly wasn't fun to stand beside the two of them in that chapel, listening as they vowed to love and cherish each other forever, when the woman I'd dated for over a decade wanted to stab me in the gut. When David came back from his honeymoon, I was happy for him, but I envied him. I'd wasted an absurd amount of time on a cruel, heartless person and I just wanted to be with someone I could really love."

Mason looked down to their clasped hands. "The day David and Regina returned, I was sitting at my desk, wanting so badly to run out of the building and into the park. Then he came into my office and suggested I date you. And I just...I knew he was right. Almost immediately. At first in my mind, but then in my heart, too." He raised his eyes back to hers. "You've brought such color to my life, Tess. From the first moment you came into it. It took me way too long to realize what you've always meant to me, but I do now. I love you. More than I have ever loved anything, or anyone, in my entire life."

She sat, stunned. A tear slid down her cheek and he reached out to brush it away. "I'm sorry," he whispered. "I'm sorry I never told you all this before. I've always believed life is supposed to be about work and success, and Malory was a failure. I failed her, in every possible way."

"No. You didn't fail her. She failed you."

"Maybe. Probably a little of both. All I know for sure is that you are the only person who's ever looked at me like I could do no wrong, and I didn't want to screw that up, too. I wanted to protect you from the horrible decisions I'd made. You asked me several times what happened between her and me, but I didn't answer because I thought you had enough to deal with, especially with me being a grouch and a robot and having ignored you for six goddamn idiotic years. I thought the only thing I had going for me was this concept you had of my actions being beyond reproach. I didn't want you to know how badly I'd failed her. I didn't want you to think I would ever do that to you. Because I won't, Tess. I swear. I would never do anything to hurt you."

"I know," she said, easing her hand up his jaw. "You're wonderful. Everything about you is wonderful. You're the strongest person I know, the most successful, the smartest, the kindest, the most loving. And the most sparkly."

He smiled as she dropped her fingers onto his arm, curling around and holding on. "All I ever wanted was to be in your heart, Mason. It was the only place I'd wanted to be for so many, many years. But when you wouldn't open up to me about Malory, I figured my heart was the only one at risk. That's why I said I only wanted an affair."

"My God. Really?"

Tess nodded. "As tense as you got at the mention of her name, I knew you still had feelings for her."

"They weren't good feelings, sweetheart. I told you so many times I didn't want her, and I just...I thought that would be enough."

She searched his eyes. "Do you remember my ex, Bryan?"

"Unfortunately."

"Do you know why I broke up with him?"

"I was kinda hoping it was because you were fantasizing about riding me like a cowgirl, barebacked across a hot desert, and he just couldn't hold a candle to that."

Tess laughed even as her gaze fell. "Yeah, well, there's that. And then there was the day I left work early to come home and surprise him. He'd told me the night before that he wanted to talk about our future, and I walked in on him having sex with his ex-girlfriend in my bed."

Mason's hand tightened in hers. "Oh, damn."

"Yeah. Apparently, I like to fall for men who have long-term, on-again, off-again exes. It's sort of my thing."

"I'm so sorry he treated you that way."

"Well, looking back on it now, it doesn't sound nearly as bad as what Malory did to you. But I was still devastated when it happened. The same basic thing happened between my parents, and I'd lived through all that pain as a kid, and I guess I never really got over it. But even so, I always wanted to have a true, loving relationship of my own. When Bryan came along, I thought he might be The One, since he was the closest thing I'd ever found to..."

Mason searched her eyes as her voiced trailed. "To what?"

Tess smiled softly. "To you."

He shook his head. "Does Bryan still live around here?"

"Why?"

"Because I would like to break both his legs."

She laughed. "I appreciate the protectiveness, but I'm okay now. I'm better than okay. You've shown me what it's like to be with a person who truly loves me and wants the best for me. I still don't know if I deserve that after how I treated you, but..."

"Tess," Mason cut in, reaching for her waist to pull her even closer. "I don't want you to ever think you don't deserve love. I didn't think I did, and I know what kind of pain that is. But I don't hurt anymore, because you changed it. You changed everything for me."

"I did?"

"Hell, yes. I've had a lot of time to think this past week. I thought so much about that first year you came to work with me. In truth, that was the last good year I remember. You came into my life and brought so much energy with you. You had your ridiculously obvious crush on me and you made me smile and laugh. Then you went out of your way to bring Ian and Vanessa back to me, to bring me a sense of family and home and connection. And I just...I adored you. I realize now that things really began going downhill with Malory during that year, probably because she knew I had feelings for you. Honestly, everyone else seems to know my emotional state better than I do."

Mason paused, tucking a stray hair behind Tess's ear. "But I still thought of you as off-limits. We just worked so well together, and with the stress of Malory and of starting the business, I believed you were better off without me. So, I watched as you moved on. I watched as you started dating other people and as you stopped babbling around me, and it was like a light dimmed from my life. After that, the next five years with Malory were terrible. I felt trapped on a deserted island, but no matter how many times I tried to get away, I always ended up back there. I think, deep down, I didn't believe my heart was worth saving."

His words ended with a shaky breath. Tess curled into him, laying her head on his shoulder. "I'm so glad you chose to get off that island."

Mason tightened his hold on her. She relaxed into his arms, listening to the calm breaths coming from his chest, letting his strength bring her peace. His hand drifted slowly across her back, smoothing up and down her spine.

"Can you promise me something, Tess?"

She raised her head. "What's that?"

"Can you promise you won't run away from me again? Because I can't imagine being without you. Not ever."

"I promise, Mason. Can you promise me something, too?"

"Anything."

"Can you promise you'll always open up to me, and let me be in your heart? Now that I'm here, I really don't want to leave. Not ever."

"I promise." With those words, his entire body settled. "Oh, thank God. This is perfect, isn't it? We're not holding anything back anymore. Everything is out in the open. Everything works out between us."

Tess stiffened. "Actually, there is something else we should..."

"No. There's nothing else. It *will* work out between us. It has to. I won't accept any other outcome."

She wrapped his hand in both of hers. "It will work out. I promise you, everything will work out perfectly. But I still need to ask you one more thing."

Mason pinned her eyes. "What is it?"

"When, um, when you thought you were going to be a father, were you okay with that? I mean...it didn't hurt you, did it?"

"Hurt me? Well, I definitely wasn't with the right woman, so that part was bad. But the father part? I liked that thought." He ran his hand down her shoulder. "Are you asking if I want kids, Tess?"

"I suppose I am."

"Is having a child important to you?"

"It's actually really, really important to me."

"Good. It's important to me, too. I'd really love for us to have kids one day. When we've had more time to discuss it, and we know we're ready, we can certainly plan for it. Maybe in a year or two?"

Tess gripped his hand. "How about in...eight months or so?"

Mason stopped breathing altogether. *"Eight* months?"

She nodded, slow and steady.

Realization hit him. He stared at her in utter shock for a solid minute. Then his eyes lit up like a Christmas tree. "Tess, are you...are you *pregnant?*"

"Yes. We're going to have a baby, baby."

In one swift motion, Mason stood, pulled her into his arms, and spun her in a circle. She grabbed onto his shoulders, squealing as his laughter rang in her ears. "This is fantastic!" he yelled, hugging her so tight that she could hardly catch her breath. "I'm thrilled! I'm ecstatic! I've never been happier!"

He eased his steel grip to see her face. "Marry me, Tess. Marry me today."

She grinned at him. "No."

"You mean no, you won't marry me?"

"I mean no, I won't marry you *today*. I have so much to do! I need to book a venue and a reception site and then there's the flowers and food and music and I'll have to fly my family in from California – they haven't even met you yet! I want everyone from the office to come to our wedding. Also, Ms. Travers and Mr. Wilks. They got engaged today, too! I want Belle and Regina to be by my side, and I know you'll want Ian and David to be by your side. And seriously, I don't care how big and pregnant I am, I *will* wear white walking down the aisle."

Mason let her feet touch the ground again. "Anything you say, sweetheart. As long as I get to call you my wife very, very soon."

Tess watched him with watery eyes. "I love you, Mason. I love you with all my heart and mind and body and soul and just...everything."

He leaned down, smiling against her lips. "I know," he said. Then he kissed her.

2 0

A GYPSY WEDDING

Mason stood in the park across the street from his office building. The sun had fallen behind several huge oak trees, and now the strings of lights hanging from nearby branches lit his surroundings, casting a surreal glow around every person he saw. But no one sparkled quite like his Tess.

He could see her in the distance, her beaded white dress catching the soft lighting. They'd been making the rounds of their wedding reception together, talking with everyone and accepting well wishes, when Ian and Vanessa had latched onto Mason's new wife and refused to let go. He understood that feeling, so he begrudgingly left her side to visit with other friends, like David and Regina, and George and Kathryn. Regina and Kathryn had spoken excitedly to him about the triple date night they wanted to have the moment Mason and Tess returned from their honeymoon, and he'd eagerly accepted before allowing them to return to their dancing. Now he stood just to the side of everyone else, alone but far from lonely, watching his bride across the sea of people.

Five months seemed like forever to wait for this day – for the moment he could call this brilliant, vivacious woman his wife – but it was worth it. Tess looked radiant and glowing and incredibly happy, and it lit him up inside. Besides, the waiting wasn't too difficult, since she'd been living with him the entire time. She'd moved back home the same night they got engaged on the steps of the Palace.

He remembered how busy Tess had been after that, not just with planning their wedding, but also with work. But then she and Annabelle were able to hire their first employee, and his sprite finally started to enjoy some free time. He would never forget the day Tess realized she was someone else's boss. She'd been so giddy, bouncing up and down in front of him. He'd just grabbed her and kissed her, because there was nothing else he could imagine doing.

Since then, Tess had come to visit him for lunch almost every day. She'd spend a few minutes with Janice, Regina, Kathryn, and anyone else around, before making her way into his office and closing the door firmly behind her. He'd look up at her from his chair, meeting her eyes as she moved toward him, his fingers twitching with need to touch her. And he would. He would savor her for every single second, and still miss her the moment she sauntered out of his building to go back to her own.

He'd offered to put a lock on his door, just to make sure she kept coming back, but Tess assured him it wasn't necessary. No one disturbed them during their conjugal visits. After all, it was the only time his door was ever closed. She did, however, insist he put a lock on his desk drawer – *because anyone could open it at any time and they would get quite an eyeful, Mason* – and he'd obliged, since that photo was for his eyes only.

His wife's laughter pulled him from his memories, the joyful sound drifting toward him across the crowd. Mason watched Ian and Vanessa laugh along with her. He could see how enthralled his brother and sister were by every word out of her mouth, and he loved how their attachment to her had grown stronger over five months of weekly family dinners. Mason always knew Ian and Vanessa would be thrilled about his marriage. What he hadn't expected was his parents' response.

Graham and Louise Tramont also stood by Tess's side, gazing affection-ately at their new daughter-in-law. Mason watched in awe as his wife turned toward them, her lips moving a mile a minute, and reached out to take Louise's hand in hers. His mother touched Tess's bulging belly tentatively before breaking into the most beautiful smile he'd ever seen on her face. Tess kept talking as she held Louise's hand on her shifting stomach. Mason saw his mother giggle. He had to clear his throat then, since it felt like something had permanently lodged there.

"Well, then. Are you happy, or what?"

Mason turned his head toward Annabelle, unaware of how long she'd been standing beside him. "I am on cloud nine, actually."

"Yeah, so is Tess. Thank you."

"For what?"

"For giving her everything she ever wanted."

He glanced back to his bride. "It's what I wanted, too."

From across the sea of guests, she looked up and caught his eye. Tess grinned at him, impossibly toothy yet ethereally beautiful, and it started that familiar squeezing sensation in his chest, the one he'd grown so accustomed to in the past six months. He watched as his wife said a few parting words to his family, and gave them each a hug in turn, before she began walking toward him through the crowd.

Belle shifted on her feet. "Before she gets here, can I ask you something?"

"Sure. Anything."

"Is, um, is your brother single?"

He refocused on Belle. "Ian? Yeah. Why?"

"Oh, no reason." She shrugged and walked off.

Mason watched her leave before turning back to his sprite. Tess glided past onlookers like an angel in her fitted white gown, the glittering fabric hugging her rounded stomach. "Hello, husband," she purred when she arrived in front of him.

"Hello, wife." Mason pulled her in as close as her pregnant belly allowed. "I must say, this wedding dress is gorgeous, but I thought you'd want to wear something a little less form-fitting."

"Are you kidding me? I love this baby. I want to show him off."

He reached to touch her stomach. "I love this baby, too. And I love *her* mom."

Tess arched an eyebrow. "I already told you it's a boy."

"You don't know that for sure; we didn't find out the sex. I think it's a girl. She's going to be beautiful, like her mom."

"Thank you for that. But it's a boy, because he already kicks the mess out of me. He's strong like his dad."

"Well, I'm going to spoil him or her silly. And if it is a boy, that's wonderful, but then I want to try for a girl. Starting tonight."

"You know, my love, you have to get the first one out before you can move another one in."

"Oh, I don't know about that. You always say I can do anything. Maybe I could start up a second one while this one's still baking. It's worth a try."

"You go ahead and try all you want to. If anyone can do it, you can. Besides, these pregnancy hormones make me ravenous for you."

"I know. It's fantastic."

She rewarded him with her sparkling laugh and he wanted to stand here forever and listen. Instead, the clinking of glasses drowned out the blissful sound. He looked up, watching everyone tap spoons against their champagne flutes. "Hmm. I think they want me to kiss you."

"Well, they are our guests, so who are we to deny them?"

He stared into her bright, eager eyes before focusing on her lips. Then he bent down and settled his mouth on hers. He meant to keep the kiss chaste – there were children here, after all – but the moment he tasted her, he forgot where he was. Especially when he felt Tess's fingers smooth into his hair and heard her whimper against his lips. She always melted into him the moment he touched her, every time he touched her. It was the best sensation in the world.

Before he could embarrass them both by taking their actions any further, reality returned in the form of whistling and cheering from the crowd. He was actually getting used to people applauding him when he kissed this woman. It was as if the universe wanted him to know he was exactly where he needed to be.

A new song started in the background and Mason finally pulled away from Tess's lips to take her hand in his. "Come dance with your husband," he said before leading her onto the floor. Although it really wasn't a dance floor at all. It was a field of wildflowers situated in the middle of the park, surrounded by white tents filled with tables and chairs, lit by fire pits and strings of lights. When they reached the center, Mason pulled her to his chest and led her in a slow sway.

Tess glanced up to his face. "No Robot dance today?"

"Later tonight. Just for you."

"Naked?"

"If you like."

"I like," she answered with a grin.

He chuckled and drew her closer. Other couples came to dance, filling in the space around them, but Mason took little notice. He breathed her in and imagined it was just the two of them. "You know," he whispered, "I've really enjoyed working on your list of fantasies these past months. Maybe we could fulfill another one today."

"Mmm. You already did."

Mason traced the side of her face with his fingertips. "You're the best thing that's ever happened to me. You know that, right?"

With his declaration, she smiled as bright as the sun. He wanted to freeze time right here, to bask in this warmth forever. But another couple bumped into them, making Tess squeak in surprise.

"Goodness, I'm sorry, dear," Mrs. Travers-Wilks apologized, her wrinkled hand coming to rest on Tess's shoulder. "My husband gets a little wild cutting a rug sometimes."

"That's certainly okay," Tess offered, greeting Mr. Wilks before turning back to his wife. "I'm just glad you're having a good time."

"Oh, the best time. You made this entire day magical. Didn't she, Mason?"

"She certainly did."

The cherubic older lady patted him on the arm. "You two just keep dancing, right into your honeymoon and beyond. And Mason, be sure to take care of this beautiful bride of yours. And your son, too."

Tess's grin overtook her face. "Yes! It's a boy! I knew it!"

"Are you *both* ganging up on me with this boy thing?" Mason huffed.

Mrs. Travers-Wilks laughed. "May as well get used to the idea." With another giggle, the godmotherly sprite twirled off with her husband.

Mason turned back to his wife, relishing the joy that lit her eyes.

"It's a boy," Tess sang.

"Just because she says so?"

"Oh, that woman knows things. Best not to question it."

He cupped her cheek in his hand. "I don't question anything anymore, sweetheart. I'm just here with you and I'm happy."

Tess leaned in, resting her head on his shoulder. He pulled her even closer, pressing her rounded belly against his body. She sighed in contentment as Mason looked out into the crowd, watching their friends and family dance around them.

A smiling David held onto a very pregnant Regina. George and Kathryn, engaged for the last month, snuggled close together. Janice and her husband-of-forty-years held their own alongside everyone else.

Mason loved that the entire staff of Field and Tramont had come to share their day. He watched the light from the fire pits cast all their faces in a warm, soft glow. Everything felt magical, just like Mrs. Travers-Wilks said. But that made perfect sense, since his Tess was a sprite and sprites created magic. That was just what they did.

She shivered inside his arms and Mason hugged her closer. "Are you cold?" he asked, knowing the breeze felt chillier since the sun set.

"I'm never cold when I'm with you. But you do make me shiver for other reasons."

"Hmm. What reasons would those be?"

"Oh, too many to count. I'm just excited about flying away together, and having three whole weeks to ourselves to..." Tess's voice trailed off, her body stiffening. She looked up with wide eyes. "Holy crap, Mason. Please tell me you locked your desk drawer before you left work yesterday. I don't want anyone idly wandering into your office for a pen while we're in Jamaica."

He chuckled. "I promise I locked the drawer."

Her body eased. "Thank goodness. Now we can go to Jamaica worry-free."

"We can. And I can't wait to have you naked and sandy."

"Oh, really? Is that a fantasy of yours, baby?"

Mason growled, his hands wandering lower on her back. "You could say that. I think that was the first really dirty thought I had about you, before I even worked up the nerve to ask you out."

"Mmm. Are you telling me that my big, bad boss had impure, beastly, lustful thoughts about his sweet little secretary?"

"God, yes. That's exactly what I'm telling you." His hands found her bottom, squeezing onto both cheeks, using the leverage to fit her body harder against his.

A gasp left Tess's throat. "You know, I'm glad you took that picture when you did. I don't think my backside will ever look the same after this pregnancy is over."

"It'll always be gorgeous. And it'll always be mine," he insisted, nipping against her lip before running his tongue across it.

"Okay, okay," David chimed in. "Hands, Tramont. Hands."

"Damn it, David," he grumbled, eliciting laughter from both David and Regina when they danced up beside them.

David chuckled. "Just save some for the honeymoon, buddy."

Mason groaned, returning his hands to the small of his wife's back.

"Tess!" Regina piped up. "Your husband already agreed to a triple date with us and Kathryn and George as soon as you're back."

"Oh, yay! That's wonderful! We should talk about what we want to do, and plan for..."

"Nope, no planning, not right now," Mason cut in.

"I agree," David said. "If you two start planning, Mason and Tess will never get to leave for their honeymoon. And I'm thinking that's something he really, really wants to do."

Mason watched in delight as his bride's cheeks flushed pink.

"Just try to practice restraint a little while longer," David advised with a wink before twirling Regina away.

Mason looked back to Tess. "You know how much I hate practicing restraint when I'm around you."

She smiled, easing her hands across his shoulders. "I'm not crazy about it, either. But I think we can make it a bit longer."

"We can," he sighed, keeping his palms pressed to her low back.

He swayed them slowly through the wildflowers, trying to occupy his mind with anything other than how much he wanted to throw her in the grass, right here and now, and have his way with her. He forced himself to look out into the distance, his eyes shifting over the other couples. Then he caught sight of something strange happening in the outskirts of the field. His head cocked when he saw Ian there with Annabelle.

He watched the pair for a time, noticing how Ian held Belle a little closer than normal dancing allowed while simultaneously grinning like an idiot. Belle's fingers played with the back of Ian's hair, her eyes glued to his face. Mason chuckled, causing Tess to raise her head.

"What's so funny?" his bride asked.

"Oh, nothing. I just think your best friend likes my brother."

Tess peered over at the couple. "Well, look at that. I think your brother likes my best friend, too. That's really wonderful, isn't it? Although, if you think that's interesting, you should see what's happening over to your left."

"What's happening?" Mason questioned, craning his neck.

"I do believe Chad Rivers is trying to pick up your sister."

"What? You mean Chad from Accounting?" Mason searched out the sight of a flustered Mr. Rivers, with both hands jammed into his pants' pockets, attempting to speak to the indomitable Vanessa Tramont. "Good Lord, that boy has no idea what he's doing."

"But look. She's smiling. In a really good way."

Mason observed the two for a moment. "You're right, she is."

"Maybe instead of triple dates when we get back, we'll need to consider quadruple or quintuple dates."

"I must say, a lot of people around us seem to end up dating or married."

"I've noticed that, too. At first, I thought it was just coincidence. But now, I think it might be something more interesting."

"Yeah? Like what?"

Tess's eyelids fell to half-mast. "What if you and I are actually descended from gypsies, and we have mystical powers that turn the people around us into crazed, wanton beings?"

Mason kissed the tip of her nose. "Tell me this involves you wearing a gypsy costume, and I'll believe anything you say."

"Oh, I'll definitely need to wear a gypsy costume. I'm an enchantress, after all."

"Hmm. Enchantress does sound fitting. I wonder what that makes me? Perhaps your manservant?"

"Do you want to be my manservant?"

"The idea has possibilities."

"Okay, then. You're my manservant. And just so you know, you're also being punished."

"Ooh, nice. For what?"

"Because you're a thief."

"Yeah? What did I steal?"

"My heart," she answered with a grin.

Mason chuckled. "Well, I'm not giving it back."

"Oh, I know. Hence the punishment."

"That does seem fair," he offered, leaning down to nibble on her earlobe. "I think I should warn you, my gypsy ancestor was a vampire."

Tess shivered. "When is this reception going to end?"

"Not soon enough, although I have to admit I like being here. I love showing off my wife to all my family and friends."

"That's because you're a people person."

"You're right. That's me."

Her eyes met his. "I love you, Mr. Tramont."

Mason smiled. "I love you more, Mrs. Tramont."

**Looking for more romantic adventures by Tina?
Visit Day and Knight Romance Publications
DayAndKnightRomance. com**

For lovers of Young Adult Romance:

Are you yearning for the softness of first love,
this time with a supernatural twist?
Set yourself on the path of *The Watching Trilogy*.

For lovers of Adult Romance:

Are you interested in trekking off the beaten path?
Take the road less traveled with *On Vacation*.

Are you craving an epic excursion back in
time and across the globe?
Explore new worlds with the *Kastle Fortunes* series.

Whatever your desire for romance,
Tina promises a voyage like no other!

Tina is the author of multiple books and the owner of the publishing company Day and Knight Romance Publications. Writing as Day for her young adult novels and Knight for her adult novels, she offers a wide variety of journeys to satisfy your appetite for romance, love, and passion. Tina enjoys couch surfing, movie theaters, steamy reads, and bonding with fellow obsessive romantics who 'ship all the 'ships there are. Fortunate enough to have stumbled onto her soulmate back in the 1990s, she has been married for over a quarter century to a man who still tells her she's beautiful, no matter how many wrinkles she grows or cupcakes she eats. They live in Virginia with their two children, multiple fish, a fuzzy kitten, and a silly puppy, who are all frankly just too darn cute.

~

Visit Tina Online:
    Facebook.com/TinaKnightBooks
    Instagram.com/TinaKnightBooks
    Twitter @TinaKnightBooks